Grace Af...

Grace sees her boyfriend Henry everywhere. At the supermarket, on the street, at the graveyard.

Only Henry is dead. He died two months earlier, leaving a huge hole in Grace's life and in her heart. But then Henry turns up to fix the boiler one evening, and Grace can't decide if she's hallucinating or has suddenly developed psychic powers. Grace isn't going mad – the man in front of her is not Henry at all, but someone else who looks uncannily like him. The hole in Grace's heart grows ever larger.

Grace becomes captivated by this stranger, Andy – to her, he is Henry, and yet he is not. Reminded of everything she once had, can Grace recreate that lost love with Andy, resurrecting Henry in the process, or does loving Andy mean letting go of Henry?

Eithne Shortall studied journalism at Dublin City University and has lived in London, France and America. Now based in Dublin, she is chief arts writer for the *Sunday Times Ireland*. She enjoys sea swimming, cycling and eating scones. Her debut novel, *Love in Row 27*, was published in 2017.

Grace After Henry

Eithne Shortall

CORVUS

First published in trade paperback in Great Britain in 2018 by Corvus, an imprint of Atlantic Books Ltd.

Copyright © Eithne Shortall, 2018

2 3 4 5 6 7 8 9

A CIP catalogue record for this book is available from the British Library.

Paperback ISBN: 978 1 78649 319 4
EBook ISBN: 978 1 78 649 320 0

Printed in Great Britain by CPI Group (UK) Ltd, Croydon CR0 4YY

Corvus

An Imprint of Atlantic Books Ltd
Ormond House
26–27 Boswell Street
London
WC1N 3JZ

www.atlantic-books.co.uk

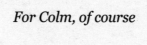

For Colm, of course

Grace took out her notebook and began to tut. She made a big deal of dragging a pen from her jeans pocket and clicking it into action.

'Damp,' she mumbled, ostensibly to herself but purposely loud enough to be heard by the two couples also inspecting this bathroom that time had forgotten but the carpet-fitter certainly hadn't; worn, once-blue fabric, not unlike the kind that used to adorn her grandmother's bedroom, was stapled all around the sides of the tub. Grace glanced up from the avocado-coloured toilet. She tutted again. 'Weak gable wall.'

In the mirror above the sink, she watched the reflections of her fellow house-hunters. One couple was inspecting the patch of ceiling Grace had just spent a good two minutes frowning at, and the woman in the other pair was making panicked eyes at her partner although he didn't pick up on this because he was too busy inspecting the boiler. Men were mad for the boilers.

'That'll have to be replaced,' said Grace, standing beside him, peering into the cupboard. 'Hasn't been serviced since

The Beatles called it a day, or so I heard the estate agent saying.'

Grace, who hadn't a clue about boilers or whether bathrooms even had gable walls, gave him a sympathetic smile and sauntered out of the unhygienic 1970s lavatory and into the 1970s kitchen.

It probably wasn't necessary to still be scaring off the competition. Grace and Henry had gone sale agreed on an end-of-terrace house on Aberdeen Street the previous week. It was right beside the Phoenix Park, which ticked more than enough boxes for Henry, and while the second bedroom was small the house had the kind of spacious, fitted kitchen that reminded Grace why she had wanted to be a chef. They were both mad about it. But they'd had deals fall through before. And while Henry wanted to hold out for Aberdeen Street – he was convinced the Phoenix Park house was meant to be – Grace knew the shrewd move was to keep looking. Just in case.

She checked her phone: 5.45 p.m. and no messages. He had fifteen minutes to get here. Henry was the master of cutting it fine. Grace, on the other hand, had been standing under the For Sale sign at this East Wall terrace at 5.20, ten whole minutes before the estate agent was due to arrive. Although she drew the line at queuing. She knew from experience that as soon as the door opened, everyone was going to charge in anyway.

An older couple stepped out of the kitchen as she was on her way in. Grace caught the wife's eye. *Riddled*, was what she hoped her stare said. *You'd buy this dump on a Monday, and it'd have fallen in on you by Tuesday.*

Actually, this house wasn't that bad. Despite its psychedelic décor and a smaller kitchen than Grace might have liked, it had a converted attic and no real signs of damp. It was worth keeping their options open.

'Don't think like that,' Henry had groaned from under the duvet that morning, trying to wangle his way out of going to yet another viewing. 'Ten months we've been looking. Haven't we served our time? We've found our house. I don't even want to consider another one.'

'Well, neither do I but reality—'

'Reality,' Henry scoffed, making a grab for Grace's bare legs as she sidestepped him again. 'We might jinx it by looking elsewhere. Aberdeen Street is going to work out, I'm telling you. I can feel it.'

Grace, standing half-dressed on the pile of newspapers that continually carpeted Henry's side of the bedroom, extracted the toothbrush from her mouth. 'Let me guess, you're going to tell me it's fate.'

'Exactly. And I feel another part of our destiny involves going to see the original *Mad Max*, which is having a one-off screening at the Savoy this evening.'

'Do you know how often house sales fall through, Henry?'

'No.' He pushed the duvet down to his midriff and grinned at her. 'But I bet you do.'

'One in four. And it's most common with first-time buyers. What if we don't get Aberdeen Street?'

'Aber-*dream* Street.'

Now it was Grace's turn to smile. 'I love it too, but we

can't put all our eggs in one basket. Until we have the keys in our hands, we have to keep looking.'

'You're right, I know you are. I'll be there before the viewing is over,' he said, finally making a successful grab for her leg and pulling her onto the bed. 'Why don't you put all your eggs in this basket?'

'That doesn't even make any sense.' Grace held her brush aloft so as not to get toothpaste on the duvet but she allowed herself to be pulled back under it.

'Jesus, Grace! You're so cold. You're bloody freezing!'

'Of course I'm freezing. I've been in our bathroom.'

'When we have a bathroom of our own, it'll have real ventilation, not just a hole in the wall. And we'll have a toilet cistern that refills . . . *by itself*.'

'The dream,' she deadpanned, before his arm reached up from below the blanket and caught her off guard. 'Hey! Give me that back. Don't put that in your— Gross! You absolute sicko, Henry Walsh. Get your own feckin' toothbrush!'

Grace pushed the flower-power curtains aside and looked out the window of the front bedroom of the East Wall terrace. 5.52 p.m. House-hunters were starting to leave; some crossed the road for a better look at the roof and drainage while others headed straight for their cars. It was threatening to rain, and still no sign of Henry's bike.

He would probably arrive just as the last lingering viewers were being herded out of the property, ruffling his helmet hair and somehow convincing the estate agent to stick around for an extra few minutes while he did a quick tour of the place. Grace envied how easily he could do that.

He charmed his way into things all the time and it came so naturally he didn't even realise he was doing it. Everyone liked Henry. He exuded self-assuredness and people wanted to be around him. And Grace was happy, proud even, that he so desperately and unremittingly wanted to be around her.

She stepped away from the window. When they moved into their own home, she would tell him how much she loved him every day. She stuck the notebook under her arm and continued into the second bedroom and then up to the converted attic. From the skylight she could see the River Liffey, flanked by lorries heading to and from the docks. It had started to rain.

'That's it, folks! Time to wrap it up!'

Grace peered down the attic stairs to see the young estate agent standing at the bottom of them. She checked her phone again: 5.59. Where was he?

Out in the front garden, Grace called him but it went straight to voicemail. *This is Henry Walsh, leave a message.* No sign of his bike from either end of the street. The last few stragglers streamed out into the rain and the estate agent shut the door behind them. Grace pushed down her hood.

'I'm waiting on my boyfriend; he's just running a little late.'

'Sorry,' said the agent, hunching forward as he pulled an umbrella from his bag. 'We're showing it again on Saturday.'

Grace nodded and followed him out of the garden. He hopped into his car and she sat on the front wall, damp seeping through the arse of her trousers and water dripping from the rim of her raincoat hood.

For feck's sake, Henry! Where are you?

The rain got heavier. She pulled her hood tighter and turned her mobile phone over in her hands: 6.07. She let out a frustrated sigh. She could feel the water on her shoulders, a slight trickle running down her arm. Grace repositioned her face to express maximum irritation. She intended to make Henry feel guilty. She was soaked. He'd better have a grovelling apology ready to go. He'd want to be arriving here with a good excuse, too. Even if he knew he wouldn't make it on time, he could have called. He could have—

A crack from above like a whip ripping the sky open. The grey clouds grew darker and the rain continued to pour. Her stomach dropped. They had fought about it so much in their early days that now Henry always called. Grace was filled with the most awful certainty that something was wrong.

'**F**eck it!'

The cyclist at the bike rail beside him looked up. 'Forgot something,' Henry told the stranger, before redoing his bike lock and jogging back to his office building. He bounded up the steps, taking them two at a time, using the handrail to propel himself onward.

'Forget something else?'

'Helmet. She'll kill me if I'm not wearing it.'

Henry went to the cloakroom, grabbed the green armour from his cubbyhole and waved it at the receptionist. 'Last time I'll be back, I swear.'

'Until tomorrow anyway,' she called after him. 'Best of luck with the house!'

But Henry was already on the staircase, winding the scarf tighter around his neck as he hot-footed it down the steps. He was dressed in a near homage to Grace. The bright red scarf she'd knitted him, and which he adored, and the helmet she insisted he wear. If he died, or suffered a terrible brain injury, what about her? It wasn't just him anymore.

9

Henry had never felt so half of something as the day he bought that helmet. It was scary to love someone so much that the end of one life could mean the end of two. He had never found the words to describe quite how he felt about Grace but he tried to show it in his actions: in being her biggest champion, in wearing a helmet like others wore a ring, in not being late for this house viewing.

He checked his watch: 5.35 p.m. Okay. If he put his pedal to the metal and didn't hit any red lights he would make it for 5.50. He only needed ten minutes to look around. Less, usually. And unless this house was significantly better than the shamelessly wide-angled photographs online suggested, his heart was still set on Aberdeen Street.

Henry unlocked his bike for the second time and stuffed *A Christmas Carol* into his bag. That was what he had gone back to the office for on the first occasion. He and Grace were reading it. Again. Even though it was February. Henry had brought it to work for a project they were designing – the book was just the right size for a mock-up – but he needed to have it back before bedtime. It was his turn to read tonight. Though she could whistle for it if she thought he was doing the voices.

Henry pushed off, pulling the scarf into position again. The sky was grey but he reckoned he could make it to East Wall before the heavens opened. He got stuck behind a group of tourists cycling two abreast down Dame Street and had to dismount his bike because of roadworks at College Green. The clock at O'Connell Bridge said 5.44. Shit. He'd take the quays. Fewer traffic lights and fewer cyclists. He looked right, left, threw the boisterous scarf over his shoulder once more and pushed right in unison with an articulated truck.

The quays were always jammed with industrial vehicles at this hour but at least they were moving, their massive wheels turning, the bolts the size of Henry's head. The cycle lane was empty. He picked up speed, recalculating his arrival time: 5.55, probably. 5.53, if he stepped on it. It didn't really matter; he just had to get there. He pushed down harder, feeling the strain in his thighs. If Henry made Grace a promise, he kept it. He loved her. Five years together and he hadn't grown tired of this same startling realisation that boomed outwards from his chest, reverberating in every part of him. He *fucking* loved her! He'd tell her when he got there. He was always telling her, but he'd tell her again. He grinned to himself. They'd get that Aberdeen Street house and properly, really properly, begin their life together. His heart swelled, driving him forward, faster. He loved this feeling; he was cycling towards her.

A splash on his wrist. Henry looked up. He didn't feel the scarf coming loose, didn't register the pull around his neck as the wind that had been holding it in the air finally dropped and the Aran wool looped its way through the spokes. A second splash, and another.

In the spokes, suddenly, all those stitches Grace had cast and caught at night, on the bus, on her fifteen-minute breaks. They had made each other's presents last year. They needed the money for their house. For their home. And now their home and Grace and their intertwined lives, spun as tightly as any threads, were caught, wrapping round and

11

round, until there was no more give. Then the brakes. A sudden halt. But he hadn't touched them.

The scarf was jammed in the brakes.

Wheels skidding, his feet down to balance but too late, too fast, too determined not to be late for Grace.

Only it couldn't be over. Not Grace and Henry. Him maybe, but never them. And that was what sustained him. That was why he still didn't believe it as his handlebars fell to the right, rain keeping time on his knuckles, skin pulled taut over them to a petrified shade of white.

His bike toppled but the truck kept coming and like it was nothing, like he was a crisp packet sucked up by the idling street sweeper, he was under. All noise, no light and still he closed his eyes because he knew now it was over and because he was scared. He was giving up. He who had promised never to give up. He who had said that where there was her there would always be him. But there was no Grace here. He was all alone and he was scared. He closed his eyes. He was sorry. He loved her and he was sorry.

The world shifted seismically but nothing tilted to accommodate it. The wheels turned, the rain fell, and all that love was sucked into a void. It was too late. He was gone.

Gone in the flutter of an eye. The eyes that saw through him and still loved him. Her eyes. Grace.

SEVERAL WEEKS LATER

ONE
· · · · · · · · · · ·

There were moments of lucidity – the sound of Dad abruptly starting up the vacuum cleaner and Mam screaming that hoovering disturbed the moths – but most of the early weeks passed in a fugue. I didn't leave the bed, never mind my parents' house, if I could help it. My social circle consisted of Mam, Dad, occasional visits from Aoife and the three other mourners I met every time I went to visit Henry's grave.

The day I came to, and regained some sort of awareness, my parents were jumping around their living room like Native Americans celebrating the arrival of rain. Everyone else's life had continued, all but mine and Henry's. Time kept passing, the sun kept rising and, as sure as spring follows winter, the moths had returned.

'I got him! I got the little bugger.'

Dad froze where he stood, right in the middle of the living room – knee bent, hands raised; an impressive yoga pose for a man with a bad lower back – and Mam, from her position on the sofa, squinted at the space above the television, the same bit of middle distance that was entrancing Dad.

Neither spoke. It was, I knew because *The Late Late Show* had just come on the telly, 9.35 on a Friday night.

'You did not get him, Arthur, look. Look! There he is now. Looklooklooklook! Quickquickquickquick!' Mam leapt to her feet, adopting the McDonnell family's preferred stance when it came to the extermination of moths. 'There he is!'

'Where?'

'There.'

'Where?'

'Theretheretherethere!'

'I see him, I see him. The fecker! I've got you now, my little friend.'

'It's the feckin' heat.' Mam grabbed the two magazines from Dad's armchair and held a rolled-up *Heat* in her left hand and *House & Home* in her right. 'The mild winter and all the feckin' central heating. I told you we didn't need the radiators on in March, Arthur. I don't see why you couldn't just use the tumble dryer to dry the clothes. You may as well roll out the welcome mat. They thrive in temperatures above twenty-two degrees.'

This was the fourth consecutive year our house had been overrun by moths and my mother, who had reactivated her library membership to read up on them, had found her *Mastermind* subject.

'Well, excuse me, Sarah,' said Dad, momentarily distracted from the assassination by this slight on his housekeeping skills. Since retiring, Dad had developed two passions: domesticity and celebrity gossip. The week he stopped being a driving instructor, he watched Lindsay Lohan's trial live on TMZ in its entirety. And he was so worried about her that he took to cleaning to distract himself. 'If you want to live in a home where you have to wear your winter coat just to go to the bathroom . . .'

'There's nowhere else I can wear it, now they've eaten two big feckin' holes in the arse of it!'

'And whose fault is that? If you'd just hang it back like I showed you, under the plastic cover, which I got special from the dry cleaner's, but no, you just throw it wherever you feel—'

'I see him! Arthur! There!'

'Shush!' admonished Dad, his head cocked like Patch used to before he went deaf and forgot he had ears.

'They can't hear us, Arthur.' Mam rolled her eyes, trying to coax me into the conversation. But I was still trying to get my bearings.

I had relinquished autonomy the moment I arrived back at our flat, drenched with rain and dread, to find two police officers at the front door. 'Grace McDonnell?' And I'd known then, not from what they said but how they stood, with their uniform caps in hand, as if they were already at the funeral.

It was amazing how long you could get away with ignoring everything when you didn't care about the outcome of anything. Emerging from that apathy in my parents' house was like coming to in a madhouse.

'Shush!' Dad adjusted his glasses, his eyes flickering from the middle distance above the telly to the middle distance above my head. 'I need to concentrate.'

Mam sent her eyes skywards again. She held her own spectacles up to her face.

'There! Arthur, behind you!'

'He's not, he is! He's—sorry, love.' Dad clambered into my chair, crushing the unopened book that lay on the armrest.

'Get him, Arthur. Go on, get him! Get the bastard.'

'Mam!'

She shrugged off the uncharacteristic profanity. 'Just checking you were still with us, pet.'

'And . . . smack!' Dad peeled his hand off the mint-green wallpaper and presented his palm victoriously. 'Mess with the McDonnells and you! Get! Squashed!'

And they both started shrieking, dancing their tribal dance around the rug once again. It was always the strangest things that reminded me how besotted my parents were with each other. They worked so hard to build this life, and they deserved these years to enjoy it together.

That was the point where I stood, something they weren't used to seeing me do without coaxing, and declared that it was time I moved on. Aberdeen Street was ready; I'd signed the last papers and the keys were mine to collect when I wanted. Henry's parents had insisted I follow through on the purchase. They didn't want the deposit money and his life insurance would help me through the first year of mortgage payments.

Mam said it was too soon; Dad said I'd be missed and that my eyesight was a vital asset in the war against larvae. But I had to go. Every time I looked at them I wanted to apologise for the new lines on their faces.

Within a week, we had moved my stuff into the end-of-terrace on Aberdeen Street that I kept referring to as 'our house'. The only unpacked bag was the plastic one stuffed with coats and scarves that had gotten caught on the spikes of the gate as Dad carried it in. It had burst all over the hallway and, ten days on, I still hadn't found the energy to pick them up.

I thought I heard Henry the first night I was in this house. Thinking I saw him was nothing new, every time I went outside I was convinced I clocked him somewhere, but that was the first time I'd heard his voice. I was in the back garden, checking that the door that led from the shed to the laneway was locked. I pulled at the iron bolt to ensure it was solid, and this shot of laughter rang out.

I recoiled from the lock as if it had burnt my hand. I didn't move another inch. I swear to God it was Henry's laugh.

My heart pounded in my chest and I felt a wave of nausea but I ignored it. I stood, still as a statue, waiting for the sound that would not be repeated. I remained like that until I started to shiver, then reluctantly I went back inside.

There were days when my only interaction was with the man in the corner shop with the Chinese–Dublin accent who called himself Pat but whose real name was Xin. I bought bread and cheese from him and he sometimes made observations but never asked questions.

'You're like a vampire,' he said, handing over the brie and baguette.

'Because I'm pale?'

'Because you only come out at night.'

But mostly I just sat on the floor in the hallway beside the mound of coats and watched as my phone flashed beside me. I'd been ignoring my mother's calls for three days now. All she wanted was for me to say, 'Yes, doing much better this evening.' And I couldn't. I considered lying back down on the pile of duffel and denim and wool. There was no end to how much I could sleep.

The phone stopped ringing and I waited for the single 'ping'. The screen flashed again: *You Have Nine New Voicemails.* She only wanted to help, like Dad when he'd offered to buy me a coat rail. Putting into action something he couldn't put into words. Just like Henry. The white glow faded and the hallway returned to dark. There was no bulb in the light fixture above me and I liked it like that. It reminded me of Ebenezer Scrooge roaming around his home in the dark, too stingy to pay for lamps.

Almost all of what Henry was carrying had been obliterated when the wheel of the articulated lorry returning to Dublin Port after a beet sugar delivery had rolled over him. All that had come back to me was his oil-stained backpack and a bizarrely pristine copy of *A Christmas Carol.* We read to each other most nights and we'd been reading that when he died. Henry was atrocious at voices but I made him do them anyway. His Bob Cratchit had me rolling around the bed laughing. We read *A Christmas Carol* every year, but never at Christmas. Too predictable.

Sitting with my back to the wall and my knees pulled into me, I opened the book to the relevant passage. I angled the page towards the living room so I might have enough light to make out the words.

'Darkness is cheap and Scrooge liked it,' I read aloud to no one, the sound of my own voice making me jump. It had been a while since I'd spoken. 'But before he shut his heavy door, he walked through his rooms to see that all was right. He had just enough recollection of the face to desire to do that.'

Beyond the front door, people were moving: coming home from work, going to the shops, heading out for a run in the park. But I stayed in the hallway. Every other room was filled with bags and boxes; throws and cushions in the sitting room, clothes in our bedroom, books in the study, and mountains of crockery and saucepans in the kitchen. I couldn't bring myself to unpack any of them. I couldn't be in the same room as them. So I stayed where I was, in the darkness, right where Henry had left me.

I would have given anything to have him back: this house, everything in it, a limb, two limbs, my sense of taste. I would have cut off the last two decades of my life. I would have watched a stranger die.

I would have watched my parents die.

I dug my nails into my arm until the dents didn't immediately disappear. The longing and aching were joined by a fresh wave of guilt. I closed my eyes until the nausea passed. But I had started down this path and I couldn't stop. Even when I opened them I saw it.

I saw him hurrying along on his bike, worrying that I would be cross with him for being late, and that stupid scarf that I had knitted that he never wanted coming undone. I saw the red wool looping into the spokes of his wheel, going round and round until it pulled him under the truck. I heard a decisive crunch as his bones were turned to dust and the squelch like a welly coming away from marsh as his insides flattened. But mainly I saw the red, spinning round, over and over, an indistinguishable mix of scarf and blood and eviscerated organs.

'Why didn't you look where you were going?'

The responding silence echoed around the hallway and throbbed in my ears.

'Why didn't you slow down? Hmm? Why couldn't you just do that?'

I remembered the last time I saw him: he was heading out the door of our flat, his big smiling head asking what the weather was supposed to be like and me saying it'd be windy and— No. No. No. No. I couldn't finish that thought.

'Henry! I'm talking to you. H—'

I choked on his name. I missed his arms and his smell and his existence. It filled me with rage how he never responded and that made my throat ache more.

'I'm sorry, okay?'

Still nothing.

'Henry!'

It was not a statement, but a plea. And I flinched at the desperation in my voice. Nobody had ever been coaxed back from the dead by a whinge and a nag.

'I said I'm sorry.'

But there was only the confirmation of night. The buzz and click and finally light as the street lamp at the end of

Aberdeen Street illuminated. My phone flashed again and I slid it away. I allowed my body to slump to the side, and though I was sobbing into the hood of a quilted jacket, sleep took no time. I was exhausted. I was gone before the 'ping' of my mother's tenth voicemail.

TWO

....

'**G**race likes *telling this story because she likes telling everyone what a dope I was.*'

'*Not a dope. More . . . cringeworthy.*'

'*Great. Much better.*'

'*We knew each other when we were teenagers. Henry lived in the same estate as a girl I went to school with and I'd met him at house parties. We even kissed once, actually, during a game of truth or dare, although Henry complained that I was the one who'd been given the dare so why did he have to suffer.*'

'*I did not use the word "suffer".*'

'*But then Christmas Eve, a few years ago, we were both in my local. The Back Bar. Henry goes there every Christmas Eve but I'm usually at my granny's. Only she was in England that year, staying with my uncle. So I go to the pub with Aoife.*'

'*You met Aoife at Grace's birthday.*'

'*Really dark hair, yeah, dead straight. That's her. She gets it from her mother's side. So anyway, me and Aoife go into the Back Bar and the place is rammed. But I see Henry*' at the bar. Half a foot taller than everyone else. And he's in a big group with Claire Maguire, the girl from school. She was the one who had all the house parties when we were teenagers. So anyway, I go over and me and Aoife are going on about how we haven't seen Claire in so long and what's she up to now, but really I've got one eye on Henry the whole time. And I can tell he's looking at me.'

'I was just keeping an eye out for my pint.'

'And this goes on for a while. Claire's not introducing us and I can't see how I'm going to get talking to him and the barman is getting ready to ring the bell for last orders so I start to panic. And Aoife can see I'm panicking even though I haven't had a chance to say anything to her but she knows I liked Henry all those years ago.'

'Best kiss of her adolescence.'

'Slim pickings in the Dublin suburbs more like. Anyway, Aoife suddenly goes: "Johnny Connors! Is that you? Oh my God, Johnny Connors." And Henry's like, "Eh, no. Not me."'

'I do not talk like that.'

'And Aoife says, "Are you sure?" Like, are you sure you are who you are? She was working off the cuff. Anyway, he says, "No, wrong guy."'

'You're making me sound like Father Fitzgerald.'

'Who?'

'From Father Ted. The boring-voice priest.'

'Oh yeah. Ha. You do sound a bit like him, actually. Anyway, then Aoife goes, "Grace, is this guy not the cut of Johnny Connors?" And I'm thinking, "Who the fuck is

Johnny Connors?" But anyway, I just go, "No, that's Henry Walsh." But I shouldn't have remembered his surname. It had been years.'

'The lips don't forget a kiss like that.'

'I'd clearly been Facebook stalking him. I think you were pretty flattered, Henry, some girl knew your name, made you feel like a big man. Big man in the Back Bar.'

'So, anyway, there you have it; that's how we met.'

'Hold your horses there, Johnny Connors. That's not the whole story.'

'Yes, it is. We've hogged enough conversation time. Let the people eat.'

'So we get talking anyway but the pub is closing and Henry says he'll walk me home . . .'

'Are they our main courses?'

'. . . which was about three minutes down the road but grand, I say, "Yeah, great thanks." We reach the bottom of my street and Henry takes my number and it's clear we're supposed to kiss but I don't want to 'cause I hate feeling like I'm in a film, like I'm just acting out the script, so I start backing up the street towards my house, saying, "See ya round." And Henry's there going, "Ehhh . . ."'

'I do not sound like that.'

'. . . clearly trying to think of something to say, so I walk slower and then just as I'm about to turn into my garden, he go—he—he goes—'

'Look at her. The supposed love of my life. Laughing so hard she can't get the words out.'

'He go— Sorry, hang on, give me a sec . . . Woo!

Composure. Okay. I'm turning into my garden and he shouts, in his big Father Fitzgerald voice . . .'

'A new detail. Great.'

'He shouts . . .'

'Here we go.'

'Let's do lunch!'

'You're almost on the floor, Grace. The waiter's going to think you've choked on something.'

'Let's do lunch?! What? Who even says that??'

'It's really not that funny.'

'Did you have your Filofax on you that night or were you going to put the appointment in when you got home?'

'Look how much joy she gets from humiliating me. You all right there, Grace? Can you breathe?'

'Let's do lunch! Oh God, it's so good. There I was thinking we were in some cheesy romance film, but apparently Henry thought we were in Wall Street!'

'Her love doth overflow.'

'Did you schedule lunch meetings with all the girls back then, or was it just me?'

'All right, honey. Just breathe. You're going to pull a muscle.'

THREE

'**I told you** we should have phoned. She's not going to appreciate us barging in on her.'

'I have been phoning, Arthur, but she doesn't answer. You're a soft touch. That girl needs some tough love right now.'

Ding-dong!

A split second of discombobulated bliss before the familiar realisation that I was indeed lying alone on a pile of coats. The voices were not dreams. They were real and familiar and less than two feet away.

'She can ignore me all she likes but she can't keep ignoring reality. She can't be late for work, not on her first day back, she's got—'

'We're three hours early, Sarah. She's not going to be late for work.'

'Am I the only one who remembers how she looked last time we saw her? She'll need at least three hours to sort herself out or Health and Safety will have the place shut down before she's so much as turned on the oven.'

Ding-dong! Ding-dong!

'Grace!' I froze as the hinge of the letterbox pushed open. I shifted nearer to the front door so whoever's eye that was – presumably my mother's; Dad hasn't bent over since 1997 – wouldn't register me. I slid right up until my back was against it. I was basically Tom Cruise in that *Mission Impossible* scene where he's trying to avoid the detection sensors.

'Grace? It's your mother.'

Silence. Then a low mumble from Dad: 'Because that was really going to make her open it.'

'Shut up, you!' Mam hissed back.

'You're leaving finger smudges all over that letterbox.'

'Are you looking for a divorce, Arthur McDonnell?' The hinges squeaked as Mam pushed it open again. 'Grace, we thought we'd bring you to work for your first day. Just to make sure you get off okay. And we want to see you, pet. We . . . we miss you.'

'We have some of Henry's stuff.' Dad cleared his throat. 'His parents dropped it over, things he'd left at their house they thought you might like. It's not much – a few CDs, a girly-looking shirt—'

There was more furtive whispering, too low for me to hear.

'Sorry. A *Topman* shirt.'

I shut my eyes to steady the involuntary lurch of my stomach. I had so few of Henry's clothes. They had given them all to charity shops in the weeks I was sleepwalking around my parents' house, lost in a stupor. The hoodie I'd been wearing for three weeks now and a coat that had gotten

29

mixed in with mine were all I had. I took a deep breath and pushed myself to my feet. I opened the door.

'There you are now,' said Dad brightly, as if I'd been held up in the bathroom and he hadn't just seen me rise from the floor through the stained glass. 'You look . . . Well, it's good to see you!'

I pulled at the hoodie and felt the greasy bun lobbing at the back of my head. They stepped into the hallway, kissing me on the cheek as they passed. They glanced down at the pile of coats, which betrayed the indent of a body, but said nothing. I didn't think my mother had it in her to say nothing. So that was what you had to do for your parents to stop passing remarks: have the love of your life die.

'You know you're back at work today?' said Mam, her face laden with concern.

'Of course I know. You really don't need to worry.'

'I'm not worried. I'm relaxed. Amn't I, Arthur? Relaxed?'

'Oh, your mother is very relaxed.'

'See?'

'I said to her last night, I said, "Sarah, will we call to see Grace tomorrow?" And she just said, "Who?" I tried to explain you were our daughter but she couldn't hear me over the sound of her Bob Marley record. So laid-back she's already fallen over, that's your mother.'

Mam turned her back on him. 'We thought we'd drive you, Grace. We can just wait while you have a shower and get ready.'

'I don't really need a shower, I was just going to—'

30

'That wasn't a question, Grace. It was an order, on behalf of the citizens of Dublin. We brought some shampoo.'

'I have shampoo!'

She shot me a sceptical look and then glanced at Dad, who produced a bottle of L'Oréal Something-or-other from the Boots bag he was carrying: 'Ta-dah!'

'And conditioner.'

'Ooo . . .' Dad pulled another bottle from the bag.

'And a razor.'

'Ahhh . . .'

I grabbed the haul from him and shot Mam a look. 'You and your lovely assistant can wait here.'

FOUR

· · · · · · · · · · · · · · ·

Dad drove and Mam sat in the back so I could have the passenger seat. We used to take this seating configuration whenever I was sick as a child. It made me feel like we were going to the doctor. Dad remarked on a white van hastily parked at the end of the road and I told him it was always there. He started tutting. In his driving instructor days, bad parking had been a particular bugbear.

'Do you know the owner?' he asked.

'Haven't met any of the neighbours yet.'

'If you don't have the patience to park, you shouldn't be allowed on the road.'

Dad switched on the radio and sang along. 'Little Mix,' he explained. 'This bit is about Zayn.' And Mam asked questions: Was I looking forward to going back to work? What was on the menu today? Did I think it'd make me feel better?

But I couldn't manage much in the way of conversation so she just stuck her hand around the side of my seat, squeezed mine and launched into a monologue about moths.

'They said on the radio this morning that there's an epidemic all over Dublin. They were interviewing this chap with a hardware shop in Cabra and he said he's sold clean out of mothballs and can't get another order for a week. I texted in to say they still have them in McGowan's on the Blackrock Road—'

'You sent that text message to me,' said Dad, his eyes still on the road.

'Did I? Well, feck it anyway! I'm always doing that. I tried to confirm my appointment for a breast check by text message last week and I ended up sending it to your father.'

Dad started to chuckle.

'I will *not* tell you what his response was.'

'The love doctor would like to reschedule for a private consultation in the bedroom, please dress—'

Mam clipped him on the ears. 'They had a scientist on the radio who thought it might be connected to climate change but yer man presenting the show is one of those climate change deniers so then the whole thing got completely side-tracked and . . .'

Leaving Aberdeen Street, we skirted the edges of the Phoenix Park and came down onto the noisy congestion of the city centre quays. Everywhere I went I saw Henry – all the places we'd been, and the places I didn't know if he'd ever been. I saw him in the lines of men who cycled into the park, the clusters who waited at bus stops, the lonely figures who visited the other graves. He was the constant mirage. And I sought it out. I did it to myself. I searched every crowd until I found him. The false hope that caused my heart to jump for the briefest moment was worth the nauseating plummet when memory came crashing in.

I watched a cyclist swerve between buses and taxis and articulated trucks. Henry had believed everything happened for a reason. But how would he explain what had happened that evening? Was he supposed to die at the age of thirty-three? What kind of reason was there for that?

The first time we met was at one of Claire Maguire's house parties. Years before 'let's do lunch' or even before our truth-or-dare kiss. Henry didn't really remember it, but I did. He was so handsome. He had heavy eyebrows and sallow skin – well, sallow on the spectrum of Irish skin tones. He looked like he should be on telly in some American high-school drama, not hanging around Dublin suburbs where the girls all had acne and the other boys were perpetually waiting to fill out. Henry towered over everyone, and he'd towered over me as we both waited for the kettle to boil.

'What are you making?' I shouted over the tinny music and drunken friends.

'Hot whiskey.' He took a container of cloves from the back pocket of his jeans and a naggin of Jameson from the other.

'Isn't that a Christmas drink? It's July!'

'I will honour Christmas in my heart, and try to keep it all the year.'

'What?'

'It's from *A Christmas Carol*. Charles Dickens. You should read it.'

'I have,' I lied, having entirely forgotten it was not originally a Muppets movie. 'Bah humbug, et cetera, et

34

cetera.' *Who tells people to read books at parties?* That's what I remember thinking. It was summer. School was over.

'There's an art to making hot whiskeys,' he continued, as if he hadn't heard me, which he may not have. It was loud in the kitchen. He grabbed a lemon from the fruit basket, threw it up in the air and caught it. The kind of move you could only get away with as a teenager.

'Go on so,' I said as the boiling water grew louder and finally clicked. 'Educate me.'

But just as he reached for the kettle, Aoife was at my shoulder asking for the cigarettes. They were in my bag so I left to go find them. And even though I hurried back, he was gone. Half a lemon sitting on the counter where he had been.

No longer interested in tea, I went and sat with Aoife and another girl as they puffed away self-consciously and gossiped about everyone around them. I was about to go the bathroom to check my eyeliner when a glass appeared at my shoulder. I turned around to see Henry Walsh proffering a drink.

'Thanks,' I said, stunned.

'Merry Christmas,' he replied and disappeared into the crowd. The girls looked from the hot whiskey to each other, wide-eyed, trying to decipher if the party line was approval or scorn.

'But it's July!' said the one who wasn't Aoife.

The next day I went into town and bought *A Christmas Carol*, the same copy that had been in his backpack that evening. I started reading it on the bus home, scouring each page for a clue to Henry Walsh.

We should have gone to the cinema that night, not a stupid house viewing. Henry wouldn't have been on the quays then. We would have met outside the Savoy, ignorant of how close to oblivion we had come. We were going to get our dream house anyway, our dream life. I made Henry come to the East Wall viewing. I made him worry about being late. I made him wear that stupid scarf.

I killed him. That was the truth. I may as well have pushed him under that truck.

'Pet?'

The traffic lights were red. It was early morning and everyone was going to work. I yearned to be like everyone else. Nausea hit and I waited for it to pass.

'Hey, Grace?'

Dad took his hand off the gear stick, momentarily, and placed it over mine and my mother's. I realised then that there were tears on my face.

'If it's too soon to go back, we can just call your boss and—'

I stopped him there. 'No, it's fine,' I said. 'I'm fine. Just – I'll be grand.'

'We'll pick you up this evening.'

'Aoife is going to collect me,' I said as the Portobello Kitchen came into view. 'We already arranged it.'

Dad pulled in outside the restaurant and Mam leaned her face forward.

'Kiss,' she said, and I planted one on her cheek.

'Bye, Dad.' And I stretched over to kiss him too.

'Good luck, love.'

36

The front of the Portobello Kitchen was as I'd left it – the 'r' broken off and hanging from the final 'o', and the second 'o' stolen, so it read: Po t Belly Kitchen. There was a sign on the door written in the style of those old 'No Irish, No Blacks, No Dogs' notices, only this version said: 'No Wires, No Macs, No Pods'. Below was another sign also in the handwriting of Dermot Gormley, my boss and the proprietor of the Portobello Kitchen:

That means NO WIFI you gobshites! If there's a laptop under your arm, keep walking!!!

I pushed the door open and made my way through the melange of old school tables, which Dermot had actually stolen from a school, a Christian Brothers place that had shut down in a cloud of disgrace, and beer barrels he'd gotten from the pub next door and just started referring to as 'stools'.

'Good morning,' said a young woman standing behind the counter. 'What can I get for you?' She was bronzed and beautiful and exuded a sexual confidence. You didn't even need the accent to know she wasn't Irish.

'I work here,' I said.

The girl frowned at me, then it dawned on her. 'You're Grace.' Then it really dawned on her. 'You're *Grace*.'

I gave her a small smile.

'I'm Christina. Tina. I'm new.'

'Hi, Tina. Is Dermot around?'

'He's in the . . . He's in his office.'

I lifted the counter top and passed through the coffee dock into the back room.

'Dermot?' I knocked lightly on the door of what had once been a storage cupboard but was now also the manager's office.

'My saving Grace!' Dermot pushed his glasses up onto his forehead and rose from a mound of dockets and receipts to give me a kiss on both cheeks. If you asked Dermot what he did, he'd tell you he was an actor, even though he'd never had a single paid gig in his life and he made all his income from running the Portobello Kitchen. 'It is good to have you back,' he said, replacing the glasses and inspecting me further. 'You look better than last time I saw you.'

'At . . . the funeral?'

'Yes. You looked dreadful.' He nodded. 'Much better now.' He led me back into the kitchen. 'Have you met Tina? Brazilian. She's new.'

'They always are.'

'I'm hoping this one might stick around a little longer. I'm paying her more than minimum wage. And I'm pretty sure her visa depends on it.'

Dermot had been a full-time unemployed actor when his father, a butcher, died and left him these premises. The idea of killing animals for a living turned his stomach so he converted it into a restaurant. He didn't know anything about cooking or management or HR (visa blackmail was a common tactic in his efforts to retain waiting staff) but he did like to eat in restaurants and he reckoned that was enough. Dermot had gone to the interior designer with a single word – 'Theatre' – and the explanation 'Because I am an actor' and they had decked the place out in cheap velvet.

And yet, entirely in spite of himself, the Portobello Kitchen was one of the most popular casual dining spots in the city. Dermot hadn't realised that, these days, the jars he was using because he was a cheapskate actually cost more than glasses in most homeware shops; the carpet that was plain dirty was seen as distressed and people thought the cabaret décor was self-aware. You could charge a lot for self-awareness in Dublin. Dermot got annoyed whenever the place was busy, which was every lunch and dinnertime, and the more he tried to turn people off, the more they came back. They thought his gruffness gave the place character. There was even a parody Facebook page dedicated to Portobello Dermo.

'Do you want to tell me about how you're doing or . . .?' Dermot winced at me like the words pained him. I gave him the benefit of the doubt and assumed the shaking head was involuntary.

'I'd rather not.'

'Thank God for that,' he said with a sigh of relief. 'Let's refresh your memory of the kitchen.'

FIVE

•••••••••••

The familiarity of the tiles and fridges and the extractor fan that Dermot had taped onto the wall himself after firing a Dutch chef who insisted it needed to be professionally fixed had a calming effect.

'Everything is much as you left it,' said Dermot, standing in the middle of the kitchen. 'The freezer still makes too much noise and the customers are as reprehensible as always. We've started keeping the eggs in the fridge and doing the sink-or-float test before throwing them out, blah blah blah. I can't remember which means they're still good but you can look it up if you're bothered. The rota is on the back of the bathroom door now. I think that's about it. I'll be gone for a couple of hours this afternoon. I have an audition.'

'I promise not to poison anyone,' I said, pulling my uniform from my bag.

Dermot shrugged. 'You can poison the whole lot of them for all I care.'

The crowds came thick and hungry right up until 3 p.m. I was slow to start but by the lunchtime rush I was in the swing of things. Hotpot heating, water boiling, bread toasting, and me crushing avocado into guacamole with one hand and stirring soup with the other. It was like I'd never been away. I enjoyed the constant busyness of my brain, and when it all calmed down there was a whole moment where I didn't think of Henry.

'One day for an aunt, uncle or grandparent. Bit of leeway there. A person could have a never-ending line of aunts and uncles.'

'You have one of each, Henry.'

'No need to tell them that. Three days for a parent. Very generous of them. It would take that long just to arrange a funeral.'

'How long do you get for me?'

'Hmmm.' Your finger traces down the page. 'Well, you're not a spouse but I guess we'd class you as a life partner . . .'

'Unless you're planning to trade me in.'

'No.' You sigh. 'I guess not.'

I flick the towel at you.

'For you I get . . . one week.'

'One week! If you died, I couldn't go back to work after one week.' A silence as I put away the last of the plates. 'Could you?' I turn around, and you are staring. 'Henry?'

'I don't even want to think about it.'

I throw down the tea towel and go over to kiss you on the head and face and neck.

'But look at this.' You clear your throat, pulling me onto your lap. 'If I die – which I think you could handle much

better than the other way around, by the way – you get money.'

'Oh? What are you worth?'

'Well, it depends on when and how, but at least €15,000.'

'Wow.'

'You don't think my life is worth more than €15,000?'

'It's not that . . .'

'Seems a bit cheap to me.'

'It's just, there was this Chloé bag in the window of Brown Thomas that I thought I could never possibly afford but now . . .'

You reach for the towel and flick it back and it doesn't quite make contact but I shriek anyway.

'Have I told you how much I hate you?'

'Yes.' I kiss you on the head, resting my hand where it fits at the nape of your neck. 'But tell me again.'

The usual resurgence came at 4 p.m.: the late lunches, early dinners and the sizeable coffee and cake brigade. I just about had the slate cleared when Tina started to deliver the 'Linner' orders.

'One hotpot, two bean soups, one special,' she shouted through the orders window that allowed me to see from the kitchen through to the restaurant floor.

Then two minutes later: 'Are we still doing the lunch special? One portion with mustard.'

And then: 'Tuna salad on flatbread, no salad, no mayonnaise, no – just tuna on bread. I'm still charging full price for that.'

I moved fast and efficiently. I could do this. Henry always said I was efficient. I used to think it was a lame thing to admire, just because he couldn't watch TV and talk at the same time. The buzzer went on the micro-oven and I removed a hotpot, placed it on the shelf of the orders window and hit the counter bell to get Tina's attention. I made three different sandwiches simultaneously and four minutes later they were lined up next to the hotpot. *Bing-bing-bing*!

I admired the tuna steak with particular pride, it was just the right shade of pink. Henry was right: I was efficient. *Bing-bing-bing-bing*. Where was she? Through the window I could see Tina talking to a man. Her skin really was as glossy as her hair, and the man— My heart jolted.

The man Tina was talking to was tall and broad with shoulders that barely curved. Just like Henry. His hair was different but that was possible and I held the hope tight.

'Tina!'

She turned, and so did he. The ringing chatter from the restaurant disappeared and everything slowed down. I heard myself gasp. I went to step forward, to start making my way to him, but the face wasn't right. I looked away, towards the floor, *breathe*, then I brought my face up again. It wasn't him. It wasn't a thing like him.

The door to the kitchen swung open and Tina came in to get cutlery.

'You okay?' she asked, her right hand hovering over a pile of forks.

'The man . . . The one who was just . . .'

'The German?'

'The one you were just talking to?'

'Yes, tall, handsome, a raspberry brownie-to-go. Tourist, of course. Too attractive to be Irish. Irish men,' she muttered, grabbing the cutlery. 'They all have the same three faces.'

I never knew when it was going to happen. I was so sure in Tesco one day that I actually called out his name. The man turned around and of course it wasn't him, but in the moment before I had been one hundred per cent positive that this was all a great mistake and Henry was not dead but actually alive and well and shopping for Bran Flakes on Prussia Street. I used to think Henry so singular, so incomparable. Now he lingered on every street corner.

When Olga arrived to take over for the dinner shift, I sidestepped her sympathies, telling her my friend was waiting on double yellow lines. In the corridor, I slipped out of my uniform and shoved it into a bag. Aoife was sitting in her battered Volvo across the road. She beeped the horn and I raised a hand.

'Well, how was it?' she asked, as I clambered into the passenger seat.

'Okay,' I said, pulling the door shut. 'Tiring.'

I told her about my parents' ambush that morning and the new waitress and how it had taken a little while but eventually I remembered how to do my job. I told her about how quickly time had passed, and I thought to mention the few minutes where Henry hadn't entered my head but I didn't. Instead, I told her about the customer who I momentarily thought was him.

'That's natural.'

'Is it?'

'Yes. I know it's not the same thing, obviously, but I remember coming back from basketball camp when I was younger and thinking I saw all the other kids from camp on the way to school for about a week afterwards. It's just what you're used to seeing, and what you miss.'

'I know it was in my head – I mean, I know that now – but at the time I'm always so sure it's him.' And as I said it out loud, I scared myself. 'I was so sure, Aoife.'

'I'm telling you, it's totally normal.'

'You're probably right.'

'Maybe you should talk to someone who's been through it?'

'I'm going to see the Three Wise Men tomorrow,' I said, and Aoife, who enjoyed hearing about my new friends up at the cemetery where Henry was buried, nodded her approval.

'And another thing, Grace.'

'Yes?'

'You need to sort out that house. I'll help, no problem, but you can't keep living like that.'

'Right.'

'And you need to get a proper night's sleep.'

'I am.'

'In a bed,' Aoife chided, giving me a side glance as she pulled out onto the road. 'We'll take it one room at a time. I'm off on Friday. What if I call around?'

'All right, okay. But now can we just—'

I didn't even have to finish the sentence. Aoife leaned over and pushed the button as the sound of the radio filled the car.

SIX

·········

'**U**sed to happen to me all the time,' said Billy.

Patsy agreed. 'I would have given you unbeatable odds Maureen was walking down Grafton Street a few weeks ago.'

'Ho ho! That was a good one,' exclaimed Martin. 'Tell Grace that one, Patsy. That'll make her feel better.'

It was Wednesday afternoon and the four of us were on our tea break. The wise men had been coming here for years, visiting their lost ones every Wednesday and Saturday and whenever else they got lonely, or bored. Glasnevin Cemetery was their men's shed, basically. I came when I could. Patsy brought the flasks and we always gathered at the graveside of Maureen O'Connell – his wife. It was Patsy too who decided when tea break was.

He took a sip of his own milky tea and placed the tin mug down on the cool marble. He waited for Martin to stop poking me – 'Wait till you hear this, Grace! This is a good one now' – and for the group to give him the attention to which he, as unofficial leader of the Three Wise Men, was accustomed.

'I was strolling down Grafton Street—'

47

Martin was already chuckling.

'I was strolling down Grafton Street,' Patsy repeated, louder this time, 'on my way to meet a man about some business.' Billy, quietly shifting back and forth in his wheelchair, winked at me. We all knew the only 'business' Patsy ever had in Dublin city was a swift one in the Palace Bar. 'And I saw this woman up ahead. I could only see her from the back, but there was something in her hair, her coat, that I would have put serious money on it being my Maureen – and you know I don't gamble easily.' I couldn't even look at Billy that time. 'Then she started to walk and I was convinced it was her. I hadn't felt as sure in years—'

'Ho ho!'

'So I went into pursuit. I started running down the street—'

'Ah now, Patsy,' interjected Billy, rolling a little closer, 'I've been running more recently than you.'

'Well, I didn't *run* in so many words, but I walked at a very brisk pace. The stick could not keep up.'

'Watch out, Usain Bolt.'

Patsy ignored him. 'By the time I got to her I was out of breath but I tapped Maureen on the shoulder, ready to accept that the past thirteen years had been an awkward misunderstanding, and she turned around and . . .'

'And?' I said, in spite of myself, in spite of knowing how the story would end. There was only one way this story ever ended.

'And it wasn't her, of course. Maureen's right here' – Patsy leaned back and placed a hand on the gravel of his wife's grave. 'The woman hadn't a patch on Maureen in the end. Couldn't have held a candle to her. And she was one of those charity collectors. I was so embarrassed about the whole business that I ended up sponsoring a rescue dog in Myanmar.'

'But it really does look like Henry.'

'All the time?' asked Patsy, taking up his mug again.

'No, not all the time . . . Always at first and then sometimes . . .' I couldn't be sure. 'Sometimes it does look like him, I think. And sometimes like maybe he dyed his hair or—'

'Audrey dyed her hair once,' interrupted Martin. 'She looked completely different. Have I told youse about that?'

'Yes, Martin. Several times.'

'Jesus, it was great,' he said wistfully. 'It was like having an affair.'

'Look, Grace, you're new to this,' declared Billy, turning his chair so as to block out Martin. 'We've had years to get used to it, you're only starting.'

'Great.'

'It does get better,' he said.

'And then worse,' offered Patsy.

'And then worse,' agreed Billy. 'But then better again.'

'Probably.'

The wise men had been coming here since they opened the new wing of Glasnevin Cemetery thirteen years ago. Well, Patsy had been coming since then – Maureen was the first person buried in this section – and Billy and Martin had been regulars since their wives died the following year. They used to be known as the Forlorn Four but the fourth fella was buried two over from Maureen now and they thought it was only respectful to find a new name. I'd given it to them, though I hadn't realised I was doing it.

It was a couple of weeks after Henry, and I'd come to visit him on my own for the first time. I was trying to fill the watering can so I could revitalise the flowers left by his parents but I couldn't get the tap to work. Patsy had shown me how to pull it up and jimmy it a bit before turning. Then Martin wandered over and said that if I ever forgot to bring flowers I could take some off Paddy Cleary's grave because his wife had Alzheimer's and never remembered what she'd brought anyway. Billy joined us then and told me that if I needed weed killer there was always some in the locker in the shed at the entrance to our wing.

'You're best getting the weeds before they start,' Patsy added. 'Lay some poison first week of May and pull them up a few days after.'

'I love the satisfaction in giving them a good tug. It's about all I get to pull these days.'

'Martin!'

'It's all right,' I said, surveying the three lads with their flasks and shovels and Patsy with a newspaper tucked under his arm. Maybe it was because Henry had been one, but I had a lot of time for newspaper readers. 'Is there anything about this place youse don't know?'

They looked at each other and shook their heads. 'No.'

'Well, actually,' said Patsy, 'we've only just learnt why it is that the residents over there' – he pointed to the only row of houses visible from where we stood – 'aren't allowed to be buried here.'

'Really?' I asked, following his gaze into the neighbouring estate. 'Why's that?'

'Because they're not dead yet!' And the three of them erupted into hysterics and started slapping each other on the back.

It was the first of many times I would hear that joke but, on the first occasion, it had made me laugh, and back then that was rare. 'The Three Wise Men,' I said, smiling, rolling my eyes.

They looked at each other again, getting excited.

'What?'

'Ho ho!' said Martin, poking Patsy before he was smacked away with the newspaper.

'I think we have it, men.'

'I think we do, Billy. The Three Wise Men.' Patsy repeated it slowly, considering it. 'That'll do nicely. Thank you . . .?'

'Grace.'

'Amazing Grace.'

And though I had always hated that nickname at school, there was something in the way Patsy said it that made me feel, somehow, better. Almost immediately, I had become an unofficial member of the gang. Martin had been a bit nervy at first about having a woman around but I promised I could top any dirty joke he told and he was soon won over. 'Amazing Grace,' Martin agreed whenever I helped him tend to Audrey's plot. 'Our lucky charm.'

I came to see them a couple of times a week. Mostly we worked quietly at our own graves, tidying them or watering flowers or often just reading the newspaper and staring into space. Every hour or so we'd meet at Maureen's plot for tea, shoot the breeze and rehash the same terrible jokes.

The buzzer went on Patsy's tiny alarm clock – which meant this break had officially come to an end.

'Right,' he said, draining his mug before handing it to Martin. 'Back to it.'

Billy put the lids back on the flasks and Martin gathered the cups as myself and Patsy rose from the graveside. The smell of Billy's coffee made me shudder. Since Henry died, I couldn't hack the stuff. We went back to the final resting places of our favourite people and alternated between diligent work and idle daydreaming. I could tell from the pen in Patsy's hand that he was working his way through the racing pages.

There wasn't a lot to do at Henry's plot. I'd already watered and straightened the flowers, and I'd finished the only magazine I'd brought. All that was left was to sit beside the temporary headstone refusing to accept that I felt no closer to him here than I did anywhere else.

'Do you need a hand?' I called across to Martin, who was undertaking some serious weeding.

'Absolutely,' he shouted back, and I grabbed a pair of gloves from the storage shed and hunkered down beside him.

'I used to leave the weeds, and the moss.'

'Yeah?' I said, burrowing a little hole in search of roots. 'How come?'

'Audrey was always shocking cold. She'd have the electric blanket on all year round, and up until the night she went into hospital she used to push her feet between my legs so I could warm them up. I thought the weeds and things might keep her cosy, you know?' He blushed. 'A little grassy blanket.'

'That's lovely, Martin.'

'It is in my foot,' he blustered, the crimson blotches rising further up his cheeks. Then after a thought: 'Don't tell the others I said that, all right? They're still mocking me about telling Billy to leave Audrey's plot alone and not to be rolling on our consummated ground. They knew well I meant the other word.'

'Consecrated?'

'That's the one.'

'I won't,' I said, dragging my finger across my chest in the sign of a promise kept. 'Cross my heart and hope to die.'

We sat there digging in silence, each building our own little stack of discarded green. Being in the cemetery may not have made me feel any closer to Henry but sometimes it made me feel less alone.

SEVEN

made my way through the mass marital breakdown that was Ikea on a Friday afternoon and pulled a newspaper rack from the pile. I'd always meant to buy one of these for Henry. Aoife held the shopping list – stopping systematically at the items I needed, ignoring any protestations.

'The minimalist look isn't working, Grace. You need a couch.'

The newspaper rack was not on The List but she let me add it to the trolley.

We shuffled through Bedrooms and Bathrooms – bed base, clothes rail, more shelving, lampshade, light bulbs, towel rack, towels, toilet brush, toilet seat—

'You really should have that one already,' said Aoife, lifting a bright yellow seat and cover from the pile. 'Even grief can only excuse so much.'

I'd been here once before, on a Monday evening, when Henry and I had first moved into our flat. I'd vowed then that I was never coming back, but that had been a mindfulness retreat compared to this. Kitchenware was particularly stressful. There were several broken plates, a toppled pile of oven gloves and a relationship combusting in the middle of Utensils.

'How are we supposed to *grow* as a couple if we never move forward?' the woman was shouting, oblivious to their children using spatulas to catapult teaspoons into the wheels of passing trolleys. 'Why are you so terrified of change? Why won't you let us grow?!'

'We do not need a pizza cutter, Diane.'

'We eat pizza!'

'Yes, takeaway pizza. From the pizzeria. WHERE THEY CUT IT FOR US.'

I was left minding the trolley as Aoife scavenged for crockery and cutlery. The slingshot children kept missing the wheels but they managed to wrong-foot a couple of older shoppers. Aoife returned with a mountain of plates and bowls and cups.

'Loads of spoons, no knives,' she muttered. 'Alanis Morissette must be running this place.'

We shuffled on, making it past the children without sustaining any injuries, and Aoife picked up a frying pan.

'Hold your horses there.'

'What?'

'Nope.' I took the thing out of the trolley and balanced it on a stack of candles. 'I draw the line at that yoke. I'm a chef; I'm not using an Ikea frying pan. I have lots of pots at home.'

'You might think about taking some of them out of their boxes so.'

Several more kitchen items were vetoed and Aoife picked up some tumblers.

'We already got glasses.'

'These are for me,' she said. 'I broke one at the weekend and I've been getting the smallest dinner portion ever since.'

'How long are you going to stay living with your parents?'

'Have you seen the cost of rent, Grace? Be glad you got out when you did. And I couldn't go back to a house share, having to be nice to weirdos who never wash up after themselves and leave passive-aggressive notes about noise levels and phantom milk thieves.'

A couple of wooden spoons were added to the growing mound. I managed to throw one of them back out. I was a woman with a mortgage, a single income and a finite amount of financial support. I could not afford all this crap.

'So I don't know,' Aoife continued. 'I didn't realise how poor I was until I broke up with Rowan. When there were two of us, rent was affordable. Now the only financial option open to me is sleeping in the twin room with my equally hard-up sister. It's like there's a tax on being single.'

Aoife McGrath and I had been friends since we were kids. But while I was an only child, Aoife was one of nine. It had taken me a while to get used to the McGrath household. At the beginning I jumped every time someone shouted – sibling at parent, parent at sibling, sibling at sibling, parent at parent – but I adapted. I learnt that selective hearing was an evolutionary requirement if you wanted to survive in a family of eleven. Screaming matches soon became the background music to us playing with Sylvanian Families on Aoife's bedroom floor.

'Get down here and FINISH YOUR DINNER!'

'I'm not hungry! And the CHICKEN IS MANKY!'

'THERE ARE STARVING CHILDREN IN AFRICA!'

'Send it to them then, and when you get locked up for POISONING BLACK BABIES WE CAN ORDER PIZZA FOR DINNER!!!!!!'

Even now her house was never quiet. Her youngest brother was still in school, and two sisters at university also lived at home. Her eldest siblings had children of their own and used Aoife's parents as a dump-and-run babysitting service. When Aoife had moved back home after breaking up with Rowan for being a useless layabout, she discovered her old bedroom had become a makeshift crèche. So she had to bunk in with her sister Sharon, who was as unhappy as Aoife about the situation.

'I thought we'd got rid of you,' she'd said, arms folded, the day Aoife turned up at the door. 'Have you no friends you can stay with at all? Are you not embarrassed to be back here at, what are you now, forty?'

'Thirty-one.'

'Well, you look forty.'

Sharing a room in your parents' house at thirty-one was nobody's idea of winning at life, but it was particularly frustrating when you were (a) as independent as Aoife was and (b) sharing with a sister who shouts 'F-M-L!!!' every time you came into the room. It didn't help either when everyone loathed the ex-boyfriend you were trying to sneak upstairs for a quick midnight shag. Even Aoife's mam had slipped up once and called him 'Moan' to his face.

'It's hard to enjoy a bit of how's yer father, when you're half thinking, "*Where is* my father?"' Aoife picked up a doormat and tossed it into the trolley. 'I wish Mam would reserve house keys for those of us who actually live there. Susan called in when we were in the middle of some Afternoon Delight to see if there was anyone she could pawn her spawns off on, and I had to shove Rowan under Sharon's bed and pretend I'd just come in from Hot Yoga.' Storage boxes, clothes hangers, some hooks for hanging paintings. 'It's getting hard to maintain dignity.'

'Maybe you should stop sleeping with him?'

'If only it were so simple.' Aoife sighed. More storage boxes, more light bulbs. 'I swear the fucker's getting better-looking just to spite me.'

Rowan was, to put it plainly, a waster. He'd start projects – writing a book, starting a band, getting a job – and then give up. Everyone was always better off than him and it was always someone else's fault. But Aoife enjoyed calling him on his bullshit, and there was the aforementioned attractiveness.

'I wasn't half as interested in sleeping with him when we were together. But now that it's forbidden, I can't get enough of his sorry-looking scrotum. I'm like a really lame Mills & Boon character.' She put more candles in the trolley, and I took them out. 'Will we get some things for the backyard?' she said. 'Plant pots? A trellis?'

Aoife battled her way into the Gardening section and I manoeuvred the trolley around a couple of teenagers running in the opposite direction to everyone else, hunting loudly for someone named Stu.

I'd tried to unpack some things the night before but gave up almost immediately and started flicking through *A Christmas Carol* instead. I never went past the bookmark, that was as far as we'd gotten this time and I couldn't bring myself to read on without Henry.

Aoife held up two pots. I pointed to the dark blue one, and on her way back to the trolley she narrowly avoided colliding with a woman distracted by her rapidly growing disdain for her partner.

'Do you even *know* what our kitchen table looks like? It's green, Paul. Green! These chairs are teal.'

The plant pot made a clanging sound as it landed on top of the one casserole dish Aoife had managed to sneak into the trolley. She blew her fringe off her face.

'They missed a trick not putting a pub halfway through this place.'

The first time I realised Henry could die was a Thursday night not long after we'd moved in together. I was reading on the sofa, waiting for him to return from football. I had checked my phone and thought, 'He's usually home by now.' At almost the same time, it occurred to me that something might have happened. It was completely irrational but it was also true: whenever he wasn't with me it was possible something had happened. I'd never thought like that before. I was shocked I'd left myself so vulnerable. Of course I knew Henry would die one day, just as we all would, but that was the first time I realised he might die on me.

The crowd thinned when we got to Ikea's warehouse section and I waited for Aoife to find the bed, couch and shelving units we had selected. Or rather, she had selected. I watched as a man helped her to take a flat pack from a ledge and slide it onto a flat trolley. Aoife gestured that she had to get something else, and I stood, drumming my fingers on the trolley handle, staring in the direction she'd gone. My neck was stiff and I realised then that I was refusing to move it. All these echoing corridors, shadows and recesses, I was afraid that if I turned my head, I'd see a ghost.

It was ridiculous, of course, but even as I realised it I kept right on staring at the point where Aoife had disappeared. Footsteps sounded like his, throats being cleared, even the jangle of coins in a pocket. It didn't take much. Aoife reappeared and I felt my shoulders relax. I quickly pushed the trolley towards her. Life was moving forward, I reminded myself, and Henry Walsh wasn't in it.

In the checkout queue, I worried about the cost again. The trolley was almost as tall as me now and I wished I'd paid more attention to what Aoife had put in there. In another ten months or so I'd have to figure out how to pay the mortgage on my own. And what if there was a problem with the roof before then, or the oven stopped working? I could not afford novelty aprons.

'This is not a hand cloth. It. Is. A. FUCKING. TEA. TOWEL.'

We'd come to a halt beside the pizza-cutter couple, who had acquired more purchases and apparently lost both their children. The man was waving a baby-blue towel in the woman's face.

'How would *you* know what a FUCKING TEA TOWEL looks like?' she retorted, taking a spatula into her own hand. 'Hmm? I'd have to draw you a map to our kitchen!'

'I swear to Christ, Diane, if I could afford to divorce you I would. What – I don't believe – what is this? Four, five, six. SIX saucepans? What exactly are you going to do with six IDENTICAL saucepans, Diane? 'Cause Christ knows it's not cooking.'

'I don't know, dear. I thought I might try lobbing them at your head and see where we go from there.'

EIGHT

. . . .

'Take.' **WHACK.** 'That.' WHACK. 'Rowan Kearns!' WHACK WHACK. 'Don't.' WHACK. 'Want.' WHACK. 'Your shrivelled ball sack anyway!' WHACK WHACK WHACK WHACK WHACK.

'I think that shelving unit's done, Aoife.'

'Just! Want! To! Make! SURE!' She threw the mini hammer down. 'Phew. This is good therapy, actually.'

I dragged my attention away from my own shelving unit. A third reading of the instructions did not explain why it looked a lot less like Aoife's than it should. 'When's the last time you, eh, saw him?'

'Last night.'

'That often? Aoife. Oh no.'

'Oh yes.'

'Where?'

'In the bathroom of the wine bar.'

'Oh, Aoife.'

WHACK WHACK WHACK WHACK.

'Well, we could hardly go to my place. *Don't let me disturb your tea there, Dad, just going upstairs for a quick ride*

62

with my ex.' WHACK. 'And his mam's always at his place so that's— What the feck is that supposed to be? Picasso's answer to a shelving unit?'

Aoife's dad was a retired builder and, of his nine offspring, she was his greatest protégée. My own dad liked to bring this up regularly and usually in the same breath as how he was a driving instructor and I still hadn't learnt to drive. It only took Aoife a few minutes to fix my mess and she was impressed by how far I'd managed to get without opening the packet of tiny wooden screw yokes that had apparently been there all along but were news to me.

'So Rowan's back home now too?'

'He couldn't afford the rent on the apartment on his own. He quit the bookshop.'

'Why?'

'Cause he didn't have a book on its shelf? I dunno. What did I have to go and shag him for?'

'Maybe it was just break-up sex?' I offered.

'We already did that. A few times. Oh, and I forgot the worst bit. He wouldn't let me sit on him.'

'Sorry?'

'When we were in the cubicle. I closed over the toilet seat and told him to sit and I'd sit on him.'

'Only way to fit.'

'Exactly. But he wanted to know why he had to be on bottom. Said it made him feel inferior.'

'Oh Christ.'

'Like, if you're that insecure, then don't quit your poxy job!' WHACK WHACK WHACK WHACK WHACK. Aoife cocked her head to one side. 'What was that?'

'What?'

'The knocking.'

'You,' I said. 'With that poor hammer. And watch my shelves, you're going to break them.'

'No, it came from the wall . . . In the hall.'

'Maybe I've a ghost.' And though I was joking, I thought of Old Marley dragging his chains through Scrooge's house and, in spite of myself, I shivered.

'Listen! There it is again.'

I followed her gaze towards the hallway but didn't hear anything. 'And I thought I was the one imagining things—'

Ding-dong!

Aoife threw me a triumphant smirk. 'I think your ghost is at the front door.'

In the hallway, through the stained glass, I saw a silhouette. It was too short to be either of my parents and Aoife was already here. I opened the front door to a woman, about eighty years of age, dressed in a heavy navy dressing gown with a scowl almost as long.

'So you haven't been mauled to death by bears.'

'Excuse me?'

'What with living across the road from Dublin Zoo and a racket coming from your house that surely no human could make, I put two and two together and presumed you had been mauled to death by bears. But you're still alive. That's good, I suppose.'

'You must be my new neighbour.'

'You're the new one, missy. I've been here fifty-six years.'

'Were we making too much noise?'

'Does Our Saviour sit on the right hand of the Father?' The woman's dressing gown opened slightly and I spied a heavy-duty nightdress. It was 7 p.m. She went on: 'I thought the wall was going to fall in on top of me. I only caught about three gongs of the angelus through all the commotion. Are you on your own?' She peered in behind me. 'I heard it was a couple buying this place.'

'I . . . it was. My partner died a month and a half ago.' *Partner*. Like we had run a law firm together. I hadn't anticipated calling Henry that until we had kids, but then I hadn't anticipated him dying either.

I expected the words to hang in the air – an awkward pause to acknowledge the death – but she just motored on like I'd said nothing of significance.

'If you need work doing, then Larry's your man,' she said, still peering into my hallway. 'He's down the end of the road. Last house, this side. You've seen the van.'

'I think so. The white one.'

'Terrible driver, couldn't park an arse on a sofa, but he knows what he's at. You need to keep an eye on him or he'll sell you a glass hammer and some rubber nails, but he made my hall table and it's still standing after that earthquake you just set off.'

'I'm sorry if we were making too much noise. I'll keep it down.'

'You can call into me tomorrow to apologise.'

'Sorry?'

'Just like that, but with biscuits. No not tomorrow, actually, I'll be out tomorrow. You can do your banging then. After eleven. I'm going out at eleven. I have Mass, then bridge. Call into me on Tuesday. You don't seem to go to work.'

'I've been on compassionate leave, actually.'

'So you're at home Tuesday.' She was already heading back down the garden path.

'I'm actually back at work now,' I called after her. 'As it happens I'm not rostered on Tuesday but I have other—'

'Good. Noon on Tuesday and bring digestives. Chocolate ones. And two Telly Bingos.'

'I don't—'

'Lotto tickets. You can get them from Pat, in the shop around the corner. You know Pat? Foreign lad. Funny accent.'

'Yes, but—'

'And make sure you get them before eleven,' she said, walking out my gate and through her own. 'They won't sell them to you after eleven on the Tuesday. Do you think you can manage to remember that?'

'I don't—'

Her door slammed and I heard various bolts and chains being secured. I closed my own door to find Aoife standing in the doorway between the sitting room and hallway.

'Nice old lady.' Aoife raised an eyebrow. 'I'll be off. I'll see you next weekend for some proper work, yeah? We need to buy paint. And sorry if I was going on earlier. I really need to stop sleeping with that waster.' She sighed as she scooped up her bag from the hallway floor. 'But there are bigger problems in the world.'

'Like grouchy neighbours?'

Aoife smiled as she pulled me in for a hug. 'Exactly. You're going to be okay, Gracie. Call me if you need me.'

NINE

made it to bed that night. Or more accurately, I made it
to mattress. The bed base was still in its saran wrap in the
hallway and the sheets still packed away. 'You've gone this
far,' I told myself as I stood beside the bedroom window and
ripped the black tape off the top box, the one marked 'Linen'.
You'd know Dad had done the packing.

The tape came away from the cardboard and I rolled it
into a sticky misshapen ball.

Would I forget his face?

I closed my eyes and Henry was right there. I saw him
handsome in that navy Aran jumper we bought in Dingle;
I saw the cheeky smile when he was convincing me to do
something reckless; I saw him during sex, serious and lost
in concentration.

How could I forget his face when I was haunted by it? I
saw him everywhere. I was not ready to let go.

It was warm and the air in the house was oppressive. I
forced the bedroom window up. For once the streets outside
were quiet. Dublin had finally fallen asleep. I tucked the
sheet in at the side and slowly I lowered myself down. I

closed my eyes to see Henry lying on his side, watching. I hadn't slept on this mattress since he left me. I spread my hand out to the right, where he always was. I left *A Christmas Carol* on his side of the bed and the water on mine; as it was in the beginning . . . I will buy a newspaper tomorrow, I decided, and I will spread it all over the floor on his side. I missed the ink on my feet. I curled up on my right to face him and let my mind wander to my favourite memory. The memory I tried to ration. The one I savoured.

So many of our first dates were in the Phoenix Park. His favourite place, and full of favourite sub-places: his favourite tree, his favourite valley, his favourite café. I enjoyed all those guided tours of Henry. I wish I'd told him that.

Eyes closed, arm stretched to the right, I floated up and over until I was looking down on the park. I sailed over the zoo – no depressed-looking lions tonight – past the tearooms and, just in front of the president's residence, over the cycle path, I hovered. I loved this bit.

I was using his spare bike and Henry, cycling slightly ahead, had slowed to my cautious pace. It was January but it wasn't cold. It was January 20, though I never told him I remembered the date. I wished I had told him that. It was January 20, it was our seventh date, and I was madly in love. I watched him cycling slightly ahead of me and I sent subliminal messages through the back of his green cord shirt. *I love you, I love you. I want to write your name on pencil cases and whisper it to myself at night. I love you, I love you.* And even before Henry turned around, I knew that this was a day. This was one of the best days. We cycled further still and the wind in my ears matched the humming in my heart. And I loved him.

'Hey!' you shout, turning your head, still pedalling.

I can't help but grin, your hair all blown to the side like a bad comb-over. You look like my dentist. 'Hey yourself!' I shout back.

Your head flicks forward to check the path and then back again: 'I love you!'

The wind pushes the words towards me, snapping against my ears, sending volts around my body. 'Well, that's convenient!' I shout back, the edges of my smile tickling my earlobes. 'Because I love you too.'

And that is it. A new reality established and the pedals never stop moving. For a moment I am worried my bicycle might actually start to levitate. And the bit that concerns me the most is not that I will have developed magic powers but that you'll suddenly know just how much you mean to me. Madly in love. I laugh but the wind is blowing against us and you do not hear.

Outside the Heritage Centre I throw my bike on top of yours and, once you have locked them, I throw myself on top of you. You take me in your arms like I am a weight you need to bear, like this is how you balance yourself now. I will hold you up, I think. And you kiss me fiercely on the mouth. This is a day, and that is so much more than a kiss.

Your face in my hair, the moisture of your lips and breath as you open your mouth to speak into the crown of my head. 'But I do.'

Half asleep I heard your deep baritone voice, and I gave an involuntary shiver from the breeze on my neck. But I didn't allow it to wake me. I drifted off and it was easy, us cycling and me telling you, somewhere in my sleep, not to go ahead. *Let's stay together*. And a wave of regret then because I was sorry. Yes, for that too. But also. I should have told you. I should have told you I remembered the date.

TEN

· · · · · · · · · · · ·

'**C**an I borrow your moss scraper yoke?' I asked Billy.
'I was going to do the edges today.'

'Knock yourself out.'

Although I'd been there an hour, I was only now getting down to some work. It was a Saturday and sunny so the cemetery's visitor count was up. 'Fair-weather mourners,' the wise men called them with no small amount of contempt. Patsy had been up and down like a yoyo, importantly directing people to where they needed to go and informing the newly bereaved that yes, actually, the watering can was supposed to be put back exactly where they found it.

It quietened down after a while and the four of us returned to our separate posts. Today I was tackling moss, or what little of it there was. Henry's stone had not been still long enough to gather it.

I had barely gotten started when a fresh wave of voices carried on the wind and we all turned to look.

'Here comes another one!' shouted Billy. 'They really need to signpost this place better.'

I stood to get a better look at the approaching tour group.

The other side of Glasnevin Cemetery was populated by the great and good of Irish history, but occasionally some group of American ancestor-searchers or Spanish students here to learn English would take a wrong turn and end up in our patch where the only notable burial was a county councillor famous for having the worst attendance record in the country.

This group of Americans – the loud enthusiastic voices, bumbags and unnecessary sunhats gave the game away – stopped inside the gate and examined their map. Patsy sighed and rose from his newspaper. 'Right.'

I watched as he talked to the tourists, gesturing back the way they'd come. Though I couldn't make out what he was saying, I recognised the tone. It was the one he used when telling us about the local history book he'd been working on since before Maureen passed away. ('It was hearing about the book that done her in,' Billy whispered when Patsy was out of earshot.)

A young boy in the group caught my eye. I waved at him and he waved back. I used to imagine what our children would look like, a funny mixture of Henry's genes and mine. His dark brown hair, my freckles, and cheeks that could have belonged to either of us.

The group turned to make their way back and I went to resume scraping barely decipherable moss from the edges of Henry's grave when something – someone – caught my eye. He was at the back of the group, walking in the opposite direction.

The air left me.

I closed my eyes and opened them again. But he was still there. He was hard to make out, heading away from the others, but it was him. It was Henry. I moved forward, just about, and started to make my way towards the entrance.

'You done with the trowel, Grace? Grace? Grace!'

I turned to see Billy coming towards me.

'Sorry, yes.' I reached down to pick up the trowel, failing to get a grip on it the first few times. 'Here,' I said, throwing it gently into his lap. Then I started to run, watching my feet as I skirted a few graves, mumbling a 'sorry' when I trampled on the late Pauline Russell. I ignored Martin's shouts and arrived at the entrance just as Patsy was heading back.

'Where . . .? What?' I shielded the sun from my eyes, moving my head back and forth in all directions. 'Where did he go?'

'Don't worry, Grace, I set them right. Told them exactly how to get to Daniel O'Connell's tomb.'

'Not the tour group, the other man. There was another man . . .'

I jogged a little further out of the gate, but could see neither the tour group nor the man.

'Grace?'

'Did you not see the tall man, Patsy? Broad shoulders? He was right here.' The frustration started to prickle at my eyes. 'Did you not see him?'

'One of the Yanks?'

'No! Not one of the Yanks. He was separate!'

'I didn't see anyone except the Yanks.'

'I must have, I thought . . .' I shook my head and swallowed hard. 'Never mind.' I strained my neck again.

'It's not him, Grace,' said Patsy gently. 'It's never Henry.'

I looked at Patsy. 'I was certain.'

He nodded in recognition. His smile was sympathetic.

'Jesus.' I threw myself down on the bench and put my head in my hands. 'Jesus!'

Patsy sat beside me.

'I never know when it's going to happen. Every time, it catches me off guard. I think I'm okay, I think it's all fine, and then suddenly it's like . . . I just lose all sense of logic.' I took a couple of deep breaths before looking up. 'Am I mad?'

'No.'

'I know he's six feet under ground,' I said, afraid to raise my voice above a whisper. I was not going to cry over a ghost. 'So why can't I stop seeing him above it?'

Patsy knitted his fingers together and stared out ahead of him. 'It's hope, Grace,' he said finally. 'That's all it is. And I reckon hope is a good thing.'

'Do you know how long we've been talking about this?'

'How long?'

'Two hours, Grace. Two hours and almost an entire packet of biscuits spent hypothesising about what great parents we'd be.'

'Nothing wrong with wanting the best for our unborn children. Multi-lingual, academically accomplished

athletes with good manners and a modest disposition don't just happen by accident, you know. One has to plan for these things.'

'Well, that is very true. I must admit I'd never considered the benefits of a foreign nanny until you ran that particular plan by me. Although I don't know how we're going to afford her, this French wonder woman with ten years' experience—'

'At least ten years, Henry.'

'At least ten years' experience and an unbridled love of housework that just cannot be quashed.'

'I used to spend my time daydreaming about men.'

'Little off topic, but all right. Thank you for sharing.'

'No wait, I'm not done. I used to daydream about men but now I've redistributed that mental space for this stuff. Like I used to watch movies and think, "I wonder how she got that body?" Now it's like, "I wonder if I could afford those floors?" I think about what our kitchen will look like, Henry, and what kind of children we'll have. I've sort of romanticised the whole juggle that comes with making that work. I have this gorgeous picture in my mind of Saturdays.'

'Saturdays.'

'Yeah. Up early, running here and there, bringing the kids to football and piano and drama, and then all of us eating lunch together. And you and me, in the evening when they're all happily tucked up in bed. We're sitting in our home, curled up on the couch, with wine maybe or popcorn, but just happy. I see this picture and it just makes me so . . . excited.'

'You big sap, Grace McDonnell.'

'I can't help it.'

'Come here and explain to me where this superhuman nanny will be while we're smooching on the couch.'

'Remind me of it, okay? When the day comes and we're sitting there and the kids are in bed and it just feels like the end of another mad Saturday. Remind me that I wished for this.'

ELEVEN

· · · · · · · · · · · · · · · · · ·

Early **Tuesday** morning, I wandered into the park in search of Henry's favourite tree. It took me a few minutes but eventually I found it, behind the deer, near the papal cross. It was gnarly and twisted with branches that went on for ever. Such was its weight, it had almost doubled over itself. Henry used to say it was sulking about not getting cast in *The Lord of the Rings*. It did look like an Ent. I took a few photographs with my phone and turned back towards home.

There were enough joggers in the park to make you feel like you were under siege. What were they all running from? That was what I wanted to know. I walked on the grass just to stay out of their path, and the sound of the breeze in the leaves above made me jumpy. I kept thinking about what had happened at the graveyard and I was on constant alert. I didn't trust my own mind. I was capable of seeing him anywhere.

If I knew I was going mad, did that mean I was actually still sane?

Henry was dead and buried. I repeated this to myself as I kicked my way back through the long grass. Most of his flesh had decayed or disintegrated; worms would be starting to digest it around now.

I looked directly ahead and thought of the photographs. I needed to show that tree to the DIY man at the end of the road, I had a job for him. Only every time I passed his house he was out. No sign of the van on my way back from the park that morning either.

So when I did call into my neighbour at noon, two Telly Bingo tickets in hand, it was mainly to get a phone number for him.

'Did you bring biscuits?' she demanded.

I handed over the digestives and she inspected them with the hand not already holding the Telly Bingo tickets. She was checking the best-before date.

'Pat said that was the brand you liked,' I offered. Pat had also told me her name was Betty and that she lived alone. He delivered groceries to her house – or 'messages' as she called them – when the bags were too heavy. She had never once given him a tip.

'Mmm.'

'So have you got a number for him?' I asked.

'Pat?'

'No. The guy at the end of the road, the man with the van?'

'Larry,' she said.

'Right. Have you got a phone number for Larry?'

'What the feck would I have a number for? Doesn't he live at the end of the street? Are you that lazy?' Betty sighed, as if she'd been all chipper before she'd opened the front door but my arrival had gone and destroyed her faith in humanity. 'It's about to start. Get in quick or we'll have missed the Home Phone Player. I hope you know how to play because I won't be missing out just to explain it to you.'

I had never played Telly Bingo, but I had the gist: it was bingo on television.

'Don't even have time to make tea first, for feck's sake,' she continued, closing the front door behind me.

Her hallway was dark but I could make out some letters on the hall table, all of them addressed to Betty O'Toole. There were three framed photographs above the table: Pope John Paul II, John F. Kennedy and a man I presumed to be her husband.

'Patrick,' said Betty, shuffling into the sitting room. 'God have mercy on his soul. Dead six years and I still expect the fire to be lit when I get home.'

The man in the picture was a little younger than Betty and wearing a suit. He looked a lot cheerier than his widow.

'Come on! It's started! And it's the feckin' blonde one presenting it. Sure you never win anything when she's doing it.

'Come on, come on,' she said. 'Pick.'

Betty was standing in the middle of a living room loaded with porcelain ornaments. Both her hands were behind her back. 'Right or left,' she said. 'Which ticket do you want?'

'Why can't I see them?'

'Because that'd be cheating,' she retorted.

'What? How? The numbers are allocated at random, and we don't know what's going to come up yet.'

'Do you know, with all that lip, it's a wonder there's any room for the rest of your face.'

I let out a heavy sigh. I just wanted to get a phone number for Larry. 'Fine,' I said and I poked her right arm.

She gave a sly little snigger as she handed it over. 'Good luck with that one.'

I didn't bother to argue.

As it turned out, neither ticket was a winner. Betty blamed me and the stand-in presenter, who she only referred to as 'The Blonde One' even though her name appeared on the screen several times, for our lack of success.

'Two little ducks, that's twenty-two.'

'Sigh.'

'Coming up next, it's forty-seven.'

'Tut.'

'Legs eleven – stairway to heaven.'

'For feck's sake!'

'It's down to chance,' I finally snapped. But The Blonde One continued to call out every number that was not on our cards, and Betty continued to curse under her breath and throw daggers in my direction.

'I am *not* unlucky.'

'Didn't your husband die on you recently?' she said, hunched over her ticket. 'You're hardly a four-leaf clover.'

I said nothing. Pointing out Henry had not been my husband seemed a bit beside the point.

'It's not *all* your fault,' she finally relented. 'It's never any good with the Blonde One. What is she wearing at all? And the Angelus barely over.'

I got up to put my crumpled ticket in the wastepaper bin when I spotted something moving from the window. I pulled back the net curtain and saw Larry's van driving onto the road.

'Larry's here,' I shouted. 'I've got to go.'

'What do you want from him anyway?'

'A table.' I grabbed my phone. 'But I want him to use a particular kind of wood.'

'Tell him I sent you. And that I need someone to clean out my gutters again.'

'Right, bye.'

'I'll see you next Tuesday,' she called after me. 'Bring the same biscuits.'

I didn't stop to argue. I jogged down the road to see the van coming to a sudden stop in a manoeuvre that was more perpendicular than parallel parking. The driver disembarked. He was a little taller than me, dressed in stained overalls and holding a sandwich in his right hand. I introduced myself and showed him the pictures on my phone.

'That's an oak,' said Larry, moving the thick ham sandwich closer to his mouth.

'Are you sure?'

'Positive.'

'I know most of the trees in the Phoenix Park are oak but this one isn't on the main thoroughfare.'

'It's an oak,' he repeated.

I studied the photograph of Henry's favourite tree with its deformed branches and peculiar shape. 'I thought it would be something more unusual. It's . . . It's someone's favourite tree, you see.'

'Ah.' Larry took a bite. 'It's still an oak.'

'Maybe look again?' I said, turning the screen back towards him.

'And . . . yep. Still an oak.'

'Oh.'

Larry gave me a smile as he continued to chew. Every time he took a bite, the butter bulged between the meat and bread. And every time he lowered the sandwich, it retreated. He was about my age, although his skin had that wind-beaten tan that made him seem a little older. His hands, given the dirt of his overalls, were remarkably clean.

'So you want a dining table made of oak?' He handed back my phone and I wiped the dust off it before putting it back in my pocket.

'Yes.'

'Good,' he said, butter advancing and retreating. 'Any other type of wood would have been near impossible to source.'

'So why'd you ask?'

'It's good for business.'

'How long will it take?' I asked.

He finished a mouthful. 'Depends. What are the measurements?'

'Maybe . . . this wide?' I spread my arms out. 'And like two or three times as long?'

Larry raised an eyebrow. The grin never left his face, I

83

noticed, it just shrank and grew as required. 'You got any concrete numbers? How wide is your door?'

'I don't . . . Well, I guess it's the same as yours, right?'

'Nope,' he said. 'This end of Aberdeen Street is older.'

I turned towards my end of the road and realised the bricks were slightly darker.

'I can call into you, get some measurements,' he offered.

'Okay, great.' And I turned towards my house.

'Not now,' he said, still leaning against his gate. A small blob of butter fell onto his chest and was immediately lost in the dried plaster and paint of his overalls. 'I've got a job on today. I just knocked home to get some tiles. I can call around Saturday, though.'

'Do you have a sander I could use too?' I said, remembering something Aoife had mentioned. 'I've got some floors to do. And actually the boiler's not heating properly, if you could take a look at that?'

'I'd have to get a plumber to look at the boiler. But I have a sander you can use.' The grin grew. 'You know how to work it?'

'Yes,' I said with more indignation than it deserved. I hadn't a clue how to work a sander. But Aoife had said I needed one so I presumed she knew what to do.

'Okay. I'll bring that around too.'

'How much will I owe you?'

'Ah,' he said, squinting up at the sky. 'We'll sort it on Saturday.'

'Great, thanks.' And I started to walk back towards my own house.

'Nice to meet you, neighbour!' he called after me.

And when I made it to the other end of the street and turned into my garden, he was still standing there, leaning against his gate, enjoying the sunshine and the last bites of his ham sandwich.

TWELVE

The days marched on and I went to the restaurant, worked on the house with Aoife and walked in the park. But I couldn't shake the feeling that I was waiting. And I kept thinking I saw him.

I fell asleep one night after reading right to the bookmark—

> 'Have you had many brothers, Spirit?'
> 'More than eighteen hundred,' said the Ghost.
> 'A tremendous family to provide for!' muttered Scrooge.
> The Ghost of Christmas Present rose. 'Touch my robe!'

—and I woke in a sweat an hour later, convinced there was an army of Henrys marching through the Phoenix Park and that I was just sitting in the house, waiting for them.

This was my reality now: waiting for someone who would never come. I went to see the wise men but half the time I was there I was looking out for the man who resembled Henry. I tried to tell myself that hadn't been him either, but

I couldn't fully shake the feeling. It was like suddenly having to accept black as white. I knew that whenever I didn't phone my mother for a couple of days, she'd get all maudlin and say how every young woman in skinny jeans reminded her of me. Was I experiencing the same thing? Was it just that I was craving him?

I thought about what Patsy said, about it being hope. That made some sense.

I'd taken to walking in the park a lot too, always ending up in the same spot.

'Hey!'
'Hey yourself!'
'I love you!'
'Well, that's convenient. Because I love you too.'

Most of the time I was fine, but then I'd wake in the middle of the night with a gasp, like it was the first breath I'd had in hours, like I was coming back from the dead.

Larry called in to get measurements for the table and said he'd take a look at a bit of crumbling plasterboard while he was there. Aoife, who had been painting the kitchen when he arrived, took this as a challenge to her abilities.

'You have a job,' I said, placating her. 'I can't expect you to do everything.'

'I just don't want him to fleece you,' she whispered back, as Larry came into the kitchen.

'That's all done now,' he said.

'What did you say your name was?'

'Larry.'

Aoife gave him the kind of stare you wouldn't get from the Special Branch. 'Larry what?'

'Larry Paul.'

'You're the chap who can't parallel park?' she said, arms folded. 'Your van is an accident waiting to happen.'

Larry responded with his signature smile before turning to me. 'I've arranged for the plumber to come next week.'

'Thanks,' I said.

'And the sander's in the hall. It's forceful enough, so if you want me to do it I could call in some evening.'

'Aoife said she knows how—'

'I've been sanding since I was twelve,' she said curtly. 'Shocking as it might be.'

'No.' Larry marked something on the back of a receipt. 'Not shocking at all. You look like a good, strong woman,' he said, and I suppressed a grin.

When he'd gone, Aoife gave me a look that said she was less than impressed.

'I could do a lot of that stuff,' she chided. 'And my da would be happy to help.'

'I don't think he's going to fleece me, Aoife.'

'If a builder sees a garden path, he'll say it needs paving and then he'll lead you down it,' she said. 'Let me know how much he's charging before you hand it over, will you?'

'I will.' I wouldn't.

'Larry Paul,' Aoife mumbled, taking back up her brush and throwing some paint on the wall. 'What sort of chancer has two first names?'

I had started to open the cardboard boxes in the kitchen so I continued unpacking. There was a box of trousers that should have been upstairs. Not that I'd missed them. I'd been wearing the same two pairs of leggings for almost two months now.

'Do you actually know how that sander works?' I asked Aoife.

'Yes. Well, I'm pretty sure.'

I looked at her. 'You said you were sanding at twelve.'

'I was. The summer we left primary school, I did all the floors in the Portmarnock Hotel for Da. I just haven't done it since, is all. Don't worry,' she said, circling the intimidating-looking contraption, 'I'll figure it out.'

It turned out Telly Bingo was on several days a week and I played with Betty when I wasn't on earlies. There was no point lying about when I was or wasn't working because she monitored all of Aberdeen Street's comings and goings with the dedication of the Gestapo from her sitting room window. When I grew a little braver, I would tell her she might as well do away with the net curtain entirely. Although I think she enjoyed the twitch.

The Blonde One, it seemed, was going to see out the spring and we often missed the Home Phone Player, the opening game of every episode, because Betty was busy critiquing her outfit.

'Imagine paying full price for that skirt and only getting half it. The gombeen!'

'In my day only streetwalkers wore lipstick . . .'

'Must be a lot warmer out in the television studio than

it is on Aberdeen Street . . .'

Betty wanted to know what age The Blonde One was and I looked it up on my phone. I found a recent interview where the presenter, who came across as a lovely woman, said she was approaching forty.

'But from what direction?!' Betty snorted as she jiggled a biscuit in front of her mouth.

Betty didn't believe in the Home Phone Player game anyway. 'It's too political,' she said, munching another digestive. 'The winners are always from the west.' She regarded me like I was a simpleton. 'If you think that's a coincidence, then you're even stupider than you look.'

Betty didn't 'believe in' a lot of things and I had learnt not to challenge them because they were built on an ideology as opaque as faith. Climate change, recycling, type two diabetes, foreign-sounding foods, deodorant, scarves on men, jeans on women and sandals on anyone would all be greeted with a scoff of disbelief. Ditto free-range eggs; any meal that called itself dinner but didn't involve potatoes; yoghurt; feminists; and gyms, mainly because she couldn't get her head around what people did in them and this made her deeply suspicious. She was only giving homosexuality the benefit of the doubt because she'd seen what that entailed on the soaps. There was a gay couple currently causing a stir on *EastEnders* and Betty was distraught that such fine-looking men would not be procreating.

'Such a waste,' she said with a wistful shake of the head. And I didn't bother to correct her on that either because I wasn't sure where she stood on acting.

But I liked being in her place. This was a home, somewhere gallons of life had flowed through, as opposed to my residence, which was very much a house. There were photographs everywhere of her grown children, all of whom lived abroad, and every inch of surface was covered in trinkets and ornaments bought by her children and grandchildren. There was a snow globe of the Virgin Mary standing beside Santa's sleigh that the Polish home-help woman had brought back from a trip the previous summer. Betty kept it beside her armchair all year round.

I talked very little about Henry when I was there and was unsurprised to learn that Betty didn't believe in grief counselling either. 'How are you supposed to get over it if you keep bringing it up?' she said. 'What you want to do is keep busy. When my husband Patrick, God have mercy on his soul, died I hadn't a minute to think never mind cry. And then by the time I had a moment, I'd gotten over it. And if it does get into your head, and you really can't get past it, have a drink. And if that doesn't work, have a couple more.'

I went to explain the theories behind talk therapy but The Blonde One had started calling out the numbers for the Snowball. In the breaths the presenter took between numbers, Betty got in key words like 'mutton' and 'lamb'. I, however, was only allowed to speak when the game was over.

THIRTEEN

The sander was broken. At least, that was Aoife's theory. Larry had given us a faulty sander, most likely as part of some sort of scam, and while she wasn't entirely sure what his game was I could rest assured all would be revealed when the bill for my table arrived.

'And if that's the kind of workmanship you can expect from him . . .' Aoife gave a scornful laugh as she shook her head at the bulky piece of machinery. 'I wouldn't be putting my legs under it in a hurry anyway.'

'Are you sure you haven't just . . . done it wrong?'

'Like how?' she demanded.

'Like, I don't know. The thing looks like a prototype vacuum cleaner to me. I could look up some YouTube videos, see if they have any tips?'

'Phone him.'

'What?'

'Phone First Name, First Name and ask him why he gave us a dud sander and what exactly his game is.'

'I haven't got a number for him,' I said wearily. Aoife was at odds with everyone at her house so she was hiding out here for the evening. And I felt like I'd been tired for months.

'Well, there you have it then.'

'Have what?'

'Doesn't leave a number? Uh-uh-uh.' Aoife shook her head. 'Larry Paul,' she spat, and I was actually impressed by how she managed to ridicule his name whilst simultaneously throwing doubt on its legitimacy, 'you could not be up to this generation of builders; cowboys, the lot of them.'

'I'm seeing him tomorrow. He's calling around with a plumber and I can ask him about it then. All right?'

Aoife gave a half-nod and went back to the Ikea couch she'd been trying to fix on-and-off since she arrived. I had, it seemed, managed to misplace one of its mini legs.

I stifled a yawn. 'I'm taking out the bins.'

In the backyard, the air was still and I could hear two dogs chatting across gardens further down the row of houses. One of the animals was fierce angry, yapping away nonstop, and the other was giving little sympathetic howls in response. It sounded like he was shouting: 'Oh I knooooow, I knooooow.'

I felt my way to the door that led from the garden shed out to the lane, stopping when my hand hit upon the iron lock and, despite myself, waiting. I stood and listened but of course there was nothing but the dogs. I pulled the wheelie bins out into the laneway and trundled them around the side of the house. The recycling one was full of cardboard and plastic from all the New House purchases, but the general waste was practically empty. It was unnecessary, a big black container like this for one person. Myself and

Betty could share a bin and still probably never have it full.

'Depressing,' I mumbled as I deposited the two bins at the front gate.

'I swear on my mother's life and all I hold dear that I am not laughing.'

'That might wash if I wasn't lying right here and if you didn't have your head on my chest. I can literally feel you laughing, Grace, as well as hear it.'

'It was a burp.'

'I'm sure.'

'I swear, Henry, I'm not laughing. Cross my heart and hope to die. Keep reading.'

'This is the kind of thing that leads to trust issues.'

'Just keep reading.'

'If you say one word about my accent—'

'Read! Please!'

'Okay. Ahem . . . "You'll want all day tomorrow, I suppose," said Scrooge. "If quite convenient, sir." "It's not convenient," said Scrooge, "and it's not fair. If I was to stop half-a-crown for—" You're laughing.'

'I'm not.'

'I can feel you!'

'You're paranoid, Henry. I'm not laughing. Keep going.'

'"If I was to stop half-a-crown for it, you'd think yourself ill-used, I'll be bound. And yet you don't think me ill-used

when—" What is . . . what is that noise? What are you doing with your throat? Grace McDonnell, you're suppressing laughter!'

'Nope.'

'The whole bed is shaking!'

'I just wanted to ask a question!'

'Oh yeah? What?'

'You know the way Scrooge has no friends, because he's such a miserly old man?'

'Okay . . .'

'Okay. Well. I'm just wondering if he, possibly, somehow, knows Jason Statham?'

'That's it, no more.'

'Maybe they play poker together, knock over an occasional bank, that kind of thing? Because that would absolutely explain the accent.'

'I'm not reading any more. Goodnight, Grace.'

'I like this vision. Sort of Guy Ritchie does Dickens. More geezer than Ebenezer. "Want Christmas Day off, Cratchit? Yuh, well, ask again and you'll be brown bread!" Brown bread, Henry. That's Cockney rhyming slang for dead.'

'Goodnight, Grace.'

'All right, all right. I'll get the light on the way back from the bathroom. I'm just going for a little Jimmy Riddle. That's rhyming slang for—'

'Good! Night! Grace!'

• • • • • • • • •

I slammed the shed door shut and double-checked the lock. From the back garden I could see all the way down the row of houses. Betty's and mine were the only ones without some form of extension. I guess it was easier to give up a chunk of your garden with the park so near.

'I sorted the sofa!' called Aoife, as I came back into the house, through the kitchen and into the sitting room to find the couch standing perfectly balanced across from the TV.

'Amazing! How'd you manage that? I thought I threw out that fourth leg?' Then I looked at the foot of the couch and saw what was holding it up.

'I found it in your bedroom,' said Aoife. 'It's the perfect size.'

'Take it out.'

Aoife looked where I was looking. 'What? Why?'

'Take it out.'

'But it's a perfect fit.'

'Take it out, Aoife!'

She dropped the complaint. 'All right.' She moved towards the couch, looking at me like she had when I'd started sleeping in the hallway. 'I'm taking it out.'

'There are other books in the boxes in the study,' I said, as she pulled *A Christmas Carol* from under the now lopsided furniture and handed it to me. It was unmarked.

Aoife went to find a substitute in the room next door and I carried the book, carefully, back upstairs.

FOURTEEN

· ·

There was going to be an inquest. In the days after Henry died, everything beyond the next breath seemed impossibly faraway. Then his mother phoned Thursday morning to say the date had been set. Henry's father was a lawyer and he explained that there had to be one if the death occurred due to unnatural causes. It often took up to a year for a hearing to be held so the fact that Henry's case was due to be heard in six weeks was actually rather quick. It was different from a court case, Isabel explained, it just established the facts of what had happened.

I missed his parents. I told them to call over, to see the house that was half bought by their son, but while Isabel seemed tempted, Conor thought it was best to leave me to it. Mam said they were letting me get on with my life. But she didn't understand that that wasn't a life I was particularly interested in getting on with. When Isabel phoned, I almost forgot Henry was dead.

'Don't cry, dear.'

'I'm not . . . Well, I am, but it's not the bad kind,' I said, standing in the yard at the back of the Portobello Kitchen. 'I'm so happy to hear from you.'

'Conor and I were just talking about you. He stopped by the restaurant the other day for his lunch.'

'I was in all week! He should have said hello.'

'He said the food was scrumptious, and he could just tell Grace McDonnell was responsible.'

I grinned, a memory swell of mealtimes spent with them and me and Henry. 'Is Conor still making his famous Sunday stew?' I asked.

'Like clockwork,' she replied, but I could hear her cutting herself short.

'Isabel?'

'I miss him, Grace.'

And I could see her then, sitting at her dining table in Donnybrook like me on the bench at the back of the Portobello Kitchen, both touching our eyes to see if they were showing us up yet again.

'Me too,' I said. 'And I miss you and Conor.'

'I wanted to invite you for dinner but Conor thought, we both thought, it would be unfair.'

'How could that be unfair? I want to see you.'

'You're young, with your whole life ahead of you. We love you, Grace. We can't hold you back.'

I knew what she meant and I wanted to tell her that no, there would be no other boyfriends, no other de facto parents-in-law, but Henry's parents were not gushy people and this was already more than enough emotion for one phone call.

'He was a good man, wasn't he?'

'The best,' I told her, and I pinched myself through the stiff starched sleeve of my uniform.

'Well,' said Isabel, rousing herself. 'We'll see you for Sunday stew maybe, one of the weeks before the inquest.'

'I'd love that. And tell Conor I said hello.'

And when we hung up I pictured her shaking herself back to the present at her Donnybrook table, standing to test the resolve of her limbs before finding there was nothing worth doing and sitting right back down again.

I wished they'd come to the house and tell me how they could see bits of him in it. Dermot had me working five days a week, varying hours, and I generally volunteered to stay late. Now that the others had stopped giving me bear hugs, I liked the silent companionship of splicing and dicing side by side.

Today, however, the plumber was calling and Simon, another of the chefs, was taking over for part of the lunchtime shift so I could run home and let him into the house.

'I'll only be an hour or two,' I reassured Simon. 'I'll let him in, show him the boiler, and come right back.'

'No worries,' he said, pulling on his uniform. 'I was coming this way anyway; I'm on after-school pick-ups this week.'

Then Tina's voice through the orders window: 'Three hotpots, one special!'

I took the docket from her and Simon took it from me.

'Go on. If you start you'll never stop.'

I shuffled out of my whites and threw an oversized jumper on over my leggings. 'Two hours,' I repeated. 'Tops.'

I was home at noon – having argued Larry down from a commitment that the plumber would call during a three-hour window to a commitment he would call between twelve and one. I waved at Betty, but she immediately disappeared behind the curtain. I ate a yoghurt and tidied the kitchen a little, washing the same plate and knife that I used for every meal. I unpacked another box of books in the study, a mixture of mine and Henry's. There were two copies of *Animal Farm*, and I opened them to see which was which. At the top of the first page of the more battered copy: *Henry Walsh. 1R English. St Malachy's Secondary School.* I hugged it to my chest.

There were two copies of quite a few books. I wondered how I'd never noticed. There was comfort in it, in the idea that our lives had parallel moments even before we knew each other. We figured out once that we had been at the same gig when we were fourteen. There must have been so many of those moments: same pubs, same parks, same long Dublin roads.

Ding-dong!

I left the books in a pile and pushed myself to my feet. But it wasn't the plumber.

'Betty.'

'Are you asking, or are you telling?'

I tried again. 'What can I do for you?'

'The postman left this.' She handed me a small brown box. 'You know that perfumed stuff gives you cancer? Nothing to do with your package, I'm just saying.'

I looked down to notice the slight tear at the edge of the

box and the bubbling brown tape spread over it. It was very like the tape used to hold Betty's remote control together. 'Right,' I said. 'Thanks.'

'No problem. It does my arthritis good to be getting up to open doors to postmen all day.'

I threw the box (prescription shampoo and moisturiser for psoriasis) up the stairs with the intention of bringing it to the bathroom later, and as it landed at the halfway point, I could hear Henry.

'Is it going to walk the rest of the way?'
'Next time I'm going for a pee, I'll get it.'

And when it was still sitting there four days later: *'Fair play to you, Grace. You must have a bladder like the Serra da Mesa Reservoir.'*

It was almost one. I considered phoning Larry before remembering I had no number for him. I was starting to think I'd have to give Betty a key, which I really didn't want to do. She'd have the black knickers rooted out of my underwear drawer and my pay cheques memorised before the plumber had arrived. And then, thank God, the doorbell went again. When workmen say they'll call within a given period, they always mean the last five minutes of said period. If you're lucky. My bag was ready to go, everything locked up, so I'd just let him in and show him where the boiler was. I opened the door to two silhouettes and raised a hand to shade the strong midday sun.

'All right, Grace,' said Larry. 'I'm legging it because I've another job I'm already late for. Andy knows what the story is, so you can leave him to it.'

Larry disappeared back down the path saying something about money and this weekend and maybe the floors. But it was all nonsense because there were no floorboards or days of the week, no new house or pipes or boiler that could only manage lukewarm. There was just him standing in the garden. And even that was being sucked away now; the modest patch of grass, the thin mesh fence that separated my property from Betty's, the broken slabs beneath his feet, Larry's voice and everything else. All sucked away. And what was left was only him. Because it was him.

Henry Walsh, alive and sun-kissed, and standing in our garden.

FIFTEEN

He **took** a step back, out of the sun, so his face was entirely visible. And still the truth prevailed.

'Henry.'

'No, mate,' he replied, though it had not been a question. 'Andy. How're you going? Sorry I'm late. You're having trouble with the boiler?'

I looked at him and those pale blue eyes looked back at me.

For a split second it was so normal. Here he was. Of course he was. Where else would he be? Then I started to spiral. It couldn't be. There was no way. He was dead. A truck on its way back to the UK after delivering a consignment of beet sugar had crushed his body under its rear wheel and the driver hadn't felt a thing. I remembered that I was a little insane lately and Henry probably wasn't there at all. It was probably just a man with similar hair or shoulders or just a man. It was another one of those, I remembered Patsy's words, another manifestation of hope. I looked at my feet and forced my eyes to close. I opened them as quickly as I could and looked up. It was still him. I could have vomited or cried or fallen to the floor but really I needed to stop spending so much time on the floor. So I forced myself to stay upright. Either I had lost my mind or it was Henry.

'You mind if I . . .?'

I nodded, because what else in the whole wide world was there to do? And then he was in the house. Our house. The house we had so badly wanted. There was a battle raging in my mind but if I could keep it at bay, then I could exist in this dream state or mental breakdown or whatever it was that had Henry moving towards me in the hallway of our dream home. But as he crossed the threshold, something shattered. It was him, and yet. Henry moved past me, not towards me, as if it was me who wasn't who they really were. He passed me and I wanted to inhale, to get his smell, but nothing worked as it should. I tried to keep my mind in place, to stop it reaching into pragmatism. If I wanted, I could stretch out and touch him. Was it another one of those dreams?

I stood to one side because, again, what else was there?

He hesitated between doors. How did he not remember our house? Henry looked to me, questioningly, but I could only shake my head. Or maybe I hadn't moved at all, but either way the hallway was spinning.

'Right . . .' And he took another step towards the stairs. 'I reckon the boiler is in the bathroom? Upstairs?'

I couldn't stop looking at him. Was it him? Henry, and not quite Henry. The skin more tanned and the hair lighter. Like Henry after a holiday, maybe. Is that where he'd been all this time? Had he been on holiday? Did he go back to Lisbon or Dubrovnik? Or had he gone somewhere new? I was in a dream and my head was floating. After a moment I followed Henry, or Not Henry, up the stairs. He turned into the bedroom mistaking it for the bathroom. How long had it been since he was here? That day in December when we came to see this place, when we fell in love with it and maybe a little more with each other and how our lives could have been. I was confused. I tried to remember the month (April) and the circumstances (Henry was dead; the boiler wouldn't heat).

He wandered into the bedroom and realising his mistake, turned. 'Sorry, wrong—'

But something wasn't right. I heard the voice from where I stood on the landing and it wasn't Henry's voice. I was as sure that it was not his voice as I was that the man who had just walked into the bedroom was him. I did my best not to panic, not to lose it completely. He didn't finish the sentence and he didn't reappear onto the landing. I no longer had any idea who that man was, the man pausing in our bedroom. I stood there looking at the doorframe, afraid that if I moved he would disappear and Henry would be gone from me. A wave of nausea crashed on all sides but I didn't look down. I didn't close my eyes. Not this time. I could not lose Henry again. I tried not to breathe.

Reality was starting to creep in, but the lack of oxygen to my brain only allowed it to travel so far. After some version of eternity, he emerged from the bedroom. Only now it was Henry again. He was holding something. He presented it to me and it reflected the sun from the skylight above.

'Is this . . .?' Henry's mouth moving, but another sound coming out. He looked up from the picture frame to my face, his eyes asking me something. He tried again. 'Is this . . .?'

And I nodded. It is us, Henry! It is us in Portugal! Our first holiday abroad. We were sitting on a wall by the sea and the sun was setting behind us. There were freckles across my nose, and his hair was almost as light as it was on this version of him that stood on the landing of the house that should have been ours. I wanted to reach out but I didn't move.

'You,' I said, barely more than a whisper. And he turned the frame to face him.

'This is you,' he said, looking at me with those same translucent eyes. 'And this is . . .' His hand moved to the man beside me. To Henry. To him. 'And this is . . .'

'Henry.' A little louder this time.

I was looking at him, and he at me, and suddenly my knees buckled. The battle of CO_2 versus reality roared in my brain. He threw out his hands and the picture fell to the ground, the frame breaking but not splintering, just a jagged line through his face, and I balanced against him. Those hands like mitts, big and strong and surprisingly capable of untangling Christmas tree lights and carrying me to bed when I fell asleep on the couch. I wanted it to be him so badly.

When I was standing, and breathing, he let go.

'What?' I said, because the oxygen had carried in reality and I was suddenly aware of where and when and, almost, who we were. But 'what' escaped me.

He picked up the cracked frame and I thought how it was from Ikea and I'd just been there and I was not going back again, no way, not for a picture frame. He held it in one hand, fingers stretching the whole way around, and he said: 'So that's my brother.'

I looked at this man and tried to figure out what he was. Almost Henry. But of course not Henry. Henry was gone. Or he had been and now he was back. Had I willed him back? Suddenly I was afraid and unsure and before I knew what to say I said, 'Don't leave.'

'I'm . . . I won't,' he said. 'Will we sit? Downstairs, maybe?' One hand holding the frame, the other still on my arm. 'Let's sit downstairs. I think I can help explain.'

Andy

SIXTEEN

· · · · · · · · · · · · · · · · · ·

had been standing on the side of the road for a full half hour before a car finally stopped. The bus driver that dropped me off told me this was as nice a day as you'd see in spring but we obviously had different ideas of what passed for spring. Could I not have packed just one pair of full-length trousers?

'Where are you for?' called the driver, winding down the window on the passenger side.

I checked the scrap of paper again. 'A house called The Sanctuary? The only address I have for it is Farmleigh, County Wicklow. Do you know it?'

The man gave a laugh. 'Yeah, I know it. Though it hasn't been The Sanctuary in years. Never deserved that name in the first place.' He leaned over to open the door. 'Hop in. I'll drop you up the road.'

He didn't have to tell me twice. I had been in Ireland four weeks. This was my third trip to Wicklow and the closest I'd come to actually reaching my destination. 'Thanks, mate.' I strapped myself into the passenger seat. 'Much appreciated.'

'You're not Irish anyway.'

'No, I'm not,' I agreed, having no interest in going through the ins and outs of my birth and ambiguous nationality. 'I'm Australian.'

'An Aussie.' The man laughed again, pulled out onto the road. 'I hear the beer is very dear down there. Is that true?'

'Dear, as in expensive?'

'Yeah. Mad expensive, I've heard.'

'I guess.' I pushed the scrap of paper into the front pocket of my shorts. 'What did you mean about The Sanctuary not deserving its name? I thought it was just a house name – like you get in rural places.'

'Maybe it's just a house now, but years ago it was a factory.'

'A factory?' The car climbed the hill and from the window, I watched the Irish countryside whizz by. There were a couple of farmhouses and a few sheep, but that was it in terms of enterprise. 'Out here?'

'Nobody from here ever called that place The Sanctuary. We knew it as The Factory. They were producing babies like they were coming off a conveyer belt. Sometimes we'd cycle up after school to try to catch a glimpse of the girls in the backyard. The story was they were only allowed out once a week. Wednesdays, I think it was. It's so long ago now I can't quite remember. I feel bad about it, a bunch of us up there gawking at those poor unfortunates. I don't think any of us would be proud of that now. Nowadays it's the only thing you hear on the radio – Mother and Baby Homes this, forced adoptions that – but we hadn't a clue. They were just women who couldn't keep their legs closed. Jesus,' he said, and I gripped the edge of the seat as he swerved around another bend as casually as if he were changing lanes, 'when I think of it.'

'Was it . . . a Mother and Baby Home?' I knew all about those institutions now. I'd read everything about Ireland's adoption history since coming here. But I still felt weird saying the name, it sounded so cosy – Mother and Baby Home – only it never fit the reality. And it definitely never occurred to me that I might have been born in one.

'Ah no,' said the driver who, I reckoned, was about twenty years older than me. 'It wasn't anything like the scale of those places. The Factory was more of a halfway house. You know?'

I looked at him. I didn't know.

'Where women in trouble went while they waited for the thing to arrive,' he explained. 'Until they could hand it over and go back to their own lives.' He shook his head. 'The stuff we used to shout at them. I do now, I feel shocking bad about it.'

'And is it still . . .?'

'A factory? No no. That stuff ended years ago. Although the foremen would have kept it up if there'd been the business, I'd say.'

'The factory had *foremen*?'

'That was their name, Mr and Mrs Forman.' He glanced over at me and laughed. 'I know. You couldn't make it up. Never saw anything wrong with what they were doing either. *God's work*. Here we are now.' The driver nodded ahead to a white and red cottage. The paint had faded and there were a few slates missing but even with that it wouldn't have been out of place on a twee postcard. This was the Ireland Mum used to get teary-eyed about when she'd had a couple of drinks. A few more drinks, though, and she couldn't say enough bad things about the place.

'It's so . . . pretty,' I marvelled as the car pulled in. I couldn't remember when I'd last described anything as 'pretty'. Possibly never.

'I suppose it is,' said the driver, observing the cottage. 'Gives me the creeps, though. What has you visiting anyway?'

'Family tree stuff,' I told him, opening the car door and then adding for no particular reason: 'I had an uncle born here.'

'Poor bastard. Rather him than me.'

'Yeah. Thanks for the lift,' I said as I climbed out.

'Oh, wait!'

The driver rolled down the window again. 'Yeah?'

'Do they still live here, the Formans? The ones who ran the . . . factory?'

'Sure do. They come into town for Mass on Sundays, and there are carers in and out to them. They never did anything wrong, technically. But sure that's Ireland for you: nobody's ever to blame, technically. They should be locked up, as far as I'm concerned.' He started up the engine again. 'Best of luck now.'

'Thanks.'

The car pulled off and I turned to have a proper look at the house where I was born.

Andy

SEVENTEEN

● ●

I couldn't remember a time when I hadn't known I was
adopted. Mum regularly told me how she got me from
a baby hospital in Dublin right before she and my aunt
and grandma moved to Australia. People found it hard to
believe that before she died I'd had zero interest in finding
out about where I came from. It was a point of fascination
in the school yard. I'd moved around enough to know that
being adopted was exotic enough to interest schoolmates
who might otherwise ignore the arrival of yet another new
kid. But when lung cancer finally got her, I suddenly felt
compelled to know. I guess it was the loss that spurred me
on. I'd always felt like something was missing and even
though I hadn't been so close to Mum in later years, when
she was no longer there that inherent loneliness had become
more acute.

Before I arrived in this country, getting information
was like pulling teeth. Tenacity and dedication were not
traits I had possessed in a long time and I was as surprised
as anyone that I hadn't just given up. I already had my
adoption certificate and Grandma told me that the 'baby

hospital' where Mum had gotten me was in south Dublin. Communication with the Irish adoption authorities had been slow to start but once it transpired my birth mother was dead, they were a lot more forthcoming. The second phone call from my assigned social worker provided me with her name and the information, which they presumed I already had, that she'd given birth to another boy about twenty minutes before me. That was what the social worker told me: I had a twin.

Understandably I was stunned, speechless actually, and the woman on the phone started stuttering and saying that maybe she'd gotten it wrong and she'd double check and come back to me. But by the time she rang back a few weeks later and confirmed that yes I had had a brother, I was no longer so surprised. I'd quizzed Grandma and she was as shocked as me, and there was no way Mum had been told, but somehow, somewhere deep down, it was like I already knew.

I had always told myself that the sense of longing I carried was due to being an only child or knowing I was adopted or having a flaky mother. And yet none of those reasons ever felt quite right. But a brother, that felt real.

'What do you mean *had*?' I asked the social worker, speaking into the phone in the dead of night in the reception of the Sydney resort where I was living and working. 'What do you mean I *had* a brother?'

The woman at the end of the line hesitated. I imagined her in an office in Dublin, looking out onto some rainy field. It was the close of the working day on the other side of the world. And then she told me that my brother had died a week previously in a traffic accident.

She had promised to come back with more information but when I hadn't heard from her in two weeks and my internet searches proved useless, I phoned the office only to be told she had gone on maternity leave. After that, I might as well have been speaking Swahili for all the information I got out of them. I hadn't expected to care this much – but then I hadn't expected to have a brother. There was something about this other life, this unknown existence on the opposite hemisphere that could as easily have been mine, that kept me going.

I took what little money Esmerelda – my mum; she'd been christened Edna but refused to answer to it – had left me and booked a flight to Ireland. I left the resort where I'd been working for six months and the woman I'd been seeing for as long, without handing in my notice to either. Maybe in Ireland I'd understand what it was to belong and I'd stop being the sort of man who thought nothing of running away.

'Hello?' I knocked on the front door of The Sanctuary, or The Factory, or whatever this fairly modest-looking cottage was called.

I waited but nothing stirred inside. 'Hello!' I shouted. 'Is anyone home?'

A few days after I arrived in Dublin, I had gone to the 'hospital' where Mum had gotten me but it was an apartment complex now. I spent two weeks unsuccessfully trying to meet someone from the adoption services. In the end I found the Adoption Rights Alliance and they pointed me in the direction of St Patrick's Guild – the religious order that had run the hospital I'd been adopted from. I'd finally started getting places but by then I was running out of money. Esmerelda hadn't left a lot. Which she'd be glad about; life was for living and all that. I stopped by a few building sites and called into hardware shops looking for numbers. I found enough nixers to get by.

I checked my watch. I had a couple of hours until a lunchtime job near the city.

I'd filled out several Freedom of Information forms but was told it could take five weeks to get a decision on my request, and even then that decision might be that the information would take several more weeks to source. So I'd started turning up at the head offices of the guild that handled my adoption. Most mornings if I didn't have a job on, I went there. I'd camp out in the foyer, badgering the receptionist and marvelling at this new-found tenacity. They threatened to call the police but I knew they were bluffing, and eventually they cracked.

I tried the front door of The Sanctuary a third time but didn't bother waiting for a response before heading around the side of the house. I looked through a dirty window into a bedroom that didn't look like it had been occupied anytime recently. The backyard was large and overgrown. There was a kennel with no sign of a dog and a shed that looked like it might collapse at any minute. In the middle of the weeds stood a statue of the Virgin Mary, dressed in her white and blue with a set of rosary beads draped over her hands. I tried the back door.

'Hello? Hell-oohh??'

St Patrick's Guild had handed over a file so immaculately presented I was convinced they'd written it up while I was waiting in the foyer, and not thirty-four years before. But the guild was known for its impeccable record-keeping – 'Like the Nazis,' said the woman at the adoption alliance, adding that the problem wouldn't be the file existing, the problem would be getting them to hand it over. But they had. A couple of sheets of paper imprinted with the neatest handwriting: *Child Two. Born to Frances Clinch, aged 19, on 2 October 1984, the second brother, twin. Both born at The Sanctuary, Farmleigh, Co Wicklow. Child One removed by private adoption. Child Two unexpected, surplus.*

'Hello!'

A flutter of wings as birds fled the adjacent tree. I started knocking on the back door and didn't stop.

'HELLO HELLO HELLO HELLO HELLO HELLO HELLO . . .'

I'd found Frances's grave and I went to visit a couple of times. I didn't feel anything in particular for the slab of marble in the middle of a massive cemetery that also doubled as a tourist attraction and was always full of sightseers searching out the historical Irish figures buried there. It just made Frances seem even less significant.

I hadn't a clue where my brother was buried. I didn't even know his name. I had tried trawling through news archives for traffic accidents in the weeks after I got that phone call from the adoption services, but without a name it was near impossible.

Had he known about me? Had my brother ever thought to go to Australia to seek me out? Had he walked up this same Wicklow road, looking for the house where we were born? I imagined a man with a similar though not identical face, and with the same restlessness I carried at my core. I imagined a man who had grown up on the other side of the world with an identical sensation that something, or someone, was missing.

When my knuckles grew sore, I stopped knocking. If there was anyone in, they weren't going to answer. I checked the time again. Was I five kilometres from the town, maybe more? How far had that car driven me? I took one last look at the house, doing my best to peer through the frosted glass at the back, and, reluctantly, left.

I walked out onto the country road, pulled the scrap of paper with The Sanctuary address from my pocket and flipped it over: 2 Aberdeen Street. I was meeting Larry, one of the men who'd thrown a bit of work my way, at his home for some local job, a boiler that needed looking at. I needed to head back to the guesthouse first to pick up my tools. I started walking in the direction I'd come. I could have done without having a job on this afternoon – if I stuck around a little longer the Formans might show up – but I needed the money. If only I could have discovered this sort of dedication in school, I might have had a career that didn't leave me so frequently skint. I checked the time again and picked up the pace. If I didn't hurry, I was going to be late.

EIGHTEEN

followed him downstairs, both of us stepping over the psoriasis shampoo and moisturiser that were now peeking out of the box because Betty had done such a poor job of covering her tracks. At the bottom of the stairs he turned into the living room and then through to the kitchen. I kept thinking I had it straight and then an obvious and inconvenient problem with the scenario would rear its head.

He sat at the table and I, automatically, went to switch on the kettle. 'Ha!' I said. And then, 'Sorry.' The point I wanted to make was that there really was no situation we Irish wouldn't try to fix with a cup of tea, even when that situation was that a man with your deceased boyfriend's face had stopped by to fix the boiler. But all I managed was to gesture at the kettle and go: 'It's just . . . Pssshh. Ridiculous.' I shook my head, and Henry smiled, though it wasn't him. It was the nose that was different; the skin and the hair and the nose.

'Your nose,' I offered in a statement that made no sense outside my head.

His hand traced its outline. 'I broke it years ago. Playing rugby.'

And I laughed because that was clearly a lie. The first time Henry met my parents, Dad asked what sports he liked and Henry said 'ABR', and Dad asked were they Spanish, and Henry said, 'No: Anything But Rugby', and Dad thought he was great gas after that.

'Sorry,' I said, unable to explain what was so funny. 'I might be going hysterical. Are you . . .?'

But I could only laugh again because each possible question was as stupid as the last. My mind was mainly blank.

'I'm not him,' he said, as embarrassed as me to be having such a conversation.

'Henry.'

'Henry . . .' He considered the word. 'I'm not Henry.'

'I know.' Which was true. I did know, now I could see him clearly. The skin and the hair and the nose. And the voice. He repeated Henry's name and it was so strange because it came from his mouth but it was not Henry speaking. The way he said it, it went up at the end, like a song, and he didn't quite pronounce the H. It was like I was making tea for a changeling. I laughed again, but he was looking at me in alarm so I decided to stop laughing. And not wanting to be rude, I told this changeling that the tea was coming. I chased the water with milk and it occurred to me that I was not making tea for who I had thought I was making tea for and it was probably too weak, too milky.

'I'm not picky,' he said. 'I don't really drink the stuff.'

What do you mean? You drink gallons of the stuff! Sometimes I have coffee, but you always have tea. You won't have a biscuit without a cup. But of course, of course . . . Grace. Concentrate.

'I'll carry those over.' He jumped from the chair and brought the cups to the table and I realised my hands were shaking, like the sails on those shitty boats at Dun Laoghaire harbour.

'Is this too much?' he asked. 'I can come back again if it is, if I've given you a shock. Hell, I've given myself a shock. I had no idea, by the way, that this was your house, his house, that this was *Henry*'s house. I just got a call from Larry about a job and I was available so here I am. Crazy, ay? Weeks I've been trying to find out anything about him and then . . .'

After a few sentences in that voice that was definitely not Henry's, I was more lucid. I could think straight.

'No, I'm sorry,' I said, sliding a cup towards me. 'Stay. Have the tea. Actually, we could probably both do with some sugar in it. For the shock.' I pushed the bowl towards him. 'So you're not Henry.' The laugh that followed *was* a lucid one because I knew what I was saying and, come on, how hilarious is that?

'No, I'm Andy.'

'Okay. Andy.' I nodded. 'But you look exactly like Henry. Almost exactly, except . . .' *The skin, the hair, the nose.*

'It's crazy, ay?' Andy observed the cracked photo frame again. 'I didn't know. I thought we might look alike but I

120

wasn't sure. There's no record of how many placentas there were at birth, that's sometimes how they tell if twins are identical or not. And obviously there was no DNA test . . . We look pretty alike though, ay?

'Twins?'

'That's right. Henry is my twin. Was my twin. I . . . I'm sorry for your loss.'

We both squirmed at that. And when I was done cringing, I goggled my eyes at him expectantly. There were too many questions and maybe he would just know which one to answer first. Henry was an only child. He has no siblings and certainly no twin. I had known no human better and more intimately than I had known Henry Walsh and if there was another, I would have known that too. Eventually, because this man was not taking the initiative, I stated the obvious: 'Henry didn't have a twin.'

'Neither did I until a couple of months ago. Not one I knew about, anyway. Mum passed away last year and—'

'I'm sorry to hear that,' I said automatically, though what I was thinking was: Isabel Walsh is alive and well and probably planting petunias in her back garden in Donnybrook as we speak.

'Yeah, thanks. When she died, I went looking for information on my birth parents. Mum would have been good with me doing it when she was alive but it was never that important to me. And then suddenly it was.' He gave an embarrassed smile, which I automatically returned. I wanted to reach out and touch it. 'I got in contact with the adoption services here and they told me my birth mum was long dead, there was no father listed and that, oh yeah, I had a twin. But then they came back and said he was dead now too.'

'Henry.'

'Right. Except I didn't know his name until a few minutes ago. I always knew I was adopted, but I hadn't a clue I had a brother. A *twin* brother!' It was his turn to laugh, albeit ruefully. 'There's no way Mum knew either. She was open about it all. I asked my grandma; she was as shocked as me.'

He turned his mug around and around but didn't raise it to his mouth. 'I should have gone looking for information earlier,' he said, staring into the cup. 'I should have. Imagine if I'd contacted the adoption services earlier, even a year before. I could have met Henry, we could have gotten to know each other. I mean . . . you don't know how that kind of meeting could alter the course of your life, do you? Maybe he would have come to Australia to visit me this year, or been held up somewhere else waiting on a phone call from me. It's possible, isn't it?'

'Sorry?' I said. I was doing my best to concentrate. 'What's possible?'

'That if we'd met, he might still be alive.'

He spoke as easily as a man complaining about the traffic or the weather, and suddenly, outrageously, I wanted to slap him. I needed a minute to catch up.

'So sorry now, Henry was . . . adopted?' And I was off again, that high-pitched laugh.

Henry was not adopted. Henry was tall like his mother and had hair like his father. There had been an adopted girl in my primary school and everyone knew before she told us because her skin was so much darker than her parents'. Henry wasn't adopted. Henry looked like his parents. I thought of the family portrait on the piano in Donnybrook. They were a handsome family. I said it out loud, just so we were all clear: 'Henry was not adopted.'

'Yes, he was.'

I couldn't figure out why the changeling was nodding, but then I realised I was shaking my head.

'Jesus,' he said. 'You didn't even know he was adopted? Did he not know? Wow.' The changeling leaned back in his chair. 'This really is a surprise. I assumed you knew that. No? You didn't know? And Henry didn't know. Wow.'

I felt sorry for him, this man who stole Henry's face and couldn't seem to get his story straight. 'No, he didn't know,' I said reasonably. 'He didn't know because he wasn't adopted.'

The man with Henry's eyes and Henry's mouth and Henry's hands looked at me and sighed. 'If he wasn't,' he said finally, 'then how do you explain me?'

NINETEEN

················

Our first time.
    Date: New Year's Eve 2012. Technically, New Year's Day 2013.
    Location: My parents' house.
    Alcohol consumed: a bottle of red wine (shared), three gin and tonics (me), two pints and a Jameson (you).
    Inebriation levels: Could still recite the Our Father in Irish and make a decent stab at walking in a straight line backwards. Possibly not at the same time.
    Soundtrack: David Gray's White Ladder.
    'David bloody Gray? Seriously?'
    'I know. I'm sorry. It's been stuck in my CD Player since 2002.'
    'Jaysus . . .'
    'Would you rather silence?'
    'What if your parents come home, Grace?'
    'I told you, they're at my auntie's party. They won't be back until the early hours of next year.'
    You're pretending to look at the books on my bookcase. I'm wondering if you're carrying a condom and, if not,

what time the Spar down the road opens until.

'If I was you, I'd just throw out the whole CD player.'

'I haven't actually lived here in six years,' I say, as you take Animal Farm *from the shelf. 'We did that in school.'*

'Us too.' You flick through the pages. 'I remember going downstairs to my dad and telling him how I had this idea that the whole story was a metaphor for the class system – I honestly thought I was the first person to figure it out.'

'Me too!' I say, sitting up straight on the bed. 'I swear to God. I did a book report outlining my "theory". That's mad. What a coincidence.'

'There's no such thing as coincidence,' you say, putting the book back on the shelf, not where you found it but frankly alphabetised bookshelves can go and shite right now. 'Everything happens for a reason, that's what I reckon.' You keep talking so I won't notice that you're coming to sit next to me on the bed.

'Even school book reports?'

'Yep. Years before we knew each other, it was written in the stars: meant to be.'

I roll my eyes, pretending I don't feel your thigh against mine. It's been a week since Let's Do Lunch. This is our third date. I know what is about to happen and I accept that I am a three-date cliché. But it's Christmas, and a Christmas romance is even better than a summer one.

You continue: 'You know one in three Irish households own this album?'

'I'm pretty sure that fact is on the citizenship test.' I turn to face you, my legs crossed into a lotus position. You're still

125

looking straight ahead. At the bookcase. 'That, and what's the bestselling single of all time.'

'Elton John. "Candle in the Wind".'

'Ding ding ding. One shiny harp-imprinted passport coming your way, Henry Walsh.'

Deciding this very Irish foreplay has gone on long enough, and emboldened by the wine, I get up from the bed. I ignore the laminated Mass card for my granddad that my mother has left on the side table. I stand in front of you and confidently straddle a leg either side. You quickly get your hands out of the way and I lower my body, careful to ensure my legs bear most of the burden. I want to give off the impression of lithe for as long as possible.

You kiss me and a warmth floods my body. Your tongue fat against mine, I pull back. I tease your lips and return to your tongue. Your hands on my side, static against the material of my tights and so secure that I almost chance lifting my feet. Almost. I edge slightly to the side, you take the hint and roll me over. You bear down on me and smile. 'How's it going?'

I'm grinning too. And there's a pause as the music seems to grow louder. You throw your head back: 'Babylon!'

And my whole body starts to shake below yours. You roll over and lie beside me, both of us staring at the ceiling, laughing and occasionally singing along in that mocking, quivering voice that makes me think of those dog figurines with wobbly heads that you see in the back windows of cars.

'I could turn on the radio?'

'But then you chance getting the News.'

'True.'

'Let's just turn it down, low.'

And so I do. And when I come back to the bed, your arms are summoning me again. I am envious of how confident you are, in a room and a bed you've never been in before.

I climb gently on top of you. We're still fully clothed and it's an hour until midnight. There's a non-verbal agreement that we have all of the time in the world, more than the old year and the new year combined, and we progress slowly. Step by step, layer after layer, whisper into whisper, until there is nothing left to hide behind.

And somewhere in a half-dream, I murmur 'you, you, you', and a year later you tell me that you heard it.

TWENTY

'**So Henry** was adopted.' A statement or question, who could say?

'We both were.' This man, Andy, took a reluctant sip of his tea with Henry's mouth and placed the cup back on the table with Henry's hand. I let my own go cold. 'Did he seriously not know?'

Maybe it was my head spinning, but it really felt like we were going in circles.

However, since a version of Henry was now sitting in front of me – if instead of being dead for the past two months, he'd been sunning himself somewhere nice – anything, I reasoned, was possible. I thought about it, I did my best, but I kept hitting a brick wall. 'He looks like his parents.'

'People who don't know say I look like my cousins. It happens.'

'He doesn't sound like you.'

'You're not born with an accent, Grace.' I flinched as Henry's mouth said my name because that was all wrong too, changing the 'a' to an 'i' sound like he was making fun. 'We were born in Wicklow, at the house of a couple that, from what I can gather, would take in unmarried mothers until they had given birth. Then the kids went up for adoption. Henry's adoption had been arranged in advance. It was a private adoption and there was a couple waiting to take him – his parents, I guess?'

I thought of Isabel and Conor. I found it hard to picture Isabel pregnant, she was so fragile, but I found it just as hard to picture her organising a back-alley adoption.

Andy continued: 'I don't know everything yet, I'm working on it. But I know we were born on October second and that our biological mother was a woman called Frances Clinch. I know she died when I was fourteen and that she's buried in Glasnevin Cemetery. She was nineteen when she had us, and thirty-three when she passed away. The same age as Henry.'

I kept track of all the inaccuracies but I let Andy finish his story. I could appreciate that sometimes you just need someone to talk to and this man clearly had a lot on his mind.

'Nobody knew she was carrying twins, I don't even think she knew. The women at these places rarely went to the doctors for check-ups – didn't want any paper trail showing that they'd ever been pregnant. Mum said she got me on short notice, a call out of the blue that a baby was available if she could take it straight away and she jumped at the chance. She kept getting turned down, you see, because she was adopting on her own. And she wasn't a great candidate on paper, or probably in reality either.'

He was very excited and he really seemed to believe what he was saying, God bless him.

Henry looked like his parents. I reminded myself of that. He had his father's hair. But despite my best efforts, cracks started to form in my resolve.

'Soon as I found out about Henry, it made sense to me. I'd always felt like someone was missing.'

I jumped in, before the dam could break. 'Okay, stop. Look, I don't know exactly what's going on here, and you seem to believe your story and you seem like a nice guy, but okay. First of all, Henry's birthday is October the third not October second—'

'That's the date we were adopted.'

'Secondly,' I refused to be thrown, 'Henry was born at home, it's on his passport.' I wasn't actually sure your birth place was on your passport but I knew Henry had been born at home and I doubted this Aussie knew anything about the Irish passport system. I wanted him to take me seriously. 'Thirdly,' and this bit I knew to be true, 'Henry never felt like someone was missing. Never. We used to talk about being only children all the time, and while I wished I'd had a brother or sister, he never did. He never felt there was someone missing.'

He did that thing Henry used to do when he was hurt, where he'd inhale quickly but you'd never hear him exhale, and I felt bad because I didn't want to wound him. But it was true. Henry had never wished for a sibling. He never missed having one.

Something else hit me then: another, third version of Henry.

'Henry is buried in Glasnevin Cemetery,' I said. 'Were you

there? I thought I saw . . .' *You, him, a ghost.* I didn't finish that sentence. 'Were you there?'

'I've been a couple of times to visit Frances's grave. South side of the cemetery.'

'About two weeks ago? A Saturday?'

'Yeah . . . I think so.'

'Was there a group of—'

'Tourists?' he offered.

I felt my head nod. But it was a big cemetery, even the south wing; he could easily have been there on a day I was not.

'Yeah,' he continued. 'And some old man telling them where to go and what year some political guy was buried and what the waiting list for the place was like. Do you remember me? I wasn't visiting Henry,' he added. 'I went to see our mother. I didn't know he was buried there. Weird, ay?'

But all I could hear was Henry's voice, reverberating in my head: *There's no such thing as coincidence. Everything happens for a reason.*

In the fog that fell between Henry's death and burial, I remembered a conversation with his parents. I'd assumed he would be buried in Mount Jerome, where both sets of grandparents were, but Isabel and Conor were adamant it would be Glasnevin and I thought that was strange because they lived on the other side of the city, but I had dropped the thought somewhere in the hazy grief.

'Were you in the supermarket near here a few weeks ago?'

He shook Henry's head. 'This is my first time in this part of the city.'

'You sure? What about the Phoenix Park?' My heart was beating faster and suddenly I was hurrying to keep up with it. 'Were you cycling there? Or, or, the restaurant! Yes! Portobello Kitchen, three weeks ago?'

'No,' he said slowly. 'Don't think so.'

'No you were, you were. Think! On Camden Street. You got a . . . a raspberry brownie!'

'Well, that definitely wasn't me. I don't eat sweet things.'

But of course it wasn't him, that man was German. Tina had said. And the man in Tesco, I had seen his face. Why did I only remember the bits where I was convinced of the lie, and not the bit where I saw the truth? But the cemetery. It had been him I saw in the cemetery. It had been him and I'd lost him. *Henry*, that was the only thought making its way through my brain. Just Henry.

'I've never properly looked like anyone before.' He was pawing the cracked photo frame again, tracing the outline of Henry just as I did. 'My cousins have hair like mine, but this . . .'

My ears were ringing and I tried to remember anything from school biology. If there were billions of people in the world, surely some of them had to end up looking similar, very similar, even if they were not related. Because how many variations could there really be on western, Caucasian males? I thought of Tom Hardy and that other actor who looks so similar, and of that other guy, Nick Nolte, who I always thought was in *Point Break* but that's not him at all, that's another guy who looks just like him.

But logic was irrelevant because here was a man with a pretty good imitation of Henry's face sitting in front of me at the shitty, temporary table that should have been our shitty, temporary table.

'Do you want to answer that?'

I heard it then, the ringing in my head was actually in my handbag. I got up and emptied the bag onto the newly constructed couch now propped up by a copy of an unauthorised Davina McCall biography that Dad had gotten me for Christmas. Four missed calls. All from Dermot. Shit! The restaurant. It was almost three o'clock. Simon had to collect his kids.

'I have to go,' I said, stuffing everything back into my bag, and when I turned back I got a fright because for a second I forgot. I had never fainted, but twice in the one afternoon that had almost changed.

Andy stood from the table like it was any other day and any other table. I had loved that face for so long, but he'd never clapped eyes on me before this afternoon. 'So I'll come back tomorrow?' he said.

The urge to throw myself at him, to push my torso against his until he wrapped his arms around me, but he picked up this strange tin box I had never seen before and I remembered. *Not Henry*. I gathered my own handbag and plastic bag of fresh whites and followed him to the door.

'Tomorrow?'

'To fix the boiler.'

'The boiler.' I nodded, because there was a boiler again, just about. And when I opened the door I found the garden path and fence and patch of grass had also returned.

'It's a lot to handle,' he observed, in the accent he said was Australian. 'Believe me, I know.'

And he smiled and I realised it was not quite the same smile but it was more than enough. I would have burned this house and everything in it to the ground for that smile. 'Your smile.'

'Is it like his?'

'I'll see you tomorrow,' I said, the garden path and fence keeping me in reality. 'I'll be home at five, if that's okay?' I wanted to laugh now that boilers mattered again, but I didn't because I was not actually insane. Probably.

'Five is good.' And he got in a car and waved and pulled away. I ran to the bottom of Aberdeen Street to hail a taxi and it was only after I was inside and I had sent Dermot a So-sorry-on-my-way text message and the car had stopped so a man with a buggy could cross and someone came on the radio talking about barbecue tips that I fully realised this was not a dream.

TWENTY-ONE

I **went back** to work and there were things to do, not least a grovelling apology. Simon had gone, he had to collect his kids, and Dermot had been left in charge of the kitchen. Nobody wanted that. Not the customers who had to eat the food; not the staff who would have to clean up the mess; and not Dermot who, though the proprietor of a popular restaurant, hated nothing quite like he hated cooking.

There had been two small fires in the fifty minutes he was left on his own and when I came running into the kitchen, apology already in full swing, he balled up the chef's hat that nobody except him ever wore because it was a costume prop stolen from some amateur dramatics group and so not at all flame retardant (it was nearly the cause of a third fire) and hurled it at me.

'How do you do this?' he exploded. 'Day in, day out, constantly *working*. Slaving away for them!' He gestured through the orders window, his voice dripping with disdain. 'And nobody even claps! Not one of them. Look at them. Look! Just sitting out there, *eating*.'

'Dermot, are you . . . crying?'

'I have been here for hours! Days probably!' He grabbed a piece of kitchen roll from the counter and blew air through his nose. 'I am an actor, I am not a pepper peeler.'

'Nobody's a pepper peeler, Dermot.'

'Excuse me?'

'We don't peel peppers, nobody does.'

Dermot flung the used kitchen roll in the direction of the fridge but it fell limply to the floor almost immediately. 'I have lines to run,' he said, storming towards the storage-cupboard-cum-office, his meaty head glowing. 'And I don't want to hear another word about this unrelenting hellhole!'

The orders were backed up and Tina was shouting from the floor. I grabbed a pile of dockets and started making my way through them. We hadn't enough chicken for the hotpot so I threw turkey in instead and nobody complained. I flew through the orders, throwing plates onto the window at such a rate that Tina could barely keep up. And then I would be in the middle of julienning potatoes or making up vegetable stock when it would suddenly hit me all over again.

The recurring realisations went something like this: *The custard is starting to curdle. I better turn it down. And I need to get the crumble from the oven. The bowl is clean, but wasn't there something else? Oh yes, that's right – my dead boyfriend's twin came for tea today and told me he was adopted. And now the custard is all over the floor and the bowl is smashed.*

I lost three ceramic dishes to this thought process but I cleared up any spillages before Dermot could see and I got no more orders wrong than I would on a typical off day. I managed to sustain an entire argument with the vegetable supplier about why we would not be paying more for weekend deliveries. Tina even complimented my hotpot when she came back from her lunch. Overall, it was more than any reasonable person could have expected of me.

It all passed in such a hectic daze that when I made it back home and found myself sitting in the window of my study, watching people walk their dogs up and down Aberdeen Street, it took me a minute to remember how I'd gotten there.

Henry had a brother. Henry was adopted.

A man in a grey tracksuit allowed his white fluff-ball to dawdle, sniffing at poles and tufts of grass. He was definitely waiting for his dog to do its business, and I doubted he was going to pick it up.

The idea of Henry's brother being in Dublin, perhaps strolling the south side of the quays while I took the same path on the north, made me shiver. I imagined us crossing the River Liffey – different bridges, only a few metres apart – or him going to Tesco and picking up a shopping basket I had placed down a few minutes previous. He hadn't been in the supermarket the time I thought I saw him, but that didn't mean he hadn't been other places. He had been to the graveyard. What about all the people who pass you by on the street when you're looking the other way? What about all the people whose faces get lost in the crowd?

And what about the inside? Was he anything like Henry beyond the face and the shoulders and the sturdy hands? Did they share a way of thinking as well as a way of moving?

There were too many questions. I would have to make a list.

By the wheel of a Skoda across the street, the fluff ball bent its legs. It quivered on its hind paws for a moment then righted itself again. I turned away. I didn't want to know.

I rummaged in one of the half-unpacked boxes along the study wall and pulled out a jar of pens. I grabbed an envelope from the floor, turned it over, thought for a second, and started to write. I underlined the incongruous title and read it back.

THINGS TO ASK MY DEAD BOYFRIEND'S BROTHER

Then I crossed out 'BROTHER' and wrote in 'TWIN' because if I was going to accept this, I might as well embrace it fully.

1.   WHERE DO YOU LIVE?

And immediately after that:

1A.   WHERE DO YOU LIVE IN IRELAND?
1B.   WHERE DO YOU LIVE IN AUSTRALIA?

And even with two sub questions I couldn't leave it there because suddenly I was thinking of C, D and E:

WHEN DID YOU COME HERE?
HOW LONG ARE YOU STAYING?

I decided to make these 2, 3 and 4. Best to retain some sense of order. I read over the list. I added a few flowers to the margin.

5. WHY DID YOU COME TO IRELAND?
    (NOT RUDE. JUST INTERESTED.
    HENRY = ALREADY DEAD)
6. HAVE YOU BEEN HERE BEFORE?
7. DO YOU HAVE ANY WEIRD TWIN
    COINCIDENCES?

I scribbled out that last one. Andy didn't know anything about Henry so how would he know if they did things at the same time or in the same way? Besides, Henry didn't believe in coincidences and I should ask questions for him too. What would Henry want to know?

7. DO YOU LIKE DYSTOPIAN MOVIES?
7A. IF NOT, WHY NOT?
7B. IF SO, DO YOU AGREE THAT THE MAD MAX
    REMAKE IS BETTER THAN THE ORIGINAL?
9. DO YOU READ THE NEWSPAPER?
9A. WHAT NEWSPAPER?
10. CAN YOU DO THIS WEIRD THING WITH
    YOUR INDEX FINGER WHERE THE
    KNUCKLE POPS OUT?

139

I'd forgotten 8. I went back and drew a little 'insert here' arrow. I thought for a moment.

8.   DO YOU ONLY FIX BOILERS OR CAN YOU
       FIX OTHER THINGS? DO YOU KNOW HOW
       TO BLEED RADIATORS?

Then, in even tinier writing, to make it fit:

8A.   DO YOU EVEN NEED/HAVE RADIATORS
       IN AUSTRALIA?

There were more questions than space on the envelope. And then there were the questions to which I couldn't get answers. What if Henry were still alive? What would it feel like for him to learn he wasn't the person he'd always thought he was? How would it feel to suddenly have a brother? Personally, I'd have loved that. Not the secret adoption bit, but there wasn't even a remote possibility of that since Mam regularly reminded me of the pains she went through in giving birth to me and Dad readily verified her version of events. Most fathers talked about the indescribable joy of meeting their firstborn child, but mine just went on about the traumatising mess. 'I didn't know what bits we were supposed to throw away and what bits were still attached to your mother.'

But the brother bit – I would have loved that.

I imagined Henry's parents, Isabel and Conor, asleep in their understated, beige four-bed detached house in a quiet estate about twelve kilometres and twenty socio-economic

140

points south of where I was sitting. How could they have never told Henry? How could he never have figured it out?

Surely he had asked, at some point over the years, what time he was born or how much he'd weighed? But then, maybe not. I asked him once how his parents had met and he hadn't a clue. Henry didn't think it was strange that he'd never enquired. He didn't know their wedding anniversary either. Was it a female thing, to take an interest in the lives your parents led before you were part of them? If so, Isabel and Conor were lucky they'd gotten a boy. If it had been me, I'd have figured it out.

I stood up to pull the curtains and felt a flutter in my stomach. This man who would come tomorrow to fix my boiler and answer questions was not Henry. I knew that. But if everything happened for a reason then there had to be more to it. Maybe somehow Henry had sent him, or the universe had done it on his behalf. Maybe Henry was as sorry to have left me as I was to have been left behind. Because who else could Andy's arrival really benefit except me who was struggling to persevere and who had been calling out for a little hope.

TWENTY-TWO

I woke the next morning with a sense of purpose. The queasiness that had been my neutral state for weeks had subsided. This was the first time since Henry left that I had a reason to get up. I arrived at the Portobello Kitchen early – although when I got there, I found it had been rebranded THE PO T BELLY ITCH. Dermot was standing in the doorway and there was a man in a retro Adidas jacket and skinny jeans scuttling away in my direction.

'That's right, buddy!' yelled Dermot. 'You better run! There's a Starbucks around the corner!'

'More pesky customers?' I said when I reached the entrance.

'That's not a customer, Grace, that's a leech. Did you see his shoulder bag?'

'Are we barring people with shoulder bags now?'

'Nothing good ever came out of a bag that slim. He'd be ordering the smallest coffee, sitting at the biggest table and producing a laptop from that yoke quicker than you can say, "Get out of my restaurant, you home-brewing parasite."' Dermot was walking in circles, his anger intensifying with every 360 degrees. 'They multiply. Like lice. You let one in and the place is suddenly crawling—' He stopped pacing. He'd raised his head and caught sight of his restaurant's new name, evidently for the first time. 'FUCK'S SAKE!!!!'

'I'll get the ladder.'

The morning was quiet, mainly because Dermot screamed at anyone who came through the door. Myself and Tina spent it scrubbing yesterday's burn marks off the wall. I wanted to ask Dermot how he'd gotten a fork lodged in the toaster but then the bell on the front door jangled and I heard him roar again and I decided against it.

'What's up with Dermot?' I asked Tina. 'Is he still mad about being made to work yesterday?'

'He didn't get the chicken gig.'

Dermot had had a rare call-back for the part of a chicken in some mortgage advert. He'd been squawking from his office on and off for days. 'So?' I said, finally giving up and chucking the toaster in the bin. 'Dermot never gets any gigs.'

'Someone called Pete got it instead?'

'Oh.' Pete was Dermot's best friend and, as they were both actors, also his arch-nemesis. They became pals because they were the only forty-plus men in their drama class. They were also the only two who, aesthetically, didn't immediately strike you as actors. This meant they were always up for the same parts. And Dermot was a God-awful actor.

At the front of the restaurant, the door jangled again.

'Out! Out!!! Parasites!'

Then another jangle as the would-be customers hurried back out. Tina grimaced at me and I giggled. I stopped immediately. I never giggled, not anymore.

It was strange carrying such a life-altering, unimaginable secret. It was like I existed in a parallel universe to everyone else. I talked to Tina like it was any other day, except maybe I was a little giddier and I checked the clock with increasing regularity: seven hours, six hours, five and a half hours until I would see Henry's face again.

Just before one o'clock, Dermot decided we were changing the menu.

'No more chicken.'

I sighed. I had made a whole batch of chicken hotpot and there was a pile of cooked meat sitting in the fridge. 'Seriously?'

Dermot glared at me, his face the colour of a Gala apple, and I backed off. 'You're the boss,' I said. 'What do you want instead?'

'I don't know . . . Steak. Can we do steak? Do we have steak?'

'As part of the lunch deal? I'm not sure that would be wise financially. But, as I say, you're the boss.'

'That's right. I am the boss. I am a successful restaurateur. I don't need to prance around in an animal costume for the amusement of others. All right.' He stood straighter. 'Well, I say steak. No chicken. Only steak.'

Tina rolled her eyes at me through the service window, but said nothing as she wiped the specials list from the blackboard.

'Everything else staying?' I asked. I hadn't the concentration for this, not today.

'Yes.' Dermot looked uncertain. 'What else is there?'

'Veg soup, sausage and mash, frittata—'

'Frittata. Is that eggs?'

'Yes. And it's all made up so you'd basically be chucking away fifty quid if you scrap it now.'

'Okay, fine. Frittata stays.'

The familiar jangle as the door pushed open and a group of office workers filed into the restaurant. Dermot growled, but at a low level, as he headed for the storage cupboard. 'Is there nowhere else for these slack-jaws to go?'

The place filled up quickly without Dermot around to discourage them. And I moved my concentration from the clock to filling orders. I was doling out the new vegetarian hotpot when Tina came into the kitchen to collect cutlery.

'I've never heard you sing before,' she said, smiling, fists full of knives and forks as she caught me off guard. 'You've a nice voice.'

I was so nervous leaving work that I couldn't make myself wait for the bus. I started walking, glancing back occasionally to see if the bus would catch up with me, but it never did and I was home at quarter to five. I was out of breath coming up Aberdeen Street. I hadn't so much spent my anxious energy as I had riled myself up. There was an argument going on across the road over a parking space. I waved to Betty sitting in her front window with some kind of sandwich.

I shoved a few Ikea instructions and plastic bags into a kitchen drawer, and stacked some empty boxes in the corner.

I changed my top – I had started to sweat once I stopped moving – and washed my face before applying BB cream. It was, I realised, the first overture I'd made to make-up since Henry died. I looked at myself in the bathroom mirror and took a deep breath.

'I'm going to meet your brother, Henry,' I told my own reflection. 'I'm going to find out everything for you. You don't need to worry.' I held my gaze in the mirror above the sink and repeated: 'There is no need to worry.'

Ding-dong!

My stomach jumped. Part of me wanted to fly down the stairs, the other part wanted to jump out the back window. I made my way down, stepping over the box of moisturiser and shampoo still sitting where I'd left it the previous day, stalling only when I saw his silhouette through the stained glass. They had the exact same shape.

'Evening,' he said as I opened the door to a distorted version of the only face I had ever loved. Countless mornings I had woken up to that face. Countless nights it was the last thing I saw. 'How're you going today?'

'Good,' I said. At least my responses were quicker than yesterday. 'Just, yeah. Good.'

Well, it was a start.

TWENTY-THREE

He picked up his toolbox and lumbered inside. He slouched slightly as he entered the house even though the doorway was a good foot taller than him. Force of habit, I thought. Just like Henry.

'I reckon I'll take a look at the boiler first? Get that out of the way before . . .' He smiled and I, no longer in full control of my own facial expressions, smiled back.

I walked back up the stairs, knocking the BB cream into a new Ikea wicker basket as I entered the bathroom ahead of him. I opened the hot press and pointed at the large cylinder with the red lagging jacket. 'There it is,' I said, for want of something to say. 'Obviously.'

'All right then, I'll just take a look.'

He started to remove the lagging jacket and root in his box for some sort of wrench. I was jealous that he had something to do.

'Do you want a tea?'

'No thanks. I don't really drink the stuff.'

'Of course. You said.' I wiped away dust from the rim of

the sink with a sheet of toilet paper, but the bathroom was too small for two activities. 'I'll be in the kitchen.'

'No worries.'

Standing at the kitchen counter waiting for the kettle to boil, I realised I was shaking my head. Henry's *twin brother* was upstairs fixing the boiler. The same boiler Henry had enquired about when we first came to view this house. He didn't know a thing about them but he thought boilers were what you were supposed to ask estate agents about, to show you were wise to their ways and that if they were looking to sell a dud, they should try the next chump. Boilers and insulation. They were Henry's go-to topics. I heard the clang of metal bouncing on the floor above me and I pinched myself through the sleeve of my ribbed sweater. I felt like a character in one of Betty's soaps. God she'd have loved this. There she was getting her kicks from a little parking tiff, and her very own *As the World Turns* moment happening right next door. I almost felt bad keeping it from her.

I made a cup of tea and pushed myself up onto the counter, dangling my legs as I drank. To nobody at all, I stated the obvious: 'This is ridiculous.'

For the next hour, I did my best to busy myself with putting away the last of the kitchen utensils. I fought the urge to go back upstairs. I got as far as the bottom step a few times but managed to restrain myself from climbing. At 6.30, when I was about to ascend with the excuse of asking if he wanted dinner, Andy appeared in the sitting room.

'All done.'

He dried his hands with a cloth and threw the oil-stained rag into the toolbox. His arms were so like Henry's. Sturdy with light hair, and one protruding vein that curved faintly around the right forearm. I knew those arms by heart. He rolled down his sleeves and cleared his throat.

'Is it fixed?' I asked quickly, my cheeks burning.

'Should be. I reset your thermostat and the water levels have started to rise. I have the heating switched on now, just to check it's all working as it should.'

'That's great, thank you. How much do I owe you?'

'No worries. It's . . . family rates.'

It was my turn to clear my throat. 'Will you have some dinner?'

'Sure.' Andy looked around the kitchen, where the only visible counter appliances still had their Ikea tags attached.

'I haven't done much cooking here yet . . . But I'm a chef. I should be able to rustle up something.'

'You're a chef? Awesome.'

'Well, I make sandwiches and hotpots. But they're good hotpots.'

'Sounds great to me,' he said. 'What are we having?'

'Em.' I opened the cupboard store for possibly the first time to find the beans, chickpeas, pasta and instant soups my parents had brought on one of their first visits. 'I'm just going to run to the shop,' I told him. 'It's only around the corner. Is that okay? Will you be all right here?'

'I'll put a light bulb in the hallway while I'm waiting.'

'That fixture is actually broken,' I said, rooting through my bag for keys and my purse.

'Then I'll fix that first.'

I looked up from my handbag.

'Really? Amazing. That'd be great. Thank you. If I could just remember where I put my keys . . .'

'Do you need them?' he asked, picking up a chair from the kitchen and walking into the hall. 'I'll be here.'

'Right,' I said, watching that familiar silhouette walk away. 'You'll be here.' Tears appeared in the corners of my eyes before I realised they were on their way. I shook them off and hurried after him into the hallway. 'I'll only be a minute,' I said and pulled the front door.

I was slightly out of breath when I got to the shop, swinging the door open as Pat looked up from his copy of the *Mirror*.

'We've no brie.'

'Excuse me?'

'No brie,' Pat repeated. 'The supplier never came this morning. So there's no Red Bull either.'

'You get your cheese and Red Bull from the same supplier?' I asked. 'Actually, never mind. It doesn't matter.' I made my way through the modest aisles. 'I'm not here for brie.'

Usually I went straight to the dairy fridge and then picked up a baguette at the till. I didn't know what else Pat sold, but it didn't take long to ascertain that the answer was 'Not a whole lot'. It'd be a good place to go to stock up your bunker for an impending apocalypse but it didn't offer much in the way of fresh produce. There was nothing with a best before date this side of Christmas, except a few pieces of fruit already starting to expire in a basket at the back. I picked up a couple of bags of ricotta-filled pasta and a packet of frozen spinach.

'Any tomatoes?' I asked hopefully.

'Beside the jam.'

I found a jar of sundried tomatoes, which would have to do. Pat rang up the lot and I could tell he wanted to ask but it was against his hear-no-evil see-no-evil code of conduct.

'I'm making dinner for someone.'

'Dinner for two,' he said, putting the four items in one of the plastic bags he's supposed to charge for but never does.

'Not like that,' I clarified.

Pat shrugged. 'I haven't seen Betty in a few days. She okay?'

I thought of her twitching curtains earlier that evening. 'She's alive.' And I took the bag.

I jogged all the way back to the house but when I got to the gate I stopped. There was light shining out from the hallway. In the ten minutes I'd been gone, this end-of-terrace house where I'd dwelled for a month had become a home. The light shone out through the stained glass of the front door like a beating heart. The whole place had come alive. I stood for a moment and admired it. It was almost welcoming. I pushed the front door, left on the latch, to find more light streaming from the study and banging coming from the sitting room.

Andy was kneeling on the floor beside the Ikea chair I'd been avoiding constructing for weeks. 'Just one more . . . There.' He placed one hand on the seat and pushed himself up.

151

'I wasn't gone fifteen minutes,' I said, unable to hide my astonishment. 'Henry could barely hang a picture. Are you sure you're related?' He looked at me and I wondered when it was going to stop taking me by surprise. 'No need to answer that.'

I carried the bag through to the kitchen and he followed.

'What was Henry like?' he asked, leaning against the makeshift table where we'd sat across from each other the day before.

I pulled the pasta from the bag. *Like you*, I wanted to say, *he was just like you.*

'I'm not sure how to answer that.'

'Sorry,' he said, offering me a smile that really wasn't his to be offering. 'I didn't know what to ask first.'

'No, it's fine. It's just . . . I've never had to explain him to anybody.' I shook my head. 'Would you believe this is the first proper conversation about him since he died that I've had with someone who didn't know him? It's so strange that *you* didn't know him when—' I flapped my arms up and down in his general direction. He looked down at his body as if he was as surprised by it as anyone else.

'What was he like?' I considered. 'He contained multitudes, like everyone, I guess. He was happy. I'd say that about him. And he was fun. He was caring, about me anyway, and loyal and he was easy-going.' I cringed. It was the speech of a best man who was only up there because the groom's mother had insisted he pick his brother. I puffed out my cheeks. 'That doesn't really make him stand out. It's hard to condense someone you know that well into a few sentences. It's like having to describe yourself. You can't. You're not objective.'

I pulled the rest of the items from the bag and read the instructions on the back of the spinach.

'It must be crazy having me here,' he said.

'Yes.'

He nodded.

'But it's good too.'

I broke up the spinach through the plastic before pulling the bag open. 'How about I cook and you can ask me questions? Not that you could really call this cooking.' I held up the jar of preserved tomatoes as I switched on the kettle. 'These don't go off for another two years. In fact, all these ingredients would probably survive a nuclear attack. Do you cook?'

'If I have to,' he said. 'But a lot of the time I'm cooking for one, and it feels like you need . . .'

'Other people?'

'A home.'

'Yeah,' I said. 'That makes sense.' And I switched on the hob for the first time since moving in.

TWENTY-FOUR

Andy told me the basics of his life in Australia. He'd been doing maintenance at a holiday resort in Sydney before coming here. But six months before that, he was working for an apartment complex in Brisbane. He couldn't settle on an answer to the question of where he'd grown up.

'All over,' he said. 'Mum was always moving, a free spirit.'

'Was she artistic?'

'Not unless you count selling crystals. But she saw herself as a troubadour, and I guess that made me her roadie.'

He'd been staying at a B&B in Harold's Cross since he got here. I told him that was near enough to Henry's parents' house, but when I saw how it piqued his interest I regretted saying anything and moved on quickly.

'How did you meet Larry?' I asked, adding the pasta to the boiling water.

'I needed to find work. I hadn't a clue how long I was going to stay here, how long it would take to find what I was looking for. I wasn't sure what I *was* looking for. I thought I'd pretty much reached a dead end until I arrived at your door,' he said. 'Must have been fate.'

'Or maybe just a coincidence,' I ventured.

'Nah.' Andy inspected the double doors that opened to the backyard, frowning at the gap at the bottom where a piece of rubber draft excluder was missing. 'There's no such thing as coincidence.'

With his back to me, or even from the side, he was identical. I felt myself doing that thing Henry did, where he breathed in sharply but snuck the air back out without anyone noticing. *No such thing as coincidence.*

'Yeah,' I said. 'Henry thought the same.'

I liked having him in the house. There was a thrill to him wandering about, inspecting the place and making everything a little more just-so. I heard the curtains coming down in the living room and pictured him reattaching the folds to the hooks, catching the one I'd missed. The sound of his step as he passed from living room to kitchen and back again. The floorboards creaked with a confidence I had never coaxed from them.

When the pasta had been spooned into the brand-new Ikea bowls, he crossed to the sink and with the heel of his hand turned on the faucet. I watched the water dividing over his fingers. His were strong hands. Henry's hands.

He wanted to know how Henry had died. He asked it like that, straight out. 'How did Henry die?' he said. 'The adoption services said a traffic accident . . .' And he trailed off.

'He was cycling,' I replied, keeping my eyes on the spinach that was done but which I continued to stir. 'To meet me.' I scooped the sundried tomatoes out of the jar and tossed them in. I saw the red scarf spinning in the spokes: rapidly, viciously, turning and turning and turning, until the whole wheel was dripping red. 'He was cycling along the Liffey, the river that runs through Dublin city, rushing to get there on time. And it was raining.'

'You don't have to tell me if you don't want to.'

I set the pan on the draining board and held a hand up to shush him, to say it was fine. 'It was a truck, a massive thing heading for the port after making a delivery. The back wheel went right over Henry and it didn't even stop. The guards caught up with the driver at the port and he said he hadn't felt a thing. Can you imagine the indignity of that? His entire life eviscerated and nobody in the whole wide world, not even the man who took it from him, felt a thing?'

I rested my hands flat against the counter until they were still again. Then I picked back up the wooden spoon and added the highly preserved vegetables to the pasta. 'Here.'

'Good on ya,' he said, taking the bowl. Then after a pause: 'Can I ask you something?'

I forced a laugh. 'Was that not it?'

He finished a mouthful and wrapped his hand around the water tumbler so his fingers almost reached his thumb. 'Do I look like a tourist?'

Now I really did laugh.

'Everywhere I go, everyone already knows I'm not Irish. Even though, genetically, I *am* Irish. How do they know?'

I considered him from across the temporary kitchen table that looked like doll's furniture now he was sitting at it.

'I look like a tourist, ay?'

'Yes.'

'But Henry didn't? How does that work?'

I tried to see his face objectively. The lines, the slight pigmentation around the mouth, the patch-free stubble. I was amassing them, the ways in which they were the same and the ways they were different. 'I don't know,' I said, genuinely stumped. 'It must be the tan.'

Most of Andy's free time – 'all of it, really' – was spent trying to uncover more about his past. He was at his most animated when he talked about this and it was easy to get caught up. It was like coming in during the ad break of one of those English village mysteries my parents were always watching and being filled in on the plot. Before the show had started again, I'd be suggesting potential endings and routes the detective might take. Only this was somebody's life. And if he'd lived, it could have been Henry's life.

Andy had the basic details on Frances Clinch and he had managed to piece together a fairly informed idea of where she had had the babies and how they had ended up where they did. Although he still couldn't understand how his mother had gotten a child.

'She was single, of no fixed abode, and her career changed as regularly as her boyfriend,' he said. 'From what I understand, she was the kind of woman they were taking babies *from*.'

He was trying to find out if Frances Clinch had any surviving family. There could be aunts or uncles or maybe even other siblings. From me, though, he just wanted to know about Henry.

So I told him how his brother had grown up an only child in a south Dublin suburb. His father was a successful lawyer and his mother had worked in the Department of Education before having Henry. 'Before Henry came along,' I corrected myself. He went to school in the city and was good, but not great, academically. People liked him. That was his biggest asset. It had done more for him than grades ever had. He made friends easily. You could bring him to a party where he knew nobody and be sure he'd be fine. He went to university straight out of school: an arts degree, then a Masters in graphic design.

'He had an easy confidence,' I said. 'I always thought it came from his parents. They were so proud of anything he achieved.'

'Lucky,' said Andy.

'Yes,' I agreed. 'But he knew it.'

We talked and talked and talked. Sometimes I'd break off in the middle of a story and laugh at the absurdity of it, and other times I'd go a whole anecdote without realising what was unfolding. It meant everything to have someone who wanted as much as I did to talk about Henry. Once I started, it was easy. There were so many stories. There were things Henry and I used to recall all the time but without him around, I had started to forget. I had almost forgotten how, when he carried me to bed, he would declare 'Last stop!' as he dropped me on the mattress. It came back to me only as I told another story. I was shocked it had wandered, even a little, from the forefront of my mind.

I told Andy about the trip to Portugal, the one where that photograph of us sitting on the wall was taken, and about the Christmas Eve he walked me home and awkwardly asked me out.

Every time I finished a story, he looked at me expectantly. His eyes didn't glaze over when I recollected the minutiae of situations he hadn't been present for or the inter-personal politics of people he didn't know. He always wanted more.

Even when the conversation verged into other territory, I knew we were both enjoying it. He had a laid-back aura similar to Henry but while his brother's resting face had been one of gentle mocking, Andy's suggested intense concentration. It was unnerving but also so disproportionately serious that it made him easy to tease. I mocked the way he put 'ay' at the end of questions that were actually statements.

'Crazy, ay?' I said in my best Australian accent and he grinned and leaned back in his chair. It was good, too, to have that face so close again.

When I heard the buzz of the street lamps illuminating outside, I checked the time.

'Eleven o'clock,' I said. 'I'd no idea.'

Andy scraped back his chair, stood abruptly and left the kitchen.

'Andy?'

I heard him climbing the stairs and presumed he was going to the bathroom. But he reappeared a few minutes later, headed straight for the double doors that led to the back garden and leaned down.

'There,' he said, when he'd straightened up again. 'Now we can all rest easy.'

I got up to look where he was looking and saw that the gap in the rubber draft excluder was a gap no more.

'You had a bit of overhang on the window upstairs,' he said, packing up his toolbox. 'I clipped it off with nail scissors.'

'My own MacGyver.' I grinned and followed slowly as he made his way through the sitting room and into the hall. From behind he was exactly the same.

'Have you ever heard of changelings?' I asked, and he shook his head. 'My ancestors would have said Henry had been taken by faeries, and that you were the changeling left in his place. You look like the human, but inside you belong to the faeries.'

'You're starting to sound like my Mum,' he said. 'Do you have a side gig selling magic crystals too?'

'No.'

'Maybe it's an Irish thing. Do these changelings sell crystals? Or the faeries?'

I folded my arms and assessed him. 'Are you the one doing the mocking now?'

'Looks like it.' He grinned. 'Ay?'

I twisted my arm around him and opened the latch on the front door. I thought too late to inhale the smell of him; my breathing pattern was all off.

'I'm on a site a lot of the week but maybe the weekend—'

'Tomorrow, or Sunday?' I said eagerly. 'I'm free.' Even though I actually had plans with Aoife, and Larry was supposed to call in to fill a pothole in the back garden.

We settled on Sunday and the Phoenix Park. I'd show

him Henry's favourite places. 'And I'll bring a few photos,' I added.

He repeated the meeting point, committing it to memory – 'Wellington Monument, Wellington Monument' – and headed down the path.

'Goodnight,' I called after him, enjoying the impact of the half-whisper on the quiet street.

When he'd climbed into the car borrowed from his landlady and driven out of sight, I shut the door gently. I allowed the moment to stretch. It expanded along the hallway, up the stairs, into the bedroom and straight through the night. I read those first few pages of *A Christmas Carol*, right up to the bookmark, and for the following ten hours, I slept like a log.

TWENTY-FIVE

'**G**race. This is a surprise.'

'Sorry, Mam,' I said, closing the door behind me. 'Are youse in the middle of dinner?'

'No, we're going out for our dinner, actually. Some place your father's been reading great things about. Just waiting for him to finish varnishing the skirting boards in our bedroom.' She rolled her eyes. 'What is it the restaurant's called again? The chicken is supposed to be excellent.' She walked over to the bottom of the stairs. 'Arthur! ARTHUR!'

'WHAT?'

I winced at the volume as she leaned on the banister and continued to bellow.

'WHAT'S THE NAME OF THE RESTAURANT WE'RE GOING TO?'

'NANDO'S!'

'WHAT?'

'NANDO'S!'

'WHAT?!'

'NAN! DOHS!'

'NANDO'S?'

'YES! NANDO'S!'

She turned back to me: 'It's called Nando's.'

'So I hear.' I took off my coat and hung it at the end of the stairs. My mother was wearing the green suit she'd worn to my culinary arts graduation.

'You know it's not like a restaurant-restaurant, Mam?'

'What isn't?'

'Nando's. It's more of a . . . it's like a fancy fast-food place.'

'Who's that, Sarah? Who is— Oh hello, love!'

Dad came down the stairs wearing his Christmas Day slacks and the shirt Mam got him for his last birthday.

'Grace says it's not a restaurant at all, this Nando's. More of a *fast-food place*.'

Somehow she managed to make 'fast-food place' sound fancier than 'restaurant'.

'Well, it is a restaurant, sort of,' I said. 'It's just very casual.'

'Have you been, Grace?'

'No, but I know all about it. They're everywhere . . .'

'Your father's been reading a lot about it. It's in all his magazines.'

'Miley Cyrus is a fan. And Robert Pattinson. And Vicky Pinkerton.'

'Who?'

'The tall lass from *Only Made in Chiswick*,' he said, taking his suit jacket from under the stairs. 'She's the one Ben Thompson cheated on in Marbella with Lettice.'

'What is it you said they were called, Arthur?'

'Who?'

163

'The sex mice?'

'Love rats,' he corrected and I remembered how glad I was not to live here anymore.

'Well, I'm not sure I want to eat in a place favoured by love rats. What if someone we know sees us?'

Dad sighed wearily. 'Vicky is not a love rat, Sarah. She's the one the love rat cheated on. She had the twelve-page tell-all in *Heat*. Remember? I showed you.'

'I don't think you did, Arthur.'

'And Niall Horan eats there. It must be fairly fancy, if all the celebs are going,' said Dad, sliding his wallet into his suit jacket pocket. 'I'm thinking about having the chicken.'

'Come on, Arthur, we'll be late,' said Mam, before turning to me. 'We've to be there in half an hour.'

'Do Nando's do reservations?'

'Sorry to be running out just as you're arriving, love. Do you want to come with us? I'm sure they can add an extra seat to the table.'

'They don't really have tables, Dad.'

'No tables?' Mam echoed in disgust. 'What sort of place is this, Arthur? No tables, no reservations, not even a restaurant really. Nothing but celebrities. Do they have chairs, Grace?'

'Of course they have chairs, Mam, and tables—'

'You just said they didn't have tables.'

'I meant not the kind where they add chairs. You share— It doesn't matter. Have fun. And thanks, Dad, but I've eaten. I'm just here to pick up a few photos and then I'll be off.'

'Oh love.'

My parents looked at each other, as if matching their sad smiles before turning them on me.

'Pictures of Henry, is it, pet?'

'Yes, but it's not . . . I'm not going to get all maudlin over them, I just . . .' There was zero chance I was telling them about Andy. Not yet. Not until I had gotten my own head around it. 'I'd like to have some.'

A horn beeped and you could make out the glow of the taxi sign through the front window. Dad took Mam's coat from under mine and held out an arm for her as he opened the door.

'Our carriage awaits!'

'The photo albums are under the bed in your room,' said Mam, linking her arm into his. 'They might smell a bit funny; we've had to up the mothball count.'

I watched them bundle into the back seat, Dad giddy with excitement. It reminded me of the time they'd gone to see *The Ring* thinking it was a romantic comedy but enjoyed it anyway because they were just so happy to be out together. They did up their seatbelts and Mam leaned into Dad as he put an arm around her. I hadn't always wanted what they had, being half of something so whole. I used to think of myself as an unyielding individual. I could be a partner but never half. It was only with Henry that I discovered the horrific elation in giving up part of yourself.

There weren't as many photographs as I remembered and it didn't upset me to see Henry grinning out from a grainy Polaroid taken on Dollymount Strand or in a photobooth strip from his cousin's wedding in Galway or the series of pictures printed out from my iPhone of the weekend we moved into the flat. I looked at his silly head peeking over an upside-down newspaper and I didn't feel particularly happy or sad or bereft. All I could think was that for thirty-three years, there had been room in the world for two of those faces.

'Get up.'

'No!'

'Take that pillow off your head, Grace McDonnell. This is the first day of the rest of your life.'

'You always say that.'

'And it's always true. Get up, get dressed, go in there and show Dermot why he has to make you head chef.'

I groan and roll over but you're sitting firmly on the mattress blocking my path.

'It's not even a proper restaurant!'

'Grace. Give me – stop – just, Grace – now. Listen.' The pillow and blanket pulled away, the sun in my eyes adding to the injustice.

'He's going to give it to Simon.'

'Has Simon been there since Day One? Did Simon invent the famous Portobello Hotpot? Did he? There are people in Cork talking about that Hotpot. Probably London, too. New York, who knows, Beijing . . .'

I make for the blanket but you intercept, sitting on the duvet before I can get a good grip.

'Henry!'

'Well, did he? Did he?'

'No.'

'No. Simon did not. You did. You're a better cook than Simon. And you're better-looking.'

'What has that got to do with it?'

'Get up!'

'Why?'

'Because it's the first day of the rest of your life.'

'So you said.'

'And because I love you.'

'Ugh! Fine.' I push the blankets back and stomp off to the bathroom. 'Fine fine fine fine fine.'

TWENTY-SIX

Despite the unusually warm weather I had forgotten I owned summer dresses until I opened a neglected box. I hung a couple of my favourites in the spare bedroom to air and went digging around for a razor. Whenever I went looking for some particular item, I tried to think like Dad. Where would Dad have packed such-and-such? This was fairly easy as my father was a lateral thinker, but the process often resulted in me casting my mind back to when Dad would have packed up our flat, Henry not long dead, me lying at home like a useless lump, and by the time I found whatever I was looking for I often couldn't muster up the sense of purpose to use it.

But this morning was different. I found a razor in a black bag of miscellaneous toiletries I hadn't missed since moving in – nail varnish, sanitary pads, hairspray, an exfoliating glove (I took that too), razor – and willingly, happily even, got into the shower.

I tuned the bedroom radio to some non-stop music marathon. I was approximately ten years too old for non-stop music marathons but I sang along without knowing any of the words as I towel dried my hair, moisturised and got dressed.

'*I love you, I hate you, I don't fffggg fffuggg you,*' I declared with unrestrained passion as I pulled the dress over my head. '*You don't bbb-da-da-da, you don't bbb-nnna me. But I doooo!!!*'

I opened the bedroom window and wiped the dust from my sandals onto the street below with an old neck scarf. '*Oooo-oooo, naaaa-naaaa, oooo-oooo!*'

I danced back to the bedside table, jutting my head from side to side in time with the music. I pushed my phone, wallet and keys into my handbag and pursed my lips while wagging my finger at the imaginary man who had done me wrong. '*No, no, no. Oooooo. Yeahhhhh! Ah ah ah ah . . .*' Then, reluctantly, I switched off the radio, ran downstairs and left the house.

I was standing on my doorstep, double checking I had everything, when a voice from behind made me jump.

'Making more noise?'

'Jesus!' I turned, my hand on my chest. 'You scared me.'

'Ah yeah. I'm sure I did.' Betty leaned over the fence. 'Will you be in for Telly Bingo this week?'

'Maybe,' I said, finding the house key and double locking the door.

'Well, don't do me any favours.'

'It's just I'm fairly busy at the moment.'

'I don't suppose it's the lad with the toolbox is keeping you busy?' she said with a smile somewhere between butter-wouldn't-melt and the-cat-who-got-the-cream. Definitely dairy related, anyway. 'Two days in a row, and he stayed a lot longer than any handyman I've ever had. Must be charging for overtime . . .'

'Have you considered offering your services to the FBI, Betty? Your surveillance skills are wasted on domestic DIY and parking bust-ups,' I said, heading down the garden path. 'Anyway, I'd love to stay and gossip, but I'm running late.'

I darted down Aberdeen Street, walking out onto the road to get around Larry's van, and turned right in the direction of the park. Every time it was safe to do so, I closed my eyes and took a few steps without looking where I was going. I imagined a thread pulling me towards the Wellington Monument and that if I allowed myself to move without thinking it would draw me there anyway. I shut my eyes and grinned as I stepped over the threshold into the Phoenix Park.

I spotted Andy in the middle of the open lawn when I was still about three minutes away.

A gang of teenagers lounged at the base of the monument and standing slightly to their right, hands in pockets, right foot worrying a tuft of grass, was Andy. He raised his head, but not like he was looking for anything, just like his neck could do with a change. He never searched around him. I couldn't have stood in such an exposed place and been so at ease. I took a moment to appreciate this and then made my way towards him. I hoped he wouldn't spot me; three minutes was a long time to be watched. He wore a black T-shirt bleached grey by the sun and shorts that went just below his knees. Henry never wore shorts. I guess he hadn't known how much they would have suited him.

He clocked me at the halfway mark and raised a hand. 'I thought it was supposed to be almost summer,' he called when I was within earshot. He hopped from one foot to the other. 'Flaming heck!'

A football landed at his feet and he kicked it back to the teenagers who let out a mocking cheer. He did not cease to exist under their gaze or melt in the sun. It was strange and wonderful and entirely incomparable to be out in the world with this face. I didn't feel bad for cancelling on Aoife and Larry. There was sadness and death and countless mornings where I feared I wouldn't get my body out of bed with the weight of it, but in that moment my heart could have cried with relief. I watched him prance from side to side and I laughed loudly. It was the most joyful laugh I'd channelled in some version of forever.

'Welcome to Ireland, my friend.'

We walked the length of the park, talking about the weather and work and the house. I told him how the mortgage was covered for another year or so and then I'd have to consider getting a lodger. He told me about the B&B and how the lady who ran it knocked a bit off his bill in exchange for him doing odd jobs around the place.

'It's great to be useful,' I said as we crossed a field of long grass.

'Cooking is useful.'

'Yeah, right.'

'It is,' he insisted.

'Everyone can cook,' I said. 'It's not useful beyond the basics. A mackerel vinaigrette isn't going to count for much when the apocalypse comes.'

'Whenever we'd go to visit my grandma, I'd spend the whole journey looking forward to whatever she was going to put on the table when we got there. It'd be the first hot dinner I'd have had in months. Don't underestimate it. A good cooked meal can be better than medicine.'

I gave him a doubtful look but he nodded emphatically. 'It can,' he insisted.

'Did you ever think about learning?'

'To cook?' he said. 'God no. I'd rather do something useful.'

He sidestepped my shove and it landed in the air.

'Who knew you were funny?'

'You might be the first.'

Andy talked more candidly when he was moving, as if the forward motion distracted from what he was saying. His mum moved to Australia a couple of days after getting him. She emigrated with her sister and mother. The other two women settled in Brisbane but his mum needed to keep moving. 'If Mum could be free, she was happy,' he said. She was a hands-off parent. The kind of freedom she was seeking for herself she wanted for Andy too. He never had a bedtime or curfew and he chose the next dinner or movie or place to live as often as she did.

'Did you like all that moving about?' I asked, picking up a branch from my path and using it to beat the grass.

'I must have, 'cause I'm still doing it.'

'So where's home, then?'

He took long studied steps through the pasture. 'I dunno,' he said finally. 'I guess I'm still trying to find it.'

We walked down the wide path flanked by trees several times the width of any human. We made our way into the valley and right back up again. He took two steps for every three of mine and our arms swung just out of time. I felt the sun on my shoulders, the gravel through the thin soles of my sandals, the cool respite when my dress blew against my legs. Despite the absence of a breeze, all down my spine a shiver vibrated.

'Was Henry like that?' he asked when we were still on the gravel. 'Did he get restless?'

'No.' He was surprised by how quickly I answered but it was an easy question. 'Henry was always on a path. He liked structure. He went from school to university to a job. He had one long-term girlfriend before me, and he wanted us to get married. We would have gotten around to it eventually. We'd have had kids and grown old together. And he was so happy with that. I never once knew him to be bored, or restless.'

Andy thought about this.

'I assumed maybe it was because we were adopted,' he said. 'Or because we were missing . . . something.'

'Well, Henry didn't know he was adopted,' I said, wanting to make him feel better.

'Yeah.'

We sat on the short grass; me kneeling up, him lying back with his arms folded behind his head, telling me about how, as a kid, he got himself up for school by never closing the curtains at night. But in his teenage years he discovered all the fun things his parental freedom so easily facilitated. He got suspended for skipping class and even though he knew his mother was disappointed, she still marched up to the school to defend him, telling the principal that the world had more to teach us than what was in books.

'Any excuse to stick it to the man,' said Andy, lying right beside me with his eyes shut against the glare of the late-afternoon sun.

At sixteen, he missed more than thirty days in a given year and social services got involved. His mother started to set boundaries then but it was too late and it didn't come naturally to either of them. He dropped out six months before finishing and moved in with friends. He worked at a hostel and sold weed and occasionally acid to 'surfies' passing through. When he was nineteen, he got busted for possession for the third time.

'I got two months.'

'Wow,' I said, unable to hide my surprise.

'What?' He turned his head towards me and squinted his eyes open. I stopped tearing blades of grass from the soil.

'Nothing.' I tried to look nonchalant but gave up almost immediately.

'I don't know anyone who's been to jail,' I admitted. 'And my drug knowledge is embarrassingly naïve. I did see Henry smoke a joint a few times when we were younger but he always held it wrong.' I cast my mind back. 'Like it was a nail he was about to hammer in, or a dart he was teeing up.'

Andy grinned and turned back towards the sky. 'I got it wiped from my record a few years later. And it wasn't all bad; the probation officer pointed me towards the building sites, which is where I trained as a plumber.'

'Would you like to have gone to university?'

He didn't respond for so long that I lifted myself slightly so I could see his face and be sure he hadn't fallen asleep.

'There was this aptitude test we did when we were fourteen,' he said, and I quietly plopped myself back on the grass. 'I got the highest in our year. The careers teacher was talking to me about financial aid and degrees and all this future stuff. I brought the results home to Mum but instead of putting it on the fridge she ripped into me for doing state-sanctioned tests. She thought uni was a way of enslaving the population. So yeah, I guess I regret that.'

'But you like plumbing?' I said awkwardly, cheerily, feeling like an auld one asking a kid if they loved their mammy and daddy.

'Sure,' he replied, his voice light again as he raised a hand to further shield his eyes. 'It's a good job for a nomad.'

This was the first day since he'd been in Ireland that Andy hadn't either been working or carrying out his own investigations. He spent his time in libraries and archives, at the adoption services, attending a support group, plaguing the religious order that had handled his case.

'My grandma can't believe it,' he laughed. 'Every time I phone her with some new piece of information all she wants to know is why I couldn't have put this much energy into keeping a job, or a woman who might make her a great-grandma.

'It just feels like I'm getting somewhere now. I'm not sure exactly what I'm looking for but I reckon I'm getting closer. You know?'

'I think so.'

'I'd really like to meet Henry's parents. They've got to know something about why Henry went to them and I didn't. That's the next step. I'd like to know what they're like, it'd help me get a better sense of my brother.'

I thought of Isabel's weak health and Conor's inbuilt scepticism. The idea of introducing them to Andy was ridiculous.

'Will we eat?' I said, clambering to my feet.

I was standing over Andy, who was still stretched out on his back, eyes closed, when I spotted it; the little mound of grass sitting just below his belly button where his greying T-shirt had ridden up. I rubbed my fingers along the skin of my thumb and felt the dirt leftover from ripping blades of grass from the earth. I'd built the same thing in the same place on the same torso so many times that I hadn't even realised I was doing it.

'What?' said Andy, able to open his eyes now that my looming shadow was blocking out the sun. 'What is it?'

I shook my head. 'Nothing.'

And as Andy pushed himself into sitting, then standing, I watched the perfect green mound go tumbling to the ground.

TWENTY-SEVEN

'Here we are.'

'This place?'

'Yep.'

'Fish and chips. Really?'

Andy looked from me to the garish neon lights above the door of the place Henry had sworn did the best chips in Dublin. Our old flat was around the corner. I hadn't been back to Gianni's since Henry died, but I could already taste the vinegar on my fingers.

'People eat this stuff sober?' said Andy doubtfully.

And then: 'What's with the yelling?'

I pointed to the upstairs floor where the windows were always open. 'There's a boxing club above it. The guy who runs the chipper – Gianni – set that up too. He left Italy in the sixties, went to America, and then came here in the seventies. Apparently he trained with Muhammad Ali.'

'Good for him,' said Andy with none of the scepticism with which Irish people usually greeted that story.

I grinned and went to push the door open but he put an arm out gently to stop me.

'Are you feeling all right?' he asked and I was embarrassed by the concern in his voice. I'd become light-headed and had had to sit down on the way here, right after we'd walked past our old flat. It was my first time back there too.

The day we moved into that flat, I ran on ahead of Henry so I could see it in its emptiest state. And when he came through the door a couple of minutes later, carrying the first load from the car, I remember thinking: 'Now it's full. Now it's a home. This is all I need.' It rained all day and when we got everything in, we ordered pizza and did not leave for twenty-four hours. That was the first night I was frightened by my own capacity for love.

'I'm grand,' I insisted, pushing the memory away.

Then I pulled Andy into Gianni's after me. 'Come on. You'll like it.'

We stood in line and I told Andy how Henry and I used to come here once a fortnight. We knew which tables had jukeboxes that worked and which ones were only there to take your money. You could feel the buzz just standing in the queue. I watched the staff shaking deep-fat fryers and compiling burgers as if they were being timed. I'd been hungry anyway but the smell made me ravenous. I was making the case for salt to an unconvinced Andy – 'You need a certain amount of sodium to *stop* dehydration, so therefore . . .' – when we were spotted.

'My friends!' the owner shouted down the queue. 'Where have you been?'

I waved back. 'Hey, Gianni!'

'What's with the bandana?' whispered Andy.

'It's part of his branding.'

Gianni had been living in Dublin for forty years but still talked like he'd just gotten off the boat. Henry, and most other people, reckoned he was putting on the accent. He only ever referred to himself in the third person, which I personally thought was a very clever form of constant brand enforcement. His multicoloured headscarves were his trademark; it was what made him one of the Dublin 'characters' that Portobello Dermot was reluctantly becoming.

Every thirty seconds or so we shuffled a little further along the line until finally we reached the counter.

'Ciao, lovebirds! Where have you been? You don't visit Gianni no more?' The white-haired Italian in the mint-green shirt and tropical-print bandana looked from Andy to me and back again. Of course, I thought suddenly, of course he thought this was Henry.

'Oh no, Gianni. It's not what you think.' I put a hand up to Andy's shoulder. 'I want to introduce you to someone.'

'You think Gianni forget? Maybe you forget about Gianni, but Gianni don't forget about you. Show me your face!' He rested his elbows on the glass counter top and held his hands out to myself and Andy. 'One face, two face! I miss your face!'

I looked to Andy for help but he wasn't responsive. Of course Gianni didn't know my boyfriend had died. The local chipper owner wasn't on the list of people you phoned in advance of a funeral. He didn't even know our names. He just knew that a woman with my face and a man with that face used to be amongst his best customers.

'This isn't . . . A few months ago—'

'You been on holidays! You,' he waggled a silver scoop at Andy, 'you get the sun. But you, bella,' he directed the scoop towards me, 'you like a ghost. You Irish all so white. The sun,' he shook his head and wrinkled his nose, 'the sun is not your friend.'

The woman in the queue behind us started to clear her throat. I tried again.

'This isn't the same man . . . I mean, this isn't—'

'Yes, Gianni,' Andy interrupted. 'Three weeks we were in the sun and she still didn't tan. Can you believe that? She never does, though, do you, dearest?'

Andy gave me an expectant smile, and Gianni started scooping chips into brown paper bags.

'No,' I said eventually, with my own quizzical expression, 'dearest. I never do tan.'

Andy moved his attention to the price list on the wall behind Gianni. He was about to order but the souped-up Italian got there first.

'You want the usual? No problem! Gianni give you the usual.'

I watched Gianni place a large bag of chips to share onto a blue plastic tray. Then he added a hotdog for me and a quarter-pounder with cheese and no salad for Henry. I'd forgotten about this happy trio. Only the burger wasn't actually for Henry, and Andy could have been vegetarian for all I knew. No salt or caffeine; he was definitely a healthier eater than me or Henry. He'd probably have wanted the salad at the very least. But then he was the one who'd gone along with the fabrication, and he'd seemed happy to do it.

I took out my wallet and handed over two notes. Gianni squeezed mustard onto the hotdog. Andy took the tray and headed for a booth.

'Keep the change,' I said, though the change was almost as much as the bill. I think I was high on the normalcy of it all.

'*Grazie*, bella!'

I lifted the tray and Gianni moved his banter on to the next customer. I slid into the seat opposite Andy in a booth by the window, one with a jukebox that worked.

'Andy—'

'Is the hotdog for me or you?'

'It's . . . for me.' I watched as he pulled two napkins from the dispenser, spread them out and took the quarter-pounder from the tray. 'The burger is yours,' I added superfluously.

'Thank God for that, ay? I couldn't tell you what's in a hotdog.' He took a bite of the quarter-pounder and chewed pensively, then contently. 'That's not bad,' he said. 'The hot chips are good too.' He gave me a thumbs-up and just like that what had happened at the counter was old news.

'Hot chips?' I raised my eyebrows.

'Yeah.'

'They're just chips,' I corrected him.

He took another bite and I reached for the bag, shaking a few into my hotdog container.

'What are you doing?'

'I want to add vinegar,' I said.

'That's all right. I like vinegar.'

'No, I want to add gallons of the stuff.'

181

He was chewing again but he gestured for me to go ahead, pour the vinegar onto the communal chips. Henry had hated vinegar. I thought it but I didn't say it. Instead, I reached for the condiment and began to pour.

I watched him watching the dispenser. I couldn't suppress the grin.

'Are you sure that's enough?' he deadpanned.

'For now,' I beamed, pulling a chip from the bottom. 'You want to get the ones right down the end. Maximum soakage.'

Andy ate mainly in silence. Every now and again he would nod his approval, mid-bite, and I'd give him a mock bow, as if I had made the food myself.

'Are you a music fan?' I asked when the eating was done.

He pushed his napkins away and sat back sated and happy. 'Sure.'

'Do you want to put something on the jukebox? This one works.'

'All right.' He flicked through the 1960s offerings, his eyes darting back and forth as one set of listings was replaced by another. 'How about Roy Orbison? "Oh, Pretty Woman"?'

'Go for it.'

He dug some coins from his pocket and put the required fifty cent into the slot. The music started as soon as he selected it. Andy counted out the beats on the table with his palm – he had rhythm, something else his brother didn't share – and I pretended to play drums with two discarded chips until they crumbled and we lost half their potato stuffing to the floor.

'That's me out of the band.'

I bent down to pick up the half-chips and must have brought my head back too quickly because my face was suddenly flush. I caught his eye and my cheeks reddened further, but Andy didn't flinch. I did my best not to look away.

Maybe life didn't happen linearly. Maybe there were parallel worlds and existences and there was one just next to my own in which Henry didn't disappear under the wheel of a truck, in which he wasn't so much a twin as one half of the same coin, the first act in a two-act play. Henry had always believed in fate and I believed in second chances.

The song ended and the spell broke but we didn't stop talking. We discussed first gigs and musical ability or, in my case, inability. We compared favourite bands and songs and books and films. It was so easy it almost didn't feel real. He hated a lot of the films Henry had liked – action movies, sci-fi, things with monsters – but I didn't say that.

I'm sorry, Henry, but I didn't mention you at all.

When we had been there so long the sun was starting to disappear, Gianni came over to the table with two mugs of tea. 'For everyone else, coffee. For the lovebirds, tea. You think Gianni forget?'

'Actually—'

But Andy took the cup readily. 'Thank you.' He even managed to drink half of it. We talked about rom-coms and coming-of-age films and our favourite actors and directors until we were the only two people left in the place and Gianni's yawns had become unignorably pointed. And we didn't say a word about the rest of it. Neither of us mentioned that he was not Henry.

TWENTY-EIGHT

' **H**enry! Henry!'

'Yeah, I'm here. Hang on. I'm coming over to you. Where are you?'

'I'm on the couch. What happened to the lights? Are they gone everywhere? Is it just us? Henry?'

'Hang on! I'm checking the window . . . Well, they're still on in the street . . . And next door. No, it's just us. That's weird.'

'You forgot to top up the meter.'

'Sorry?'

'You, Henry, you forgot to top up the meter. Again. I have fish in the fridge for tomorrow night's dinner and now it's going to go off. I told you two days ago to check the meter! You said you were going to do it on your way out to work.'

'Yeah, okay, I forgot. I was late that morning.'

'And that evening?'

'Lay off, Grace.'

'Jesus Christ!'

'Relax, I will go downstairs and top it up now. It's not a big deal.'

'It is a big deal. If I ask you to do something once, you forget. And if I ask you more than that, you say I'm nagging you. I shouldn't even have to ask in the first place.'

'I forgot one thing.'

'It is not one thing! You always forget to put out the bins; I'm the only person who ever cleans the bathroom. Or the kitchen. If I don't ask you, it doesn't get done. I shouldn't have to ask, Henry! You're not my child, you're my boyfriend. We're supposed to be partners.'

'Okay, Grace, you are blowing this way out of proportion. It's one thing. It'll take me five minutes to fix it. Why are you bringing everything else into it? Are you looking for a fight?'

'Of course I'm not looking for a fight! Most of the time, I'm keeping my mouth shut so as not to start a fight!'

'Most of the time?'

'Yes. Pretty much every day there's something that you say you'll do but you don't, or that I really wish you would just know to do but you're blind to it. Like the fridge. Have you cleaned the fridge once since we lived here?'

'I'm not arguing with you about this.'

'There is black mould on the top shelf.'

'I'm going downstairs to top up the meter and then I'm going to bed.'

'Don't do that, Henry.'

'Don't do what?'

'Don't walk out on an argument. It's childish and it solves nothing. You're not the injured party here.'

'I made one mistake!'

'It's not about the bloody electricity. It's about everything. It's okay now it's just the two of us, but what about when we have kids? What then? Am I going to have to give you a list of chores like you're a babysitter or something? That's not a life I want.'

'If I'm so terrible to be around, Grace, then you should probably just break up with me.'

'Oh for God's sake, Henry, I'm just trying to have a conversation about our future. I want us to be a team.'

'Well, I don't really feel like I'm on a team right now. So I'm going to go and top up the meter. If that's okay with you? May I be dismissed?'

'Grow up, Henry.'

'Goodnight, Grace.'

TWENTY-NINE

'Tell us,' said Billy.

'We're here for each other,' added Patsy. 'That's what the group is about.'

'Solidify.'

'He means solidarity.'

'Right,' agreed Martin. 'I do.'

'Just tell us.'

'There's nothing to tell,' I insisted for what felt like the hundredth time.

'It's not just your absence,' said Patsy. 'Although that has been noticed.'

The three of them mmm-hmmm-ed.

'Or,' he continued, 'that the last time we saw you here, you weren't even *here*. You were off wandering in the next section.'

'East Section Three,' said Billy, narrowing his eyes.

'Enemy territory.'

'They're not our enemies, Martin. They're dead!'

I had come to the cemetery the previous week in search of Frances Clinch's grave, which I knew from Andy was in the neighbouring section. It was true, though, that other than that visit, I hadn't been up to see Henry's grave or the Three Wise Men in over two weeks. I'd been spending all my free time with Andy.

I'd brought cake from the Portobello Kitchen but it hadn't distracted attention. The wise men were suspicious.

'And there's something else,' said Patsy, getting the group back on track. '*You're* different.'

'How am I different?'

'You're happier.'

'I was always happy.'

'No,' said Martin, wagging his finger. 'You were always . . .'

'Pleasant,' offered Billy.

'Yes, pleasant. But now you're sort of . . .' Martin searched for the word. 'Glowing.'

The other two nodded their agreement.

'This *is* the first time you've ever brought cake,' said Billy. 'I mean, you've brought restaurant leftovers before, sure. A bit of lasagne or a few slightly stale scones. But cake . . .'

'I resent that. My scones are not stale. And I'm not glowing.'

'Martin thought you were off with a new man . . .' said Patsy.

'I resent that even more.'

'. . . and Billy thought you'd done yourself in.'

Billy nodded. 'I knew you'd turn up eventually. I just thought it might be in a hearse.'

I sighed and took a step back.

'Ah now, don't be getting offended,' said Billy.

'No, it's just, the smell of your coffee.' I made a gagging noise.

'Have you stopped seeing Henry everywhere?'

'Not really,' I mumbled, draining the end of my lukewarm tea. 'Anyway! Enough about me – what about youse? What have I missed?'

'There's a new woman gone in beside Ted Brangan.' Billy motioned towards the far corner of our section.

'That's good,' I said. 'You were saying he'd be getting lonely.'

'And Martin's been dating.'

I looked at Martin. 'Have you really?'

'I have,' he said, visibly chuffed with himself. 'I set up a profile on one of them internet sites and they came flocking.'

I looked to the other two for verification.

'He brought one of them up here last week,' said Billy.

'What? On a date? To a graveyard?'

Martin looked hurt. 'She wanted to know about my hobbies.'

'Of course. Sorry.'

'She didn't laugh at any of my jokes,' said Billy, who had clearly not forgiven this slight.

'But she did ask if we did eco-burials,' added Patsy, equally affronted and making 'eco-burials' sound like 'swingers' retreats'. 'She wanted us to put in a composter, for all the old flowers.'

Martin's cheeks grew redder. 'Her name is Larissa. She's an environmentalist. And a vegan.'

'She sounds great,' I said. 'And I think the composter is a wonderful idea.'

'You have to move on sometime, don't you?'

'You do,' I agreed, putting my arm around him. 'You absolutely do.'

I did consider telling them about Andy. It would have been easier than telling a lot of other people, since they had never actually met Henry and so would be able to look beyond the physical similarities to see how much it meant to me, how much I liked having someone around with such a visceral connection to him. But ultimately it was easier to keep it to ourselves, for another while anyway.

We stopped going into the city centre. It was too much of a risk. Some man who worked in a chipper was one thing, but what if we ran into someone Henry had actually known? What if we were spotted by a work colleague or an old school friend? What if we bumped into Conor and Isabel? So we stuck to the edges, to the suburbs and the parks, where nobody ever got too close to anybody else. Mainly, we stayed at Aberdeen Street. Andy mentioned Henry's parents again but I managed to bat it away. After a while, he seemed happy to forget about external factors too. And in the scraps of time he was away from me and not working, I think he continued searching for information. But I didn't ask about that.

'Do you mind that everyone thinks the Irish are a nation of drinkers?' he asked one evening as we took a different route through the park.

'Do *you* mind that everyone thinks the Australians are a nation of racists?'

'That's really the perception, ay?'

'Well, not just that,' I reasoned. 'Also that you have no culture.'

'Awesome.'

'And that you all go surfing.'

'Not true, but not as bad . . .'

'And that you're all descended from murderers and outlaws who were sent there on prison ships,' I added pleasantly. 'Except for the Aborigines, of course. But you exterminated most of them.'

Andy considered this. 'Huh. You see, I thought we'd be a fun nation; all crocodile wrestling and didgeridoos.'

'Didgeridoo? Was that not Rolf Harris's instrument?'

'Yeah.'

'Rolf Harris who was arrested and jailed for—'

'Yeah, all right,' he interrupted. 'Point taken. Mate, now I wish *we* were the nation of alcoholics.'

'Well, you are that too. Only when you get drunk you start throwing around slurs. Whereas we Irish just,' I crossed my feet and began to hop on the spot, 're-enact *Riverdance*.'

'That doesn't look anything like *Riverdance*.'

'Like I said,' I called behind as I jigged off through the trees, 'youse don't know a thing about culture!'

It was never not enjoyable. We talked about everything. Less and less about Henry, but I guess that was natural. There was only so much to say. We painted a few rooms and I started teaching him to cook properly. We lounged on the couch and watched boxsets. Nothing we did was special, particularly. It was all just normal stuff. We were watching

The Slap, an Australian drama he'd seen before but didn't mind watching a second time.

There was a restlessness to Andy and I could feel it surfacing when he talked about the past. But when it was just him and me, sequestered away on Aberdeen Street, it was gone; he was at peace.

'Stop shifting!'

'Sorry,' I said, pushing my feet flat against the inside of the sofa arm so my toes straightened out. I turned them slightly to the right and pressed down on the baby ones.

'What are you doing?'

'Sorry,' I repeated, irritated. 'Henry used to pull my toes out straight for me. I can't get the same stretch on my own.'

Andy sighed and got up from his seat on the armchair and moved towards the couch. He pulled my legs up and sat under them. He took my left foot in his right hand and pushed the toes straight. 'There.'

'Ah!' I said, throwing my head back. 'Bliss.'

'You're weird, Grace.'

'Shush now and do the other one.'

The episode ended and we allowed the next to start automatically. About halfway through Andy got up and headed into the kitchen.

'Tea, please!' I shouted after him, pausing *The Slap*. My phone beeped and I dug it out from the side of the couch.

What is the story?? Are we painting this Saturday??
Are you visiting your aunt again?? ARE YOU ALIVE??
The paint will be growing mould by the time we get

around to using it. Your pal (in case you've forgotten my name) Aoife

I started two replies and deleted them both. There was a voicemail but I didn't want to hear it. I had been avoiding Henry's parents. They'd invited me to dinner twice and I never responded. The inquest was in two weeks. I stuffed the phone back down the side of the couch.

Andy plodded back into the room barefooted and handed me a cup that looked like a tea bag had taken a dip in it but decided the water was too hot and hopped straight back out.

'The kitchen's coming together nicely,' he said.

'All down to your abilities with a roller. Is there any tea in this tea, or . . .'

'What's wrong with it?'

I peered into the cup. 'I can identify hot water and milk. But traces of the third crucial ingredient are modest.'

'Ha ha.'

I went to get up to make myself another cup but he took the vessel from me. 'I'll do it. You keep watching. I remember this episode anyway.'

'No it's fine,' I said, pushing myself up. 'Honestly. I'll make it.'

'I've got it.'

I made a swipe for the cup but he held it aloft and headed for the kitchen. 'Just keep watching.'

'No, Henry, I'll do it!'

He stopped at the door. I put my hand over my mouth but it was too late. The word was out and it was echoing back and forth in the space between us.

'Andy. Sorry.'

He didn't move. With his back to me, I couldn't see his face.

'I wasn't even – I don't know why I said that.'

'It's fine.'

'Andy.'

'That's my name.'

'It just came out. I didn't even think. I wasn't even thinking about him, I just, I wasn't thinking at all.'

'Grace, it's cool,' he said, finally turning. 'It was bound to happen. It would be weird if it didn't.'

'I'm sorry.'

'Don't worry about it,' said Andy and he smiled. 'It's all good. Now, I'm going to make the tea.'

THIRTY

••••••••••••••••

'**I spent a** *night at my parents' house. Why is this a big deal?'*

'I didn't know where you were, Henry!'

'You knew I was having dinner there. Where else would I have gone?'

'I thought something had happened on the way home. I woke at five a.m. and you weren't here. I went to phone you but then I saw you'd left your phone here. Why didn't you just let me know you were staying over? Text me or something?'

'Because I left my phone here, like you just said.'

'You could have used Isabel's or Conor's. Or you could have just picked up the landline and dialled, instead of having me phone your parents' house at six in the morning. It was embarrassing.'

'You were embarrassed? I'm the one who looks like his girlfriend doesn't trust him!'

'Don't do that. It's not fair and you know it. Why didn't you just call?'

'Because I'm not a child, Grace! That's why. And you're

not my keeper. If I want to spend the night at my parents'
I'm allowed.'

'Of course you're allowed. When have I ever stopped you
from going anywhere or doing anything? That is not what
it's about. It's about having some consideration. It's about
thinking about someone other than yourself. Not calling
was just selfish, Henry. You were being selfish.'

'And you are being dramatic. I'm just going to presume
it's because you didn't have enough sleep. I have to go to
work. I'll talk to you later.'

The second cup wasn't much better than the first but I drank
every last drop of it. I even smacked my lips a few times.

'Grace,' he said, back sitting under my legs, 'you're trying
too hard.'

'What? It's an excellent cup of tea.'

'Can I have that in writing?'

Andy really did seem fine. I don't know why I couldn't just
let it go. I hadn't even been thinking about Henry – I often
didn't when we were hanging out; sometimes, and I know
this sounds impossible, I even forgot the connection – but
it had just come out. I had said it out of habit. Henry was
the person who I'd spent the most time with, whose name
I said the most; my brain was obviously thinking, 'Well, it's
been a fair while since I've put the neurons together to make
that sound *Hen-ry* that she loves so much, this seems like a
good time to get it out there, right?' Wrong.

I wanted to explain this to Andy but I didn't think he'd thank me for bringing it up again. We had already moved on. But that didn't sit right either. How could he be so fine about it? People who grew up as twins in normal circumstances were undoubtedly used to it. But these weren't normal circumstances.

I liked being around Andy because it reminded me Henry had existed but it also allowed me to forget he was gone. Did that make sense? I was sick of pitying looks and softly spoken How-are-yous. I didn't want to be a tragic figure. I just wanted things to be normal, like how they were before. I was less sure what Andy got from it but I knew he was happy so it was fine. I didn't need to question it. The credits rolled on the second episode and I couldn't have told you a single thing that had happened. I put the whole incident out of my head.

'Let's cook,' said Andy, standing from the couch and holding out a hand to pull me up after him. 'Well, you cook. I'll chop.'

I followed him through to the kitchen and we took our stations. We had established an evening routine where we stood side by side at the worktop and I doled out instructions. Andy had mastered the difference between slicing, dicing and chopping, and was now reluctant to proceed with any knife-based task without knowing exactly what size was desired.

'These small enough?' he asked, halfway through the first red pepper.

I leaned over. 'They look good.'

'Garlic?'

'Two cloves,' I said, pushing the utility knife towards him. 'That'll work better.'

'I was seeing a girl once who would string garlic up with twine and hang it all around her house.'

'Interesting.'

'She was into vampires,' he said, brow furrowed as he tried to get the cloves as fine as possible. 'She had two dogs and she called them Bella and Jacob, after the *Twilight* characters.'

'I thought Edward was everyone's favourite.'

'Yeah, he is, and hers too. But she was *such* a fan that she didn't think either dog deserved the name.'

'Wow.'

'Weird, ay?' He turned to rinse the tomatoes and despite the garlic the smell was overwhelming. His smell. Sweat and aftershave, dirt and dust, and lingering after the faintest whiff of something sweet. It was so close to Henry's. It took me by surprise and I swallowed it down.

'Look!' I grabbed two slices of pepper, stuck them either side of my mouth and waited for him to turn back from the sink.

'Did she vont to suck your blood?'

He watched as my fangs fell to the floor. 'No, but she did *bat* her eyelashes.'

'That's terrible.'

'I apologise,' he said, grinning now too. 'I really shouldn't make jokes about ex-ghoul friends . . .'

'Oh God.'

'It's nobody's fault it didn't work out; sometimes you're just not their blood type.'

'Stop!' I shouted, lowering my head to the counter. 'Do you just have these stored up somewhere?'

'I'm done, I'm done,' he said, lifting the knife again.

He returned to slivering the garlic and I took two chicken breasts from the fridge. I upturned them onto the white chopping board.

Andy sighed and I glanced over at him suspiciously.

'This is what happens when I talk about vampires,' he said, as if talking to himself. 'For some reason it always gives people a pain in the neck.'

I chucked a nearby tea towel at him and it landed on his shoulder. Somewhere at the back of my mind was a memory, another time I'd thrown a tea towel at those shoulders . . .

Andy tied it around his neck like a mini-cape.

'Application accepted,' he said. 'I hereby promote you to president of the Irish branch of my international fang club.'

THIRTY-ONE

'**I**s the clock broken?'

Tina rolled her eyes. 'No,' she said evenly. 'The clock is not broken.'

'Every time I look at it, it says the same thing: "Almost five o'clock but not quite. You're going nowhere yet, Grace."'

'Maybe you should stop looking at it.'

Dermot had been shouting 'NO!' at everyone who walked through the door for the past hour (Pete's chicken commercial got picked up for syndication) and the restaurant was empty. I wiped down the worktops for the fourth time in as many minutes and tried not to look at the clock.

'Have you your phone on you?'

Tina eyed me doubtfully. 'Why?'

'What time does your phone say it is?'

'Grace!'

'Just check.'

Tina made a big deal of pulling her phone from the back pocket of her dark, sprayed-on jeans.

'Well? What does it say?'

'It agrees with the clock. Almost five but not quite. Now will you please relax?'

'I am relaxed.'

I was not relaxed. Andy was in the city centre. He had a job at Trinity College this afternoon and I was meeting him at the front arch afterwards. It was stressful enough to think of him spending hours at one of Dublin's most popular tourist destinations without imagining him idling at the arch a minute longer than necessary. Trinity was slap bang in the middle of the city and the front arch was a popular assembly spot. Henry and I used to meet there. I'd thought about letting him make his own way to my house and just seeing him at home, but I had visions of him getting lost and taking wrong buses and generally spending far too much time traipsing busy streets.

I drummed my fingers on the counter and wiped the prints away again.

What if Henry's parents decided to go into town for a bit of late-night shopping? I imagined Isabel arranging to meet Conor at the front arch and him getting held up at the office. I pictured her standing there alone, thinking about whether or not to bother with the Brown Thomas sale, when her dead son moseys into her path. If Isabel saw Andy, she'd fall to pieces and he wouldn't have a clue who this shrieking woman was. It was impossible not to keep checking the clock.

'Where the heck is Simon?' I exhaled.

'What is going on with you, Grace? Your body's in the kitchen but your mind . . .' Tina made a gesture to symbolise my mind being blown away.

'There's nothing to do here. I don't see the point in hanging around for the sake—'

The jangle of the café door opening and Dermot's responding bark: 'NO!'

Tina rolled her eyes.

'NO! OUT! No parasites, no— Oh, it's you. Fine then. If you must.'

I looked through the orders window.

'Simon!'

I pulled off my whites and was stuffing them into a bag by the time he came through the kitchen door.

'We're in for a busy night, I see.'

'Dermot's heading home shortly,' I called from the storage-cupboard-cum-office where I fished out my handbag from under a pile of napkins. 'It'll be business as usual after that. See you tomorrow!'

I was out the door before I remembered to tell him we were out of kale.

I jogged down Camden Street onto Aungier Street, past a stag party shouting at each other from either side of the road in thick Liverpool accents. I slowed to a walk as I weaved my way through a massive group of Spanish exchange students. It was a Thursday and the pubs were already heaving. I thought of how nice it would be to sit outside a bar and watch people go by but of course we couldn't do that. I'd be collecting Andy and hopping straight on a bus, maybe even into a taxi. It was fine. We could always have a drink at home.

When I got to Trinity, he wasn't there. I checked both sides of the arch and then my phone. I was five minutes early. Grand. Better I was the one hanging around than him. I half-read the noticeboards, turning my head after each advert to check the entrances. There were a lot of personal notices looking for language exchange partners: Spanish students seeking English speakers, Irish students seeking French lessons. Some of them matched up. Did people even read the little cards before sticking up their own?

I looked left and right. Still no sign.

A familiar feeling niggled. A recollection of an earlier sensation: when he wasn't with me there was always a possibility that something had happened.

In the corner of one noticeboard was an old photograph: *Class of 1954*, it said underneath. Did all students wear suits to university in those days? I moved closer and scanned the rows of black-and-white faces for any female graduates. When did women start going to university? I tried to think of the oldest college-educated woman I knew. I had a great-aunt who'd been a teacher but I wasn't sure if she'd—

'Grace.'

I smiled with relief at the sound of my name. I spun around and, without a thought in my head, I kissed him.

THIRTY-TWO

t wasn't a long kiss. There weren't any tongues. I just planted my lips on his and left them there for a second, maybe two. It was probably in that latter second that I realised what I'd done.

I'd done it a thousand times before. Heard my name, turned around, saw what I expected to see, and kissed him. I hadn't been thinking. I'd just moved closer, arms like magnets pulling me towards him, one on either side. It came so naturally – as instinctive as building a mound of grass on his stomach or saying his name – and I was on Henry's lips before I realised they weren't Henry's at all. My mouth on his mouth, sending that faint jolt of excitement through my body. It wasn't his voice that had said 'Grace' and even though it had the same waist, tailor-made to accommodate my arms, it wasn't his body. I was right there, right at Andy's lips, when reality came thundering through.

'Oh.' I said this still a hair's breadth from his mouth. I was afraid to pull back further. I thought of vortexes and alternate universes. For as long as it didn't come to an end, maybe it could be reversed.

'Grace.'

The blood was pounding in my ears. I felt sick and faint and I really thought that this time I might drop. Oh God. I straightened my knees. Oh God, oh God.

It felt as if we were frozen there for eternity. I didn't know where to look and yet at such close proximity, there really weren't a lot of options.

'I'm sorry,' I said.

I couldn't read the look in his eyes. They were too close. I closed my own. I was no longer dizzy but there was a strong chance I might still vomit.

I took a step back. 'Oh God.'

'Grace.'

'Fuck.'

'Grace.'

'Fuck fuck fuck fuck fuck.' I placed a hand against the cool stone of the under arch and doubled over slightly. This wasn't happening. I couldn't have done that. I wouldn't do that. Remember Henry, Grace? More than just a face. Henry: the love of your life, the man you would do anything for, who would do anything for you.

'Are you all right?'

My head bent towards my knees. 'No,' came the sound of my muffled voice.

Inside my skull, the blood continued to pound. It was rhythmic, keeping time, repeating the same message: Henry Hen-ry Hen-ry Hen-ry Hen-ry.

'Grace, it's cool.'

'I didn't mean to. I wasn't even— Oh God.'

'No worries.'

I brought my head up with a rush of blood.

No worries? No fucking worries? Who says 'No worries' anyway? Henry would never say 'No worries'. How could I have thought this surfer dude, this plumber fraud, this *Australian* was Henry? Nausea, self-loathing, pity; I put my head back down and allowed it to come. Good enough for me.

Andy said something but I couldn't hear it over the crashing down of everything around him. What was I doing? What *was this*? All those times I'd met Henry under this arch and we'd sauntered into the evening air for nachos and wine or shopping or nothing-in-particular, never thinking those nothing-in-particulars were finite. Never thinking a time would come when I would want so desperately to meet him under this arch, and he would not come. I could wait here for ever and he would never show up. The best he could do was to send a changeling in his place.

'No. Sorry,' I said, standing up straight and interrupting whatever it was he'd been saying. 'I'm sorry.'

And with that, I was gone. I turned left and threw myself into the crowds of people making their way through Trinity's front gate. I knew I shouldn't leave him standing there, I knew how risky and stupid it was, how easily he could have been spotted, but I couldn't stop. I was scared and I had to get away.

I did my best to slow my pace as I pushed through the masses. Why was the whole of Dublin heading in the opposite direction to me? I didn't know what I was doing or where I was going. I crossed to Dame Street and kept heading west until I got stuck in a crowd of people queuing for a bus. I looked behind in case Andy had followed and then, panicking, I jumped on one of the buses.

A woman stood to allow me to sit near the back. I must have looked as awful as I felt. I managed a 'thank you' as I took her seat and squeezed my eyes shut until it hurt. I pictured Andy standing right where I'd left him. It didn't matter how many people had Henry's face, there was only one of him. How could I have forgotten that? I looked out of the window and was vaguely aware that I hadn't a clue where this bus was going.

But I didn't think I *had* forgotten. I knew Andy wasn't Henry. I hadn't meant to kiss him. I could never. But habit, instinct, reflex – whatever it was – had taken over and I had ruined everything. I had sullied Henry's memory and destroyed whatever this unprecedented thing was with Andy. I leaned my head against the glass but it did no good. This time I couldn't stop it. I grabbed the plastic bag that was slipping across the floor in time with the bus's motions. I fumbled it open and with a force that lunged my chest forward, I vomited.

The man beside me got up and the woman who had offered me her seat sat down in his place.

'You all right now, pet?'

'Fine,' I mumbled, a burst of sweat giving way to shivers. I wiped my mouth with the back of my hand.

'Was it something you ate?'

I shook my head.

'Dodgy fish?'

I looked into the bag of vomit in the hope she would take a hint. Nobody wanted to talk when they had just been sick. She peered over my shoulder.

'I find,' she said, 'that anytime I have fish out, I know I'll be seeing it again before the night is over.'

I stood up, grabbed the bag, and rang the bell for the next stop.

THIRTY-THREE

'**F**irst Name, First Name is here.'

Larry appeared in the doorway but Aoife refused to move from the middle of it so he sort of bent around her as he waved.

'Long time no see,' he called. 'You got the light fixture sorted, anyway.'

'Yes,' I said as Aoife turned back in to the hallway, noticing for the first time that the bulb was illuminated. 'My dad called over to do it,' I added quickly.

Aoife remained unconvinced. She knew the only bulb with which my father was familiar was the UV one he used to inspect the carpets for hidden stains. I should have said Mam did it. I kept my focus on Larry.

'I've got the table in the van, anyway. I'll just bring it in.'

'I'll help you,' I said, physically moving Aoife to one side as I hurried past her without making eye contact.

It was two days since I'd left Andy standing under the Trinity arch and I had thought about nothing else. In the month since he'd shown up on my doorstep, this was the longest we'd gone without seeing each other. I had fretful dreams where Henry and Andy started to blend into one and my waking hours were spent looking for him on the street, in the lunchtime crowd at the Portobello Kitchen or thinking at any moment, even now with the house full, that he might knock on the door. I went to search for traces of him online before realising I didn't even know his surname. I'd never thought to ask. I read through the B&B listings for Harold's Cross, checking a few on Street View, but there were too many and even if I came across the right one, there was no way for me to know.

Forty-eight hours and I was already starting to doubt if he'd ever existed at all.

Larry climbed into the back of the van and I stood at the open doors as he undid cable ties and restraints. 'Do you do much work with that plumber you brought around to mine?' I asked casually. 'What was his name again . . .?'

Larry kept rummaging. I held the doors open.

'Andy!' I exclaimed, as if hit by an epiphany. 'That was it. Andy something.' I waited for Larry to fill in the blanks. 'What *was* his surname?'

'I've gotten him in for a few bits all right,' came the voice from the darkness. 'He's pretty good. Why?' Larry stuck his head out into the daylight. 'Was there a problem? Is your boiler back on the blink? I can take a quick look. I actually meant to say to you about getting in a few shelves for the hot press. I could get them next week? Or if—'

'The boiler's fine,' I interrupted, desperate to keep the conversation on track. 'He did a great job. So good, actually, that I thought it would be handy to have his details in case

I needed any other work done, or if a friend was looking for a recommendation.'

'Ah, he's only passing through. Going back to Australia soon – next month, I think. No point getting attached. Anyway, he's not on the books. That's why he's so cheap. So better off not mentioning him to anyone. Don't want him getting into trouble.' His head emerged from the van again. 'You didn't tell anyone about him, did you?'

'I can honestly say I am the only one who knows he exists.'

Larry gave me a conspiratorial wink. 'Better if he remains a ghost.'

'Yeah,' I said, somehow mustering up a smile from the empty pit in my stomach. Andy hadn't said anything to me about going back to Australia, nothing concrete anyway. I grabbed the legs of the table as Larry began to feed it out of the van.

Aoife came down the garden path to help, sighing loudly. Betty, too, emerged for a gawk.

'You haven't been in to see me for weeks,' she shouted from her doorway. 'You could have said you weren't coming. You know well they don't sell the Telly Bingo tickets after eleven o'clock. So if I don't know you're coming, that's it over for me.' Betty walked down her path, drawing closer as her voice remained at the same volume. 'And The Blonde One's been gone for a couple of weeks. You know I always win when she's not on. You probably owe me money.'

'How do I owe you money?' I asked, not sure why I was bothering.

'Compensation for winnings lost.'

211

'What about all those tickets I bought before? If anyone owes anyone, Betty, you owe me!'

'I'm not paying for those,' she scoffed. 'You only ever buy duds.'

'How's it going, Betty?' said Larry cheerfully, but the older woman ignored him. Her focus was very much on me and the various ways I had done her wrong.

'I could have fallen over in there, broken my ankle and be lying dead on the kitchen floor for all you'd know. Or care. That's the problem with your generation: it's all about yourselves.'

Aoife and I shuffled forward holding the front of the table and Larry brought up the rear. We manoeuvred our way around my neighbour. 'Betty,' I said, as we mounted the kerb, 'you had that front door open almost as soon as I'd come out my own. There's nothing wrong with your ankles, or your ears.'

Betty inspected the table. 'Something else that'll make an unholy racket, no doubt. You stomp around in that house like nobody ever paid you a slip of attention in your entire life . . .'

Aoife kicked my gate open and the three of us shuffled up the garden path.

'. . . and we both know that's not true.'

'What isn't?' I huffed, trying to keep a grasp on the table as I mounted the step into the house. I'd had a headache all day and this was not helping.

'That nobody's been paying you any attention,' sang Betty. 'You're getting plenty of attention these evenings. How's your fancy—'

I slammed the front door behind us, cutting her off mid-sentence. My head was throbbing.

'What's she on about?' asked Aoife, as we lowered the table to the hallway floor. 'What attention?'

'Who knows? Here, Larry. If you leave it down there, we can just sort of rotate through to the kitchen.'

The other two shimmied it through and Aoife put on coffee. The smell made my head worse. I stood in the hallway and listened to Larry and Aoife's muffled bickering. A low good-natured rumble followed by a high, irritated dressing-down and then silence before the rumble tried again. Where was Andy? I closed my eyes and massaged my temples but it didn't do any good. I was exhausted.

In the kitchen, Aoife had a tape out and was measuring the new addition, noting down dimensions as she went. I saw the table properly for the first time. I did a quick tour, taking in the smooth finish and sturdy legs. The carpentry was impeccable.

'It's gorgeous,' I said, meaning it.

'It's two inches narrower than requested,' corrected Aoife, standing dangerously close to Larry as she snapped the tape measure back into place.

'It's slightly narrower because that was the wood available,' he explained. 'And it ended up being a little shallower than expected so I wanted the proportions to match.'

'You needn't think you can skimp on the wood and expect Grace to pay full price.'

'I'm not charging full price.'

Aoife scoffed. 'That's what they all say, Larry David.'

'It's Larry Paul.'

'Sure it is.'

'It's perfect,' I said. 'Thank you very much, Larry.'

'I'm fairly proud of it myself, I have to say.'

'I'd send it back.'

I got halfway through jotting down Larry's bank details when I had to put the pen down. 'Sorry, Larry. I've a thumping headache. Give me one minute.'

'Not a bother,' he called after me as I headed out to the hallway and climbed the stairs to the bathroom in search of painkillers. I could hear Aoife asking for a receipt.

I emptied the black bag that contained all the miscellaneous, unpacked items I had survived perfectly well without since moving into the house. The whole lot came tumbling to the floor. Nail varnish, blister plasters, foundation that came free with something and was six shades too dark, sanitary pads, hairspray, a plastic beaker, nose pore strips, hand cream and, underneath the box of tampons, paracetamol. I popped two tablets into my mouth and picked up the plastic beaker. I ran the tap and placed the beaker underneath as I surveyed the odds and ends scattered on the bathroom floor. This was the kind of stuff you were meant to just throw out.

I could hear Aoife complaining about paintbrushes and when I got back downstairs the two of them were making a start on the study. Larry insisted he had nothing better to do that evening and was happy to help with the painting. Aoife did most of the talking. Her mother was wrecking her head, her sister Sharon had started a petition for her to move out

– 'Literally. She's got a page up on Change.org' – and she was still seeing Rowan.

Larry occasionally threw in his two cents and Aoife dutifully took umbrage at whatever he said.

I made occasional overtures towards conversation –

'Is that not the biggest load of shite you've ever heard, Grace?'

'Mmm.'

– but mostly I concentrated on my brushstrokes, making little deals in my head.

If I manage to get from the skirting board to the cornice in one smooth swoop, Andy will turn up.

The number of strokes it takes to complete this area to the left of the door is the amount of days it'll be before I see him again.

Two, three, four . . .

Aoife thought Rowan was sleeping with a woman he used to work with at the bookshop. She'd been talking about it for most of the first coat.

'. . . I can't be sure if there's actually something going on or if he just wants me to *think* there's something going on. It's possible he's just talking about her a lot and is not *actually* seeing her. I know she likes him, and he knows I know that, so he might just be using her to make me jealous when it could as easily be anyone at all, you know?'

'Mmm.'

'And because we're not actually going out and I effectively hate his guts and know him to be a waste of my energy, I can't really care. So then I can't ask anything and therefore

215

it's impossible to find out what *is* actually going on.'

'You should probably just put him out of your head,' I said.

'I would but he keeps putting up pictures of the shop on Facebook. He doesn't even work there anymore! Why's he still hanging around?'

'Unfriend him,' I offered. The headache had finally subsided but there was something else troubling me.

'And let him know he got to me?'

'Mute him so,' I said, only half-listening.

'What's the point of muting him if he doesn't *know* I've muted him? He needs to know how irritating he is.'

'Doesn't sound like he's worth it,' mused Larry, who I'd almost forgotten was in the room.

Aoife broke off mid-stroke and turned slowly. Sinisterly, even. 'Did I *ask* for your opinion?'

'Just thought you might like a male perspective,' said Larry, who never stopped painting. His relaxed tone made Aoife sound all the more manic.

'Every man thinks every woman could use a *male perspective*, as if there were none of those about already. You're grand thanks. We're allowed to drive and vote and work now, so I think I can figure this one out on my own.'

'Grand so.'

'And you can wipe that smugness from your voice too. We were having a private conversation?'

Larry shrugged and, about thirty seconds later, started whistling. I had never heard him whistle before – and he'd spent hours in this house doing whistle-inducing activities. Aoife turned and stared; the irritation radiated from her.

When Larry left, Aoife went out back to wash the brushes and I stayed in the study, perched on the stepladder. How long had it been since those assorted bathroom items had been scooped up from our old flat and thrown into a black bag? As long as Henry had been gone, when I first moved home. Three months. There were several weeks after Henry's death that I could barely remember at all, except that I'd spent most of the time in my parents' house in bed. Exhausted and heartbroken and refusing to face the world. It was grief. I thought of the headaches and nausea, the sudden aversion to coffee and the constant want of bread and cheese. Although granted, that last one had been there before.

Aoife reappeared in the doorway, dripping clean paintbrushes in hand. 'Is it the inquest?' she asked, her face softening now Larry had left. 'It's totally understandable if you're nervous, Grace. You've been doing great. I'm very proud of you. And if you want me to come with you to the hearing I will.'

'Thank you,' I said vaguely, trying to do the maths.

'Is it Larry? He is very annoying. I can tell him to stop calling around. I'd actually be more than happy to do that. You just give me the word. Grace?' Aoife took a step closer. 'What's up? Besides the obvious, of course. And not that that's not enough. I mean, you're entitled to stare forlornly into the middle distance for the rest of your life as far as I'm concerned.'

'Aoife,' I said as another wave of nausea, different from the others, swept through me.

'Yes?'

I looked up at her and felt the blood drain from my face, a swishing in my stomach that I hoped really was in my stomach. 'Aoife,' I said again.

'*Yes?*'

'I think I might be pregnant.'

THIRTY-FOUR

● ●

have a thing about doctors. Doctors, hairdressers and waiters. I don't know why, but I always wanted them to like me. So ideally, we would have gotten off to a more innocuous start with some nice, blameless ailment that, if undetected, didn't throw my intelligence so justifiably into question. Thrush, for example, would have been perfect. That's what I was thinking as I looked around the surgery, trying to avoid eye contact. I'd have killed for thrush.

'Have a think,' said the doctor again, turning the calendar to face me. 'It helps some people to have a visual aid.'

'I really have no idea,' I told her. 'I'm usually not this stupid, honestly. I got three As in my leaving cert. Including Biology.'

'Take your time, Grace, there's no rush.'

'I don't know.'

We had been going around in circles since she confirmed my pregnancy by having me pee into a container a few minutes earlier. She'd delivered the prognosis with a cautiously upbeat formality I presumed all doctors used in

219

these situations, not having a clue if they were confirming someone's wildest dreams or darkest nightmares.

I looked around at the certificates on the wall and the family photos on the desk. There were more pictures of her dogs than her children. One, two, three – yep. Four versus three. To be fair, the golden retriever was very cute. When I brought my gaze back she was still smiling expectantly, notepad in front of her.

I sighed. The height chart by the door was starting to look like one you'd get in a police interrogation room.

'Doctor,' I started.

'Call me Rachel.'

'Rachel,' I corrected, 'I'm not being smart but if I had the wherewithal to remember menstrual dates, do you not think I would have been here a lot sooner than this?'

Dr Rachel smiled harder. I was losing her. If she was a waiter, she'd be in the kitchen right now spitting in my food.

'Like I said, though,' I added brightly, not willing to admit defeat entirely, 'I know the date of conception. Is that not better? More exact?'

'And like I said, Grace, that's not how we calculate it.'

'It's all I've got.' And I repeated what was fast becoming the most significant date of my life: 'February nineteenth.'

The morning Henry left for work and never came back, we had sex. I remembered because weekday-morning sex was not our usual routine. And also because he died later that day. The weekends were always up for grabs, day or night, but on weekdays we were traditionalists: bedtime or not at all. We hadn't done it in a few days and as I climbed on top of him that morning, toothbrush abandoned to the folds of the duvet, I had a vague doubt about my pill-taking but I didn't dwell on it. Kids were on the near-future agenda, right after the house. We talked about them on an increasingly regular basis and had semi-consciously gotten more lax about birth control. Less than twelve hours later Henry's organs had been ripped to shreds and I hadn't thought about the contraceptive pill since.

In my early twenties, I was so paranoid about taking that little white tablet at exactly the same time every day that I had an alarm set on my phone. What a difference a decade makes.

'It was in the morning,' I added. 'If it helps.'

'It doesn't.'

The doctor flicked through her desk calendar. She circled something with a pen then returned to her computer. 'Thirteen weeks, give or take.'

'There's definitely no take,' I said. 'It couldn't have happened any more recently than February nineteenth. And I'm almost completely certain it wasn't any earlier.'

Dr Rachel was one of those two-finger typers where the slow clackidy-clack made each letter sound accusatory. I bit my lip as she typed out whatever it was she was noting until I couldn't take the passive accusations anymore.

'It wasn't a one-night stand, if that's what you're thinking.'

She looked up from the computer.

'Dead boyfriend. Partner,' I clarified. 'Dead partner.'

The typing stopped. I started to feel hot. Why had I said that?

'I'm very sorry to hear that, Grace,' she said. Her voice was soothing and sympathetic, which only embarrassed me further. 'My deepest condolences.'

'Typical man, ha? Get a woman into trouble, then feck off.' I laughed but she didn't, so I stopped. I suppose it wasn't very funny. 'I know you must think I'm a complete moron not to have noticed, but Henry had just died and my period has never been regular. I'm pretty sure there was a *bit* of blood.' I wasn't sure actually. I hadn't a clue about anything. There was a big black hole where my memory of those weeks had been. It only started to come back around the time Andy appeared. 'I'm really not that stupid,' I said again. I wished she'd write that down: *Not stupid, just in mourning.*

Which made me think that there had to be some gag about the similarities between morning sickness and mourning sickness, but now was probably not the time to develop it.

'I've seen it all, Grace. Honestly.' She smiled kindly. 'Three months is nothing. There isn't a week goes by without a woman presenting herself at A&E with what she believes to be a burst kidney or a bad case of food poisoning only to be turned around and redirected to the nearest maternity hospital with an updated diagnosis of contractions.'

That, actually, did make me feel a bit better.

'After Henry died, my mind was gone. It was like it just checked out. I forgot to eat and shower, I lost all track of time, never mind counting the days of the month.' My whole body was still burning and, despite my best efforts, I was getting upset. 'I lost weight, then I gained more back. My body went rogue. There were symptoms, yeah, when I think

222

about it now.' I'd been going over these since Aoife forced me to take two pregnancy tests two nights before. 'If you knew what you were looking for then there were symptoms; but if you were looking for something else, well then there were plenty of signs of that too.

'I thought it was grief. Grief made sense. I was tired, a lot. And in the first few weeks, if I could avoid starting the day, I did. Entire days spent lying in bed, thinking about him. I could fall asleep anywhere.'

Dr Rachel started typing again.

'But I was in mourning,' I insisted. I had rationalised these things as my body yearning for Henry. I hated the idea that they had all been about something else entirely. It felt like a betrayal, as if I hadn't suffered his loss at all. 'Wasn't that grief?'

'It was probably both,' she said. 'Did you experience any nausea?'

'Plenty of it. But I've always felt my emotions in my stomach. When other people talk about their hearts flipping or dropping; for me, that's my tummy. So yeah, I was sick a lot but I just thought . . .' I exhaled loudly, puffing out my cheeks. I hated crying in front of doctors, and hairdressers and waiters, but this power balance had long tilted.

'I had some headaches, and the smell of certain things, just. Ugh.' The thought of coffee was enough to turn my insides. 'But I never thought . . . Look,' I said, though she wasn't the one who needed convincing. Dr Rachel didn't require my excuses. 'I felt sick every time I thought about Henry, but that was all the time. So I was always nauseous.

On the scale of things, it was a welcome distraction. Not vomiting was easier to concentrate on.' I spread my hands across my stomach. 'Is it all right?'

'Well, you're over the worst bit. Symptoms should abate now the first trimester is done and the risk of miscarriage is significantly lower, so that's good. But we'll get you in for a scan at the hospital and then we'll know everything for sure. We should also get you started on prenatal supplements as soon as possible.'

'Maybe it won't be so bad,' I said. 'I can already think of some positives to being pregnant. One: you get to eat more calories. I mean, you *have* to. Isn't that right?'

'Not as many as people think, but yes, there is a slight, gradual increase.'

'So that's good. Two: you have an excuse to nap all the time. Before I just thought I was depressed – I mean, I think it's fair to say I *was* depressed. But I was also pregnant. So now I don't have to feel bad about sleeping. Staying in bed is not good when you're depressed, but it *is* good when you're pregnant. Right? So that's a definite plus.'

'Grace—'

'Three! Now this is a niche one and only holds for a small window of time. BUT in a few months, when I actually look pregnant, and people say whatever it is that people say, like "when are you due" or "do you want this seat", I'll be able to act all offended and say, "What? What are you talking about? I'm not pregnant." So that'll be fun. Yeah.' I gave another loud exhale and presented Dr Rachel with the brightest smile I could manage.

'If you want a referral for someone to talk to, about this or other things, I can give you that too.'

'You know,' I said, shaking my head and attempting another conspiratorial laugh though I had no doubt my face was red and blotchy, 'this is probably the only three months of my adult life where I could have been unknowingly pregnant and the baby might not actually end up with foetal alcohol syndrome. I haven't exactly been out partying since Henry died. Whereas normally . . .' I gave her my best girls-just-want-to-have-fun smile. It fell to a death somewhere in the half-metre between us.

'I realise I don't know you yet, Grace, but I'm sure this is a shock, especially given what happened to your partner. Have you family who can provide support?'

I thought of my parents who had just gotten their lives back, of Henry's mother who in the first few weeks after her son's death had been in more denial than me and who had never had great health anyway. And of Andy, who I hadn't seen in four days.

'Like I say, I have heard it all . . .'

'I doubt it,' I said quietly.

She dragged her pad across the desk and started to scribble. 'These are some vitamins you should start taking as soon as possible . . .'

'What if I don't keep it?'

Dr Rachel readjusted her glasses. I admired her unwavering professional demeanour. 'As you know, abortions are not yet available here,' she said. 'If you're travelling to the UK, they can be carried out up to twenty-four weeks. If you get the procedure under fifteen weeks, it can be less invasive. Which would mean making a decision relatively soon.' She fixed her spectacles to her nose. 'All right, Grace?'

'Yep. Got it.'

How could I have a child? In a few months I'd be struggling to meet my mortgage repayments. I was already struggling to take care of myself. When Henry and I talked about kids, I used to worry they'd get my chin and his forehead and both our eyebrows. You know the way parents always think their children are gorgeous? That wouldn't be me. I had no difficulty identifying ugly kids. I kept imagining giving birth to a big hairy brick, but Henry told me to stop slagging our unborn child. 'All that matters is that they're happy.' That was what he said. 'We just have to give them our happiness.'

But this thing could never be happy. Not when it was formed inside a body consumed by such powerful grief that it had, just one day, early on, taken to pausing abruptly when crossing the road. For the first few weeks of its gestation, it had lived in a place that was more sadness than consciousness, more despair than bone or flesh. That sorrow was overwhelming and it had to transfer. It just had to.

Dr Rachel took out a Filofax and returned to her computer. 'Do you know where you'd like to have the baby, if you do?'

'In a . . . hospital?'

'Which hospital, Grace?'

I named the first maternity one I could think of and she handed me a form, told me to fill it in and send it off. 'You should get a letter from them in a week or two with appointment dates. You can get booked in for your first scan while you consider your options.'

Then she gave me the list of prenatal vitamins and stood from her chair as I gathered my belongings and thanked her.

'Best of luck,' she said, putting a hand on my shoulder as I left the room.

'What about Assumpta?'

'You're just trying to piss me off now, Henry.'

'What? Assumpta is a lovely name.'

'Assumpta is the name of a deeply pious and unhappy woman.'

'Assumpta is my aunt's name!'

'And no doubt she has swollen knees from all the praying.'

'You've never even met her, Grace.'

'Of course I haven't. Assumpta is not the name of a people person. Assumpta is more of a cat person. Cats and nuns. That's Assumpta's social circle.'

'All right. Forget Assumpta. Elizabeth. What about Elizabeth?'

'Are you having an actual stroke?'

'What could possibly be wrong with Elizabeth??'

'It's already taken.'

'By who?'

'Mmm, by the queen? Of England? Grace and Henry are regal enough without adding Elizabeth to the mix. We

227

might as well hang a Union Jack over the door and be done with it. They'd burn us out of our home. We'd have to leave the country on St Patrick's Day, Henry. And I'm one of the few Irish people who actually like St Patrick's Day.'

'We're going to have to start putting a forty-minute time limit on these conversations because that seems to be the point at which you stop making any sense.'

'All right. I've got one: what about Aoife?'

'Too many vowels.'

'Eimear?'

'Can I get a consonant please, Carol? Oh. What about Carol, Grace? Or Caroline? Actually, no. Now that I say them out loud, I'm not so into Cs.'

'No vowels, no Cs. You might give me a list of pre-approved letters when you get a minute?'

'This is fun, isn't it?'

'What?'

'All of this, Grace. Plotting. Making plans for our future.'

'Yeah, it is. It really is, actually. Our whole lives ahead of us, as they say. I can hardly wait.'

I was in the pharmacy beside the doctor's surgery buying vitamins before I considered what I was doing. What was the point in having a healthy foetus if I wasn't going to keep it? The woman behind the counter did a little shimmy as she ticked the supplements off the list and handed me the bag. 'Is it your first?' she asked in a low voice.

I nodded, taking the bag and stuffing it into my jacket pocket.

'I hope it all goes well for you, love,' she beamed. 'You'll do great.'

I bought a small carton of microwaveable soup in the supermarket next door and headed home.

THIRTY-FIVE

· ·

Not having siblings meant I had very little experience of babies. I didn't hold one until I was twenty-one and hanging out at Aoife's house while she reluctantly babysat a gaggle of nieces and nephews and one of them started to cry.

'Pick it up,' she said, already busy with a howling toddler.

I stared into the basket at the pudgy pink creature, flailing its arms and legs about like it was a woodlouse that had gotten caught on its back. 'How?'

'Just . . .' Aoife made a cradling motion.

'I don't know what to do. I've never done it before.'

'Pick it up and hold it like it's the bottle of wine you get from the off-licence just as it's shutting. Lie the back along your arm, support the neck, cradle it snugly and whatever you do don't let it fall because it's past ten o'clock and it's too late to go back for another one.'

I managed it in the end, and the child did stop crying. Still, I thought, lying in bed on Aberdeen Street staring at the ceiling, it probably wasn't great that my maternal instincts were so closely aligned to the protection of alcohol.

The alarm clock said 7 a.m. I'd been awake since five. Suddenly I had permission to sleep my life away and I couldn't do it. I kept going over my ever-expanding bank of new realities: the non-existence of Henry, the new existence of Andy, the potential existence of a baby. If money got really tight, I could always book a slot on *Ricki Lake* or *Jeremy Kyle* or whichever of those chat shows where people got up out of their chairs and pointed fingers at family members was still on the go. *He's No Baby Daddy . . .. He's My Baby Uncle.*

I missed Andy more today than I had yesterday, and more yesterday than the day before that. Or maybe it was Henry I missed. Or maybe the baby was making me feel things that weren't actually there at all. My emotions, according to multiple internet searches, were no longer my own. What I did know for sure was that every time I heard footsteps on the street outside, I froze, listening, as they inevitably faded away again. The house felt lonelier than it had before.

I must have dozed off because suddenly the doorbell was ringing and the clock radio said 9.03. I freed my body from the sheets and dragged it into standing. I felt bad getting Aoife up so early. My crisis pregnancy would still be a crisis in a couple of hours.

Ding-dong!

'Coming,' I shouted, doubting if she could hear me through the open window. 'Coming, coming!' I threw Henry's hoodie on over the mini-marathon T-shirt I had slept in and pulled on leggings, both legs getting caught on my ankles. I was too hot before I'd even left the bedroom.

'Coming, coming, coming!'

I quick-stepped down the stairs, leaping over the beauty products still sitting there. The shampoo and moisturiser were halfway out of the box. Perhaps they'd given up on me and were making their own way to the bathroom. Henry, I thought as I landed on the bottom step, would have found that funny.

'Coming, com—'

As I reached for the latch I heard Betty's voice, but it wasn't her standing on my doorstep. It wasn't Aoife either. The fractured silhouette was too tall. My heart pounded. I pulled the door open.

'. . . could take a look at my drain so. It makes this awful sound whenever I'm doing the washing-up. It's a sort of *gurr-gurr*, like the noise my late husband Patrick, God have mercy on his soul, his stomach used to make whenever he had more than two pints. Smithwick's. Insisted on drinking the stuff but couldn't digest it at all. Here she is now. Nice of you to join us. Sure at this rate, you might be dressed by dinnertime.'

Andy was standing directly in front of me. I stared up at him, my heart racing. He had come back. I hadn't ruined everything, not entirely. My smile got wider and wider. I was so glad to see that face. Betty leaned over her fence.

'Morning,' I said.

'Morning, afternoon . . . What's the differ . . .'

'How're you going, Grace?'

My stormy stomach lay calm. 'Hello,' I said, and then again for good measure: 'Morning.'

He was wearing the same cargo shorts he always wore and a T-shirt so white it deepened his tan. His stubble had grown out, a day or two off a beard. It suited him.

'New T-shirt?' I studied his face, trying to work out if we were okay.

'I was running out of clothes,' he said, holding my gaze. 'Do you like it?'

I nodded.

'Yeah,' I said. 'It's nice.'

I kept my eyes on his. *Forget the kiss,* I tried to convey. *Let's forget it ever happened.*

He moved his head up and down slowly until we were nodding in unison. I grinned and he grinned back.

When I finally glanced away Betty was studying Andy's plain T-shirt. She looked from him to me and back to the white cotton again. Then she leaned further across the fence and poked him on his bare arm.

'I'm out tomorrow,' she told him. 'It'll have to be today.'

'What's that?'

'My *drain.* You were going to sort my drain. Jesus Christ!'

'Most people just call me Andy, but all right . . .'

'Listen, buster, do not get smart with me. The lack of respect that emanates from this garden on a good day is enough to knock a body out. Sweet mother divine. It does not need your help.'

'Betty, you can't just demand people do things—'

'It's cool.' Andy rested a hand on my shoulder and turned back to my neighbour. 'I'll call in and have a look now, all right?'

Betty shrugged, like he was the one putting her out. 'I hope you're going to bring some tools. I don't just want you staring at the yoke and stroking your chin.'

'I have them in the car.'

Andy rotated back to me: 'I'll have a look at the drains and be in to you in half an hour.'

'Hasn't even looked at the thing and already knows how long it's going to take,' Betty muttered as she disappeared into her hallway. 'Sure is there anything the lad can't do? Mind reader, plumber, expert T-shirt buyer . . .'

Andy raised a hand to me and smiled as he rounded my garden into Betty's and followed her inside.

'I hope you're going to pay him,' I shouted in after them.

'I think you've paid him enough for the whole street!' And she slammed the door shut before I had a chance to respond.

I closed my own door, pulling off the hoodie and wandering into the kitchen for a glass of water. Sitting on a worktop in the direct path of the morning sun, I phoned Aoife.

'How are you feeling today?' she said, the sound of yelling in the distance behind her.

'Good, yeah. It's sunny.' *And Andy is only a few metres away.* 'I think I'll go to the park,' I added, enjoying the warmth of the rays through the patio windows. 'The sun is out and I have a whole Tuesday where I'm not working. Might have a picnic. It'd be nice to be outside.'

'That's great, Grace, but I wasn't enquiring about your sunbathing roster. I more meant how do you feel about having another life growing inside you?'

I squinted as the sun grew stronger, and turned my head to the side.

'What are you going to do about that?' she probed.

'I'm going to not think about it.'

'Wonderful plan.'

'Just for one more week. The inquest is next Monday and that's enough. I want a bit of time before that. Just a few days of blissful ignorance.'

Aoife said nothing.

'I've been avoiding Isabel's calls for weeks,' I said, only half changing the subject. 'Then last week she sent me a curt, formal letter with the details of the hearing. I think I'm in her bad books.'

'Why are you avoiding her? I thought you got on well?'

'We do,' I said, picturing Andy next door, gripping tools with hands identical to Henry's. 'I just—'

'Hang on,' she said. A door slammed behind her. I could hear muffled shouting then the sound of her hand moving off the receiver as she came back on the line. 'One of Lorcan's offspring ate Sharon's diamanté ring. The offspring shat it back out this morning but Sharon's still demanding a new one. Lorcan offered to sterilise it but she's not budging. She's calling his child – honestly haven't a clue which one it is, boy or girl I could not tell you – anyway, she's currently calling it an emotional eater.'

'Okay . . .'

'To its face.' Aoife sighed. 'I really need to move out. Hang on . . . What? WHAT!? No! DETTOL! It's under the sink! NO— Give me patience! I better go, Grace. Enjoy your week of delusion. Call me if you need me, or else I'll talk to you when you're back in the real world.'

I hung up the phone and went through the house opening curtains and windows. I climbed the stairs, threw off my pyjamas and pulled on a loose dress. I sprayed dry shampoo at the roots and pulled my hair into a ponytail, then I rooted the tartan rug out from the hot press and found a basket and flask under the stairs. Six days of delusion, then I'd face up to it.

I was boiling the kettle for a second time when Andy rang the doorbell again.

'Did she pay you?'

'It depends,' he said, following me into the hallway and through the house. 'Is criticism a currency?'

The loud creak from the floorboard as he stepped from the living room to the kitchen was the best thing I'd heard in days.

THIRTY-SIX

For two days we did everything together – roaming the park, all our meals, watching TV – and for the two after that, we met back at my house every evening after work. Andy would stay until one of us, usually me, started to fall asleep. He always talked about leaving earlier, about going back to the guesthouse to do some research or go through files, things to do with Frances and the adoption, though he never said exactly what they were and it didn't matter anyway because he always stayed. He didn't mention the kiss and I kept schtum about the life form developing inside me and in our agreed silence the bubble quickly reformed around us.

Andy was the only person I wanted to be around. He was a bridge between the life I had chosen and the one fate had given me. He was the gentlest reminder of Henry and also that Henry was gone. I told him how Henry and I used to read together at night and that we'd been halfway through *A Christmas Carol* when he died. I let Andy read, up to the bookmark. I listened as his Australian inflections retraced Henry's steps, looping the same tongue around the same letters. I smiled as Scrooge's nephew arrived at the shop, and mouthed along for the first *'Bah!' said Scrooge. 'Humbug!'* Andy was great at accents, dropping his own brogue for an English twang every time a character spoke. My heart ached for Henry and this talent that had skipped him and gone to his younger brother.

We watched late-night news and cooked. I taught Andy how to make a proper cup of tea and the best way to sauté peppers and he showed me how to bleed radiators. I found Henry's old slippers in a box and Andy took to wearing them around the house, and when we watched television he automatically took my feet in his hands and stretched out my toes. Even though Andy was the strangest thing to have happened in the past few months, which was saying a lot, these were the times I felt most normal.

But for everything that was discussed, something else went unsaid. He brought up Henry's parents a few times and I managed to brush it aside. I didn't tell him about the inquest. Andy stopped talking about his plans in terms of staying or leaving Ireland and I didn't ask because I wasn't sure what answer I wanted.

Larry called in once. He thought he'd seen Aoife's car on the road, which sent me into a minor panic, but it turned out it belonged to Betty's home-help woman. He was mildly taken aback to see Andy doing the washing-up in my kitchen. But it was more 'you sly dog' than 'oh look, the second coming'. My life was divided into those who'd known Henry and those who knew Andy and I did my best to keep the groups apart. When Larry went into the study to inspect the finished paint job I slid the cracked photo of me and Henry sitting on a wall in Lisbon into a drawer, and I left it there.

I loved how at ease Andy was in quietness. He was the kind of person who'd leave a party without you noticing, but once you did you'd be sorry he was gone. All my life I had felt responsible for the gaps in conversations. I tried to emulate what Andy did, forcing myself to drop the habit of a lifetime and embrace the voids. It was like discovering a superpower.

'Are you nearly finished?' I asked, after a good twenty minutes in which both of us had been too absorbed in the task at hand to speak.

Andy pulled the piece of sketch paper and the book on which he was leaning it towards his chest. 'No peeking.'

'I'm not peeking!' I protested, squinting dubiously at my own portrait. 'Are you at all sensitive about your chin?' I asked. 'I've been trying to shade a bit off, but I appear to be adding depth.'

It had been my idea to draw and, having done fruit and our own hands, we had moved on to each other. But looking from the real life Andy to the Popeye portrait resting against my knees, which were bent into me on the couch, I was regretting my choice of recreational activity.

'You should be good at this,' said Andy, as he continued to switch from pencil to pen and back again, never taking his eyes off the page.

'Are you trying to intimidate me?' I demanded. 'All that, "Oh look, I need so many different *textures* to express myself." Pen, pencil; pencil, pen. It's like the art world equivalent of the haka going on over there.'

I kicked him gently but he lifted the book from his lap so his secret portrait would not be disturbed.

'The haka is New Zealand, Grace. Not Australia.'

'Yes, and it's intimidating wherever it's done.' I tried rubbing at the chin with the side of my thumb. This caused the stubble to expand into a beard. There was, I thought, a touch of the Arab about the man I was drawing.

'What do you mean I should be good at this?' I said. 'I haven't an artistic bone in my body.'

'I mean it should be easier for you. You're more familiar with the subject.'

Andy kept on shading and I looked down at the page again. I was about to ask him what he meant, and then I realised. It hadn't occurred to me that I might be drawing Henry. I had studied the details of Andy's face and tried, in vain, to replicate them on the page; the faint sun blotches, the ever-so-slightly crooked nose. These were all new to me. I wasn't drawing a dead person. When I looked at Andy I didn't see Henry, not anymore. I was thinking only of the man in front of me.

'I'm drawing you,' I said, still studying the page. 'And I've known you as long as you've known me.'

I felt him look up then, but I kept my eyes on the drawing.

'Grace?'

'Mmm?' Still not moving my gaze.

'Look up.'

'No. Why?'

'I need to see your eyes. For the picture.'

I stared up at him slowly, steadily, worrying about how long he spent sizing them up and how much he might see.

'All right?' I said, and he nodded slowly.

'I think I have you now.'

The room fell quiet again and I did a bit of work on the nose but when it started to look like he had two I knew it was time to admit defeat. 'Are you nearly done?' I asked, when another fifteen minutes had passed.

'Almost . . .' He raised the pen and extended it towards me as if measuring my face, then he brought it back to the page. 'Okay, that's it. I've immortalised you in ink.'

'Well, you shouldn't have gone to the trouble because . . .' I lifted the sketch pad from my knee and winced as I turned it around. 'Sorry,' I said. 'It looks like I drew with food.'

'All right,' he said, lifting his own page and tapping the end of it lightly on the book he'd been leaning on. I did a quick intake of breath and as he turned the page around I suddenly shut my eyes.

I didn't want to know how he saw me. I didn't want to know if he could tell what I was thinking.

'Grace?'

I thought of how he'd looked into my eyes and I refused to open them.

'No.'

'Come on!'

I inhaled, slowly this time, then bit by bit I opened them. I exhaled in a far less dramatic fashion. 'What is that?'

Held in the air beside Andy's delighted face was a drawing of a stick woman with some sort of rod in her hand. There was a tree behind her, a full sun in the sky and her stick legs were crossed like she needed to pee.

'That's what you spent almost an hour on?'

'Yip.'

'You know you're turning pink?' I said, raising my eyebrows as he nodded, incapable of speech in case he wet himself laughing. 'And what, if you don't mind me asking, am I holding?'

'Wooden spoon,' he yelped.

'Naturally. And her legs?'

He pursed his lips together and the sight of his rosy mug ready to explode at any moment made me burst out laughing, which obviously caused him to fall to pieces too. Our bodies went loose, flopping in unison on the couch, colliding in the middle. Andy was literally holding his sides.

'I can't draw, I'm sorry,' he hooted. 'I never could.'

'Well, at least I'm thin,' I said, when I'd regained some composure. 'But seriously, though, what is going on with her legs?'

'Oh,' said Andy, frowning as he turned the page back around to himself. 'She's doing *Riverdance*.'

'Ah.' I nodded sagely. 'Of course.'

THIRTY-SEVEN

Saturday morning we went to a market held by the Polish community in the Phoenix Park. None of the other shoppers spoke English and all of the signs were in Polish, which was why I decided it would be safe for us to go. We weren't going to bump into anybody.

We walked from stall to stall, holding up everything, presenting them to each other. Things we might buy, like eggs and bread and a tea cosy shaped like an old woman. And things we couldn't believe anybody would buy, like coasters covered in glittery shamrocks, a money box that burped when you inserted a coin, and some sort of fish soaked in sour cream.

It was the most beautiful morning and I was happy. I could feel the contentment humming inside me. The whole way back to the house, I swung the plastic bag that held six eggs and the tea cosy. Andy told knock-knock jokes and I laughed even when they weren't funny. I didn't mention Henry, not once. I hadn't mentioned him in days.

I suggested to Andy that he buy the paper and he went into Pat's shop while I waited outside. Back at the house, he sat reading at the table, while I cracked the eggs slowly, ceremoniously, into a mixing bowl.

'Is it weird that I feel like I know you?' I said, after half an hour of comfortable silence.

Andy looked up from the newspaper spread across the polished oak. 'No,' he considered. 'It makes sense that you'd feel that way.'

I nodded, and returned to the mixing bowl and the eggs I was beating.

'But it doesn't make sense that I'd feel the same,' he said.

'You do?'

'Yeah.'

I watched as he formulated thoughts. Slowly I was learning to read him.

'I feel like . . . this could have been my life.'

'Like Henry's life could have been yours?'

'Not Henry's life exactly. But this life.' He made a grand sweep with his hand from his seat at the table. 'Every adopted kid thinks about an alternate life. I remember when I was about eight building a tent in my grandma's kitchen and thinking, "I could be camping in another grandma's kitchen."'

I smiled.

'When I learnt to ride a bike, I had the strongest sensation that there was another version of me learning to ride a bike somewhere else, with his mum. Not a brother, but actually me: the me that would have been if I hadn't been adopted. Or maybe if I'd been adopted into a different family.' He went back to the paper. 'It's hard to explain.'

'No,' I said, pushing the bowl to the side and leaning across the counter. 'Go on.'

I wanted him to say what I was thinking, to articulate the thing I couldn't put into words.

'I always had the strongest feeling there was another version of me, in a parallel world or whatever, doing all the same things but a little different. Is it possible that I knew somehow? Twin intuition? Because even though I knew about Frances, the alternate life I imagined was never with her. The life I imagined was like this one, with people like Henry's parents. What if I'd gone to them, Grace? What if I'd grown up in Dublin and been introduced to five-a-side soccer and had parents who valued education and wanted their son to have a secure life? What if I'd gone to Henry's school and had Henry's friends and met . . .' He trailed off. I glanced away.

'I feel like I know this life,' he said. 'Not the Frances life. *This* one. Like this was my alternate life.'

Hadn't I thought something similar, about parallel worlds and alternative lives? And maybe, too, this was mine. Henry but more careful with his words, Henry but less sure of his place in the world, Henry but better at accents. Henry but more cautious on a bike.

'Sorry,' said Andy, embarrassed. 'I've had a lot of time to think.'

A large drop fell from the kitchen faucet, and I jumped as it hit the basin and reverberated.

'It does that,' I said, slightly too loudly. 'Sometimes it just lets this trickle out, no matter how tight I have it turned.'

Andy moved towards me, needing half as many steps as I did to cross the room. I backed away from the sink, his smell caught in the breeze created by our movements. He took a screwdriver from his box and started to twist at the tap.

The muscles on his back moved below the surface of his T-shirt as he forced the top off the tap. I had never known Henry to as much as change a light bulb. There was something so arbitrary about it, the accident of birth. A split-second decision as babies, and their futures were decided. What if Andy's restlessness had nothing to do with not being in the right place? What if he'd never managed to settle because he hadn't been in the right life?

'You need a new washer.'

'Okay.'

'I can bring you one tomorrow.'

'All right. Thanks.'

He pieced the tap back together and threw the screwdriver into the box.

'I was thinking I might go to the graveyard,' I said. 'If you wanted to come?'

'To see the wise men?'

I smiled. 'They'll probably be there, yes, drinking tea and pontificating.'

'I have been granted an audience,' he said, brushing the hair from his forehead. 'I'm honoured.'

'Yeah, well, be warned. They will tell you the same awful graveyard jokes they tell everyone and Patsy will give you a history of the entire place.'

'Great.'

'Not just our section but the whole cemetery right back to 1823 when Daniel O'Connell began his campaign to find the impoverished Catholics of Ireland somewhere to bury their dead.' The amateur historian's voice was ringing in my head.

Andy grinned. 'I'll be sure to take notes.'

THIRTY-EIGHT

• •

'Until **1832** the impoverished Catholics of Ireland had no place to bury their dead. Nine long years it took O'Connell to build this place and now it's the largest cemetery in Ireland. Have you heard of Charles Stewart Parnell? No? Well, he's one of our most interesting residents. Some remember Parnell for his politics, others for his extramarital affair, but around here he'll always be the man who was so paranoid about grave robbers digging up his body and selling it to science that he asked to be buried under a pile of peasants teeming with cholera . . .'

I threw Andy a told-you-so look and he jiggled his eyebrows until I laughed. He was enjoying himself. He nodded as Patsy continued his history lesson and he followed the older man off in the direction of the storage shed.

'. . . I think we have a copy of the plans somewhere . . .'

We'd been there half an hour and Patsy had already laid out the 'political context' for Glasnevin Cemetery's foundation.

'So that's Henry's brother,' said Billy, when the pair of them were out of earshot.

'Yep.' I drained the end of my tea and reached down for the flask to top it up.

'I'd love shoulders like that,' said Martin wistfully. 'Does he look like Henry?'

'You could say that.'

'I don't remember you ever mentioning a brother,' mused Billy, still staring in the direction of the storage shed though Patsy and Andy had both disappeared inside it now. 'In fact, I could have sworn you said the two of you were only children. How come he hasn't been up to visit? Or has he? I've never noticed him, anyway. Have you, Martin?'

Martin shook his head. 'I'd remember those shoulders.'

'They weren't close,' I said.

'I see. And what's with his accent?'

'Did he watch too many Australian soaps?' offered Martin. 'I know a fella whose son never watched anything but *Friends* and now "like" is his every third word and he says "math" instead of "maths".'

'How's the love life going?' I asked, steering the conversation away from Andy.

Martin shook his head forlornly.

'Don't mention the war,' said Billy.

'What happened?'

'She gave him his marching orders due to an unethical dinner.'

'Oh, Martin! We went through this.' Martin had phoned me from Tesco the previous week. He was cooking for the vegan eco-warrior for the first time. Billy had given him a couple of recipes but he had still managed to tie himself into knots. 'I told you: beefeater tomatoes, fine. Beef salted almonds, no.'

'I got all that,' he said crossly. 'And the dinner was fine – don't get me wrong now, it was absolutely disgusting, but it was vegan, so grand. She liked it. Only then she went to the fridge to get milk for the tea. I'd bought sorta milk and everything—'

'Do you mean soya milk?'

'I do. Soya milk and everything, but when she came back from the fridge she pulled a calculator from her rainbow-y woollen bag yoke and started going loopers.'

'Why?'

Martin squeezed his eyes and rubbed the sockets like he was experiencing a migraine. 'I don't know. It didn't make any sense to me. She kept clacking on the yoke and said our dinner had travelled around the world three times to get to our plate. I tried to explain I'd gotten it all in the Tesco Local except for the special milk, which I'd gone to Clarehall for, and even then that was only a five-minute spin up the road. But she kept going on about thousands of miles and all these countries I'd never heard of. I haven't been further than Blackpool!'

I put my arm around him.

'It was very stressful, Grace. I don't mind telling you.'

Patsy and Andy came back up the slope. Patsy was carrying a wrench and saying something about drainage. I experienced an emotion akin to pride as I watched them. I was glad they were getting on.

'He's going to take a look at the tap,' said Patsy importantly. 'I'd do it myself only I have to look after my back.'

Martin grinned at Billy, but Billy wasn't looking in his direction.

'So you're Henry's brother,' he said.

'That's right,' agreed Andy.

'He already told you that, Billy. And I told you. How many times do you have to hear it?'

'It just seems strange. What's with the accent?'

'Well, I grew up in Australia,' said Andy, glancing in my direction.

'Patsy!' I said, nudging the ringleader and clapping my hands. 'Why don't you tell Andy about the people in the houses over there?'

The four men turned towards the only visible housing estate.

'Oh yes,' said Patsy, pointing in the same direction. 'See the people living in the houses just yonder? Well, they can't be buried here.'

'Why not?' asked Andy, following our gaze.

'Cemetery rules.'

'Was there a falling-out?'

'No,' said Patsy, as Billy winked at Martin. 'Because they're not dead yet!' And the three of them dutifully fell around the place in hysterics.

'I'm going to fill the watering can,' I said, safe in the knowledge that the subject had been changed.

I carried the container to the tap and jimmied it a little like Patsy had taught me. My foot kept the can upright. I watched the four men from a distance and felt happy. The seal had been broken on the wise men's joke repertoire and a few of the punchlines travelled on the breeze. 'The plot thickens!' I heard Martin shriek, using Billy's chair to regain his composure as the seated man tried to shove him off. If we could keep the conversation off Andy's exact origins, I'd happily spend all night up here.

My phone beeped from my pocket but I ignored it. The inquest was in two days and it was all anyone wanted to talk about. Aoife kept texting to say she was free to go or to provide comfort afterwards – originally she said wine, but then she sent me a baby emoji and changed her offer to tea. Mam kept checking exactly what time it was at and if she should wear anything in particular. Dad told me some socialite's father's inquest had been held in the same building. He also wanted to know what they should wear, so he'd have time to get it dry-cleaned.

I hadn't heard from Henry's parents since I got that formal letter from Isabel. I bit the bullet and sent them a text – well, I sent it to Conor, I wasn't brave enough for Isabel – saying I'd call to the house beforehand. He hadn't told me not to so I assumed that was still the plan.

There were four sets of flowers on Henry's grave and I recognised none of them. I needed to visit more often. Two were from Isabel's garden – she always used the same silver pots – and another was from the Astro Turf Lads, the group Henry played football with on Thursday nights. I smiled as I closed the card. The last bunch was the least impressive: store-bought tulips, probably from the garage beside the cemetery. I opened the attached card. Unlike the other, which had a note saying they missed him and hoped he was doing fewer slide tackles where he was now, this one just said: *From Andy*.

I watched them across the cemetery where the dynamic had changed. The wise men were the ones doing the listening now. I put down the watering can quickly and shouted across. 'Andy!' He stopped talking and looked over. 'Are you going to fix that tap?'

He said something else to the men who nodded in agreement, then he headed towards me.

'Hey,' I said, meeting him back at the tap.

'Hey.'

'I see you've been up to visit Henry's grave.'

'Yes,' he said, bending down beside the water source. 'One day you were at work. Is that okay with you?'

'Of course, yeah. I just . . . I was thinking if you ran into Henry's parents . . .'

'Well, I'd much rather meet them properly, but you don't seem to want to set it up.'

'I do, I will,' I promised. 'Soon.'

'I want to meet them, Grace,' he said, firmly enough that it couldn't be ignored.

I nodded and he went back to inspecting the spout.

'You seem to be enjoying yourself,' I gushed, pushing the awkward moment along. 'And they definitely like you.'

'Well, they love you,' he said, smiling reluctantly. 'Amazing Grace, they keep calling you.'

'And what did you say?'

He shrugged. 'I mean, she's all right . . .'

'Ha ha.'

253

We went back to the group and Andy told the men to try putting some oil on the tap before doing anything more drastic. Patsy said he had suspected as much all along but it was good to have a second opinion.

'Well,' he said, clearing his throat at the other two, 'I'd better be off *home*.'

'Me too,' said Billy.

'Oh yeah,' said Martin, copping that 'home' was fairly transparent code for 'a swift pint at the Gravediggers'. 'Me too,' he almost shouted. 'I'd better be off home too.'

They shook hands with Andy and told him to come back anytime. 'We're always here Wednesdays and Saturdays,' said Billy. 'But most other days too.'

'You'd be surprised how much there is to be done around here,' clarified Patsy.

Andy and I watched them go, Martin poking Patsy and Patsy pushing him away. It was cooler now but there were still a few hours of daylight left. We turned back to each other.

'So . . .'

'So . . .' agreed Andy. 'Do you want to see where Frances Clinch is buried?'

'Yes. I went searching for her once but it's like a needle in a haystack when you don't know where to look.'

'This way.'

I followed him out of our section and into the neighbouring mass of graves. This was where I had been looking the time the wise men gave out to me for being in enemy territory. These ones were a little older but still within the last century.

I could make out all the names and a lot of them continued to have visitors, judging by the flowers.

'Did the wise men tell you why the cemetery has such high walls?' I asked.

'No. Oh wait, yes they did. Because everybody is dying to get in.'

'That's my favourite one.'

We had only been walking a couple of minutes when Andy stopped. 'Here.'

We were standing in front of a plain black slab with three people's names, dates of birth and dates of death etched into it. There were no flowers save for a row of dandelions growing near the headstone. From the dates of birth I deduced that the other two were Frances's parents. My arm brushed against Andy's.

'Was she an only child?'

'Dunno,' he said. 'Be kind of fitting if she was, though, ay? An only child has twins and manages to make both of them only children too.'

'When I was a kid I thought the saying was lonely child,' I told him, reading the names again. 'I'd tell people, "I'm a lonely child."'

'Me too,' he said.

I kept my arm against his. 'Henry never did.'

A significant crack ran diagonally down the tombstone but the lettering had held up: Jackie and Tom Clinch. I guess that made them Henry's grandparents. The bed of the grave was more moss than pebbles. Before Andy's visits, I doubted if anyone had stopped at this plot in years

– maybe not since Frances had died. Then I noticed the date of death and gasped. 'Her parents died after her,' I uttered, horrified.

'If the parents had gone first, they probably wouldn't have been buried here. They weren't from Dublin.'

I glanced back the way we'd come and couldn't believe how close it was to Henry's grave. So this was why Isabel and Conor had buried him here when their families were both interred on the other side of the city. Surprisingly considerate for people who'd never bothered to tell him this woman existed. I read the names and dates again. 'Poor Frances.'

'Yeah.'

I rolled up my sleeves and scrambled around to the edge of the grave.

'What are you doing?' asked Andy, still standing at the foot of it.

I reached into the centre and with both hands around the stem, yanked the first stubborn weed from its bed. 'Making amends.'

THIRTY-NINE

·····················

'**D**o you take milk with your tea, Grace? I forget.'

Conor gave me a look, apologising for his wife, and shouted through to the kitchen. 'She takes a large dollop, dear. Even I know that.'

'It's hard to remember all these little things,' said Isabel, appearing at the dining table with the bone-china tray, 'when it's been so long.'

I leaned over to help take the jug and matching sugar bowl but Isabel got there first. 'It's all right, Grace. You're the guest.'

I had served Christmas-Eve dinner at this table on several occasions. I had spent a bank holiday weekend running up and down those stairs with basins and clean towels when Isabel was particularly sick with her stomach and Conor and Henry were away at some relative's stag party. I hadn't been a guest in this house in years.

The box of pastries I'd brought sat ignored and unopened on the table that was eternally set for a dinner party, even though Henry's parents rarely socialised. And while Isabel was making a very clear point about how long it had been since they'd seen me and about the many unreturned phone calls, Conor was acting like everything was fine. We could as easily have been gathered for morning coffee as for the inquest into his son's death.

'Scooter! Scooter! Down, boy. Leave Grace alone.'

The old Labrador slumped from my knee to the carpet and plodded over to Conor. I wasn't used to affection from the Walshes' dog. I was used to being in this house with Henry and when that was the case Scooter only had eyes for him. 'Blind as anything now, aren't you, boy?' said Conor. 'Only recognises people by their smell.'

'Your flowerbeds are beautiful, Isabel,' I said, craning my neck to see out into the back garden. 'So much colour.'

'Those,' she said, throwing an indifferent glance towards her beloved garden as if the plants had sprung up by accident. 'Gardenias. They've been there for months. But I suppose you wouldn't have seen the garden since the pansies, or was it even the lavender?'

'I'm sorry I never made it over for dinner. I was busy. With work, and the house, and you know how it is now—'

'You don't owe us a word of an apology,' said Conor, placing a hand on the one I had outstretched towards his wife. 'You have your own life to be getting on with, and we're happy to see you doing that. Isn't that right, Isabel?'

'Mmm.'

'Well, I wouldn't say I'm getting on with my life,' I said hurriedly. 'I haven't been . . . I'm just . . . I'm doing my best.'

'We all are. Isn't that right, Isabel?' His voice sharper this time. 'I'm telling Grace how we're all doing our best.'

'Well, of course we're all doing our best,' she snapped, but softened when she finally looked at me. 'We all find a way to survive.'

I returned her thin smile with grateful gusto. I should have called, should have visited, but if they'd known the truth they wouldn't have wanted me to; I'd have been coming with questions, not cakes. Isabel was wearing the linen shirt I'd picked out and Henry had bought the previous Christmas. Fitted when she modelled it for us on Stephen's Day to prove she didn't need the gift receipt, it now hung from her thin frame. Henry and Conor spent a lot of time worrying about what Isabel's health could handle – foreign trips, big parties, going back to volunteer at the Oxfam shop after bouts of illness – but they never considered she'd have to handle a public inquest into her son's death. Had Conor ever considered she might one day be subjected to a private inquisition into her son's adoption? My gaze wandered back to the family portrait on the piano taken at Henry's graduation and the broad smile and tall stature shared by all three of them. How could they never have told him?

'Exactly,' said Conor, as if the wrongs of the world had all been resolved. 'Now, who'll have tea?'

'I just wish the driver would say sorry,' Isabel blurted out. 'If he could just say sorry I know I'd feel so much better, I'd be able to sleep.'

'Not this again.'

'Well, why not, Conor? We've given our word we're not going to sue; I'm not interested in their money. I just want him to acknowledge the part he played in our son's death.'

'Isabel.'

I made a great lunge for her hand.

'We talked about this,' continued Conor. 'They're not going to say sorry because that would be admitting culpability.'

'His blood was encrusted on their tyres, Conor! Of course they're culpable!'

I looked at the cup of tea before me, the milk forming a wispy skin in the centre, and waited for the nausea to pass. *Please don't tell me I'm going off tea now too.*

'If he could just apologise I'd be able to sleep at night, I might be able to get up in the morning. And you would be able to spend a whole day at the office without worrying you'll have to come rushing home because your useless wife can't find the willpower to sit up straight.'

'Isabel . . .'

'How could he not *need* to say sorry?'

This was not the kind of household where dirty laundry was aired. Nor was it a place where you registered another's tears. I followed Conor's lead and removed my cup from its saucer, the other hand still on Isabel's. I couldn't stomach the tea, though, so I just hovered it there in front of my mouth, elevated in the air.

'We have been over this,' said Conor sternly. 'Over it and over it and over it. They're not going to admit culpability.'

'I just want an apology!'

'Or say they're sorry, because it would leave them open to a civil case. They will accept the coroner's ruling – which will say that he died by misadventure; they were at fault but ultimately it was an accident. That will do us.'

'It won't do me! How could it. How can I . . .?' She took her hand away from mine and wiped at the side of her eyes where brown, perfectly applied eyeliner was starting to pool. 'I can't . . .' She blew through her nose. 'I don't know if I can take this.'

'Please, Isabel, no dramatics today. It's tough for us all. Have some sugar, it'll help.' He pushed the bowl towards her and she looked from it to him, her eyes round. 'Oh, come on. I didn't mean it like that. We're hardly going to avoid sugar – the s-word, Isabel – for the rest of our lives, don't be so—'

But before he had finished the sentence Isabel stood from her chair, the dainty white china bowl in hand, and hurled it at the piano nobody played but which has been in Conor's family for generations. The bowl smashed into a dozen pieces just inches from the family portrait. I thought how lucky it was that the cover was always closed; you'd never get the sugar granules out from between the keys.

Conor said nothing, nor did I. I had never seen her act like this. Isabel did not act out. I had certainly never known her to take any sort of stand against her husband. She stormed out of the room and upstairs.

'Sorry,' said Conor, looking suddenly tired as he rose from his chair and started to collect the pieces of china. He grimaced like Henry, though I suppose that could as much be nurture as nature. 'It's been tough.'

'Of course,' I said, hating how much like an outsider I sounded. 'Trust me, I know. It's been tough for me too.'

We collected the larger shards and I got the dustpan and brush from where they always were under the stairs, and swept up the glistening grains. When Isabel came downstairs fifteen minutes later, she didn't say a word, just walked through the front garden and climbed into the waiting taxi, leaving the door open for us to follow.

FORTY

The **driver** asked if we were off anywhere nice and
the curtness of Conor's responding 'no' was enough
to ensure the rest of the journey passed in silence. The
coroner's court was held in an old Victorian building beside
the city's bus depot and not far from Custom House Quay.
If I'd gotten in the taxi first I would have told the driver to
avoid the stretch of road between the austere building and
the river. I didn't know the exact spot where Henry lost his
life, just that he was 'approaching Custom House' when he
was sucked under the wheel of the truck.

What would we be doing today if that had never happened?
I'd probably be at work, texting Henry to arrange what was
for dinner that night. Or maybe he'd be texting me, checking
in on the two of us, me and our unborn baby. Would our
house look any different? Would Henry have made a mark
on what little decoration there had been? Perhaps if he'd
been here we'd have gone the whole hog, knocking down
walls and ripping up floorboards. There was a version of me
that had the energy for that, who relished it even – the adult-
endorsed destruction. I watched the side of Conor's face, his

gaze directly ahead – was he worrying about what route we would take too? He'd have been at work. Isabel would be in her garden or maybe on one of her volunteer days. The taxi driver would be on another job in another part of the city. The coroner would probably still be sitting, a different devastated family in the gallery. Would Andy have come anyway? Of course he would. Why wouldn't he? Sometimes I forgot he hadn't actually been sent as a replacement.

In the end we didn't pass Custom House. I could see the building, an impressive hangover from the days of British colonisation, as we crossed a bridge over the Liffey in a matter of seconds, but neither parent turned to look. Isabel was sitting up front with the driver so I couldn't see her face, but her head didn't move. I wanted to reach my hand around the side of the seat, like my mother had done, and apologise for all this pain.

'Nineteen forty, when you're ready.'

Conor handed the driver a twenty and we slipped out of the car. It was starting to rain and we ran straight into the building made of burnt red bricks. The lobby was crowded with people: a few firemen in their office wear; guards; people in suits; others in casual, everyday clothes; and my parents standing close together in the corner, wearing what they had worn to Nando's.

A woman with a small ring-binder notebook sat at the entrance deleting files from a Dictaphone. I hadn't considered there would be journalists. I hadn't properly considered any of this. Mam and Dad made their way through the crowd and I gave them both a hard embrace.

'Arthur, Sarah,' said Conor, holding out a hand.

'How's it going, Conor?' said Dad, shaking it heartily. 'Nice to see you, Isabel.'

'Arthur,' she responded with a nod. 'Sarah.'

But Dad wasn't leaving it at that. He engulfed Isabel in a hug, almost knocking the woman's delicate balance.

'Excuse me a second,' said Conor as a man from the sea of suits raised a hand in his direction. 'That's James, from the firm.'

'We had a peek in the courtroom,' said Mam. 'Gorgeous room. Absolutely gorgeous. You'd know the English built it.'

'You give the English credit for everything good in this country,' said Dad.

'If we'd built this place ourselves, it would have been made of wattle and daub and it'd have fallen down within the month. This place has been here for well over a hundred years, Arthur. And that's down to the English.'

'Probably funded it with all the potatoes they stole from us during the famine.'

Mam threw an arm around Dad. 'He's very worked up today,' she said to me. 'We both are, to tell you the truth. How are you doing, pet? Are you holding up?'

'I'm all right,' I answered, taking the hand she was holding out to me. I had a sudden desire to crawl into Dad's pocket and have Mam tell me everything would be okay. I hadn't felt that yearning in years, not since I'd switched my allegiances to Henry's pocket.

Conor returned and introduced the man in formal wear. They worked together. 'They're running a little late today,' said the lawyer, shaking each of our hands in turn. 'Having trouble finding jury members. The guards have gone out to see if they can round up a few people.'

'What?' exclaimed Isabel. 'From the street?'

'Sometimes,' said the lawyer, whose name I'd forgotten as soon as I was told it, 'if jurors fail to turn up the guards have been known to approach members of the public who happen to be passing. They need at least six jurors for a traffic accident hearing. It's not unheard of for guards to phone up friends and family asking them to come down and sit in on the hearing.'

'Ridiculous,' muttered Isabel.

'It is a bit,' agreed Dad.

'If you all wanted to go and get a cup of coffee, it'll be at least another half an hour. This isn't the most comfortable place to wait. There's a coffee shop in the bus station across the road. I can give you a call when they're ready.'

'Isn't there a waiting area, for members of the family?' asked Mam.

He shook his head. 'And just to warn you, it's not uncommon for family members to end up sitting beside witnesses when the court is particularly busy, which it looks like it will be today.'

'Witnesses?' said Isabel. 'Who . . .?' She looked at Conor. 'You mean we could be sitting beside the *driver*?'

'It's unlikely,' said the lawyer, catching Conor's eye. 'European Hauliers have enough lawyers with them to keep the driver entirely surrounded, but the courtroom will be busy so I'll save you seats. There are a few journalists

266

here too. Usually this sort of case wouldn't attract much media interest but with the rise in cycling deaths this year . . .'

'Okay, James, thank you,' said Conor. 'We'll head over to the station. You have my number.'

When Andy left my house the previous night, after dinner and some documentary that I half-watched, he didn't say anything about hanging out today. I assumed he assumed I was at work and I hadn't said anything to contradict that. I hadn't slept much. I kept waking up with questions burrowing into my consciousness. It was like my brain knew the reality respite was up and suddenly it was spewing queries about bonding and breastfeeding and whether people could be born sad. Google had very few answers. I had sent the form off to the maternity hospital and was waiting to hear back.

In the bus station café, I looked around at our two sets of parents. The four of them dressed in their Sunday best and no sign of Henry. If this was going to happen it should be at the top table on our wedding day, not in the dingy surrounds of a bus depot where pigeons paced the floor like they were anxiously waiting on a delayed service.

Mam made chit-chat about how much the roads in Ireland had improved since we joined the European Union and how when she was a young woman it took more than four hours to get to Galway. Conor and Dad made an effort to contribute – one mentioning a busy motorway, the other agreeing – and Isabel sat staring at her uneaten scone, not listening to a word. I told them about the time Henry and I got the bus to Galway for our second anniversary, all dressed up for dinner that night only to fall asleep for the entire journey and arrive sticky and damp.

'I bet you both looked lovely,' said Mam. 'Henry was always a snazzy dresser.'

'I don't know about that now, Sarah. He had some fairly funny shirts.'

Mam slapped Dad on the knee. Conor and I smiled.

'He didn't get his sense of fashion from me, anyway,' said Conor. 'That was his mother.' But Isabel didn't bite. 'You always looked good together,' he said, and I smiled back at his paternal pride though it almost broke my heart. It was wrong, the five of us here without him.

There was a lull in conversation and we stared at Conor's phone lying in the centre of the table.

'I remember the first time I took Henry on a bus,' said Isabel suddenly. 'He wanted to sit upstairs right at the front above the driver. He thought he was flying. "Look, Mammy! We're flying! Look, Mammy! Look!"'

My parents smiled and Conor nodded fervently. 'That's right, that's right. I remember you saying that.'

'How did you get him home from the hospital?' I asked before I could stop myself. 'When he was born, I mean? How did you get Henry home?'

Isabel looked up from the scone and considered me before turning to Conor. 'It was a home birth,' she said, breaking into a disorientating smile. 'I'll never forget it. How could I? Rain lashing down outside, my whole body exhausted, and

I don't think I've ever been so happy. Do you remember, Conor?'

'I—'

But then his phone rang and we all stood, eager to get this over with.

FORTY-ONE

The courtroom was as high as it was wide, and while that was very high it wasn't particularly wide. It was packed. The only group I distinguished before we took our seats was a row of about six men wearing identical T-shirts with bicycles and some text across the front. Conor's lawyer colleague had saved us a red-cushioned pew at the front. The wedding theme prevailed. Marriage hadn't felt so urgent until Henry died. Losing a boyfriend sounded like teenage carelessness; 'husband' would have focused people's understanding much better.

An industrial-sized box of tissues sat at both ends of the bench. '1,000 Facial Tissues' was printed along the side in a practical black font. There were identical boxes dotted all around the room. I imagined a storage closet, somewhere else in the building, heaving with these state-sanctioned tokens of sympathy.

A woman in legal regalia came over and shook our hands. She was telling Conor and Isabel that it wasn't usually so crowded and Henry's death had become 'a bit of a cause'.

I kept my focus straight ahead until the court clerk called for us to rise, and the whole room got to its feet.

The coroner walked out from a side door and climbed to an elevated throne-esque seat. Her hair was swept haphazardly to the side. 'We are here to call an inquest into the death of Henry Walsh of 144A Thomas Street, Dublin 8,' she said and I pictured the address as it had been written on the postcards and bills the shopkeeper downstairs used to drop up to our flat. 'If I can just see the family are present?'

Conor's lawyer friend raised a hand.

'And I believe you have legal representation?' He nodded and she launched into a description of how proceedings would go. We were here to establish the identity of the deceased, the date and place of his death and the circumstances in which it occurred. The jury would return a verdict of how he had died.

I observed the jury, sitting in two rows to the right of the coroner. A man and a woman at the end were holding hands. They must have been two of the people wrangled into taking part last minute. Would they leave the court with a greater appreciation for their own lives and for each other? I felt like Tiny Tim at Christmas Mass, making the other worshippers feel better about themselves because they were not the ones with gammy legs. Things might be bad, but I was the reminder that they could always be worse.

'In the coroner's court nobody can be blamed,' she continued. 'It's only to clarify those circumstances I outlined.' No criminal or civil liability could be established; the family could ask questions; the minutes would be recorded. The judge looked like she was behind on her sleep, a few strands of hair now sticking up. She could have been hung-over, or maybe she was just tired of repeating herself.

She checked that the doctor who'd carried out Henry's autopsy was present and then she called the first witness, a guard, to the stand. He placed his right hand on a Bible presented by the clerk and agreed to the oath. The coroner asked painstakingly detailed questions even though this guard had not been at the scene of the incident but only called to the hospital afterwards. He wasn't one of the ones who'd been standing outside the flat that evening, hat in hand, when I arrived home soaked to the bone.

The guard attested that 'the deceased's father, Conor Walsh' had come to the mortuary at the hospital and made a formal identification. The whole thing seemed pointless. What did anything matter if it happened after Henry was dead?

'Next we have Conor Walsh.'

I looked down the pew as Conor stood, tugging at his cuffs slightly. I didn't know he'd be taking the stand. Had he offered or been asked? Could I have gotten up? Could I have told them all about the scarf that was too long and the East Wall house we didn't need to visit? Conor swore on the Bible just as the guard had done. Then he produced an A4 page from his breast pocket and began to read.

'My name is Conor Walsh. I am the father of the deceased. Henry Walsh was the only son of myself and my wife, Isabel Walsh. We loved him very much.' Conor, who spoke with the formality of a man used to giving presentations, hesitated.

He glanced from the page to Isabel, but she was staring hard at the ground.

'I was at my office – McDermott and Walsh, 24 Pembroke Grove, Dublin 2 – on the evening of February nineteenth when I got a phone call from a member of An Garda Síochána whose name I didn't remember but who I now understand to be Sergeant Montague,' he said, going off script and nodding to the officer who had just abdicated the stand. 'He told me that a man whom they believed to be my son, Henry Walsh, had been involved in a road traffic accident. He asked if I would be available to identify the body. They had contacted his girlfriend, Grace McDonnell, but did not believe she would be physically able to make the journey to the hospital.'

I looked up from my knees to Conor in horror. I did not remember this. I had next to no recollection of the time after the guards were at the doorstep except that somehow I had ended up at my parents' house. Had they asked me to go to the hospital? To identify the body? Had I put his parents through that too? Conor smiled kindly at me, as if to say it was all right. I opened my mouth and closed it again.

'I travelled to the Mater hospital immediately, deciding not to phone my wife until I had made the formal identification in case it was an error. I remember being surprised by how light the traffic was. The taxi driver told me it was mid-term break and that always made it easier to cross the city. I was met at reception and brought through to the mortuary. I was greeted by a guard, Sergeant Montague, and a doctor who explained what was about to happen and asked if I was ready to go in. The staff at the Mater were very considerate and professional. I wish to put that on record. Myself and my wife are very grateful for that. I followed the guard through to the room and could immediately see that it was Henry. He was covered with a white sheet and the doctor explained that the truck had done serious damage to his organs. But his head was visible. I identified him as our boy, Henry.

'I appreciate that some people would prefer to remember their child as he was, but I'm glad I got to see Henry like that. Every time I think about the manner in which he died, and how terrified he must have been, I remember him as he was that very last time, all covered in white. He looked so peaceful. And I'm glad too because it has helped me to accept that he is dead. It is a difficult thing for any parent to accept.' I looked down the row at Isabel who was still concentrating on the floor. 'I do, however, regret that I didn't say goodbye, out loud, to him. I was disorientated in the mortuary and I was outside again before I realised I hadn't told him how much we loved him. It felt foolish to ask to go back in. That was the last time I saw my son.'

Conor looked up from the page first to Isabel, then to the coroner. I wondered if anyone had ever been sick in this room.

The coroner thanked Conor for his statement and offered her sympathies. Then she asked him a long series of questions about Henry's cycling habits, whether he had also been a motorist, what he'd been wearing at the time of the accident, and so on and so forth. I didn't see the purpose of most of it. I kept thinking about the exact moment Henry's heart had stopped beating.

'Boyzone.'

'Yeah, but which one?'

'All of them.'

'All of them? Your first crush was five grown men?'

'They all brought something different to the table, and they were being sold as a collective so I think it's fair enough that my ten-year-old self and her burgeoning sexuality saw them as such.'

'I have to say, Grace, I'm feeling a little inferior here. Five grown men. How will I ever keep you satisfied?'

'All right, so, who was your first crush?'

'She-Ra.'

'Who?'

'He-Man's sister.'

'I'm sorry now, but your sexual awakening was a cartoon character?'

'At least I had a bit of fidelity. Ten-year-old Grace, already plotting her way to polygamy.'

'We're not talking about me anymore, Henry. We're talking about you. You and the little tent that a 2D animation used to build in your pants.'

'You're so crude, Grace.'

'Oh, I'm sorry. Did I insult your girlfriend?'

'I used to get up every Sunday morning to watch He-Man. They were on mad early, but I was committed. I had this friend and every time I went to his house, I'd ask if we could watch the He-Man Christmas Special, 'cause She-Ra was dressed like Mrs Claus in that one.'

'You kinky little weirdo!'

'I didn't know why I wanted to watch it so badly. But when he said "no", I'd actually start crying. I'd beg his mam to put it on. Sometimes my friend would get pissed off and go out on the road to play and I'd just sit there on my own watching He-Man and She-Ra try to save Christmas.'

'This is both incredibly pathetic and incredibly charming. Hang on while I look up this She-Ra woman, check out the competition . . . This one? How the feck was she supposed to save the world in that! Her boobs are one high-kick away from falling out. But she's not bad-looking, Henry, I'll give you that. For a cartoon.'

'Well, you know, if you were thinking about what you might wear for my birthday . . .'

'Except her boobs aren't real.'

'Excuse me?'

'They're not. Look.'

'Of course they're real.'

'See how they're holding up that top? They defy gravity.'

'She-Ra lives on Eternia, Grace, not Earth.'

'So?'

'So gravity works differently there.'

'I see. Well, my deepest apologies, Henry. That makes perfect sense, now that you say it.'

Proceedings dragged on with the coroner double checking every fact. There was a steady line of witnesses – firemen, doctor, forensic specialist – and photographs with markings from the scene of the accident were blown up on a massive television. The one that sat enlarged on the screen the longest was a close-up of the side of the footpath and the mangled bicycle. There was a space between them where Henry's body had been and my imagination seamlessly reinserted it. In the spokes of the wheel which lay on its side, bent in two but still connected to the bike frame, you could clearly make out the red wool.

The coroner took a break but we all stayed where we were and the photo remained on the screen. Two weeks it took me to knit that scarf. If I'd spent five days less, maybe none of us would be sitting here.

When the judge re-emerged, she called a Candice Sweeny to the stand. I looked around the room to see a woman of about seventy making her way to the front. Candice, the judge informed us, had been approaching Custom House on foot, going west to east, on the evening in question. She was the one who called the guards. She was the last person to see Henry alive.

FORTY-TWO

My image of Henry's death was so vivid and I had relived it so many times that I'd forgotten it wasn't necessarily true. In that image Henry had been all alone. I peered down the row at Isabel and Conor but neither seemed taken aback by this woman's existence.

Candice climbed carefully to the stand. She had grey-blonde hair and wore a navy blue skirt suit. Her statement was shaking in her right hand and she used the left one to keep it in place.

Candice had spent the day in town shopping for an outfit for her granddaughter's First Holy Communion. She was on her way to get a bus home. She'd been walking slowly because she had several bags in her hands. It had started to rain and although she was wearing a gabardine her shoes were slippery. The road was in her peripheral vision. She had been approaching Custom House when a cyclist who had been there a moment ago suddenly disappeared. Her voice quivered through the statement and I squeezed my eyes shut, willing it to stop.

She told the court what time of evening it was and how far she'd been from the bus stop. She described the moment she realised the cyclist hadn't disappeared but fallen. He was lying on the side of the road, immobile. I kept my eyes closed and swallowed a silent burp. She kept apologising to the family and I found myself getting annoyed at how illogical this was, as if witnessing it could somehow have made it happen.

Candice mentioned twice that his helmet had still been attached to his head. She noted how the truck had trundled on and left the scene by the time she got to the cyclist's side. She never referred to him as 'Henry', only ever as 'the cyclist'. Another man whose name she didn't know had caught the name of the company written on the back of the vehicle and pulled Henry off the road and onto the footpath. Candice tried to speak to the cyclist but he didn't respond. She repeated how it took her several seconds longer than it should have to phone 999 because her hands kept shaking, and when she got through she couldn't fully hear the voice on the other end so she just kept shouting their whereabouts until the line went dead.

'I am so sorry for the delay,' she said, as the trembling page continued to knock against her hand. 'I want to apologise to the family. My hearing is bad in my right ear and I was in a panic. The rain made the quays noisier than usual, but it's not an excuse. I could have been faster. I am so sorry for that.'

Candice told the court how she'd taken off her raincoat and placed it over Henry's body. She said again how sorry she was for our loss. We all had her deepest sympathies. She thought about him every day, she said. He had a kind face. She was glad he had been so loved. She was sorry for our loss.

I opened my eyes and blinked hard as the clerk helped her down from the witness box. She was pale and shook. I doubt she'd had much sleep either. My mother squeezed my hand and Dad tore a tissue from the industrial box. They were both in tears but I felt only frustration. I wanted to get up and go to Candice, tell her how she needed to stop saying sorry, that I was the one who should be apologising to her.

Then, when I thought maybe we were done, the coroner called the driver.

'George Shopov!'

Several men stood and confirmed that they were European Hauliers' legal representation, though the coroner had yet to ask. A thin man with sallow skin dressed in a short-sleeved shirt emerged from their fold and walked to the stand. He was entirely unremarkable. That was what struck me most. There was something deeply insulting about a man half Henry's size being responsible for his death.

'Is the translator present?' asked the coroner.

A woman in large glasses and a pinstriped suit nodded.

George put his hand on the Bible, the translator read the words and he agreed. Then the translator read out a statement on behalf of George. I could feel Isabel shuffling further up the bench. She was being robbed of her apology in plain view and she didn't know how to stop it.

George's statement was the shortest, shorter even than the guard who had been at the hospital when the body was identified. The translator read his name and address, originally from Sofia, Bulgaria, now living at a rural home outside the town of Mullingar in the middle of Ireland. He'd been resident here for a year. She gave his employment record, all clean, and confirmed he had been driving a tanker in Dublin on the evening in question – a return trip to the UK after making a sugar delivery – and that he had felt nothing. The first he knew of the accident was when he was stopped at Dublin Port.

Isabel's protests grew louder. Conor hushed her but she kept mumbling. Conor whispered something to the lawyer and then back to Isabel. The coroner asked George several questions but even she, a woman who seemed to thrive on minute details, grew tired of the three-way translation system. When she was wrapping it up, Conor's lawyer stood and stated that the family would like to ask a question.

'Go ahead,' said the coroner.

'The family wish to know if the driver feels remorse for what happened.'

The woman in the pinstripes translated and George was about to respond to her – and I think what he was going to say was yes, yes he did feel remorse – when one of the haulier company's lawyers stood. 'We'd like to advise our client not to respond.' The translator said something else. George replied to her and she told the judge: 'No comment.'

Conor's lawyer sat. Isabel started making noises but the coroner was talking again. There were closing comments and advice to the jury as to the ways they could rule. She advised us to stay where we were because she didn't imagine it would take long and we had all had a very long day as it was. If she was hungover she looked like she was reaching the stage where the promise of multiple pizzas was the only thing sustaining her.

A few minutes later the jurors were back and they ruled as Conor had said they would: Death by misadventure.

The back rows were standing and moving towards the door before the coroner had returned to her chambers. It made me think of Mass, where nobody's supposed to budge before the priest has left. There was an immediate bottleneck at the entrance but nobody in our bench moved. A young woman approached Isabel – a campaigner maybe, or a journalist – but whatever she wanted was declined and Isabel was the first of us to rise. My parents were red-eyed and forlorn. I felt sick to the pit of my stomach. But Isabel was livid. Conor got up to follow her and I, with one hand on my midriff, forced myself to do the same.

I twisted my frame to look behind. The bodies pushed towards the door and I found myself squashed against a guard. The woman directly behind me was carrying a bag of pear drops. The crowd pushed me forward and I was out through the heavy door before I registered what I thought I saw.

Henry, I thought as I stumbled through the door but immediately corrected myself: Andy. But he couldn't be here. He didn't know it was on. I looked behind again but it was no use; this was a one-way system. Up ahead Isabel was fighting with Conor. It had only taken a few hours of going back to a time of Henry and the people who knew him for Andy to start to evaporate. He was the ghost now, the one who existed only in the corner of my eye. I rebuked myself and followed Henry's parents out onto the street.

'How could you!'

Isabel had freed herself from Conor's grasp and was launching her thin body through the horde of lawyers gathered in a corner outside the court. 'I'm talking to you!' The Luas whizzed by and a few junkies looked up but kept walking. Histrionics from well-heeled women mustn't be uncommon outside this building.

'Why won't you say sorry?! I'm not going to sue, I swear on my own life, it's the only life I have to swear on now. We told your employers we have no interest in a civil action. I just want an apology. Please!'

'Isabel!' Conor was marching after his wife and I followed, although neither of us managed to infiltrate the suits as well as she had. She was standing in the middle of the lawyers, opposite the driver who glanced from her to the outer-ring. He looked terrible, like he wouldn't mind being hit by a truck himself. 'Mrs Walsh,' he said in heavily accented English, 'I am—'

A hand went to his chest. 'Mrs Walsh,' said the suit who owned the hand, 'we appreciate what a difficult time this must be for you . . .'

The fire fell from Isabel as the lawyer stood in front of the driver and he got sucked back into the throng. She wouldn't be getting her apology, neither in court nor outside it. Her face turned wan and grey.

283

'I just wanted . . . A single kindness . . .'

She shook her head as she whispered the words, and Conor led her gently by the arm. I'm not sure she could have stood on her own.

'We should go home. Thank you for coming, Sarah, Arthur,' said Conor as my parents appeared at my side.

'Of course.'

'And take care of yourself, Grace.'

'I'll call you during the week,' I said hurriedly, as Isabel winced at some internal pain.

'If you like.' His arm outstretched, a taxi stopped. Conor bundled his wife into the back of the cab and climbed into the front seat.

'Would he not get in beside her?' My mother shook her head as the car drove off. 'The poor creature.'

'I'll just be a minute,' I said, leaving my parents on the footpath and hurrying back into the building. I was light-headed but kept it together. I marched down the corridor, avoiding anyone semi-official-looking who might tell me the premises needed to be vacated. There were still people leaving the courtroom. I saw one older man with a flask, but no sign of Andy. Of course I had imagined it. All this had brought me back to the weeks after Henry's death when I willed him into being in every crowd and around every corner. I must have—

'Are they gone?'

I jumped as he emerged from the bathroom.

'What are you doing here?' I hissed, pulling Andy into a corridor recess. 'Are you completely insane? They could have seen you! What were you thinking?'

'He's my brother.'

'For all of a few months!'

'I want to see his parents, Grace. I tried to find an address for them but couldn't. You keep saying you're going to introduce us but you don't.'

'Well, did you see them? Did you? Did you see his mother – the tall, thin woman who looks like she's heading for her own grave? How could I tell them? They're barely functioning as it is.'

'I might be able to help.'

I guffawed at that. 'You're wearing trousers,' I said, only noticing then. 'I've never seen you out of shorts.'

'They belong to my landlady's husband. Are his parents still here?'

'They're gone. Isabel was in a state. Jesus.' I put my hand to my forehead and walked in a circle. This was another one of those tropes learnt from movies: how to behave in a legal corridor. 'Were you in there? Where were you?'

'Right at the back, with the journalists.'

'Jesus! My parents are still here, they're right outside, unless they've come looking for me. What if they see you? You'll give them a heart attack!'

'I'd like to see—'

'No. No shagging way. You have to get out of here.'

'I'm not leaving without . . .'

'What, Andy?' I realised how rarely I said his name. I had too many secrets and I was struggling to contain them. The corridor began to spin. 'I'll come with you, just . . . give me five minutes to get rid of my parents. Although what am

285

I going to say? If I say I'm not feeling well they'll insist on bringing me home . . .' I concentrated on a spot on the wall and the spinning slowly stopped. 'I'll tell them I have to go to work. An emergency. Just' – I checked the corridor in both directions – 'wait in the bathroom for another ten minutes, then come outside. All right? Okay?'

After a silent stand-off in which I half expected him to refuse, Andy turned and walked back through the door of the public toilets.

Andy

FORTY-THREE

In the beginning, it was all about information. I wanted names and dates and facts. I'd always had a linear brain. I did well at maths and science and anything that involved hands, no matter how much school I missed. Of course, the problem came when I didn't make it in on the days of tests; then all that natural ability was like a tree falling in the woods with nobody around to hear it.

Tracing my way back was like a sprawling jigsaw puzzle, where one right piece led to another and then another. Frances's name led to her grave, which gave me her parents' names, which led to parish records and the location of the village in the west of Ireland where she'd grown up. 'Your home place,' the woman at the archives office had said, although she was probably just thankful to have found an answer that would allow me to stop badgering her.

I took to the research with no problem. It was addictive and infuriating. I kept thinking, though I knew it was a pointless thought, how good I would have been at this sort of thing, if I'd had a chance. Every answer led to five more questions and you never knew which ones were dead ends

287

until you'd travelled down them. I constantly thought I was getting closer to whatever it was I was searching for, but I never actually got there. I visited the village where Frances was born, the house where she'd had me, and the building where I was given up for adoption. And I never felt anything. I had slipped off my shoes and stood on the overgrown patch of land in the west of Ireland that had once housed my birth mother, the place my blood ancestors came from – my 'home place' – and still I felt nothing. I was as lost there, barefooted in a field on the edge of the Atlantic Ocean, as I had been my entire life on the other side of the world.

And then, on a day I was cranky because I thought I was being pulled away from a serious lead, I met Grace. Every time I stepped through that front door, I got a glimpse at what could have been. I stood in the void left by Henry, looked around at his life and it made sense. I almost recognised it. That was when the question changed. It was no longer: 'Where did I come from?' Now it was: 'Who could I have been?'

Grace took me on tours of the park and though it was impossible to say I remembered it, none of it felt unknown. Henry's favourite places could have been my favourite places. She told me stories and it was like my memory was being jogged. I looked at that photograph of them sitting on the wall by the sea in Portugal and I could taste the salt in the air. I could smell the fish from the small waterfront restaurants just out of shot and I almost remembered how Grace had looked at me on the walk home. I know it's crazy. Trust me, I know. But we sat together on the sofa and it was like we'd always been there. I'd spent my life wandering the wrong hemisphere looking for a place that felt like that. Sitting in that room, beside her; it felt like home.

I'd been telling myself I was going to fix the top step for Mrs O'Farrell for days but it was always dark by the time I got back to the guesthouse. Monday morning, I had no jobs on and Grace was at work, so I sat down to see if I could stop the squeak. Mrs O'Farrell brought me out fruitcake, even though it was twenty minutes after breakfast, and told me there'd been a few messages that week. She'd tried to catch me but she was always in bed by the time I got back.

'I hope you're not working too much,' she said. 'Those files in your room are multiplying; they're getting difficult to clean around.'

'I haven't added to them in weeks,' I told her.

'Well, good.' She put the plate of fruitcake on the step beside me. 'There were three calls. Your grandmother phoned twice, nothing important, just thought she'd try you since she got the time difference right. She reckons you're developing a bit of an Irish twang, but I don't hear it myself. And then a Rose Banville called on Thursday, from Tusla – is that how you pronounce it? She said to phone her back when you got a chance.'

I picked up the house phone, dialled the social services number from memory and asked for Rose. Six months ago the only phone number I knew was my grandma's. But I was different these days; I barely knew myself.

'Well well well,' said Rose by way of greeting. 'A few weeks ago I couldn't arrive into work without seeing you skulking around the lobby. Now *I* phone *you* and it takes four days to call me back? What has happened to the Andy Cunningham we all came to know and loathe?'

'I'm taking a different tack.'

'Oh yeah? Not pestering underpaid civil servants and elderly clergy members anymore?'

'My focus has switched from information to experience.'

'I hope that's not a euphemism for necking Guinness in Temple Bar.'

'Why are you phoning?'

'Your brother.' The sound of her shuffling pages at the other end of the line. 'Henry Walsh's inquest is being held today in the coroner's court on Store Street.'

'An inquest?' I repeated, jogging my memory on what an inquest was. 'I didn't know there was an inquest.'

'Yeah, sorry. You know this place, I know nothing until I'm told and even then I'm lucky if it's not too late. I just got news of it on Thursday. I did phone you . . . It starts at noon.'

I looked down at my shorts and the grey T-shirt I'd worn at least one day too many. 'That's soon.'

'It's fine, these things never start when they're supposed to.'

'And anyone can attend?'

'Anyone can sit in,' Rose hesitated. 'I'd tell you to give it a bit of thought, consider if you really want to go or not, but I know I'd be wasting my breath. So just . . . be careful. Okay? From what you've told me, you look a lot like the dead man they'll all be there to hear about.'

I considered phoning Grace but she rarely answered when she was at work. You think they'd have told her about an inquest, but then I guess she wasn't family, technically. And technically, I was. Anyway, I was tight on time. I tidied up the tools from the front step, borrowed a pair of Mrs O'Farrell's husband's trousers, took a taxi as far as Trinity College and walked the rest of the way.

I hurried through the city, over the River Liffey and down towards the bus depot. I pulled out the map again. I'd been here. This was near where the accident happened. I brushed more hair into my face, pulled on the woollen cap I'd bought from a street vendor and lifted my collar. The more time I spent on these streets, the less my face felt like my own. In this city, it belonged to someone else. And I felt it too, the longer I was here the more I was morphing into a different person: a halfway point between Andy and Henry.

My grandma wanted me to come home. She thought I'd had enough. The Irish lilt she heard in my accent worried her, like I was no longer happy to be myself. 'You're loved,' she said. 'Come back to the people who love you.' But 'the people' was two, and my aunt lived in Perth now and rarely visited. And even though sometimes the more I found out the worse I felt, I couldn't stop. The longer I was here, the more distant my family felt. That old life was slipping away.

It was quarter past twelve when I got to the courthouse. The place was rammed with people waiting for something to happen. I pushed my way through the crowds, careful to keep my head down, until I reached the back wall where I wedged myself into a corner. The man beside me had a bag of mint humbugs and the woman beside him was sucking pear drops.

'You come here often?' she asked, leaning over her companion to offer me a sweet.

'I'm good, thanks. And no, never been here before. Why . . .?' I looked at them. 'Do you?'

'About twice a week,' she said, and the man nodded.

'There are *journalists* here today,' he whispered, nodding to the row in front of us. 'Must be a good one.'

'That'll be the family now,' said the pear-drops woman, and I followed their gaze to the group coming through the door. And there, at the rear, was Grace, glancing once to the side before taking a seat in a bench near the front. I presumed the pair to her right were her parents, and the others were Henry's. I watched closely but I didn't get a good look at them before they sat and the clerk was calling us to attention. And though I felt a stab of betrayal, my body tensed with protective loyalty.

I listened intently as Henry's father talked about his son and I watched the back of his mother's head, bent towards the floor for most of the proceedings. I had a right to meet these people who could so easily have been my parents.

The inquest dragged on. Some people left. A couple of journalists skipped out early and the man with the humbugs took to scrolling through Facebook on his phone. I half-listened to the testimony, but my attention was on Grace and on Henry's parents. I felt a responsibility towards them. Because I was responsible for their loss, in a way. If I'd been there and Henry had been where I was, it never would have happened. Henry had this perfect life and he'd just thrown it away. I got angry when I thought about how easily he'd taken it for granted. It was left to me to make amends.

Frances Clinch's choice had resounded through the core of the earth and out the other side. And I kept thinking, I couldn't get this thought out of my head: How Henry had been in the wrong place for one moment, and I'd been in the wrong place for thirty-three years.

FORTY-FOUR

●●●●●●●●●●●●●●●●●●●●●●●●●●●●●●●●●

Despite the evenings I had spent googling B&Bs in Harold's Cross, I didn't recognise this place. It was an imposing dark-brick structure with stairs up to the front door and a large 'Vacancies' sign on a picket in the front yard.

'It's stuck,' said Andy. 'Even when the place is full, it's like that. I've offered to fix it but the landlady likes it, for some reason.'

He led me up the path and steps, talking more than usual. He stopped on the porch to search for his key. He was, I thought, a little embarrassed.

'It's nice,' I said, him still searching. 'I love these old houses.'

'She'd answer if I knocked but no need to disturb her, I have it somewhere . . .'

'Won't the landlady mind you having a guest in?'

'She never minds about that,' he said, putting the key in the lock.

'Oh. Right,' I said, missing a beat, doing a poor job at hiding my surprise.

'Or she doesn't seem to anyway,' he added hastily. 'With the others. Mind that step, it creaks.'

I nodded at his too-late qualifier and tried to put the image from my mind. When I was a kid, if I couldn't see someone I thought they didn't exist. Where did I think Andy was when he wasn't with me? Set to 'Sleep' in a storage unit somewhere, waiting for an appointment with me to power him back on?

'Up here. I'm on the first floor.'

The room did a better job of covering his tracks. There was zero trace of the female touch. He kicked some clothes under the bed and hastily pulled back the half-drawn curtains. There was a musk I recognised as Andy's and almost Henry's – grit and soap and prevailing maleness – only amplified. It was stale and invigorating all at once. He opened the window.

The bed was carelessly made and a couple of creased T-shirts lay half consumed by a sheet at the end of it. Belongings were sparse but the dark furniture was too bulky for the room and, combined with several teetering towers of paper, it gave the impression of clutter. There were a few books on the desk: *Maps of Ireland*, the collected poems of W. B. Yeats, *Tracing Your Irish Ancestors*. But mainly it was paper: loose pages, bulky files, Post-it notes, cardboard dividers, several notebooks. If this was a spy novel, the case would be cracked in this room. His toolbox sat in the opposite corner to the door with a pair of overalls folded beside them. In this whole place, those dusty garments were the only items stored neatly. A couple of photocopied newspaper articles lay on the large dresser facing the bed but I couldn't make out what they said.

'That's my file, from the social worker,' said Andy, following my line of sight to a blue folder beside the printouts. He stood behind me, leaning against the wall by the door, and though the side of my left calf was pushed against the cold wood of the bed frame, there were only inches between us. If you removed the furniture this bedroom would be as big as my own but, with everything twice the size it needed to be, there was barely room to bend down and stroke a cat never mind swing one.

The sunshine showed up the dirt on one window pane but not the other. Andy gazed at the dresser. The intimacy of the situation made us both uncomfortable. The door to the en suite was ajar, the light left on from earlier. I spied his toothbrush, yellow and chunky, perched gingerly on the side of the sink. For some reason, this made me blush.

'Why didn't you tell me the inquest was today?'

My face reddened further. 'Should I have?'

'He's my brother.'

I let my annoyance at this statement pass. 'I don't know how to get hold of you,' I said. 'I have no phone number for you. I didn't know where you were staying until now. You call me from some borrowed mobile or landline—'

'Here.'

'Or you just turn up. I don't even know your surname.'

'Cunningham.'

'Okay,' I said before registering it. *Cunningham*. So ordinary. But what had I been expecting? 'Well right, now

I know.' He leaned to the side and shut the bathroom door, never moving his feet. The compactness of the room accentuated his size. 'How did you know it was on today?'

'My latest social worker told me,' he said, walking over to the dresser and absent-mindedly flicking through the piles of paper. He held up a plastic pocket. 'This is everything St Patrick's Guild had. They were never actually a home for mothers, or an orphanage, you know. They were more of a holding pen, for babies. And they kept very neat files' – he pulled out the pages so I could see – 'like the Nazis.'

What must it do to someone, to discover who they are when they've already spent thirty-three years being someone else? I wanted to reach out, as I had been doing to people all day. I wasn't sure if we offered our hands in times of sadness to comfort others or to reassure ourselves that we were not alone, but I wanted to place my hand on his bare forearm, to feel the muscle and veins and flesh of it. I also wanted him to stop talking. I didn't want to know.

There were a few sheets of paper that had fallen from the dresser to the floor. On the back of one page was a question mark, drawn as long as the page itself. The house was quiet and there was no noise from the street below. It was just me and Andy and, somewhere in the middle, Henry.

'Frances Clinch contacted St Patrick's Guild via a private residence in County Wicklow on the morning of October third. She had given birth to a baby boy the night before that was not expected,' Andy read from one of the sheets. 'Frances Clinch had already given birth to one child, a boy whose adoption had been agreed.'

'Henry.'

'She was not expecting twins. She wished the baby to be removed from her care as soon as possible and placed with another family. She made no further requests.' He placed the sheet on the dresser. 'That's it,' he said. 'No great mystery. Had a child, didn't want him, gave him away to whoever would take him quickest. I've been to that house in Wicklow. I was there the day I met you. Frances stayed at it for a few months, I think, waiting to have Henry.'

I sat beside him on the bed. 'She didn't know you, Andy.'

'She didn't even know *about* me. Henry was in her thoughts the entire time she was pregnant, but for the whole nine months I didn't exist. She was going to give him away, yeah, but at least she knew he was there. I didn't exist in her mind or anyone else's, not until the moment I came out of her. That must have been a shock.' He gave a hollow laugh. I removed my hand from my stomach.

'I existed to her for less than eighteen hours. Can you believe that? That's how much time there was between my birth and my deposit at the hospital, as they call it here. Less than eighteen hours. Of course Henry got the better life. He's the real one, the one who existed, and I'm the substitute.'

'Andy—'

'And no wonder Mum finally got a baby. They would have given me to anyone.' He dropped his head, defeated. 'I'm moving on from this stuff now. It's endless and it leads nowhere. It doesn't matter anymore.'

I budged over closer and pushed my arm and hip and thigh into his. I wanted him to know he was not alone. I held my hand out and he rested his palm flat against mine, like the gentlest high-five.

'I never needed anything from anyone until I came here. I never cared that much, about anything. But once I started, it was endless. The more I know, the less I know. You could wade through this stuff for ever and never get anywhere, so I'm done. I've moved on.'

'Moved on to what?' I asked reluctantly. I didn't like seeing him like this. I wished he would stop.

He lifted his head and looked at me. That face with the remnants of one I had loved like no other. I fought the urge to reach out and press my thumbs lightly over the lids of those pale blue eyes.

'I know enough about who I was,' he said finally. 'That's over, it's done. We only get one life but that doesn't mean there's only one path. There are a million ways to live.'

My gaze swept over the modest array of possessions scattered about the bedroom. There was a backpack against the wall with an airline tag still around the strap. That was the bag he'd brought to Ireland; it was the kind most people brought to the gym.

'Let's not stay here,' I said, turning back to him with a sudden burst of enthusiasm that all did not have to be lost. 'Let's go back to mine and make a big dinner and listen to music.'

'I need to meet his parents, Grace.'

And I need to press my mouth against yours and feel your arms across my back, and have them be yours and his and one-and-the-same.

I curled my fingers, digging the nails into the flesh of my palms. How was it he'd come back to me and still I could not have him?

'Okay,' I said. I gave up, I had to. He was always on the verge of slipping away again.

I got up from the bed, clearing my throat as I reached down to where I'd thrown my bag inside the door. I scrolled through my contacts, stopping at Conor W. Isabel was better on the phone, but probably not today.

'It's ringing.' I held it up to him, so he could see that I really was phoning them. I prayed it would go to voicemail.

'Grace.' Conor's voice not exactly cold, but wary. 'What can I do for you?'

'I wondered if I could call around tomorrow.'

'Is something the matter?'

'It's . . . I can't really explain on the phone. But it's important. I need to talk to both of you.'

'Isabel has been in bed since we got home. I don't think she'll be up to—'

'It's *really* important.'

Andy was still as a statue. He didn't dare to breathe lest he miss a beat of the conversation. His eyes flicked at each of Conor's responses, as if he was already taking their willingness to meet as a reflection on him.

'All right. In the evening.'

'Good,' I said breathlessly, not realising I had been holding mine too.

'I'm in the office all day but I'll be home around seven. I'll make sure Isabel is here.'

'That's fine, thank you. We— I'll see you tomorrow.'

I put the phone back in my bag, and hesitated over it. Did he want me to go now? Should I pick up my things and leave?

But Andy was standing, stuffing money and keys into his pockets.

'Come on,' he said, stepping over me to open the door. He took my hand in his, cold and sturdy and coarser than the one I knew before. I had taught myself not to hear his accent or the quirks of his speech, shortening words into a language of fun. And at the same time I had brought myself to focus on his nose – his skin and his hair and his nose – to know that he was different. Andy was him and not him.

'Grace?'

His eyes were kind and knowing. My stomach flipped then settled completely, quenching an unease that had festered since morning. It had been a long day. His thumb stroked the back of my hand. I was shocked by the intimacy of it but I didn't pull away. I wanted to cry with exhaustion and relief.

'Come on, Grace, let's go. I'll even cook.'

FORTY-FIVE

....

We stopped outside a house with a For Sale sign in the garden.

'How much would that place cost?'

'A lot,' I said, stepping out onto the street of the quiet estate to do a quick scope.

'Half a million?' Andy sized up the generously proportioned property. 'A million?'

'Do you actually want to know how much the house would cost? Are you thinking of buying?'

'Just making conversation, passing the time.'

'Well, I'm happy for the time to drag on, thanks very much.' The road was empty. I guess most of the commuting residents were already back home, preparing to tuck into their dinners. 'All right. You wait here,' I said. 'Behind the tree. I don't need the neighbours going into hysterics. His parents should get first dibs on that.'

'Did Henry grow up here?'

'They moved here when he was born,' I said, pushing him towards the tree. 'They were in Clontarf before, I think, on the north side of the city. Most of the people living here knew

Henry all his life. They were at his funeral. They dropped food into his parents afterwards. They sent Mass cards. They're not expecting to see him loitering in Rosedale now or ever again.'

'More people would recognise me here than in any housing development in Australia,' mused Andy. 'That's crazy, ay?'

'Insanity.' I rounded on him. 'How can you be in such a good mood?' Ever since I'd set up this meeting the night before, Andy had returned to his usual self, as if a weight had been lifted from him. Meanwhile, my stomach was in the kind of knots that meant I hadn't eaten since breakfast, although I was still taking the vitamins. I kept looking behind me, afraid Conor or Isabel was about to walk out their front door.

Andy leaned against the tree where I had instructed him to remain until I had delivered the greatest shock these people had received since the last one. He scrunched his face up at the evening sun. 'It's going to be okay,' he said serenely. 'They'll be glad to see me.'

I let out a hoot, regretting it immediately and hoping nobody peered out their window to see where the noise had come from. 'I'll be about fifteen minutes, maybe twenty, maybe—'

'Maybe none, I know. But there's no way they won't want to see me. I know it.'

I made my way slowly towards the house. Both Isabel's and Conor's cars were parked outside.

'Good luck,' Andy hissed. I turned around but he was

303

obscured by the tree. Why did we both feel I was the one who needed luck?

The shrubs in the front garden were perfectly pruned. There wasn't as much as a slug on the path and you could, as they say, have eaten your dinner off the porch. I made my way, as slowly as was reasonable, towards the door. Scooter was barking before I'd rung the bell, and I heard Conor telling him to be quiet.

The door opened to Isabel's tall, thin frame. Conor was coming up the hallway behind her still shouting at the dog in that gruff tone you hoped humans only ever used on animals.

'Hello, dear,' said Isabel, not looking any better than when I'd seen her the day before but not looking any worse either. 'Conor said you'd be calling.'

'Let her in, Isabel.'

The door pulled back and I went to step inside but Scooter, whose movements had rarely been more than a plod the past year, bounded past me through the threshold, over my feet and down the garden.

'Scooter! Scooter!' Conor was out the door after him. 'Get back here! Scooter!' Conor strode rapidly down the path – he would never run, not in front of anyone anyway – and I realised too late what was happening. I started to go after him and the dog but the course of events was unstoppable. Conor froze at the end of the garden, only his side profile visible to me and Isabel as he stared agog in the direction of the barking.

'What is it?' said Isabel, first to me, then to her husband.

'Conor? What is it?' She went to make her way down the garden path too but I put an arm out to stop her.

'Wait.'

'Hello, boy. Hello.' The Australian accent clear and distinct.

'Who's that?'

I didn't know what to tell her so I told her nothing. 'Wait,' I said again.

'Hello, sir.' Andy's voice travelled over the neighbour's bushes and up the path.

'Conor?'

But her husband could not hear her. He was going through the same things I had gone through that bright afternoon when Andy appeared on my doorstep. I strained to listen as if I might just hear the blood pounding in his ears, blocking out all external sound.

'Conor,' I said, finally breaking away from Isabel and rushing down the path. 'This is Andy, Conor.' I tried to get it all out as quickly as possible. 'Andy is from Australia. He came to Ireland looking for his brother. This is Andy. It's not Henry.' Why did it sound like I was lying? This is Andy,' I repeated, slower. 'He's Henry's twin brother. He grew up in Australia. He's here to find . . . He's looking to find out about where he came from. He was adopted, Conor. Like Henry was. They were twins and they were adopted.'

I stood directly in front of Conor, speaking into his face, trying to obstruct his line of vision and break the spell. 'It's not Henry. It's not him, Conor. It's his brother.' Still he did not move.

'How's it going?' said Andy from behind me, more nervous than he sounded earlier. 'It's a real pleasure to meet you.'

'What is going on?' Isabel called from the step. 'What are you saying about Henry? Who are you talking to? Conor? Conor?' There was no point impeding her, the inevitable was in motion. Isabel came down the path towards us, watching her step as she went.

If the neighbours weren't at their windows already, they would be now. You could only hear a scream like that once. It was the noise of a banshee, the sonographic expression of unspeakable sorrow and it made my blood run cold. There were months of pain in that scream, and for the first time I considered that my own loss may not have been the greatest.

I caught Isabel by her right arm and finally Conor moved, getting his hand under her left one just in time.

FORTY-SIX

stood in the immaculate, cream living room, walking from mantelpiece to couch before getting up again and retracing my steps. Andy was perched awkwardly on a dining chair. I gave him a reassuring smile but neither of us spoke. We were waiting.

Conor and I had all but carried Isabel into the house. Andy offered to help but it was better if he kept his distance. She kept repeating the word 'no', and Conor had taken her upstairs. That was twenty minutes ago. The door to the front room was open and occasionally I wandered into the hallway. Indistinguishable panic wafted down the stairs, but the only words I made out were Isabel saying: 'But I had him, I had him. I remember.'

Conor must have given her something because when they finally reappeared in the living room she was calm. Tranquil, even. They came in, Isabel smiling, Conor frowning, and sat. Isabel on the sofa, Conor in the armchair by the window and Andy still on the dining chair as if on a pedestal, an object of curiosity. With the four of us now present, we continued to exist in silence. Isabel stared at Andy, he stared at her and Conor focused on the window.

'So Henry was adopted.'

I think all three of them had forgotten I was there.

'No,' said Isabel.

'Yes,' said her husband.

She didn't correct him.

'Right, and he had a twin?' I looked to Andy. He'd wanted to come here, these were his questions, but someone had to get the ball rolling. I tried again: 'Andy was his twin.'

'We didn't know,' said Isabel vaguely. 'He had a twin . . . Did he? We didn't know. You didn't know, did you, Conor? You didn't know there were two?'

'Of course not,' her husband snapped back. 'Of course I didn't know.'

The room returned to silence. Isabel stared at Andy in amazement, contorting her face in response to whatever was going on in her head. I concentrated on the photograph of Henry in his graduation cap and gown and the sound of Scooter barking frantically from the back garden.

'We had been trying for a baby for years.'

'Isabel.'

But she ignored her husband. 'I got pregnant easily, but it never stuck. My body kept letting me down.'

'You don't have to tell them this.'

'We hadn't talked about adoption until a girl at Conor's office got pregnant. We said we'd take care of everything and she'd give us Henry. It was very simple. Do you remember, Conor?' But he wasn't looking at her. 'She was delighted that we wanted the child. She had no plan, did she, Conor? She didn't know what she was going to do. We said we'd find somewhere for her to stay, look after everything, Conor would make sure she got her job back. She didn't know anything about nutrition; she could barely look after herself. She was only a child. Wasn't she, Conor?'

Andy continued to sit immobile, watching Isabel as her mouth moved. I presumed he was taking this in.

'And did she go to live with you?' I asked.

'She told her family – and Conor told everyone in the office – that she'd been posted to France for six months. They all thought it was very glamorous, didn't they, Conor?'

'And she came here?' I pressed gently, not wanting to disrupt her flow now answers were coming so readily.

'We didn't live here.'

'To Clontarf, then? Did she go to live with you in Clontarf?'

Isabel looked at me like I was stupid. 'How would we explain that to the neighbours?'

'Then where?'

'The house in Wicklow. It had a name . . . What was it called, Conor? Father Clogher, long dead now, he was our parish priest in Clontarf, he found a nice couple in Wicklow and they looked after her. She was happy there, wasn't she, Conor? They were a really nice family and they were really good to her. Isn't that right, Conor?' Isabel didn't look at her husband as she sought these confirmations. She was talking to me but her gaze never left Andy.

'We saw the place for ourselves,' she said. 'She asked us to call in a couple of weeks before Henry was due – the only time I ever met her – on our way to the airport for our holiday. We had to collect her postcards. Remember, Conor? They had pictures of general seascapes on them so you couldn't tell where they were from. It was very clever, wasn't it, Conor?'

Conor didn't as much as flinch but I was getting irritated on his behalf. Andy was still just watching, not saying a word.

'What postcards?' I asked, doing my best to quash my frustration. 'Why was his mother giving you postcards?'

'I'm Henry's mother,' said Isabel sharply.

'I know. Sorry. But this girl, Frances? Why was she giving you postcards?'

Isabel relented. 'She only had two requests and that was one. It was very clever. I remember being impressed. She had two postcards and she wanted us to post them for her from abroad, from France. One was to the crowd in work and the other was to her parents in Sligo. We'd been talking about taking a final holiday as a childless couple anyway so it worked out well. I've always loved Paris.'

'And?' I was growing impatient, worried Isabel's tranquil lucidity would start to crack. 'Why did she want you to send the cards from abroad?'

'For the postmark,' said Isabel. 'So they'd think she was in France. She said the postmistress where she was from would have the thing read and the contents told to half the village before her parents ever received it. Everyone in work would think she was off on a glamorous sabbatical and everyone at home would think she was having a wonderful time in

France. Very clever. Wasn't it very clever, Conor? Do you remember I said that at the time?'

I didn't know what Isabel had taken, Valium maybe, or perhaps it was just the shock of the situation, but it was like she was under a spell. She was so pliable I could have folded her up and stored her under the couch.

'What was the other requirement?' I asked. 'What was the second thing she asked you to do?'

Isabel looked at Andy and her smile wavered. 'She didn't want Henry to know. Ever.'

'That he was adopted?'

'She didn't want him ever coming looking for her. He was ours.'

Isabel looked at her husband as he continued to stare out the window. I tried to catch Andy's eye but though he was watching the action he wouldn't engage. I had no idea what he was thinking.

'But isn't there an adoption cert?' I asked. Andy would know more about this stuff than me, if he'd just open his mouth.

Isabel went to say something but stopped herself. She shook her head.

'Or a birth cert?'

Finally Conor turned. He shot his wife a warning look. She shook her head again. 'He's ours,' she said simply. 'We have the birth cert to prove it.' Then Isabel smiled, staring just beyond Andy. 'Father Clogher signed it as our witness. A home birth at our house in Clontarf. That's where I gave birth to Henry, and then we moved.'

I was losing her. 'And you never told Henry?' I asked.

'No,' said Conor, calm and unapologetic and final. His single-word offering to the conversation.

'A cul-de-sac is a great place to raise a child,' said Isabel. 'No traffic, lots of other children.'

The four of us sat there as this meaningless statement fluttered around the room. I was out of questions. Then Andy finally spoke.

'And what about me?'

Isabel studied the source of the question. I put myself in her head and felt the marvel at the foreign accent on familiar lips.

'What did you know about me?' Andy pressed, his focus firmly on Isabel.

'Nothing,' she said finally, her voice barely a whisper. 'We were abroad, in Paris, when she went into labour.'

Then Conor delivered his first full sentence since we'd sat down: 'We didn't know there were twins.'

Tears started to form in Isabel's eyes.

'She gave me to a religious order, St Patrick's Guild.'

'She should have given you to us.'

Andy too was blinking hard. Isabel met his gaze and held it. Conor and I barely existed.

'Maybe she thought you only wanted one.'

Isabel's eyes shut in pain. 'Why would she think that? Why wouldn't she have given us both? Conor? Say something, for God's sake!'

'What do you want me to say, Isabel? How should I know? This isn't any less of a shock to me.'

Scooter's barking had turned to a whine. He was scratching faintly at the back door.

'Were you . . .? Was your life good?' asked Isabel, guilt splashed across her face.

'Can't complain.'

She nodded as if his answer was more satisfactory than it was. 'And you grew up in Australia?'

'I did.'

'I'd say that was nice,' she said. 'Don't they have Christmas Day on the beach there?' She was like a taxi driver or someone making idle chit-chat in the supermarket queue. 'Sounds idyllic,' she agreed, though Andy had said nothing. 'You're so like him.'

She stood from her seat, approaching him slowly, her hand outstretched. 'Can I?'

Andy nodded and gently she touched the features of his face. I turned away in embarrassment. Scooter's scratching got louder. I heard Isabel's gentle sobs.

'I broke it playing rugby,' he said. I kept my eyes trained on the only piece of fluff on the entire cream rug, waiting for it to end.

'I can't believe you're real. It's a miracle.'

My vision started to blur. I imagined what would happen if I stood and announced my pregnancy. Instead, without looking up from the rug, I said: 'I'll make tea', then moved quickly into the kitchen. My cheeks were burning. I stuck on the kettle and threw my weight against the back of the kitchen door. I'd already been through it all, I'd done my time. I wasn't interested in reliving the experience. I just wanted us to leave.

I stood for a few minutes while everyone in the room next door caught up. When the water was boiled I slowly made a pot of tea, allowing it to brew, searching for biscuits in what Isabel called 'the goodies press'. The most exciting thing in the whole cupboard was oatcakes. The box of pastries I'd brought the day before had probably been binned without either of them so much as peeking inside.

I loaded the tray, adding the oatcakes still in their packaging, and carried it through just as Isabel had done the previous morning. Conor was sitting where I'd left him but Isabel and Andy were at the dining table with a photo album opened in front of them. I caught a glimpse of Henry in a nappy sitting in a suitcase. I had seen these photographs before. The tray clattered to the table and they looked up. I started to pour.

'I'm okay, dear,' said Isabel.

I gestured the pot towards Andy.

'I don't drink tea, remember?'

'You don't drink tea?' exclaimed Isabel.

'Well, sometimes you do,' I said, recalling the evening in Gianni's chipper. But he didn't hear.

'Not really, no,' he told Isabel.

'We'll have to change that, won't we, Conor?'

Conor said nothing. I brought him over a cup and saucer and left them on the footstool in front of him.

I poured myself a cup, if only for something to do, and was relieved to find I hadn't gone off it. I walked aimlessly around the room, sipping from the thin rim. I was fuelled by unease and growing irritation. I didn't want to be here in the house Henry grew up in, going through all the same realisations I'd been through weeks previously, watching it dawn on these people as it had dawned on me. I wanted to be back at Aberdeen Street cooking dinner and decorating, laughing and talking. I wished then that I'd told Andy about the baby.

I washed the crockery that hadn't needed to be dirtied in the first place and a couple of other odds and ends around the kitchen. I filled Scooter's water bowl. Walking back from the kitchen to the living room, I heard Isabel laughing. The photo album had been joined by another. She'd accepted it all so readily.

I caught Andy's eye over Isabel's head. *Will we go?* I mouthed, and he did a half-nod half-shrug. Then he returned his attention to whatever picture Isabel was showing him.

'I suppose it's time to head,' I said loudly.

'If you think it's best, dear,' replied Isabel, standing from the dining chair. 'Thank you for coming.' She was walking towards the hallway to see me out, something she hadn't done since the first time I'd called to this house.

'Ready?' I said, peering around her, and Andy went to stand.

'Oh, he doesn't have to go too. Do you?' She turned to Andy and I recognised the familiar reluctance to say his name. 'You can stay a little while longer, can't you? I've so much I want to know. How you found us, for one.'

Andy looked at me and I raised my eyebrows.

'I can stay a little longer,' he said.

'Oh, wonderful!'

'But how will you get home?' I asked.

'He'll be fine, Grace, you go on. We'll take care of him.'

'I'll talk to you tomorrow,' said Andy, and I could think of no further argument.

Isabel took the opportunity to usher me into the hallway and out the front door. She pulled the latch across and drew it open. 'Thank you for bringing him back to us,' she said quickly, not realising her slip of the tongue as the door closed in front of me.

I stood there speechless in the evening twilight. 'Do you like rice pudding?' I heard her say as she turned from the frosted glass back into the house. A low inaudible response followed and then, 'I knew you would!' A door opened and shut somewhere inside, and in the garden there was a sudden breeze. I made my way down the path, looking back to see Conor immobile in his seat by the window.

I walked slowly out of the garden, turning right, past the house with the For Sale sign and out of the estate. From the mouth of Rosedale, the Walsh home was entirely obscured by hedges and trees. Was Andy being polite or had he wanted to stay? Surely he wouldn't rather hang out with Henry's parents than with me. Didn't he realise how weird that was? Didn't he know he was a ghost in that house?

I waited at the side of the road as two suitable buses passed me by. Aberdeen Street held none of the appeal now that I would be in it all alone. It seemed so cold, like it belonged to late November and not the last days of May. I got on another bus entirely, one that was heading for my parents' house.

Conor

FORTY-SEVEN
∙∙∙∙∙∙∙∙∙∙∙∙∙∙∙∙∙∙∙∙∙∙∙∙∙∙∙∙∙∙∙

knew Frances Clinch was pregnant before she told me. She'd been spending chunks of her workdays locked in the women's bathroom on the first floor and the rumour mill had carried word the rest of the way. The gossip must have reached Frances's ears too because the day she came in to tender her resignation, she was doing so with immediate effect. She would not be working out any notice and if that meant sacrificing her last pay cheque or forgoing references, then so be it. It was a Wednesday, the last one before Christmas, and she'd be leaving on Friday and not coming back.

It took me all of eight minutes to get the real reason out of her, and as many minutes again for her to offer us the child. I'd like to say it was my years spent cross-examining and bartering that extracted the information, but the poor girl was desperate to tell someone. She hadn't an ally in the world.

I didn't coax the child off her. Let me be clear about that. There was never the faintest possibility she was keeping the thing. And I was in two minds about the whole business myself. I still wanted a child, of course I did, I wasn't one of those men who just went along with their broody wife's whims and before they knew how they were going to afford it all had acquired a football team of offspring. Children were something I'd given some thought to. I had always wanted them. Well, that's not true, not always, but from the day I met Isabel. We were a solid match and I knew she'd be a great mother. She was loving and thoughtful and we had shared values. But her body, as she put it, let her down. The miscarriages had taken their toll and I was beginning to think we should stop trying, hedge our bets and thank our lucky stars for such a happy and love-filled relationship.

But then Frances suggested we take the baby. She'd rather that, she said. A girl from her village had given her child to the nuns and, if even half the stories were true, she didn't want anything to do with that. The child would be ours, she told me, and that would be the end of that.

Isabel agreed immediately. As I recall it now, I was only halfway through telling her about the predicament of this poor secretary who'd sat before me that afternoon in admirable stoicism when Isabel made the suggestion herself. It had been at least two years since I'd seen that kind of hope in her. I told Isabel I'd take care of it all, and I took her silence to mean it would never have been any other way.

Father Clogher, too, seemed to know where I was going before I had arrived at my question. He said to give him forty-eight hours and in less time than that he was back with a name and address for an older couple near Roundwood.

Good Catholics, always happy to help another parish. Father Clogher drove Frances there himself. Isabel and I were watching *The Late Late Show* the other night and there was an elderly man in the audience talking about how his mother had been taken from her village to a Mother and Baby Home in the dead of night. The local priest had put his mother on the crossbar of his bike and cycled her there. Seven months pregnant and she sat like that for nineteen miles. Isabel and I didn't say a word, we never spoke about it, but I imagined she was experiencing the same sense of outrage. Ours wasn't anything like that. It wasn't a forced adoption. Frances wanted nothing more than to be rid of the child. She presented herself to Father Clogher's parochial home at 11 a.m. on a sunny Saturday afternoon and he drove her to Roundwood in his parish car, which, if I recall correctly, was a rather spacious Renault 18.

Isabel and I bought this house on the other side of the city. We told the old neighbours we were 'expecting a child' and that we needed more of a family home. We didn't lie, we just fudged the details. When we ran into a few of them over the years, as was bound to happen, Henry's exact date of birth wasn't a topic of conversation. They just said what a loss we'd been to the road and that we should call around for lunch some Sunday. We said we would but never took any phone numbers.

Isabel was full of energy in those months – preparing for the baby's arrival, nesting. We bought a crib and toys. Isabel read baby books and I painted the new house. She left the room when I opened the tins; there was lead in the paint and that was dangerous for expectant mothers. She even developed cravings: liver and Mr Freeze ice pops.

'Maybe it's psychosomatic,' she'd say hopefully.

I knew it was nonsense but I said nothing. I just hopped in the car and went to the butcher's. Over the years, I think Isabel convinced herself she really had been pregnant. Once when Henry was fifteen and refusing to tidy his room, his mother shouted up the stairs after him: 'I went through labour for you!' And then she looked at me and rolled her eyes. Forgetting I knew the truth, or maybe just forgetting the truth.

We never once mentioned it, never alluded to it, even in our most intimate moments, lying side by side over the years, keeping ourselves awake worrying about his grades or health or moods. Henry is ours and that's it. Was ours. I forget sometimes. Emotions have not been my forte but I loved him like it was a form of breathing.

Maybe if Isabel had been the one taking the Formans' phone calls it would have been harder to fool herself. I paid for Frances's living expenses and a recommended donation for their Christian generosity, and they provided me with a couple of telephone updates.

The first report, a month after she'd been with them, was that all was well. Frances was blooming, Mrs Forman told me down the line of the pay phone around the corner from my office. 'I think it'll be a boy,' she said, and I felt a pride that was entirely irrational but which I did not dismiss.

The second phone call was generally upbeat too; there was still some occasional vomiting, which was rare, and Frances was bigger than Mrs Forman was used to, but nothing to worry about. So I didn't mention it. Mrs Forman was a trained midwife and Isabel was sick at that time, stomach problems again. Part of me worried if the physical strain of caring for a child would be too much.

The last phone call, a month before she was due, was more alarming. Mrs Forman was 'a little concerned'. Frances was very big and still sick but of course she hadn't been to a doctor so she couldn't say for sure but there were old wives' tales about large pregnancies and late illness and now Mrs Forman wasn't superstitious herself . . . And on and on. She wasn't the kind of woman to come straight out and say something so I did the plain speaking for her and maybe I was a little too direct, but I'd been up all of the night before with Isabel who still wasn't showing signs of improvement. I told Mrs Forman that my wife would not be able to care for anything other than a healthy child. It wouldn't be fair to either of them. That was our arrangement, and we were delighted to have entered into it.

Nobody ever told me Frances Clinch was carrying twins. I want to make that clear. I never knew. Those words were never said.

Frances didn't came back to work, though I had kept her job open. I suppose she wanted a fresh start. I saw her one last time, when we stopped by the Formans' place to collect the postcards. She had written them on the backs of photographs of nondescript seaside settings. I didn't tell her Paris wasn't by the sea. I presumed none of her family would realise either.

Chere Maman,

That's 'Dear Mammy' in French! I am having a lovely time. The city is so pretty and everyone at work is really nice. The manager says he'll be lost when I leave. He has even offered a promotion to make me stay! But I think I'd miss you all too much. The <u>Mona Lisa</u> is even better in real life and I can see the Eiffel Tower from my bedroom window. I'm looking at it right now. Tell Daddy and everyone I said hello and that they're to try not to be too jealous of me. I hope it's not raining too much at home!

    Lots of love,

    Franny

We read the postcards on the way to the airport but didn't say a word about them, just bought a couple of stamps at a *tabac* and posted them en route to the Musée D'Orsay, enjoying our last holiday just the two of us. Father Clogher had it registered as a home birth at our old house in Clontarf and he sealed the parish record in Latin. We did our best by Frances and we made it so Henry would never again know what it was to be unwanted. We gave him a better life.

I have dealt with historical adoption cases through the firm. Harrowing, horrendous stories of women held against their will and nuns who made them scrub floors and bathroom walls until the moment they went into labour. Ours was nothing like that. The stuff you hear in the news would make you sick. The kind of stories that should have the entire country taking a good hard look at itself. To be a part of those cases would have been unthinkable.

FORTY-EIGHT

. . . .

managed fifteen minutes of the murder mystery my parents were watching before taking myself off to bed. Neither of them asked why I was home, just if I wanted a hand removing the crates of mothballs from my bed. Mam helped me transfer them to the floor and when I got under the covers, there wasn't an inch of carpet exposed. I felt like I'd been embalmed.

'Well,' said Mam, standing in the doorframe, 'you should be safe from attack tonight anyway.'

'Will you turn off the light?'

The room went dark. 'Night, pet.'

How long had Andy stayed at the Walshes'? If Isabel made rice pudding and they went through a few more photos . . . that couldn't take more than an hour. Andy wouldn't have dinner because we ate before we got there. Unless he wanted to be polite. I tossed and turned and dozed off sometime after 3 a.m. but was awake again by four. What if he'd stayed over? But then he'd never spent the night at mine, so he was hardly going to spend the night there. What was he going to do – sleep in Henry's old room? Of course he hadn't stayed.

Mam left early the next morning to go walking with a friend and Dad was making avocado and parsnip breakfast fritters from Ed Balls' new cookbook. He washed the last saucepan, dried it, folded the tea towel, placed it delicately on the draining board and sat down at the table with a sigh of profound contentment. 'Now.'

He might have stayed over. The Walshes had plenty of guest bedrooms. What if he did and what if he was still there now? I was worried and jealous and unbearably put out. He was slipping through my fingers and I couldn't keep my grip.

'Eat up there, Grace, before it goes cold.'

'It must be great to be retired,' I said, straightening the plate in front of me. 'Nothing to worry about anymore.'

Dad guffawed. 'No work to worry about. Still plenty of other things to occupy my mind.'

'Like me?'

'Yes. And how your mother never manages to put the towels back in the bathroom after a shower.' He smiled at me over his fork. 'We haven't heard as much from you lately. Hadn't seen you for a while before the inquest. Everything good?'

I stuffed a fritter into my mouth. 'Busy.'

'You're dead right. Best way to be. You look well, anyway.' And Dad went back to cutting up his breakfast, relieved to have completed the task Mam had left for him. He'd asked and I was fine, just busy. That was enough information to report back.

'These are nice.'

'Arra they're grand. Claudia Winkleman's are miles better.'

He drove me to work, singing along to the radio all the way, and the restaurant was full of singing too because Dermot was preparing for a musical theatre audition. I stayed a little later than necessary and abandoned the bus for a slow walk home. I couldn't help hoping Andy would be waiting on the doorstep, which of course he wasn't. But he did say he'd call. Yesterday when I left, he said: *I'll talk to you tomorrow*. I had this terrible pain in my stomach at the thought of him still in Rosedale, maybe wearing a T-shirt and socks that had belonged to Henry because he'd slept in his own clothes and then hadn't left at all.

The hallway was cold, though not as bad as I'd imagined. It was like when I was a kid and we'd get back to our house after a week's holiday: it didn't matter if the central heating had been left on timer, it needed body warmth to heat it back up. There was a letter on the mat and on the back, it said: *This came to my house. Betty.*

I pulled it open, surprised it hadn't been done already. It was from the hospital. My first scan was booked in for two Mondays time. I went upstairs and stood in front of the bathroom mirror. I pulled my T-shirt back and turned to the side. Maybe . . .

I boiled the kettle and placed some pasta in the saucepan, then I took a container of leftover sauce from the fridge and poured it onto a pan. I waited. I considered sitting in the hallway and wallowing. It had passed the time before. Only the coats were no longer in a heap on the floor and I knew this was a different kind of loneliness, more aimless than bereft. I picked up *A Christmas Carol* from the couch in the living room and opened it at the bookmark.

> 'Have you had many brothers, Spirit?'
> 'More than eighteen hundred,' said the Ghost.
> 'A tremendous family to provide for!' muttered Scrooge.

I flicked back through the earlier passages, letting my fingers get jammed in the pages, and when I heard the water start to bubble over, I closed the book and went back to the kitchen.

'Right,' I said to the empty room. Then I left the house entirely and knocked on Betty's door.

'Would you like some dinner?'

'What's wrong with it?' she said, holding onto one side of the door. 'Did it fall on the floor? Do you need a guinea pig to make sure it's fit for your consumption?'

'No,' I replied patiently. 'I've made too much and just thought you might like to join me if you haven't already eaten.'

'I have. Dorota made me a lamb cutlet and roast potatoes.'

'Oh. Right,' I said, having forgotten the home-help woman came on Wednesdays. 'That's fine so. Just thought I'd ask.'

'But,' said Betty as I turned to go, 'that *was* two hours ago, and I am meant to eat regularly, with my blood sugar and everything.' She opened the door a little more. 'What is it?'

'Pasta arrabiata.'

'Sounds foreign.'

'Look, it was just a thought. If you're not—'

'Go on so.' She sighed. 'Bring it in. And you can use your own plates. You needn't think I'm washing up.'

'I was thinking you'd come into me?'

Betty looked aghast. 'I'm eighty-two, Grace. Do you want me to do everything?'

We ate in relative silence in her front room with the television on. I checked my phone every couple of minutes, alternating between having it face up in case I missed something and face down because I was irritated by my own obsessiveness. In the break between *Coronation Street* and *Fair City*, Betty told me how she was certain the Hegartys were the ones leaving their rubbish at the end of the road. 'They wouldn't pay you a compliment never mind pay their bin charges,' she said. 'And they must be doing it at night, which is doubly sneaky. So you may keep that curtain open!'

I could have left but I had no desire to sit in the house next door on my own. I kept imagining Andy at the Walshes', that even if he had left they'd asked him to come back again to eat with them, a proper formal meal. I pictured him taking up the dinner invitation that I kept declining. I had declined it because of him and he just went ahead and took it? I turned my phone over again and then threw it away from me to the other side of the sofa. He could have been anywhere.

The credits rolled on *Fair City*, and when Betty didn't say anything about me leaving I stayed for the next soap too.

Someone was screaming at someone else in a pub when my phone finally rang and Betty threw me a look like she wished I'd never been born. I picked it up and hurried into the hallway.

'Hello?' I said.

'I can still hear you!'

'Hello,' I said quieter this time, moving down towards the kitchen.

'Grace?'

I could tell from the background noise that he was outside. It was the quiet static of an enclosed space, a garden maybe. And I saw him there, standing among Isabel's flowerbeds, the phone pressed to his ear.

'Can you hear me?'

'Yes,' I said, closing my lips as quickly as I'd opened them. I was annoyed at myself now too. Barely a day had passed and already I missed that voice and its stupid melodic tone.

'I wanted to call earlier but I was crazy busy all day.'

'Right.'

Busy how? Busy with what? Busy with who?

I pictured him accompanying Isabel on one of her walks, strolling down to Dun Laoghaire harbour to see Conor's boat. I envisaged them from the back, both tall with good posture, as I'd seen that image in real life many times before.

'I'm walking home,' he added.

'Home from where?' I said, more irritated than I was probably entitled to be.

'From work . . . Is everything all right? I was on that site down by the gas company today. We were meant to get off at six but of course it dragged on until eight. I can't talk too

330

long; I'm on one of the guys' phones and he's about to hop in his car.'

I didn't say anything and my irritation didn't diminish, it just shifted its focus from him back to me.

'What are you doing?' he said eventually, aware that something was off.

'I'm at Betty's. Having dinner.'

'Oh right. That's nice. Do you . . .? Will I call over?'

'Well, it's pretty late now so,' I said, clamping my mouth shut mid-sentence.

'Tomorrow evening?'

'I'm working,' I said, growing more frustrated with him and me and the whole situation.

'Friday?' he offered.

'Nope.' I told myself to get a grip. I was trying to punish him, though I knew it wasn't fair, and in the end I was punishing myself. 'Sunday evening?' I suggested.

'I promised Isabel I'd go to theirs for dinner.'

The sound of a car alarm filled the silence as I digested this information.

'But any other day,' he said. 'What about Saturday?'

'Can't.'

'Really? Sunday night is the only time you're free?'

'Yep.'

'Well then, why don't you come to dinner too? I'm sure Isabel won't mind.'

I bit my lip hard. As if he had a clue what Isabel would or wouldn't mind. As if he knew her.

'No thank you,' I said curtly. 'Anyway, I have to go now. I'll see you around.'

'See me around?'

'Yep. Bye now.' And I hung up with as much aggression as one could expend on a touchscreen phone. Then I went back into Betty and watched through blind frustration as some woman told a man with loads of tattoos that she was leaving him.

FORTY-NINE

preferred being in Betty's so much more than being alone in my own house that I came back the next day too. I was on a late shift so I called in before work and helped clean her windows, something I had yet to do in my own home.

'There,' I said, climbing down from the stepladder. 'All the better to spy out of.'

She made me tea and we sat and gossiped about the neighbours – well, she gossiped, I still didn't know who most of them were – and then I left for the Portobello Kitchen.

On Friday, at around noon, I knocked on her door for the third day in a row.

'Is this one of those old people scams?'

'What are you talking about?'

'You. Not being able to get enough of me.'

I sighed. 'No, Betty. This is not a scam.'

The door didn't budge. 'I heard a thing on the radio about how this young person in England started calling to his elderly neighbour every day and everyone thought he was just being Christian but then the old woman died and the family discovered that she'd signed over her house, car,

333

stocks, shares in all these airlines – because her husband had been a pilot – everything, to the neighbour who'd been calling and slowly brainwashing the poor woman for months.'

I had a house I couldn't stand to be in alone, a dead boyfriend who'd half come back then left again, and a leech sucking all the nutrients from inside me. I was in no humour for this.

'Because I don't have any stocks,' added Betty. 'If that's what you're thinking.'

I reached into my back pocket and held up the two Telly Bingo tickets. Like flashing a private member's card, the door finally opened. 'I don't have shares in any airlines either,' she said as I stepped into the hallway.

'Good to know.'

Betty did the usual no-peeking tickets-behind-her-back routine and gave the sly grin she always gave when I made my selection, as if somehow she knew what numbers were going to come up.

'If it's not a scam, then what is it?' she demanded, settling back into her chair. 'Three days in a row. Is it because the toolbox man hasn't been calling around? Has he jilted you? Is that it?'

'No.'

'You're awful unlucky with the men, aren't you?' she said, not unsympathetically. 'One dies, fair enough. But to lose two of them . . . You'd have to wonder, wouldn't you?'

'Would you?'

'Ah, you would,' she said decisively. 'Have you given any thought to my theory that you might be cursed?'

'I'm pregnant,' I snapped, if only to shut her up.

'Yah,' she said with a deep intake of breath. 'They say these things come in threes all right.' She didn't miss a beat. It was almost impressive. The woman was unflappable. 'That'll send a man running, sure enough.'

'It's not his,' I said. 'It's Henry's – my partner. The one who died. Not my husband, Betty. My partner.'

Her face softened slightly. She put her bingo ticket down. 'As you may or may not know, I don't believe in sex before marriage . . .'

'I did not know that but I can't say I'm surprised.'

'. . . but I do believe that a child is always something to be celebrated. New life is a great thing, Grace. You should be very happy.'

'It doesn't feel so great to me,' I said, folding my arms across my stomach. 'Not when I'll be doing it all on my own.'

'I raised my first two on my own for a while after their father died. It was tough,' she agreed. 'I wouldn't recommend it.'

'I thought your husband, Patrick—'

'God have mercy on his soul.'

'Right. I thought he only died a few years ago?'

'He did.'

'So how were you raising your kids on your own? They were well grown by then.'

'I got married when I was twenty-one,' said Betty, taking a slurp of tea. 'To Joe O'Toole, the handsomest man Crumlin has ever produced. He was our local postman and all the women used to go into hysterics when he'd ring the bell at them. They'd be almost throwing their knickers at him as he cycled by. I don't think we had a single day of sadness the four year we were married. I got pregnant straight away with Joe Junior, then a year after him Trisha came along. I used to go to church every day and say the rosary because I knew I'd been too lucky and something bad had to happen. Then one Thursday Joe headed off to work and he never came back. He was hit by a bus five minutes from home.'

'Oh, Betty.'

'Joe Junior was three, Trisha just gone two. So Joe's brother Patrick came home from England where he was working on the sites, and he took up the responsibility. I'd always got on with Patrick. He was groomsman at our wedding, and Joe and him were shocking close growing up. The next year, myself and Patrick were married and we had Louise and Anthony. He was a good man and we got on well. He was a great father to all four of them. I told Joe and Trisha about their dad but sure it didn't mean much to them; they couldn't remember him. Far as they were concerned Patrick, God have mercy on his soul, was their da.'

'You married his brother?' I said in disbelief.

Betty rolled her eyes. 'That was the done thing. No big swinging mickey. If one man died, another decent family member stepped up. Plenty of children were raised by uncles and aunts. Family is family.'

'Wow.'

'I wasn't anything special, Grace. You do what you have to do to keep going. But I'll tell you this, I couldn't have raised those children on my own, Joe Junior was a terror.'

Betty was not a woman for tact but I must have looked particularly stricken because she quickly added: 'Not back then, I couldn't have. Things are much different now.'

'Because women can work?' I hazarded.

'Where the feck would I have found the time to work? No. Because youse have dishwashers. And disposable nappies.'

The Telly Bingo opening sequence began to roll and Betty flung her pen at the telly. The Blonde One had appeared on the screen.

'Ah, for feck's sake!'

'Keep the shower curtain closed over!'

'It is closed.'

'I don't want you to see me. I'm hoping to keep some romance in our relationship after this.'

'I can't see a thing, Grace.'

'If I spy even a gap – ow! Ow! Ow ow ow!!!'

'It's pretty slippy in here.'

'You're sitting in a bath, Henry Walsh. I'm sitting on a toilet doing what feels like pissing razor blades. So pity about you. Do not touch that curtain! I don't want to see more than your arm peeking out.'

'I'm not.'

'Just keep holding my hand, please.'

'I am.'

'It's sore.'

337

'I know, Gracie. I'm sorry.'

'Tell me something – ow! – tell me something to keep my mind off it.'

'Can you imagine what we must look like? Imagine someone from room service came in and stood at the bathroom door. A couple of supposed lovebirds on a romantic weekend away, only it's four in the morning and she's sitting on the toilet seat and all you can see of him is an arm sticking out from the side of the shower curtain.'

'Ha. Was that a yawn, Henry Walsh? Don't you dare fall asleep. Do you know how you get a urinary tract infection? Sex! So this is your fault and we're both going to sit here sharing my pain until it's late enough, or early enough, or whatever, to go to a doctor.'

'Your pain is my pain, love of my life. If you're pissing razor blades, I'm sitting in a bath with a wet arse.'

'Don't make me laugh!'

'Can I switch hands? My arse really is going numb.'

'Okay, just don't let go for long.'

'I won't.'

'And don't touch that shower curtain.'

'Count to five and I'll have a hand back in yours.'

'One – two – the curtain, Henry! – three—'

'There.'

'Four, five.'

Betty got the lucky line, which was worth two euro more than usual so she said there was a chance that sitting in the same room as me wasn't exactly like having a family of black cats cross your path. She gave me her winning ticket and told me to put it towards the baby fund. I wasn't sure how many disposable nappies I'd be buying with seven euro, but it was a nice gesture.

I had no idea how much nappies cost, or baby food, or what you were supposed to buy before a baby was born. Because the baby would be born, I accepted that with no great feeling of celebration as I walked to the supermarket on Sunday afternoon to do a shop for Betty. Not because the thing growing inside was half me, but because the other half was Henry.

I made omelettes for myself and Betty and only went into my own house to get pepper. I kept my phone in my back pocket but it didn't ring. Andy would be having dinner with the Walshes now. Maybe he'd moved out of the B&B and gone to live with them. I pictured the three of them playing happy families in the bright and airy modern home with its high energy rating and underfloor heating.

'You should be getting plenty of rest,' said Betty, dipping a slice of toast into the eggy concoction.

'I am,' I said, slightly taken aback by the spark of compassion. 'Thanks.'

It turned out the soaps, like football and world news, never stopped. They differed slightly each night but there was always at least three on. I was starting to get a grasp on some storylines, and Betty gave me character backgrounds during the ad breaks. The implausibility of some of the plots made me feel a bit better about my own situation.

'Was that . . .?' Betty leapt from her armchair. 'I think that was one of the Hegartys . . .' She scuttled over to the window and picked up a pair of binoculars I'd never noticed before. 'I knew I'd catch them. If these feckin' things would just work . . . Jesus!' There was a bang on the window and Betty jumped back. 'Jesus, Mary and all the feckin' saints!'

I got up from the sofa and looked out. I could just about see him. 'It's Andy,' I said.

'Who?'

'The toolbox man.'

FIFTY

'I **did call** here first,' said Andy, when we were safely locked away in my own kitchen. 'Then I remembered you were in Betty's the other day and the curtain was open so . . .'

'She's keeping an eye out for the Hegartys.'

'What's that?'

'Illegal dumpers. Allegedly. That's why the curtain is open.' I shook my head. 'Why aren't you at dinner?'

'I was, but I left.'

'Wasn't there dessert?'

'There was,' he agreed. 'But to tell you the truth, I'm not so big on that rice pudding. It's not really pudding at all.'

'No,' I agreed. 'It's mainly rice. So I guess you don't want anything to eat?'

'Nah. But I'll take a cup of tea if it's going.'

'Really?'

He grinned and my heart slowed slightly. I remembered how the evening sun lit that face. 'What can I say?' he replied. 'Isabel's been getting to me.'

'Have you seen a lot of her since we visited?' I switched

on the kettle and did my best not to sound accusatory.

'I've been over every day.'

I nodded to the kettle and pretended to untangle the cord.

'But that's only six days. I reckon it does Isabel good having me around. Although Conor doesn't seem so happy about it.' Andy shrugged. 'I like hanging out with her. She's nice, and it takes her mind off things. She's pretty obsessed with that lorry driver, ay? She showed me his home address and everything. It's only a two-hour drive from Dublin. She's talking about paying him money to apologise.'

'Why isn't Conor so happy about it?'

'Who knows? He doesn't say. Isabel was asking about you this evening,' he said, stepping forward to take a cup. 'Good on ya. She said you should come for dinner. She's really a great cook.'

I sipped from my cup. I knew what kind of a cook Isabel was. I had eaten dozens of her dinners. I knew the entire repertoire. She declared everything she made to be 'good for a growing boy'. Never mind her 'boy' hadn't gotten an inch taller in fifteen years.

'And my travel visa's up in two weeks. Isabel reckons I should go down and assert my citizenship, then I can stay as long as I like. She's looked into it. She says it's relatively straightforward.'

The cosiness between them creeped me out. That was the most honest way to put it. I took solace in Conor's objection, though I wasn't proud of it. I didn't want to be on the opposite team to Andy. But at Henry's funeral Isabel kept talking about him in the present tense, as if he were still alive. I imagined Conor didn't think this new-found bond was particularly healthy.

Andy poured part of his tea down the sink. 'I still need a lot of milk,' he said and reached for the carton. 'Isabel wants to show me more of Ireland. There's a spot she is sure I will love, further down the coast, by the sea.'

'Wexford.'

'That was it.'

'They have a holiday home there. Henry loved it.'

'She was talking about us going next week,' said Andy. 'They're members of some wine club and they get all the bottles delivered there. Isabel's planning to cook veal. She says it's the speciality of the local butcher.'

'Kill the fatted calf, the prodigal son has returned.'

I could feel his eyes on me but I didn't look up from my cup.

'I'm sure you could come,' he said carefully. 'I know she'd be happy to have you.'

'I can't,' I retorted immediately, dismissively, throwing my own tea down the sink. 'I can't drink wine and I can't eat undercooked meat.'

'I'm sure it's not—'

'I'm pregnant.'

I placed the upside-down mug on the draining board and exhaled. Finally I looked up. Andy was staring at me, his face unreadable. I had a flash of what it would have been like to tell Henry, and it made me desperately sad. Standing in this kitchen informing him he was about to be a father; the unexpected elation; him suddenly laughing loudly, me

343

laughing too; the two of us collapsing onto the couch, a different couch, a couch Henry had a say in, high on the excitement and possibility of it all. We'd have so much more than baby names to discuss then. I took another deep breath and pushed the image away. Back in the real world, Andy blinked.

'You're pregnant.'

'Fact.'

'Right now.'

'Yep.'

'I knew it.'

'Sorry?'

'Well no,' he corrected, 'I didn't know it but,' his gaze diverted, 'I knew there was something. This makes sense.'

'Well, I'm glad one of us thinks so.' I wrinkled my forehead as I watched him go through some sort of epiphany. 'It's Henry's, if you're wondering. I haven't been shagging my grief away.'

He smiled. It wasn't a laugh but it was good enough and, despite myself, I smiled back.

'I only found out a couple of weeks ago, which is fairly embarrassing given that I'm now fifteen weeks' pregnant. They reckon. My first scan is Monday week but, you can kind of see it.' I lifted my top and turned sideways. 'Can you? There?'

Andy didn't say anything and when I glanced up I expected to see a look of deep scepticism, the current bump was probably only decipherable to me, but no. Andy was gazing at the tiny swell that had appeared in the past couple of days like it was magic. Nobody else had looked at my stomach like that. Even I hadn't looked at it like that. It felt good.

His eyes were on me and all of a sudden I felt important, unknowable, mythical, like I was Earth Mother and the world would hear me roar. I was proud to be seen so completely, as I really was.

'You can touch it if you like,' I found myself saying, the Beyoncé moment clearly gone to my head. 'You'd be the first. Not that you would necessarily want to touch it, of course. It's kind of like rubbing a bald man's head, isn't it? Bit weird.'

Andy moved slowly towards me, brushing his right hand on the leg of his trousers before extending it towards my stomach. His palm was cool. It sent a shiver through me.

'Wow.'

I grinned. 'It's not that impressive currently. I'm bigger than this when I need to pee. But I'm reliably informed it will grow.'

Andy took a step back and looked at me, all of me. That expression hadn't just been for my belly. I felt my whole face blush and I started to talk quicker.

'I don't know how I'm going to afford it or what exactly I'm going to do. Well, be a single mother, I suppose. Not exactly the plan but sure there you are. And if I have to sell this place then so be it, I shouldn't lose any money on it, hopefully. I got pregnant the day he died. Can you believe that? Well, the doctor explained I didn't actually get pregnant that day because interestingly the way insemination works . . . Too much information. Sorry. I haven't really talked to anyone about this yet. It's exciting. Well, I did tell Aoife, and Betty, but Betty doesn't believe in sex before marriage and I wasn't going to get into the nitty-gritty. So anyway, it's all a big mess but there you are. You're going to be an uncle,' I said, leaning back against the counter. 'Congratulations.'

'Or a father.'

I faltered. 'Excuse me?'

Whatever calculations Andy was doing seemed to be adding up rapidly. He was a man on the verge of an answer. 'I could be an uncle,' he said slowly, his eyes dancing across my face, 'or I could be a father.'

'You could . . .? Sorry, now. What?'

'I had a single mother,' he said. 'It's not easy to do on your own.'

'So I've heard.'

'Then don't.'

'Don't what?' I said.

'Don't do it on your own. Let me help.'

'Help.'

'Let me be the father.'

I stared at him. 'What?' He didn't blink. 'No, no way,' I continued. 'That's insane.'

'No it's not. It makes sense,' he said, far too calmly for my liking. 'It makes total sense, Grace. This is why I'm here. I wanted to do something to help, to make up for Henry and this is . . . I don't even feel that surprised. It's like déjà-vu. You say Henry believed in fate; well, me too, and here I am. The answer is so obvious.'

'Andy, you're not the father. I mean, I know I'm a powerful kisser, but those two seconds at Trinity's arch weren't quite enough to impregnate me. Andy,' I said again, catching his eye, not used to saying his name, 'Henry is the father.'

He held my gaze. His brow furrowed and for the first time since the day we met, I could have sworn he was Henry.

'Henry was the father, for a few hours. And then he died. But I'm here. I can take his place. He's my brother and I'd like to do what he can't. Let me do what he can't, Grace. Everyone deserves a second chance,' he said and I did not know if he meant him or me or Henry or the child.

I thought of Betty and the uncle who had come home from England to stand in and raise his brother's family.

Andy laughed, an elated sound that came from the belly but also the heart, and suddenly I was the one wading in déjà-vu. The laugh. It was exactly as it had been in my mind's eye.

'Let me do what he can't,' he repeated. 'Let me be the child's father.'

FIFTY-ONE

made two further rounds of tea and Andy drank almost half of each cup. He even ate a couple of biscuits. Intentionally or not, he was making a good stab at transforming into Henry.

We talked rationally and calmly. He tried to convince me why his idea was not the most insane twist in my own personal soap opera. I sat and listened and remained unconvinced. Occasionally I wavered. How many women had men of whom they had no carnal knowledge begging to be allowed to raise their fatherless children? Granted this was a particularly 1950s' way of thinking but even with the aid of dishwashers, not doing it on my own had its appeal. What swayed me more was the notion that this child might know some version of its father, and that I might continue to know some version of him too. Because although I kept repeating that the child was Henry's, it was – just like everything connected to Henry now was – somehow part of Andy too.

Andy was sincere and funny and calm. And there was more than those quantifiable attributes. He had something that did not have a name, the thing that made me want to stand beside him and breathe deeply. He only saw the things his brother had been given that were denied to him, but he had qualities Henry had never possessed. He had a heavy load and he carried it lightly, responsibly. He did his best for people. I could see, now that there was something to compare it to, that Henry had been a little spoilt and it had done him no favours.

It was great too to have someone who was excited. Not a best-foot-forward attitude, but a let's-kick-all-our-feet-in-the-air-with-delight. I hadn't thought I was going to get that, from anyone. I hadn't thought like that myself. The last time I'd been excited about the prospect of a child was when Henry and I sat around our flat having conjectural conversations about names and whose genes were stronger. That had been great, but this was real.

'And what would we tell the child, hypothetically? Who would we say was his or her father?'

'Me,' said Andy, sitting on the other side of the table I'd had built in memory of Henry. 'Initially. He or she is going to look as much like me as him. Even if something went terribly wrong and it needed an organ or something, I'd probably be as likely a match as he would. And then when he's older, or she, we can tell it the truth. When it can understand . . . I hate calling it "it".'

'What if you started to regret your decision? What if you resented us and wanted your own children?'

'It's not necessarily one or the other, Grace. Everything is possible. The future is unwritten.'

I thought of Betty, and of Frances Clinch, and of Andy and Henry too. I imagined all of Ireland's lineage written out in perfect sets of family trees – only when a magic marker was rubbed over the chart, all these secrets were exposed and unseen lines started to fly across the board making connections between relatives entirely unknown to each other. I imagined a world full of near-doubles, doppelgängers in different towns, cities, countries and all the blood relations who did not look alike. It was a wonder more of us didn't end up accidentally marrying our cousins.

'But how would it work?' I said. 'Where would we live? How . . . would we be?'

'We'd live here. I'd sort out my visa and get a proper job. We'd raise the kid here, in a happy home.'

'And my parents? Henry's parents?'

'They'd understand. They would,' he insisted. 'They'd know that the kid was loved.'

'And what about us?' I asked, looking at him without an ounce of embarrassment. 'How would *we* be?'

'We'd be. . . however we wanted to be,' he said simply. He had no hesitation. He was confident on all of this. 'There are no rules for happiness, Grace. No road map for this life. There are a million ways to live. I said it already, but it's true. I didn't fully appreciate it before but now I do: we get one life, but there's more than one path.'

We went round and round, and though what Andy was proposing was undoable, I didn't want the conversation to end. I didn't know what I wanted. There were too many hormones in my body for this. I had read a post on a New Mothers Blog where HoneymoonMammy87 was finding it impossible to make a level-headed decision about what colour to paint the walls of her marital kitchen; she couldn't tell what she liked and what was just hormones spending her money. Different circumstances, admittedly, but I knew where she was coming from.

'When I came to Ireland I didn't know what I was looking for,' he said. 'Even when I met you, when I found out about Henry, I was getting closer but I never quite reached it. I thought maybe it was you and his parents and all the other parts of this life that could have been mine. And it is, in a way. I was getting closer. And then . . .' He smiled like every part of him was alight with hope. 'I can do this,' he said simply. 'I want to do this.'

I smiled, waiting for him to come to, to say the jig was up. But he didn't.

'Everyone needs a family, Grace.'

He was talking about the baby but he meant himself too. Suddenly I could see both sides and I understood better. I was more comfortable with it, knowing it wasn't an entirely selfless offer. Andy needed a family too.

'We get on,' he added, and I laughed at the understatement.

'You're the only person I want to be around,' I said.

'I know I'm not the same,' he said carefully, tapping out the words on the table with his fingers. 'But I'm the closest thing.'

It was easier to be part of something than out in the cold on your own. It was nicer too. So when he reached for my hand, I let him take it, and when he said we'd talk more in the morning, I nodded. It was after midnight. He kissed me on the head as he made his way to the door and I knew not everything in the world was rational because I almost whispered, 'Thank you.'

'You can stay if you want,' I said instead, as he removed his lips from my crown. I felt him hesitate. 'In the spare room, I mean. Because it's late. And we're going to talk in the morning. I'm not working until the afternoon. Unless you have a job on tomorrow. Do you, have a job?'

'No,' he replied, lingering a moment longer. Then he straightened up. 'Do you want me to carry you?'

'Yes!' I said, before he'd finished asking. I stood from the chair, my bones heavy with tiredness, and I turned to face him.

'Like this?' he said, and went to wrestle me.

'No,' I laughed. 'On your back, you dope. A piggyback.'

'All right then; one, two, three, hup! All aboard! Watch your head.' And I ducked as we left the kitchen, though it wasn't quite necessary. 'If our passengers want to look to the left, they will see one of Ikea's finest couches. Oooo! To the right we have: The Television. Ahhhh! No flash photography now please, ladies and gents.'

I laughed the whole way into the hallway. Partly because it was funny but partly because once I started, I didn't want to stop. His back was warm and strong and though Andy began to feign exhaustion as he climbed the stairs, I knew he could have carried me for miles. I could have fallen asleep right there.

'Were there always this many steps? Flaming heck!' He plodded dramatically upwards. 'To the right, you'll see the mid-stairs art installation. This piece is entitled: *Shampoo Half Out of the Box*. Made with mixed materials.'

He crossed the landing, me still laughing, and with his left arm holding me up, he reached forward with the right and turned the handle to my bedroom door. 'Now, this is the last stop, folks. If you could make sure you have all your belongings with you . . .' He lowered himself towards the bed and released me with the softest bounce. I lay there grinning, happy, looking up at him, the street lamp lighting the room like a crime noir. It made his face grainy, a digital photo that had been blown up and printed out on ordinary paper. My laughter slowed and stopped. The room was charged, like maybe there'd be thunder.

'Thank you for the lift.'

'All part of the service.' He loomed large above me and it looked like he was about to say one thing when suddenly he snapped to attention: 'Heck! I forgot! The baby.'

'That I was having one? Really? That's one hell of an attention span you've got,' I teased, pushing myself into sitting.

'I just flung you down there, like a sack of coal. It completely slipped my mind. Is it all right? It can't become . . .?'

'What? Angry? Bruised? *Born?*'

'. . . dislodged?'

'I think the baby can take it.' I placed a hand over my stomach. 'This child is made of strong stuff.' I was

353

enjoying this new-found sense of maternity, as if somehow I knew what I was doing. A protectiveness surged through me. Earth Mother once again. Or maybe it was just the hormones.

'Glad to hear it,' said Andy and he moved towards the door. 'Okay well, sleep well.'

'You too,' I said.

'Goodnight, Grace.'

'Night.'

'Goodnight, bump.' And he closed the door softly behind him.

I lay back on the bed and watched shadows move across the ceiling. I was resting but I was also figuring out my next move. Nice as it was to be carried to bed, I still had to clean my teeth and use the toilet. Quite desperately, actually. I was a bi-hourly urinater now.

This was the best I'd felt about the pregnancy since I'd found out. The problem was tomorrow when we had to step into the world. That was when it always fell apart.

I heard the light switch flick next door and the floorboard creak as he returned to the lowdown bed that had never been slept in before. I got up, went to the bathroom and emptied my fairly empty bladder. I put toothpaste on my brush and watched myself carefully in the mirror, trying to read my own face.

'Now,' I said self-assuredly, like my dad often did, and I began to brush. Then I watched as my face crumbled. With the brush lodged in my mouth I put a hand either side of the basin and leaned over slightly to take a deep breath. I took a moment before I went back to eyeballing my frightened face, scowling at its dramatics. 'We'll be fine,' I told her sternly, whispering. And I wiped the tear from my right cheek and kept on brushing.

FIFTY-TWO

. . . .

'I'll **give** it a try.'

Andy looked up from the newspaper he had spread across the table to where I stood by the kitchen door in my mini-marathon T-shirt, leggings and bedhead. There was fresh bread and a pot of jam I hadn't seen before on the counter. He had been up a while.

'What's that?' he asked, taking a slurp of tea. I was struck by the familiarity of it all.

'Last night, what we discussed, I mean if you still—'

'You'll give it a try?'

'Yes. If you still want to.'

He pushed back his chair, grinning, and crossed the room to envelop me. I filled my senses with the glorious smell.

'Yes, yes, yes! Of course I still want to. Ah, Grace.' His happy words shimmied through my hair and I could have sworn I'd been here before. 'We'll do it our own way,' he said. 'No pressure.' Then he released me and rubbed his hands together.

'Now let me prepare for you my breakfast special.'

'*You* have a breakfast special?' I said, sitting at the table, pulling the magazine out from under the broadsheets. 'A couple of weeks ago you couldn't peel an onion.'

'It's a little Australian delicacy, you may or may not have heard of.'

I watched him carving slices off the fresh loaf. 'Is it jam on toast?'

'Pffff!' He slid the slices into the toaster and broke the seal on the jar. 'Grace, what do you take me for? What I am preparing for you is a sophisticated meal of hot bread with sweetened forest fruits.'

'My apologies,' I said, smiling. 'I'll have three slices of toast. I mean, hot bread. And be generous with the sweetened forest fruits. Thanks.'

We ate jam on toast and perused the papers. It's possible he was reading, but I perused. I hadn't the concentration for paragraphs. I kept looking at Andy, then glancing away when he raised his head. I felt like a pathetic teenager. On the umpteenth occasion, he was ready for me. I looked up and he was staring right back with a dollop of jam at the end of his nose. I snorted tea out of mine. I wished we could stay here, in the house, for ever.

But the time always came to leave. This morning I was accompanying him to apply for his Irish passport. We could probably have gotten the forms online, but I think it was about doing something to mark a commitment, a joint act that said we were going to try.

'Hang on!' I said, as he went to open the front door. 'There are two things I need to verify before we go out there.'

'Okay . . .' He took his hand off the latch. 'What's the first one?'

'Sex.'

He thought about this. 'Fine, but not on any main roads.'

'Are we going to have it? Is that what we're doing here? I mean, it'd be weird if we weren't but it would also be weird if we were. Not that I don't find you attractive, obviously I do, it'd be like having sex with Henry, probably. And that's the problem too. That would be weird. Good, but weird. So what's the story with that?'

'With what?'

'Sex!'

'Personally, and generally speaking, I'm in favour of it.'

I didn't laugh.

'I don't know, Grace. Do I find you attractive? Of course I do. Would it be weird? Probably. More for you, I'd say. You don't look like the love of *my* life. Well, maybe you do but that's . . .' He cleared his throat. 'Anyway! We don't have to. I didn't presume we would. We can cohabit without copulating. Like I said, a million ways to live.'

'So we don't have to?'

'No.'

'But we could?'

'Someday, sure. If you want.'

'Right.' I nodded slowly, cringing. 'Sorry.' I reached for the latch. 'Okay, let's go.'

'And what was the other thing? You said there were two. Sex and . . .?'

'Oh right,' I said, thinking. 'Yeah.' I looked at him. 'We're going to have to tell people.'

'Are you telling me or are you asking? Because I already know that.'

'Just verifying,' I said, nodding. 'Yes. Tell people. We are going to have to tell people.'

'So you said.'

'Like Aoife.'

'Right.'

'And my parents.'

'Okay.'

'Right,' I said, my head still bobbing.

'Right.'

I nodded definitively, bolstering my resolve. 'Right,' I said again. 'Let's go.'

We walked through the city side by side, yapping and laughing. People looked at us as we passed and at first I was worried but then I realised it was only because we seemed so happy. I kept grinning. We played 'would you rather'. I asked the questions and Andy gave decisive answers: rather lose an arm than a leg, have no sense of smell than no sense of touch, always be a little too hot than a little too cold. He followed my lead across roads and around corners as we made our way through Temple Bar. I kept forgetting this wasn't his city.

'Okay,' I continued, 'would you rather have the same song stuck in your head for ever or fall asleep at the end of every film you watched? And I mean *every* film.'

'What's the song?'

'To be confirmed.'

'Well, it depends, because some Beastie Boys number, awesome. But if it's Michael Bolton, say, or Abba or something—'

I halted on the cobblestones. 'What's wrong with Abba?'

Andy began to count on his fingers. 'Em . . . Let me see . . . Everything?'

'Abba are one of the greatest bands ever created.'

'That's the problem; they were created.'

'Ugh. The manufactured pop whinge. Are we not past this? Abba came from a non-English-speaking nation to dominate the English-speaking world. They had eight number ones, in a row, in the UK. They have their own museum, an entire museum dedicated to them. They're the reason *Mamma Mia!* exists – a film you'd think you, Mr Who's Your Daddy, would appreciate. They made the Eurovision Song Contest semi-credible, for Christ's sake! What more do they have to do?'

'Record a song that isn't the same simplistic words repeated over and over?'

'It's their second language!'

'You know how Abba get classified?' he said. 'And I mean this as the greatest insult: Family Favourites.'

I gasped in disgust. 'What's your least favourite Abba song?'

'"Dancing Queen". No wait! "Money, Money, Money". That may be the worst song ever written.'

'All right then,' I said and started walking again. 'The song that will be eternally stuck in your head is the global number-one hit "Money, Money, Money" by the under-appreciated Swedish band Abba.'

'Cheers.'

'Don't mention it.'

I was having the best time. Even out on the streets our plans felt possible. There was a wedding party coming out of City Hall and all the taxis beeped as they drove by. Tourists stopped to take photos of the bride. One taxi driver rolled down his window and shouted, 'It's not too late, love! Quick, hop in!' and everyone laughed.

'I guess they said I Do, I Do, I Do, I Do.'

'Don't.'

'What?' he grinned as we strolled on down Dame Street.

'Leave Abba out of your godforsaken puns.'

'But that's the Name of the Game.'

'You're basically taking the lord's name in vain right now. You know that, don't you?' I glanced over at him. 'And knowing you, you're not done.'

'Knowing Me, Knowing You?'

'I will actually have you deported.'

I was still smiling as we entered the passport office. Andy took a number from the queuing system and we sat in the plastic chairs. I didn't even do a sweep of who else was in the vast impersonal waiting area.

Through the large street-facing windows, I watched the people passing by. A woman with a pram – I registered so many more mothers and pregnant women now that I was 'with child'; a young lad with headphones; a pair of older women laden with shopping bags, one of whom reminded me of Candice Sweeny, the woman from the inquest. I would like to have talked to her, if I hadn't had to run off in search of Andy. A group of men passed by in suits and ties, and when one of them turned to speak to another I could have sworn it was Chris Walters, a college friend of Henry's. My heart stopped. I held my breath as I waited for the group to pass only for the man to turn again just before disappearing out of view. He no longer looked a thing like Chris.

'We're 141,' said Andy, turning the ticket over in his hand. 'They're on 123. At least we're moving.'

'Good,' I said, turning away from the window, concentrating on him.

'I'll have to tell my grandma I'm staying,' he said. 'I was just thinking that.'

'Of course.'

'Tell her I met a girl.'

I smiled.

'I'll tell Larry, and some of the guys from the sites. Should be able to pick up some more work easily enough. Isabel will be glad I'm hanging around,' he said. 'I almost know as many people here as back home. Not that it really feels like home anymore anyway, not like here.'

I listened as he grew more excited and slowly I realised what was actually at stake. I had only really been considering my own position but the objective truth was that Andy had more to lose than me. I was a ticket to a whole new life, to someone else's old life. I offered some stability, finally. I let the responsibility press down briefly then I shook it away.

'I should phone Isabel. I said I would when I left yesterday evening.'

'Okay,' I said noncommittally. But he was still looking at me. 'You want to use my phone?'

'Do you mind?'

I could hardly say no, not unless I wanted to admit to some irrational, pseudo-Greek jealousy. I took my mobile from my bag, unlocked it and handed it over.

'She's listed under Isabel W,' I told him as he stood from the plastic chairs, leaving the queue ticket with me.

'It's okay,' he said, already pressing the keypad. 'I know the number.'

FIFTY-THREE

Some people are numbers people, I knew that. They see a car registration plate and they can recall it two days later. It was no big deal. Andy was probably one of them. I watched him through the large window as he stood on the path outside with one hand stuffed in the front pocket of his cargo shorts and the other holding my phone to his ear. I knew my parents' phone numbers off the top of my head. But then they were actually my parents, and I had known them for more than a week.

'Grace!'

I turned in my plastic chair to see my neighbour strolling down the row of seats, heading in my direction.

'Larry,' I said, caught completely off guard. And behind him, was it? Oh God. 'Aoife.'

I glanced to the window where Andy was listening intently to whatever Isabel was saying, then I turned back quickly. I didn't want to draw anyone else's eye.

'What are you doing here?' I said, standing as they came closer.

Larry had his usual easy smile but Aoife kept looking

around her, towards the window it seemed. Had she clocked Andy? Did she know something was up? Was she worried she'd seen a ghost, that she was hallucinating?

'I'm off to Mallorca for my brother's wedding in two weeks,' said Larry. 'Only realised yesterday my passport was out of date.'

'Right, right . . .' I shifted my position, coaxing them to move with me so they were the ones with their backs to the window. I kept my eye focused on the automatic doors behind them.

'And you?'

'Oh yeah, same!'

'You're going to a wedding?'

'Yeah. No. No no,' I said, laughing far too loudly as I put a hand on Larry's arm, gently rotating him a little further. 'Sorry, no. Just yeah, didn't realise my passport was out of date either. So' – I held up the 141 ticket – 'just waiting to get it renewed.'

'Where are you going?' asked Aoife, who still looked shifty.

'Me? Nowhere.'

'What do you need an emergency passport renewal for so?'

'Oh I . . .' I turned my head to the side as I pretended to cough. Andy was still there, on the phone, chatting away happily. He saw the woman yesterday. How much was there to say? 'You know me, just like to be prepared.'

Aoife did know me and so she also knew 'be prepared' had never been a particular mantra of mine, and definitely

365

not to the point of spending a hundred quid fast-tracking a passport for absolutely no reason. That she didn't challenge this admittedly pathetic cover story only made me more nervous. She knew something was up. She had seen him. She must have.

'How's it going, anyway?' asked Larry, taking a seat on one of the plastic chairs as he settled in for a chat. Then he arched his forehead. 'How's Andy?'

'Who?' said Aoife, still standing.

'The plumber,' Larry told her. 'Remember I told you about him?'

'Oh yeah. The *Australian*.' She made eye contact now, finally. 'You never told me about this lad, Grace. I hear he's been hanging around your house, doing the washing-up. Are you seeing him?'

I scrunched up my face and shook my head fervently. 'No! I mean, it's only been a few months since . . .' I turned my head and cleared my throat again. Andy was no longer there. I turned back and looked past them towards the double doors. Nothing, and then there he was, outside, approaching. 'I have to go!' I barked, grabbing my bag and Andy's newspaper.

'But you're only three from the top!'

'Here,' I said, and shoved the queuing ticket into Larry's hand. 'I left the oven on.'

I legged it down the row of chairs and out the front of the building before Andy could make it inside. I collided with him in the hallway between the two sets of sliding doors and shoved him back outside.

'Fuck!!!'

'What are you—'

'Larry's in there,' I said, keeping my hand on his chest so he moved backwards and I pushed forward. 'And Aoife. I mean, Jesus! Aoife. This bloody city. It's too small! No, not that way. We have to go this way, away from the window.'

'Grace, we have to go back in. We were almost at the top of the line.'

'We can't go back in there. Did you not hear me? Larry *and* Aoife! And Aoife knew. She definitely knew. She couldn't look at me, she was incredibly shifty and Jesus! She knew.'

'How could she know?'

'I don't know, do I? Maybe she guessed.'

'She did not guess, Grace. Nobody guesses this. Come on,' and he went to walk back towards the building.

'What? No. I'm not kidding. I'm not going back in there and neither are you. No way. And I gave Larry our ticket.'

'Grace!'

I dragged him further up the street and down a lane at the side of a pub.

'What happened to telling people?'

'Not in the passport office!'

'Where would you suggest would be a suitable venue?'

I rolled my eyes.

'I'm not mucking about, Grace. You said you were going to give this a try and you gave up at the first hurdle.' The frustration was audible in his voice as he threw his head back and exhaled loudly. 'Did you even consider that Aoife being shifty might not be about you at all? She had just run into you, and she was with Larry. You didn't know they were dating or whatever, right? This was the first time you'd seen them together. So she was probably a bit embarrassed. She probably thought she was the one caught out.'

'Wait,' I said, leaning against the wall of the lane. 'They're *dating*?' I put my hand to my mouth. 'Really?'

'Well, I don't know, but why else would she be accompanying him to the passport office?'

I looked at him, my eyes wide, as it dawned on me. Andy just shrugged.

'I had no idea,' I said. 'I didn't even ask why she was there, I was too busy . . .'

Andy pursed his lips, presumably in a bid not to say 'I told you so'.

'I'm sorry,' I said, after I had digested the new turn of events. 'I got a fright. If it was up to me, we'd never leave the house.'

This, I could tell, had not been the right thing to say.

'I am going to tell them,' I clarified quickly. 'I just wasn't prepared.'

Andy threw back his head like he was saying he reluctantly believed me, but I knew that really he had no choice. And as I stood there, leaning against the wall, I couldn't imagine a single suitable time or setting in which to tell Aoife or anyone the truth. I couldn't imagine the circumstances in which I told them that Henry had a twin, that we'd been hanging out all these weeks in secret and that we were making wild plans to raise Henry's child together.

'Isabel was asking for you.'

'Yeah?' I was trying to imagine telling my parents. But that was another blank. I could see their faces, listening, but I couldn't quite picture me saying the words.

'We're going to go to Wexford on Saturday for a couple of days. Doesn't sound like Conor is coming, but she invited you.'

'I can't go to Wexford,' I said vaguely. 'I have work and . . .' I thought about asking him to stay, to spend the weekend locked up in Aberdeen Street, plotting and dreaming and nesting, instead of posturing like some sort of tribute act in the holiday home where Henry had spent countless summers. 'I can't go.'

'We thought you'd say that,' he said with a half-smile, and I grimaced at the notion that he and Isabel were now a 'we'.

'Will you come to dinner on Friday instead, the night before we go? Can you make that?'

'Friday. . .' I thought through my roster, but Friday was wide open. 'Yeah, I can make that.'

'Awesome,' he said, and I returned his smile.

'Yeah.'

And I told myself that the sinking feeling, the sense of something falling away, was just the baby stretching out.

FIFTY-FOUR

'So let me get this straight,' said Martin, pacing back and forth slowly in front of Maureen's grave, making the most of this rare foray into the spotlight. 'This man, the so-called brother' – Martin drew quotation marks in the air with his fingers – 'wants to raise your child. Congratulations again, by the way, Grace, I'm over the moon for you. He wants to raise his brother's child?'

'Help raise,' I said patiently. 'Yes.' Patsy and Billy had already grilled me. I was hoping the facts might stick the third time around.

Martin kept pacing. He put his hands behind his back, the fingers interlaced. 'And he's not just Henry's brother, on a point of accuracy. He's Henry's *identical* twin brother?'

'We're not one hundred percent sure on that. But yes, they do look alike.'

He retraced his steps. 'Curiouser and curiouser.'

'Not really, Martin. We've already been over this. Twice.'

Martin unlocked his hands and held them up in a don't-shoot gesture as he took a step back. Billy rolled forward. I sighed loudly.

'So,' said Billy, stroking a beard he did not possess, 'Henry's twin, who you never knew existed because Henry never knew he was adopted, turns up out of the blue and basically wants to take his dead brother's place?'

'Now you're trying to make it sound ridiculous.'

'It doesn't take much trying,' he replied. 'Not from where I'm sitting.' The other two joined in for the collective mmm-hmm-ing. 'When people ask how you want to live your life, is the answer: with a man who looks like my dead boyfriend by my side? Don't make that face, Grace. I'm just painting a picture.'

'Isn't it important to have an open mind?'

'Sure is,' agreed Billy. 'Just not so open your brain falls out.'

This was me telling people. It wasn't quite family or lifelong friends but it was a start. I was standing in Glasnevin Cemetery, confessing the complicated intricacies of my life to a trio of men who could get an hour's conversation out of which visitors did and didn't put back the watering can correctly. And if that wasn't giving it a try, I don't know what was.

'I don't think it's completely mad,' said Patsy, taking a sliver of the chocolate cake I'd brought. 'Well, not from your point of view. Him, though . . . It's quite the offer, raising someone else's child.'

Billy concurred. 'I barely wanted to raise my own.'

'I'd bring up someone else's child,' mused Martin. 'I think that'd be great.'

'Anyway,' I said loudly, returning the conversation to its point, 'now you know. And if he comes here with me again, you're all to be nice and civilised.'

'Of course,' agreed Patsy. 'It'll be good to have someone who can give me a hand with what needs doing around here.'

Billy snorted, but when Patsy looked over he was pretending to choke on his coffee.

'Do you think women would like that?' pondered Martin.

'Like what?'

'If I offered to raise their children.'

'No, Martin,' said Billy, 'I don't think so.'

'Why not?'

'Because it's creepy.'

'Grace doesn't think it's creepy, do you, Grace?'

'I do a bit,' I said.

Martin looked wounded. 'Oh yeah,' he sulked, picking up another slice of cake. 'Some exotic chap with great shoulders offers and it's all dandy. But poor Martin makes the same suggestion and he's a creep.'

'What did your parents say?' asked Patsy.

'I haven't told them.'

'Ah.'

'Yet. I haven't told them yet. I have told Henry's parents. Well, not about the baby, but about Andy. They've met him. Henry's mother likes him. A lot. And I will tell them about the baby too, soon. What?' I demanded.

Patsy had the same look he got whenever the red-headed tour guide who said this section was added in 2014 instead of 2004 came by with a group. It was an expression that said he was fighting a serious inner battle to hold his tongue.

'Nothing,' he said, shaking his head.

'Just tell me. What is it?'

'Well,' said Patsy, only semi reluctantly, 'are you sure?'

The other two turned to look and I waited for him to elaborate.

'God knows I spent many months thinking my Maureen might just turn up at the door someday. But if ever it did happen, and I saw her lovely face through the pane of glass, and then I opened the door to find it wasn't actually her at all, well, I don't know that I'd thank you for it.'

Billy stared over at his own wife's plot. Martin stuffed his hands in his pockets and shook his head.

'Yeah,' I said evenly. 'I'm sure.'

'All right then,' said Patsy brightly, patting me on the shoulder. 'Consider us only delighted for you.'

Pedalling through the park, careful not to fall behind but comfortable at my own pace too. Convinced the borrowed bicycle will suddenly take flight. I could have followed you for ever, sustained by the periodic turns of your head that allow me to see your face. What a face.

'Hey!'

Your hair blown into a terrible comb-over, and the big smiling head on you.

'Hey yourself!' I shout back.

You look away and I am preparing to freeze-frame that image until the next turn, whenever that might be, when your head flicks right back again: 'I love you!'

I don't just hear the words, I feel them; the wind pushes them into my ears and swirls them all around. 'Well, that's convenient!' I shout back, worried now about flying bikes and also that my heart might burst. 'Because I love you too.'

I don't know about near-death experiences and people's pasts flashing before their eyes, but in that moment, I see my future. A blur of you and me, laughter and fights, tired and happy, kids and holidays, work and life, all of life, and yes, somewhere in the distant future, death. I strike a deal there and then. I sign up for it all.

Outside the Heritage Centre, my bike thrown on top of yours and me thrown on top of you. I will hold you up, Henry. That is what I'm thinking. You kiss me and it is still ringing in my ears: I love you, I love you, I love you. You saying it, me saying it, and both of us breathing it. Your chest against mine, our hearts count it out in beats: I love you, I love you, I love you.

And you must feel it too, our bodies must hum with it. Because your face is in my hair, the moisture of your lips and breath as you open your mouth to speak into the crown of my head: 'But I do. I do.'

I felt the weight of the baby all that afternoon, burdening me and making me doubt myself. I was slow in the kitchen, which Dermot was quite pleased about. The customers were irritating him more than usual today. 'Did they always chew this *loudly*?' But I was constantly apologising to Tina who bore the brunt of diners complaining when they got the wrong food. The third time I messed up – sending a vegan burger that wasn't even on the menu to a customer who'd ordered a steak sandwich – I went out to correct the mistake myself, bringing the right dish with me.

'Sorry about that,' I said, taking up the vegan burger and placing the steak in front of the woman. 'My mistake.'

'Grace?' she said, pushing her head down to catch my eye. 'It's Claire Maguire.'

'Claire. Oh my God, sorry. I wasn't even looking. Hi! How are you?'

'I'm good,' she said, smiling. 'Just moved back from Hong Kong last month. My husband got a job here so, happy days.' She raised her arms in a silent cheer. 'This is my sister Angela.'

'Hi,' I said to her lunch companion. 'We've probably met. I used to go to a lot of parties at your house. God, it's been ages. Years. When was the last time I saw you? It must have been . . .'

'*Johnny Connors! Is that you? Oh my God, Johnny Connors!*'

'*No. Not me.*'

'*Are you sure? Grace, is this guy not the cut of Johnny Connors?*'

'*No. That's Henry Walsh.*'

'. . . one of those Christmas Eve drinks,' she said, finishing my sentence. 'At the Back Bar. It must be, what? Three years ago now? Four?'

'Five,' I clarified. 'It was five and a half years ago.'

'Five years. Wow. Time flies. And how are you? Wait, no. Jesus, that's a stupid question. I was so sorry to hear about Henry. I still can't believe it. I would have gone to the funeral only we were still abroad then.'

'Oh no, no worries,' I said, growing hot under my chef's whites as I attempted a laugh. 'I was barely there myself.'

'It must have been awful. I can't imagine. Grace's partner died in a cycling accident,' she told her sister. 'Henry Walsh. Do you remember? He lived at the other end of the estate.'

'Oh yeah,' said the sister. 'That was your partner? I'm so sorry.'

'Thanks,' I said, the back of my neck burning.

'You must be devastated.'

'Oh, you know,' I said, not quite looking at the sister. 'Anyway, I better get back to work. It was really nice to see you.'

'So great to see you!' exclaimed Claire. 'Give me a shout if you ever want to get a drink. Well, not for another couple of months!' And she slid back her beer-barrel stool to reveal the bowling ball she was smuggling under her top.

'Wow,' I said, feeling the sweat form on my hairline. 'Congratulations.'

'Took a while, but . . .' And she did her silent 'happy days' cheer again. 'Look me up – I'm on Facebook!'

'Okay. Nice to see you, Claire. And congratulations. Again.' Then I turned on my heels and power-walked back to the kitchen, the vegan burger falling from its plate as my shaking hand tried to place it on the counter.

'Fuck,' I said, tears of anger rapidly making their way to the surface. 'Fuck!'

'You all right?' asked Tina, coming into the room behind me.

'I dropped the burger.'

'It's cool, Grace. Nobody ordered it anyway.'

'This city,' I blustered as my nose began to run. 'It's too god-damn small!'

'I've been saying that since I got here,' said Tina, picking the chickpea mush up from the floor. 'You run out of Tinder options in a lunch break. But you probably didn't mean it in that way,' she called after me as I made my way to the bathroom and pushed open the door. 'Too small for what? Grace?'

But I didn't respond. I just leaned over the toilet bowl and vomited.

For two of them, I thought as I slid down onto the floor. This city was too small for two of them.

FIFTY-FIVE

sabel got to the door before us, holding it open as we made the rest of our way up the path. Somewhere behind her, Scooter was working himself into a frenzy.

'Come in, come in. How are you, dear?' she said, catching me by surprise as she gave me a peck on the cheek. It had been a while since she'd greeted me like that. She stepped towards Andy as his arms opened. 'Hello, sweetheart!' she enthused, and he rested his chin on her head. It was exactly what Henry had always done. I didn't recognise Isabel's dress and her hair was recently cut. She looked as well as I'd seen her in months.

'Oh,' she said, inspecting the wine bottles as I handed them over. 'Were they out of the usual?'

In the five years I'd been coming for dinner at this house, I'd always brought the same two bottles of rioja. It had become a fun tradition. Today I was carrying merlot.

'I thought it might be good to try something new.'

'Well,' she cleared her throat and placed the bottles on the sideboard, 'I'm sure these will be worth trying too. Come on through. I'm almost ready to serve.' She ushered us into the sitting room.

Conor stood from his armchair and I got another kiss on the cheek. 'Hello, Grace,' he said. There was a pause before he extended a hand to Andy, all the while looking beyond his son's doppelgänger. I followed Conor's line of vision to Isabel who stood in the doorway nodding at the handshake.

She asked Andy to help her with the plates, leaving Conor and me to make small talk.

'Am I imagining it, or is the room different somehow?' I asked, doing a quick 360, trying to locate the anomaly.

'Bit cleaner maybe,' Conor replied, 'if that's possible.' His statement was punctuated by a loud laugh from the kitchen, and he moved closer to me. 'This is no good,' he said with a quiet ferocity. 'It's too confusing. She thinks he's . . .'

'What?'

'Conor,' said Isabel, making us both jump as she appeared again in the doorway. 'What did you do with that bread I asked you to buy?'

He looked from Isabel to me and then back to his wife. 'I must have left it in the car,' he said wearily, and Isabel stood waiting until he went out into the hallway and we heard the front door open. 'Everything all right, dear?'

'Fine,' I replied, in spite of my growing unease. I flashed her a smile. 'Thanks.'

Isabel went back to the kitchen and I watched from the window as Conor sat in the passenger side of his BMW and stared directly ahead with the bakery bag in his hands. The low mumble of Andy's voice from the kitchen and Isabel's airy laugh. If we stayed two hours that would be enough. Two hours and then we could go home.

Andy brought the plates through from the kitchen. He put ours side by side and I gave him a look of relief as I shimmied into the adjacent chair. Under the table, he squeezed my hand and I only pulled it away when Conor went to pour the wine. Not the wine I'd brought, that was still sitting in the hall.

'None for me, thanks,' I said, reluctantly covering the glass with my flattened hand. 'I'm just getting over a cold.'

Isabel led the conversation. She asked me about the restaurant and how the house was working out. I told her about all the jobs Andy had done on it and watched as she beamed with pride. Andy told them about his plans to claim his Irish passport and a few leads on steady jobs. They discussed their plans for Wexford, what time they would leave in the morning, what they'd do, whether there were walking boots in the holiday home that would fit Andy. I watched Conor throughout the meal, bending further and further over his plate. He didn't speak until we were on dessert and Isabel was dishing out the neighbourhood gossip.

'Two weddings on the road in one summer,' she ruminated, spooning the syrup over her poached pears and watching as it trickled back onto the plate. These comments, like most of what she said, were directed towards Andy. 'David Reilly married an English woman, a doctor, last month, and then the couple who moved into Roger Fagan's old place have their ceremony in a few weeks. Have you met them yet? Your father and I are invited to the afters. It's on in Wicklow somewhere, I think.' Then she gave a knowing grin. 'If there was ever a house that could do with some love, eh? Poor old Roger.'

I looked around the table but Andy didn't flinch. I was starting to think I'd imagined it when Conor let his cutlery crash to his plate.

'Excuse me?' he demanded, rounding on his wife.

'Yes?'

'His father? I am not his father,' Conor spat. 'We are *not* his parents.'

Isabel brushed him away. 'Oh for heaven's sake, Conor. It was a slip of the tongue. Too much wine. Don't be so dramatic.'

'I don't think she meant—'

'I'm sorry now,' said Conor, interrupting Andy without looking at him. 'And of course he hasn't met the new couple, Isabel. He'd never set foot in this estate until last week. And if he did go banging on doors, introducing himself, there'd suddenly be a lot more houses up for sale in Rosedale because half the neighbours would have died of cardiac failure!'

Isabel narrowed her eyes, but Conor kept right on.

'And I don't know why you're talking about David Reilly when he, *Andy*, this new acquaintance of ours, has no idea who David Reilly is.' Conor turned to Andy, though he was still speaking for his wife's benefit: 'David Reilly went to school with our son, Henry. They played hurling together after school. Do you know what hurling is?'

Andy shifted in his seat. 'I don't think so.'

'No, I wouldn't expect you have that in Australia. It's a popular Irish sport. Our son Henry was very good at it when he was a young lad. I used to bring him to matches on Saturday mornings. I spent hours watching from the sidelines, come rain or shine. Often it was the best part of my week. You should look it up. Hurling. It's an interesting part of Irish culture.'

Isabel slammed her own spoon onto the table and stared at her husband like she was willing him to burst into flames. I would have crawled out of my skin if I could, crawled under the table, across the cream rug and all the way out the door.

Isabel and Conor were good people but they constructed their own realities. They had kept Henry in the dark like it was nothing. It wouldn't be long before Andy was 'son' and Isabel was 'mother' and everyone had convinced themselves that Henry and Andy were the same person.

'The pears are delicious,' said Andy finally, and Isabel picked up her spoon again.

'Good for a growing boy,' she retorted with a warm laugh. Conor bent further over his plate, took one more mouthful and pushed back his chair.

'Where are you—'

'Bathroom.' And he slammed the door behind him.

I volunteered myself and Andy to clear the table and quickly started stacking the dirty plates while he struggled to keep up with the glasses.

'What was that?' I hissed when the kitchen door was firmly shut behind us.

'What?' asked Andy, letting the glasses slip onto the counter before pulling open the dishwasher. 'It's half full,' he muttered and began to remove the few clean cups and plates.

'She referred to Conor as your father!'

'It was a slip of the tongue.'

I watched agog as he continued to empty the dishwasher. 'Does she call you Henry?'

Andy shrugged, taking the dirty plates from me. 'You've done it.'

'Once! And not on purpose! I realised straight away and I felt terrible about it. She acts like it's no big deal.'

'I look like him, she's used to saying his name . . .' He slid the plates into their holders. 'I really don't mind.'

I had so many arguments but I couldn't find where to start. 'Can we go?'

'Now?' he said, standing from his dishwasher duties. 'Really?'

'It's been two hours.'

He exhaled in disbelief.

'What?' I demanded.

'I don't count how long we spend doing your things, Grace. I don't put a limit on how much time we spend reading the paper. I don't have a clock running when we're walking in the park or reading *A Christmas Carol* or whatever.'

'Do not put that on me,' I exclaimed. 'You like doing all that stuff too. You're always reading the paper, even when I'm not. You *ask* to do *A Christmas Carol*.'

'I ask because it makes you happy. I know those things remind you of Henry' – he raised a hand to stop me interrupting – 'and that's okay, I don't mind. I want you to be happy. Same with Isabel. If she calls me Henry, I'm not going to make her feel bad about it.'

I turned my head away. It was too ridiculous.

'Or with you,' he continued, bending his head towards me as I tried to avoid eye contact. 'When you absent-mindedly press your feet into my hands while we're watching telly, I don't push them away. Grace?' I scrunched my eyes closed but he kept talking. 'No. I stretch out your toes.'

The kitchen door opened and Isabel appeared holding a glass. 'Forgot this,' she said, and I took it from her.

'Thanks.' I handed it to Andy who slid it onto the dishwasher shelf just as the front door slammed. 'Is that Conor?' I asked. 'Is he gone somewhere?'

'He won't listen. I try to tell him something and it turns into another argument. Only a saint could live with that man. Sorry,' she said, smiling meekly at Andy. 'I know I shouldn't speak badly about him in front of you. It's not fair.'

Andy pushed the dishwasher shut with his leg and threw an arm around her, not registering that when she said she shouldn't speak badly 'about him' she meant she shouldn't speak badly 'about your father'. She used to say the same thing to Henry. Isabel pushed herself into her pseudo-son and the happiness that flooded her face made me look away.

'I was explaining it to him, my idea of paying the driver for an apology, but he wouldn't listen. I know we can't just write the man a cheque but I don't see why we couldn't make some sort of contribution, flights to visit his family in Bulgaria or pay off a bit of the mortgage or the rent or whatever he has out in that farmhouse in the middle of bog-sodden Ireland. I don't want anything on the record, not the apology, not any financial transactions. I just need . . .' She exhaled the end of her sentence into Andy's chest.

Or maybe Andy did register it. Maybe he knew exactly what Isabel believed.

'Did we stack that right?' I said abruptly, not waiting for an answer as I brushed past them and pulled the dishwasher door open again. 'I just . . .' Down on my hunkers, I started to distribute the cutlery more evenly. My stomach felt too tight in this position, like the baby was being squashed, but it was better than standing up, better than witnessing it. I could not condone this make-believe.

It frightened me how readily Isabel could fool herself. She treated Andy as if he were Henry. The way she looked at him made my skin crawl. But most uncomfortable of all was the sudden and whole realisation that, when she looked at him, she could have been me.

I pictured Aberdeen Street as we had left it earlier that afternoon; a mound of teabags at the edge of the sink, day-old newspapers strewn across the floor, a rug thrown over the couch and Henry's slippers lying on their side in the hallway where they had been swapped for real-world footwear. It was, had I thought about it in the time before Henry's death, exactly as I'd expected our home would look. Only it wasn't our home, not mine and Henry's.

It was so easy to fool yourself when the only other people present were willing to go along with the pretence too. Aberdeen Street wasn't safe because the world couldn't interfere. It was safe because there was nobody present to contradict us. The world wasn't there to observe.

'I have to go,' I said, shutting the dishwasher finally.

'But I thought we agreed—'

'You stay,' I interrupted. 'I'm tired, I need to go home. But you stay. Thank you for dinner, Isabel,' I said, moving towards her before Andy could interject.

I stood before Henry's mother and saw only myself, determined and lonely and bereft of a piece of life that got bigger the longer it was gone. I abandoned the established peck on the cheek and engulfed her into the firmest of hugs. I held her like that until she started to shift. Then I picked up my bag and left.

FIFTY-SIX

●●●●●●●●●●●●●●●●●●●●●●

I **heard Andy** jogging behind me but I was almost out of the estate by the time he caught up. I didn't stop walking until he had run ahead and was standing right in front of me.

'Is it the baby?' he asked, and I couldn't help being impressed by how not out of breath he was. 'Is everything okay?' he pushed. 'Is it anything to worry about?'

'No. No, I'm fine. I just . . .' I threw my arms up. 'It's weird in there. It's like a shrine to Henry and you're the only exhibit.'

We had both stopped moving now and Andy relaxed a little.

'It is weird, ay? I know,' he said. 'She can be weird but . . . What am I going to do? I can't imagine what she's been through. I mean, can you?'

'Yes.'

'Okay but, you know what I'm saying. She just . . .' Andy shook his head. 'I'll talk to her.' He bent down to catch my eye and smiled. 'Okay?'

'I ran into a girl from school at the restaurant on Wednesday.'

'All right . . .'

'She was pregnant. I said wow and congratulations, and I meant it. But, for a split second, I was also thinking, "What must it be like to be pregnant?" Because I forgot. I forgot that I was pregnant.' I put my hand over my stomach as if to block the ears that it may or may not yet have developed. 'Somewhere I was reasoning that what this woman has, with her husband and their jet-setting life and meeting people for lunch to celebrate the impending arrival of their first child, that's not me, that's a completely different thing to what I'm experiencing.' I blew air quickly from my mouth.

'I thought, "I'm not *really* pregnant, not like her." Y'know?' I said, just about.

He reached for me but I took a step back, shaking out my whole body, fingers and feet and everything, trying to make it feel less like it was folding in on itself.

'And it made me think about what you said about Frances not knowing you were inside her. Because I didn't know this thing was here for so long, and now I do know and I have this constant lingering shame. And you're right that I haven't told people about you and I should have.'

'It's okay, Grace. You can take your time.'

'No, see,' I rallied, dismissing his platitudes. 'That's shame too. I can't square it with myself, I can't make it sit right. And that's not fair on you. I know you think Henry got everything.'

It was Andy's turn to avert his gaze now but I made him look at me.

'But he didn't,' I continued, putting my hand up to coax his chin back to me. 'Henry didn't have the truth. And it breaks my heart to think he never knew where he came from. I can't lie to this kid. Isabel and Conor are great, but that whole house is built on secrets and I can't continue them. I see Isabel this evening and it's scary. But she's just like me. She looks at you and she sees Henry. She *wants* to see Henry.'

'I know you see Henry when you look at me. That's okay, I don't mind,' he insisted. 'It makes you happy. I *want* to make you happy.'

The skin, the hair, the nose.

'That's not true,' I said. 'I don't.'

He waved my words away. 'Not just my face. I see it in you like I see it in Isabel. I know you think that a little bit of him is in me, and I don't think that's mental.' He sped up before I could interject. 'I think it too. We were formed side by side, nine months, and one decision gave him this life and me mine. It could easily have gone the other way, and that has to have done something to us. Why did I come here now, after he was dead? It's fate. This life doesn't feel alien to me. It feels like it's mine.'

'Andy.'

'Isabel and Conor look more like me than my mum ever did. There are things I almost remember, just from stories you've told or places you've brought me.'

I shook my head but he nodded faster as if willing me to agree with him. He wouldn't be stopped.

'Isabel took me out to see Conor's boat at the harbour one

389

afternoon and she couldn't get over how, though she hadn't steered me, I just knew how to get there. There were two roads down to the sea and while she usually took the other, Henry had always taken this one. She couldn't believe it. That's my reality here, Grace. My days are one long déjà-vu.'

'I don't . . .' I said, moving towards him with no idea how to finish. 'It's not real.'

'Are you telling me you don't feel that?' he challenged, putting a hand on mine; the coarse skin, the smooth nails, the smell that was only half his own. 'Tell me you don't feel like you're getting a part of him back. Hmm? I don't mind, I really don't mind. I *want* to give that to you.'

He was offering what I had wanted. He was proposing to make the impossible possible. He would make it so Henry was never fully gone, so he'd never fully left me.

I studied his face, serious and sincere and vulnerable, but beyond the flesh and bone, I couldn't see Henry. He didn't remember the night we first had sex, how it took a few goes to make our bodies fit. This wasn't the hand that had held mine as I sat on the toilet all night with a UTI and he sat dutifully in the bath. He wasn't the man who had turned to me on a bike, the wind making a mockery of his hair as he told me he loved me and changed reality for ever.

'I see you as you,' I said finally.

I watched him watching me. And I kept watching as my acceptance dawned on him.

'What if I had come along before Henry died?'

'If I'd never met Henry, I would have met you and thought: "This is it."'

'That's not what I asked.'

'Andy . . .'

'What if Henry hadn't died, and I'd turned up?'

'I'd be glad you got to know your brother.'

'And us?'

'Andy . . .'

'You have no problem calling me by my name now.'

I concentrated on my feet. 'If Henry was still alive, I'd be a different person.' Then I raised my head and spoke slowly. 'If you're a version of Henry, then I'm as much a version of the person I was before. I used to be cheeky and funny and constantly excited about things. You wouldn't recognise me. I used to laugh all the time. Sometimes I can't believe I'm the same person. I should have a different name. I should need a different tongue to speak that name.' I swallowed hard. 'Grace and Henry. That's how it goes. I can never be Grace and Someone Else.'

'Yes you can,' he said eventually.

I shook my head, knowing what was coming next.

'Just never Grace and Andy.'

And the sob was out, like a gulp, a last-ditch attempt not to drown.

In that moment I felt him leaving, a magnet pulling the wall of my chest towards him as he prepared to disappear. I didn't want him to leave. I wanted to tell him to stay, but if I did I knew he would, and I couldn't keep my half of that deal.

'It doesn't mean you have to go. You could still stay, be here.'

He nodded.

'Get your passport, get to know Henry's parents.'

'Yeah.'

I reached out momentarily but I could see him checking out, his face set to self-preservation, and I dropped my hand again.

'Mind how you go,' he said softly, his words drawing a tender line under it all.

And I turned and left him standing there, at the mouth of Rosedale, visible to anyone who came in or out of the estate. Maybe they'd drive straight past him and hours later find themselves thinking about the boy who played hurling and visited his parents and then one day ceased to exist.

FIFTY-SEVEN

I was washing the windows in the kitchen, shaking out my arms after each section of the double doors, and the music was blaring. I'd been cleaning all morning, vigorously scrubbing the bathroom, bedroom, and now the kitchen. Taking it one room at a time. It was like therapy. Plus, it needed to be done. Mould had started to appear on the bottom of the bedroom windows and the dust balls in the living room were morphing into tumbleweeds.

I thought about nothing, except whatever was pissing off Gwen Stefani.

I only heard the phone because it happened to ring as one track faded out and another prepared to fade in. I leaned over to pause the CD player with my right hand and picked up the mobile with my left.

'Hello?' I said, only realising how breathless I was now I actually had to speak.

'Have you seen him?'

I held the phone away from my ear to see the caller ID: Isabel W.

'He was supposed to be here at nine a.m. That was the agreed plan. Then ten a.m. came and eleven and it's coming up on noon now and still no sign. I phoned the B&B but the landlady says she hasn't seen him. I don't know if she's telling me the truth or not but if he's not there and he's not with you . . . Is he with you?'

'Andy?' I said, both superfluously and pointedly. I pictured Isabel standing in the middle of her living room, the non-phone hand on her narrow hip, cringing at the crudeness of the name. But we were too far gone for this. We didn't need another game. 'No,' I relented. 'I haven't seen him since your house yesterday.'

'He ran out of here after you and never came back,' she said fretfully. 'I presumed he'd brought you home or you'd had an argument or I don't know, but that whatever it was, our appointment still stood. It takes some time to get to Wexford and I hate arriving with half the day gone. I mean, we'll just have to make the most of it but really, you think he could have called.'

I looked around at the basin and kitchen roll and various foods I had to put back in the fridge once it dried a little. I couldn't feel anything, not like before. I had no sense of how near or far he was.

'Do you think he's all right?'

I pictured her biting her lip, knitting her brow until the crease in the middle needed time to smooth out.

'I'm sure he's fine.'

'I bet you Conor has something to do with it. I bet he said something, told him not to come. He just sat watching me pack all morning and then when he didn't show up Conor didn't seem the least bit surprised. He keeps telling me to leave it, puts on he's only thinking of me but he's delighted, of course. Conor never wanted him here in the first place. I know this is down to him. It has to be.'

Embarrassed by the gap in conversation, Isabel gave a half-laugh.

'I shouldn't be bothering you with this,' she said with a breeziness forced to the point of audible strain. 'I'm sure it's nothing. He probably just slept in. He'll be along any minute. I'll let you go, Grace. I'll get him to phone you from Wexford, let you know how we're getting on – if there's a minute. We've a lot to fit in, you know. It is quite the packed itinerary.'

'Oh, I'm sure,' I replied, but my own breeziness was even faker than hers and it proved too great an ask for both of us.

'He's gone, isn't he?' she said quietly, as the pretence fell away.

'I don't know,' I told her truthfully.

'I have this awful feeling, Grace. I think he's gone.'

When the call was over, the stereo came bellowing back in. I turned up the volume two more notches and it stayed like that for the rest of the day. I scrubbed and swept and washed, and listened to music from the time when I first knew Henry. It was the only kind I had on CD.

On Sunday, I went to see my parents. I phoned ahead to check they'd be in and Mam said there was some reality TV love rat opening a hardware store in Celbridge and Dad was considering going to give the chap a piece of his mind and also to avail himself of the half-price offer on all new mops. I told her to ask him not to, that I was calling around and I had news. She said she'd try but, as I could no doubt appreciate, she couldn't promise anything.

When I arrived, Dad was there. 'Arra it's grand,' he said, serving up a bowl of stew and insisting I eat it. 'He's opening another place on Tuesday.'

He was batch-cooking dinners for the week and Mam was watching some English murder mystery. I waited for her to come into the kitchen. She was wearing Dad's glasses, probably because she couldn't find her own, which were sitting on top of her head.

'Go on so,' she said, removing one set of spectacles. 'What's the news?'

'I hope it's good news,' clarified Dad. 'And if it's good *and* bad news, maybe you could start with the good?'

I looked at them both, standing there, waiting. Then I took a deep breath and blurted it out.

'I'm pregnant!'

I said it with such gusto that the silence that followed seemed particularly deafening.

Mam hesitated. 'Are you sure?' she said, glancing at Dad.

'You know it takes two people to make a baby,' he added helpfully.

'Oh, for God's sake! Yes, Father, I am aware. The baby is Henry's. Will you stop looking at each other! I'm not making it up. I'm almost sixteen weeks' pregnant.'

'Really?'

'Yes! If you look . . .' I turned to the side and pulled my top tight across my belly. There was almost a proper tiny bump now. 'See?'

'Oh!' said Mam, suddenly coming alive. 'Oh Grace! Oh! We're going to be grandparents! Arthur! Oh oh oh!' Her excitement continued to escalate as she started clapping her hands and hurrying towards me.

'Oh Grace, this is the best news! This is absolutely the very best news in the entire world!' She threw her arms around me and the emotion in her voice radiated from her body. She let go of me almost as quick. She was hopping about on the spot. It was not unlike her moth assassination dance. She was shrieking and laughing and hopping and clapping. She pumped her arms in the air in an infinitely superior version of Claire Maguire's silent 'happy days' cheer. There was nothing silent about what my mother was doing.

'Mam,' I said, laughing, as she continued to whoop and holler, 'calm down. It's not your baby!'

'But you're my baby, Grace! Oh, I'm just so bloody delighted! This is brilliant!' And she was laughing again now, laughing and crying and hugging me tight.

'Dad?' I said, when Mam had loosened her grip slightly. He was still standing where Mam had left him, at the counter in his I Taught Mary Berry apron.

'Arthur? You're looking a bit pale.'

'I . . . I just—' He put the ladle down and frowned. I knew he was giving himself a good talking-to. I looked at Mam and the two of us started to grin.

She let me go and I walked over to him.

'Dad . . .?'

He held up an arm as I got close, telling me to stay back. 'I think,' he said, still frowning at the stew. 'No,' he rebuked himself, speaking purposefully. 'I know. I know, that this is the best thing that has ever happened.'

'To me, to you, to . . .?'

'To anyone,' he clarified, his tone as serious as I'd heard it. 'This is the best thing that has ever happened. Ever. This . . .' He started to wag a finger as he reached his point. 'This is the circle of life, love.'

I threw my arms around him and Mam skirted back around the worktop too. We stood like that, in a circle of happy, communal tears, until the alarm went on the oven, and Dad removed his chicken and broccoli bake.

'You're home early. I haven't done a thing about dinner before you ask— Henry? What's up? What is it?'

'I saw a drawing in this book at work and it made me so homesick, I had to come back.'

'What do you mean?'

'This new kids' series we're doing the design on. I was trying to get the proportions right. Then I stopped and looked at the image and it gave me such a fright, Grace. It was us.'

'In the book? How? Come here to me, you funny man.'

'It was a love story about a boy and a girl. It never said

they were in love, they were best friends, but I knew that one day they were going to grow up and fall madly in love with each other.'

'How did you know?'

'Because they were you and me. The little girl looked just like you and the little boy was me, and they were riding their bikes home from school and he was trying to hold her hand.'

'Sounds dangerous.'

'It could have been us riding home from school.'

'But Henry, we didn't know each other when we were children.'

'That's what gave me such a fright. All those years before I met you, all that time wasted talking to everybody else.'

I laugh then, because I can't help it. 'Well, I'm flattered, but it was hardly wasted . . .'

'That's how it felt, when I saw the picture. I thought of all the years you existed in the world and I didn't know you. It made me feel sick. I had to come home. I didn't want to waste any more time.'

'Well, I'm glad you're here.'

'What are you doing this evening?'

'Nothing. Why?'

'Can we go to the park?'

They wanted me to stay the night, but I knew if I did they'd never let me leave. Mam was going to join me for my first scan the following day and I let Dad drive me home. But as soon as he had pulled out of Aberdeen Street, I turned away from the house and headed for the park.

I would never, I accepted as the sky grew dark and the number of cars began to diminish, walk through the Phoenix Park and not think of Henry. These trees belonged to him, the cycle paths mapped our journey. I walked through the soft grass, shivering sympathetically as the wind rustled the leaves overhead. I had a photograph of him, standing somewhere here, mimicking me with a cheesy smile. I was glad there was a place where he still resided. Somewhere I could bring his son or daughter to show them a bit of their father's soul, when a box of bones buried among thousands of other boxes of bones couldn't quite suffice.

It was after eleven when I started to nod off. I was sitting on the couch with the blanket at my feet and *A Christmas Carol* open on my lap. I whispered the dialogue, making a stab at the voices, but the rest I read in my head. The Ghost of Christmas Past had brought Scrooge back to his childhood home when my head started to droop. I jerked myself awake again. Just another page or two and I'd take myself off to bed.

'You recollect the way?' inquired the Spirit.
*   'Remember it!' cried Scrooge with fervour. 'I could walk it blindfold.'*

I used my finger to keep my place as I looked up from the page. Apart from what the reading lamp provided, the room was dark, and there was no noise outside. But still I knew I was waiting. I sat like that a moment longer. And when the doorbell went, coming up to midnight, I was already on my feet.

FIFTY-EIGHT

He stood at the doorway, almost the reverse of how I'd first seen him two months before. Back then it was the light, and disbelief, that stopped me from viewing him properly. Now his face was obscured by darkness.

'I'm sorry it's so late,' he said, as my vision adjusted to the night sky and his silhouette developed features. I marvelled at how that accent had grown on me.

'Come in.'

I stood to the side to let him enter and remembered how when he first came here, I could barely move.

Perhaps it was the witching hour, the time at which Scrooge's ghosts came calling too, or maybe because a version of it had already happened, but the whole thing felt like a particularly wonderful dream.

'I know you're usually in bed by now,' he said, and I left the door open so we'd have the street light as I felt around for the hallway switch. 'I wanted to say goodbye.'

The light snapped on overhead and he closed the door. I could see him clearly now. The skin, the hair, the nose. The mouth, the pale eyes, the heavy eyebrows, the whole face.

He was wearing the trousers he'd had on at the coroner's court.

'Your trousers,' I exclaimed. 'And your shoes! You're covered in muck, Andy!'

Andy looked down at his feet. 'Heck!' he grumbled, and began to pull off his trainers. He left the shoes by the door, two lumps of encrusted dirt falling from the soles as he placed them side by side. Then he began to roll up his slacks. As he folded the material, the muck that had dried in cracked slightly. 'You don't get this problem with shorts,' he muttered.

'Where were you?'

'I had a couple of things to take care of before I head off. All done now. I just have to drop Mrs O'Farrell's car back to the guesthouse. And I guess give her back these trousers, if she wants them. I'm leaving tomorrow.'

He'd said that already, hadn't he? But I heard him this time.

'For home?' I asked. 'For Australia, I mean?'

'Nah.' He looked at me as a smile slowly formed. It was the same mouth. God, I still loved that mouth. 'I'm going to travel the world,' he said.

'Good for you,' I told him, trying to work out if I meant it. 'I'm happy for you.'

'Are you?'

'I think so.'

He nodded. 'Good.'

We walked through to the sitting room.

'This place smells like a hospital,' he remarked.

'I've been cleaning.'

'Removing all trace of me?'

I tilted my head at him but his face seemed to say he was kidding.

'Isabel was looking for you,' I said, remembering. 'She phoned yesterday when you didn't show up for the Wexford trip.'

'I know. She phoned the guesthouse too.'

'Have you told her you're leaving?'

Andy shook his head. 'Can't,' he whispered. 'You were right, Grace; I shouldn't have met them. I was only thinking of myself.'

'No,' I said emphatically. 'I was only thinking of *myself*. She should have met you. And even if they never told Henry the truth, I'm glad they had to tell someone. I'm glad I know.'

'I've done my best to make it up to her, anyway.'

'How?'

'Just something.' He shrugged, pulling at his rolled-up trousers. 'You'll see, probably.'

'I'm sorry, Andy.'

'Don't, Grace. There's no need. We said it all the other day and I'm not here to rehash that. I just wanted to say goodbye, and to thank you.'

'Thank me?' I gave a little laugh. 'For what?'

'For showing me what home is.'

I grabbed my right wrist with my left hand and told myself I could not touch him. We stood in the centre of the sitting room, the reading lamp shining only over the couch and a halo of brightness on the floor by the door to the hallway. I liked him best like this, in the half-light. He could be whoever he needed to be.

'I'm glad I came here, and that I met you,' he said. 'I'm glad I got to see all this. I don't regret one path untaken, only that I could not walk them both.'

He smiled then, making light of his poetic solemnity, and I sat down on the couch and patted the spot beside me.

'I've got my first scan tomorrow,' I said, smiling now too.

'Oh yeah?'

'Yeah. I'm excited. Aoife's coming.'

'Great!'

'And my mam.'

'You told them. Awesome. Were they thrilled?'

'Yeah.' My heart swelled at the thought of Mam's celebratory rain dance but I didn't want to say too much. I didn't want to rub it in.

'Go on,' he insisted. 'Tell me!'

And if there was pain in his eyes, then there was pleasure there too. It was a great thing, how this baby could exist in spite of everything.

'They were delighted,' I confirmed. 'Dad said it was the circle of life, which is just about the best way to view the whole thing. I know it seems ridiculous, because I didn't do anything except fail to take contraception seriously, but they were really proud.'

'Of course they were,' he said with a smile that could break my heart. 'I'm so happy for you.' He put a hand on my lap, palm upwards, and I covered it with mine.

I stifled a yawn. 'Sorry,' I mumbled, biting it down. 'Long day.'

'I'll go. I wanted to say goodbye and I've done that. I have the car to return anyway.'

'No! Don't!' I pleaded, suddenly aware of the finality of this. 'Not yet.'

'Is there anything I can do? Any last little jobs, maybe show you how to grout the shower?'

'I'm good for grouting,' I said as the panic seeped away.

I allowed a silence to descend and I set about committing him to memory. I took in the width of his hand, the callus on his left index knuckle, the rough terrain of his skin. I breathed in, deeply, and closed my eyes. I made an imprint on my body, in my nostrils, on the underside of my eyelids. Then I opened my eyes slowly and looked. I took in the face, feature by feature, fine line into deep line, and I locked that away too. This face that was almost Henry's. This person who had been there in the beginning, long before Henry had ever known me, had ever known anyone, even himself.

Then, when I had tattooed the 3D image onto my brain, I picked back up the book from the other side of Andy, and put it on his knee. 'You could read?' I said tentatively, allowing him to say no. 'If you have time.'

'I have all the time in the world,' he said and squeezed my hand tightly. I closed my eyes before any tears could escape. He cleared his throat and he began to read.

'Marley was dead, to begin with. There is no doubt whatever about that.'

I felt him glance up from the page, but I kept my eyes shut. I nodded my silent encouragement, then curled my legs under me, leaned my head back and allowed the story, and with it the night, to bundle me up and carry me away.

FIFTY-NINE

was walking in the park and it was snowing. We'd had a lovely Christmas dinner, roast potatoes and the prize turkey from the poulterer's around the corner. Aoife was up ahead, wearing a top hat and calling my name, only the closer I got she started shrieking. It was a high-pitched song like a piano scale or a car alarm or a ring tone. It was a ring tone. My phone was ringing.

I was awake now, on the couch, all alone, and my phone was ringing. I shook myself, and the blanket I didn't remember being on me fell to my waist. There was no sign of Andy where he had been, beside me on this couch, just a moment ago . . . Only it wasn't a moment ago. It was morning now. Had he been here? Had he called last night, or was that a dream too?

The phone was still ringing. Ringing and ringing and ringing. I felt down the side of the couch. I looked on the floor. There, at the foot of the sofa, beside the overturned book.

'Hello!' I shouted into it, still trying to lift the fog of sleep and looking at the caller ID before I put it fully to my ear. 'Isabel?'

'Oh Grace, Grace! Where have you been? I've been phoning you! You'll never guess what has happened!'

My first thought was that Andy had called to her. That he had left here and gone there . . . If he had been here at all. I shook the blanket off myself completely and clambered to my feet. I rubbed at my eyes as I made my way into the hallway.

'I've been asleep.'

'Yes I know, sorry, sorry. It's very early, it's just' – I pulled the phone away from my ear to check the time: 7.09 a.m. – 'phone call at six o'clock this morning. At first I thought it was something terrible, that there'd been an accident and someone was dead only Conor was in the bed beside me . . .' her excitement died away momentarily. 'And well, there isn't anyone else.'

'Sorry, Isabel, I missed that,' I said, pressing my feet flat against the cool wood of the hallway floorboards as I tried to concentrate. 'Who phoned you at six o'clock this morning?'

'The driver, Grace! The driver from European Hauliers!' I stopped looking around for clues to Andy's presence and gave Isabel my full attention. It was difficult enough to follow as it was. 'He did it, Grace!' she prattled. 'He apologised. I mean, I couldn't understand everything he was saying, but he definitely said he was sorry. I got that bit. And I could tell he meant it. I actually felt sorry for the man. He sounded quite emotional.'

'Why?' I said, staring at the floor, trying to make something click.

'Well, I don't know, because he knew it was the right thing to do, I suppose.'

'But why now?'

'I don't know, Grace,' she said, not slowing down at all and sounding annoyed that I couldn't just get on board with what had happened. 'It wasn't really a *conversation*. I couldn't understand everything. He said something about "night" and "dead" and "Henry Henry Henry"' – I knew Isabel was worked up but I still grimaced at her particularly awful, potentially racist, impersonation – 'Something gave him a fright, I think, last night. A bad dream. If I was as isolated as him, only pigs and cows for company, I'd be easily frightened too. I think he said he saw Henry, but it was hard to follow. You know how it is when you've had a nightmare, even when you do have a full grasp of the English language. Whatever it was, anyway, was enough to bring his conscience around.'

The early-morning sun formed a pool near the front door. I moved closer so I could soak up its warmth, but two steps away I stopped. There, beside the door, were the two clumps of muck that had come off Andy's shoes when he'd removed them the night before.

He never said where he'd been before arriving at mine close to midnight. All I knew was he'd had his landlady's car and he was covered in dirt up to his shins.

I stood there, between the clumps of dried mud and the pool of early-morning sun, and it started to slot together. Andy mentioning the driver's address, how it was only a two-hour journey from Dublin. Isabel mentioning that he lived in a farmhouse, how the place was surrounded by bogs.

410

Andy standing in my hallway, as I was now sure he had been, having recently stood in muck.

I pictured the driver as he was at the inquest, a slight man in a short-sleeved shirt, only now he was standing at the window of a stone farmhouse, holding the curtain back as he stared out into the night in heart-stopping terror. I know I'd never been to his home but that didn't stop me imagining, just like it had never stopped me seeing Henry's bike spinning helplessly out of control.

I pictured the driver at his window in the dead of night. And staring back at him, standing alone in the muddy field at the front of his house, was the same man he had run over almost four months earlier. I imagined the driver's shock, his utter alarm that he was now being visited by a ghost, and I felt a deep well of empathy for him.

I had believed him in court, in the end, when he said he hadn't felt his wheel hitting Henry. I had never once blamed the driver. I never even considered it. I blamed only myself and sometimes Henry.

'I'm happy for you, Isabel,' I said, meaning it, as I wandered back into the sitting room.

'Do you think *he* had something to do with it?'

I stopped in the threshold between hallway and living room. 'I think he's gone,' I said simply.

There was a pause.

'I know.'

'I'm sorry, Isabel.'

'I just liked having a bit of him still.'

'Me too,' I said.

411

'But now he's gone, all of him.'

I kneeled back onto the couch. 'Well, not quite.'

'Oh yes, his spirit, and as long as we love Henry he'll still be with us, blah-de-blah, but I mean really, Grace.'

And then I told her. I told her about the circle of life and I had to move the phone away from my ear until she stopped shrieking. Then I had to wait for her to run upstairs and wake Conor. She put him onto me as she tried to calm down but he hadn't said a word before she grabbed the phone back again.

I kneeled on the couch and grinned, rolling my eyes in delight as I adjusted the proximity of the phone speaker, volume dependent. They wanted to call over, and when I said they couldn't because I was going for a scan, Isabel wanted to come too. But I said no. She would be a wonderful grandmother and this child would be loved, but he or she would be mine. I said I'd call around that evening with a printout of the scan. Isabel kept coming up with things she could do for me in the meantime. She practically had my mortgage paid off by the time I managed to hang up.

I folded the blanket and hung it over the arm of the couch, then I picked *A Christmas Carol* up from the floor. The bookmark had been moved. It was no longer where it had been for the past four months, lodged about a third of the way through. It was right at the back of the book, on the page that read 'The End'. Had Andy gone beyond the agreed point? Surely he had just closed the thing and left as soon as I'd fallen asleep? I flicked through the last few pages to find sentences already swirling in my mind: Scrooge shouting at the young boy on the street, the prize turkey hanging in the poulterer's, the quick synopsis of how seeing a few ghosts had been the making of him. I put my hand on the couch where Andy had last been and recalled the image I had stored away.

Ding-dong!

'You're not dressed!' said Aoife, tramping into the hallway. 'You never even ran that mini-marathon, Grace. You just happened to help hand out the T-shirts. Go and put something on, will you? We need to be going in ten minutes.' I could tell she was as excited as me.

'Hi, Grace,' said Larry, coming in behind her. 'I'm going to be your chauffeur.'

'He insisted,' Aoife clarified.

'I just know how she hates to be away from me,' he teased, throwing an arm around her and though Aoife rolled her eyes, she didn't move away. If anything she pushed a little closer.

'Okay, two minutes,' I said, and turned to run up the stairs.

'Are we driving your mam too?'

'No!' I called down, grabbing my hairbrush from the bed. 'She's meeting us there.'

I stood in my room, trying to decide what one wore to see the first image of their first child. Leggings? A dress? I grabbed a dress from the end of the bed, brushed my hair and pulled it back. I stood in front of the mirror and smiled. I kept staring at my reflection but I couldn't lose the smile.

'We are loved,' I whispered, and with both arms wrapped around my middle, I gently squeezed.

Then I slipped my feet into sandals and skipped down the staircase to find Aoife and Larry kissing at the foot of it.

'All right, lovebirds,' I called, skirting past them as Aoife shoved Larry away. 'Let's go. I have a baby to see.'

EPILOGUE

was about 300 metres away, a whole section and a half of the cemetery between us, but there was no doubt it was him.

'Shushhhh,' I said, rocking the buggy gently though there wasn't a sound coming from it. I had pushed the thing into the far-flung corners of the graveyard, trying to induce sleep before we went to pay Henry a visit.

I hadn't seen him in almost sixteen months, not since the night he came to say goodbye. I hadn't talked about him either. Only Henry's parents knew and no better people to ignore awkward truths. As far as I was aware he hadn't been back in Ireland. And I doubted he was staying now. I watched him from where I stood beside a large oak and I understood. He was here to acknowledge the only thing they still shared. Even those who had known them would mark their birthday tomorrow. Only Andy, and me, knew that today was the day they had entered the world, and tomorrow was the day they were adopted.

'That's your uncle,' I whispered, still pushing the buggy back and forth. 'That's your daddy's brother.'

Though it did my heart good to see him, I had learnt to let ghosts remain ghosts and concentrate on the newly living. I moved back a little, obscuring myself and the buggy behind the tree.

There was nobody else in Henry's section, but then there wouldn't be. Visitors were sporadic on weekdays, with the exception of the wise men. And as given to delusion as I could be, I knew I would not be seeing them here today, or tomorrow.

Footsteps drew nearer behind me. I turned to see a woman of about fifty making her way into this neighbouring section.

'Hello there,' she said, holding up a pot plant in greeting. 'Lovely morning.'

'It is,' I agreed.

'Oh!' she exclaimed as I turned the buggy around. 'Would you look at that!' She clasped her hands to her heart. This had been one of the best things about becoming a mother, the way people now looked at me as if I was proof that the world still contained wonder. 'Does it run in the family?' she asked. 'Isn't that what they say about twins?'

I bent down to fix their matching hats. 'They do say that, although the truth is it only counts if it's on the mother's side and I'm not a twin,' I said. 'But their father is.'

The woman looked at me in amazement and shook her head. 'Well isn't that something. What a coincidence.'

'There's no such thing as coincidence,' I replied but the woman was too busy cooing at the buggy to hear.

'Like sleeping angels.'

'Ha! For about another twenty minutes. I'm hoping to have them dropped off at my parents' before they wake.'

'Lucky grandparents,' she enthused, leaning into the buggy for a closer inspection. 'Two boys?' she whispered, looking back up at me.

I nodded, and she beamed at them.

'Well, have a lovely day,' she said. 'Here's hoping the weather holds fine.'

'Hopefully,' I agreed, thinking of Martin and how he was probably sitting in his kitchen right now worrying about whether the sun would still be shining by the time he said 'I Do', or whether Patsy had anything embarrassing planned for his speech. I'd have to get going soon if I wanted to drop the boys off, get home to change and make it to the forest on time. They were having an eco-wedding.

When the woman left, I turned the buggy back around but Henry's grave was all alone. I looked in the surrounding plots and traced my sight along the path that led to the main entrance. There he was, walking out the gates in long, easy strides with his hands pushed into his shorts pockets. Not a ghost at all but a fully-formed man. Andy kept walking, getting smaller and smaller. And I watched as he disappeared, the way normal people do.

The End

ACKNOWLEDGEMENTS

A heartfelt thank you to everyone who helped me with the research for this novel, especially Susan Lohan, Louise Roseingrave, Ian Wright and Christine Monk. Thanks to Liz Parker and Juliet Mahony, agents extraordinaire, and to Sara O'Keeffe and the whole team at Corvus. I also want to acknowledge this peculiar country I call home. For better and for worse, *Grace After Henry* is entirely of Ireland.

Read more from bestselling author,

eithne shortall

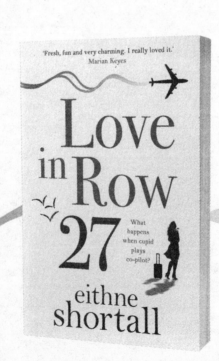

'Fresh, fun and very charming. I really loved it.'
Marian Keyes

Love in Row 27

What happens when cupid plays co-pilot?

eithne shortall